French Expressions Series

Claude Roy, *The Distant Friend*

Julian Green, *Adrienne Mesurat*

Anna Lorme, *A Traitor's Daughter*

Rabah Belamri, *Shattered Vision*

Adrienne Mesurat

Julian Green

Translated by Henry Longan Stuart

Revised by Marilyn Gaddis Rose

HM

HOLMES & MEIER
New York   London

Published in the United States of America 1991 by
Holmes & Meier Publishers, Inc.
30 Irving Place
New York, NY 10003

First French edition published under the title *Adrienne Mesurat* in 1927 by Librairie
Plon. Reissued 1986 by Editions du Seuil, © Julien Green, 1986. First English-
language edition published as *The Closed Garden,* © 1928 by Harper & Brothers, New
York and London; © 1955 Mary M. Young.

BOOK DESIGN BY DALE COTTON

This book has been printed on acid-free paper

Library of Congress Cataloging-in-Publication Data

Green, Julien, 1900–
   [Adrienne Mesurat. English]
   Adrienne / Julian Green : translated by Henry Longan Stuart ;
revised by Marilyn Gaddis Rose ; with a new preface by the author.
      p.   cm.
   ISBN 0-8419-1193-2 (acid-free paper)
   I. Title.
PQ2613.R3A6513   1991
843′.912—dc20   90-41295
                                                                    CIP

MANUFACTURED IN THE UNITED STATES OF AMERICA

Contents

Author's Preface *(1973)*

Psychoanalysis has been mentioned in connection with *Adrienne Mesurat*. Well, let's look into the matter. I'm willing to try.

I once proclaimed that I knew nothing about psychoanalysis when I wrote my novel. I cannot say that now. In 1920, I was a neurasthenic dreamer, pining away with passion in one of the most beautiful spots in the world. I was glum and studious, living through the saddest hours of my life at the University of Virginia. I hadn't the slightest idea that it could have been otherwise, and yet an old gentleman was shouting at me from his apartment in Vienna. Young men, like curly-haired Greek heroes, were bearing his message; all around me they repeated mysterious phrases ringing with barbarous words like *complexes, repression,* and *libido.* "Listen, please listen," Freud implored. "You silly fool. Stop your suffering. I can explain everything. . . ." Nothing could be done, I was deaf.

However, as a result of seeing *Introduction to Psychoanalysis* dragged in everywhere, I followed the advice of two or three ecstatic friends and finally gave that big book a cursory glance. What did I think I'd find there? No doubt, some things that shouldn't be read—what out-of-date manuals loftily called indecencies. My disappointment was immense. I could not understand how students could get excited over pages so hard to read. What were these complicated and repugnant childhoods, those filthy infants filled with lust? Nurseries were becoming places for orgies where the potty reigned. It all ended in some kind of incestuous passion for the mother and a desire to kill the father. Thank God, there was nothing in all that that could apply to me, and I bestowed on myself a profound *satis fecit*, a discharge from possible guilt. *I* was pure with the solid walls of the Catholic Church guarding my precious person from the defilements of this world, and I remained alone, proud; no one understood me.

Still, here and there in the work of that suspect author I was struck by what he called his cases. These were confidences, or, rather, confessions, disturbing because they were obviously sincere. A man in pain spoke in these naked texts. Without knowing exactly what he was turning over in his mind, I was touched by the tone, the crudeness of the confessions, the will to speak truthfully, but there was nothing for me in all that, I said to myself, closing the book perplexed. More than a reading, my first exploration of the Freudian universe was a brief plunge into its shadows, but since I retained only an undefinable malaise, I forgot it. How bookish and cerebral all that seemed compared to life, especially my life, a story whose key remained undiscoverable.

I wasn't like the others. All my troubles could be summed up that way. Now, my desire to be like the others and to find a home with them sometimes came over me with a kind of violence. As a child, I had experienced the sadness of never being able to be part of a group and to have fun with the same things, but I was comically awkward. I laughed by guesses, in hopes. It was obvious I didn't understand. The rules of the simplest games went by me. Blindman's-bluff, capture-the-flag, hopscotch were alien, and I stayed by myself, amazed by the sudden vacuum that formed around me.

Later in the upper grades, it was pretty much the same thing, and it was no different when I saw myself in uniform in 1917, first wearing khaki, and then sky blue, and yet the uniform by its very nature assured me, allowing me to blend into a group. Externally, at least, I looked like everyone else. The differences did not show. I knew instinctively that differences brought bad luck. However, they were part of me. You might have said that they watched over me, not as guardian angels, but like Fates.

When I returned home to rue Cortambert in 1922, I thought I had lost this sense of my solitude. The family group formed again around me. I knew the special idioms of the language which set us apart from the others, all the others in the world. We had our slang. We could effortlessly understand allusions that remained devoid of meaning for any outsider.

In that comforting milieu, why did I feel the desire to escape? Was it possible that the vacuum would turn up there too? "There especially," whispered the Fates.

Sometimes I would study the graveyard. That's what we called a group of photographs which covered a section of a wall panel in our dining room, bringing together grandparents, uncles, aunts, even cousins, all dead. I would consider this world, gone forever, with the gloomy attentiveness that accompanies boredom. In front of those mute faces I could intuit the amount of nothingness in all human life. Yet it was among them that I sought—without great conviction—a link with the person I was. But I didn't find any Between them and me, no resemblance: I was outside the group. In that gentle-eyed woman whose black hair was worn in bands over her ears, I could see only a stranger, although she was close to me in blood. Similarly, that old gentleman with the white mustache and upright, imperious manner was my immensely rich grandfather who crushed with a glance the penniless little pup judging him. And the others, the others . . . All that was my oppressive family, my tribe, heaps of bones in a far country. I myself was living, lively, proud of my hands which could arrange words in a sense that was mine alone, proud of my eyes which could uncover a new world in the world of everyday. . . .

In 1926 I had finished my first narrative and was wondering what I was going to put in the next one. Everywhere I was told that a second novel had its risks. Now what worried me was not the fate of my second book but the very possibility of producing one, good or bad. I didn't have a subject. *Mont-Cinère* (Avarice House) had been supplied by my memories of America and the huge house that burned down in Virginia while I was there.

At that moment my imagination wasn't working. To stimulate it a little one chilly April afternoon I settled down in my room with a stack of aquamarine paper and several carefully chosen pens. Silence. The city noise did not reach that courtyard where a feeble little palm tree tried to grow. I studied it unsympathetically. To me it symbolized neurosis and spleen. But I had to get down to business; I didn't have time to daydream;

I had a novel to write, at least to cover two hundred pages with my even hand. Unfortunately I had nothing to say. I yawned. Perhaps it would be easier in the living room.

There, at least, I would not be alone. My father was reading *Le Temps* in the big armchair with the yellow and white flounced slipcover. My sister Anne had made that slipcover, and I remembered that the flounces bothered him. I had hardly sat down when I was distracted. Moreover, there was conversation going on around me. A novelist was really not taken seriously. Mary was of the opinion that the water in the tulips should be changed. In our apartment there were always flowers nearly everywhere. A room without flowers was a dead room, Anne was asserting.

"Couldn't you be quiet long enough for me to read this article?" my father asked.

"And while I'm trying to find to get my novel started," I said to myself.

At that moment Lucy entered, a picture of mystery. She glanced darkly at us and stalked across the room like a grenadier.

"Lucy, I can tell you're lost in thought," Mary said chattily.

No answer. Lucy never gave herself away. She disappeared as she had entered, then returned to go sit in front of the fireplace.

Closing my eyes, I tried to concentrate. A subject for a novel. How does one go about finding one? Today, nearly a half-century later, I ask the same question somewhat differently. How could a twenty-five-year-old writer escape from the novel surrounding him on all sides in the bright, peaceful living room where he was preparing his storms?

To tell the truth, I vaguely felt my characters' presence, but I didn't want to meet them in the familiar faces who watched me writing. It seemed a dishonest way to find models. According to my views then, you had to reinvent life. That's what creating was. Everything was to come out of my head. It was forbidden to look around. Life wrote its novel; I didn't have the right to lean over its shoulder and copy.

Actually the more I delayed in the living room, the more my book grew in that invisible region where works take shape. One of my reveries of those days pictured novels composed from one end to the other with the words placed in the desired order, in expectation that in time someone would discover the whole thing. Then it would only have to be transcribed. This vaguely platonic notion charmed me, and although I couldn't possibly take it completely seriously, it had an effect on me. It would be a mistake, I thought, to make an outline. That would risk writing the wrong book or disfiguring the good one if by chance an author got his hands on it. The only reasonable method was to dismiss all methods and to *find* the book, sentence by sentence. A writer had only to sit in front of the blank page and when the moment came—sometimes very long in coming—to let the pen take over. It would start with an image because an image was indispensable—and, as might be expected, the image would come directly from the imagination but corresponding to a reality.

Here the difficulties began. If the image was false, the author might not notice being led astray. It might be necessary to begin over, once, twice, even several times. Something finally alerted the author that he was on the right path. This was the moment of intoxication that I compared to the Pythian beginning to prophesy. The gift would gain strength, that of seeing and making visible. At night I thought about the next morning's page with a kind of frenzied impatience because I knew that page with un-known contents would be there with letters I would summon from the magic library.

What I was completely unaware of was that those books which I thought I invented, that is, discovered, truly preexisted in me, not in some kind of terrain of ideas but inside me. Futile to look in the depths of a mir-ror or in a family graveyard to encounter the *unknown*. It gave itself away on every page. In all innocence the author unmasked the guilty party, and the guilty party was the author.

What is the point of entering into all that detail unless it helps eluci-date the genesis of a work? Wasn't my problem like that of any other nov-elist who wonders where his novels come from? In the back of my mind, like so many geological layers, my poorly understood reading of Freud was acting, although it didn't touch me.

I hated psychoanalysis instinctively, but in Paris in 1926 I could no more prevent hearing it discussed than at the University, six years earlier, and I breathed in the nefarious and stultifying atmosphere. Everybody had complexes, and characters in a novel docilely followed fashion. For my part I didn't know what I was going to put in my narrative, but in me the unknown barred the door to Oedipus. That didn't touch me either.

After several false starts, I gave up working in the living room or even in my bedroom. The vacation season found me in an Alsatian village. Even calling it a village is a bit much. I had gone with a friend first to Orbey where we spent a day, and it was there in a hotel room that I wrote the first page of my novel. From time to time the piercing noise of a sawmill would cut the silence into fine slices. To that was added the horror of a wallpaper where I could see regularly spaced red disks which reminded me relentlessly of the necks of guillotine victims. We left the next day for a remote spot where we could discern, if I remember correctly, the peak of Linge which was the scene of violent battles in 1917.

You could not say the place called Hautes-Huttes was a village. There was a single building, the inn, on the road that led to the immense meadows which gently sloped down to the bottom of a valley. In all Europe we could not have found a more peaceful spot. Working there was delightful. My friend wrote his novel, and I wrote mine, the one with the first page "given" to me in the room with the sinister wallpaper.

At Hautes-Huttes the silence was pervasive, almost disturbing. I was happy to hear the song of a stork that tried all by herself to imitate the Orbey sawmill. Sometimes you could also hear from a wheatfield nearby the whispering of a stone sharpening the reaper's scythe.

Every time I glanced up from my page, I admired the idyllic landscape which seemed to speak only of happiness. Under the sparkling blue sky, hills, woodlands, pastures bordering gold and russet fields. It was a big event when one or two carts would pass in the space of an hour. I would run to the window, glance out curiously, then return to my novel, and what would I find?

Silence. I was at rue Cortambert, as should have been expected. I carried that nearly provincial street with me. I could in fact be in Alsatia; I breathed the air of our apartment and observed someone studying our graveyard, hands behind the back

Someone . . . not me, certainly. A young woman, the heroine, safe and secure, I realized. The unknown was arranging things as it would, I was tranquil. Did the heroine have a mother? No anecdotes in that area, the unknown decided. The heroine had lost her mother in childhood. As a result none of those stupid complexes would disturb the limpidity of my narrative.

So I could proceed blindly without risk. "Blindly," that was truly the case. However, someone was calling the young woman from a nearby room, asking her to change the water in the flowers. Like our family. But what readers would suspect it? I continued intrepidly. Everything was where it should be in this story which scorned current taste. The father was still missing. Adrienne surely had the right to have one. He wasn't far away. I called him "old Mesurat."

From that moment began my long game of hide-and-seek with Uncle Freud. Since the chapter was difficult for me to handle, I judged its beginning rather unpromising, lacking verve, even interest. Despite that, I persevered, intrigued precisely by what was dreary as well as true in that first page. Could so many things be hidden in the heart of a young woman gripped by boredom? She must have a secret.

A year later when the book was out, someone claimed that Adrienne was none other than I myself. These words struck me like a thunderclap, and to aggravate this revelation, my father, who had had the time to read the novel a few weeks before his death, declared with a somewhat sad smile, "Obviously I'm old Mesurat." I wasn't around when he made that statement, but my sisters cried out, "What do you mean, Papa! Because you read *Le Temps*? A simple coincidence!" They hadn't read Freud. My father hadn't either. His name was not uttered. It would have taken only that to make me desperate.

I easily persuaded myself I wasn't Adrienne Mesurat. People had simply picked it up to apply to me Flaubert's dictum on Madame Bovary. You can call yourself Madame Bovary, if you like, Flaubert, but I refused such bizarre *travestissements*.

As well as I can remember, the critics did not make any allusion to the psychoanalysis I had imbibed, imbibed more deeply than I knew, perhaps. Whatever the case, from the Surrealists came the murmur "automatic writing," and I had the feeling that they were on the right track. To tell the truth, I didn't know exactly what they meant by automatic writing, but it still wasn't necessary to understand it in order to guess, and the term "automatic" seemed to fit up to a certain point. I let my hand go as it pleased, and the sentences came out by themselves, not without a struggle, however. In order to begin writing I had to put myself in a state of perfect immobility, by which I mean internal immobility. Does this expression convey what I mean? It's the best I can find.

Something was working loose, getting free. I was expecting a kind of click which always accompanied this indescribable phenomenon, because, in the end, what does a click mean? That's what it was, however.

I knew that at a precise minute, what I now call the unknown would guide my hand, and slowly the words I needed would arrive. Several of my novels—not all of them—were written in this way. *Adrienne Mesurat* and *Leviathan* (The Dark Journey) from one end to the other, then *Moira* and some parts of *Chaque homme dans sa nuit* (Each in His Darkness). I wrote *Epaves* (The Strange River) all alone, if I may put it that way, and also *Varouna* (Then Shall the Dust Return). *Minuit* (Midnight) and *Le Visionnaire* (The Dreamer) benefited relatively little from the intervention that I describe, although it resists analysis. In *L'Autre Sommeil* (Another Sleep) the reality of the facts complicated my problem, and I experienced the agony of transposition. Almost nothing was *given* to me, the unknown having only to do there with the autobiographical truth unfurled in fiction.

I haven't mentioned *Le Voyageur sur la terre* (The Pilgrim on the Earth), which in my eyes remains the most mysterious of all my narratives because I wrote it without understanding very much about it. Indeed, up to the end, I believed in the reality of one of the characters who could only have been imaginary and there was something unexpressed in that story which escaped me totally. T. S. Eliot, who talked to me about it, was the first to throw a little light on that murky novelette. In that respect he saw it more clearly than Gide, whom my "Pilgrim" had pleased for purely literary reasons.

Years went by, and I thought no more about "Pilgrim" than I did about *Adrienne Mesurat* when Marc Schlumberger reported to one of my friends Stekel's opinion of the novel, which he presented to his students as a psychoanalytic novel written by someone who understood nothing about psychoanalysis. At first this formulation left me indifferent. What I had heard about psychoanalysis made me shrug my shoulders. Especially unacceptable to me was the famous Oedipus complex we were hit over the head with. Where I was concerned, I was certainly sure that there was nothing in me to concoct any psychological confusion of that sort. Where my father was concerned, in fact, everything seemed as ordinary as could be in our relationship from my childhood to his death. If I once found it a little difficult to talk to him, it was because to me he seemed more like a grandfather than a father. The age difference did that: forty-seven years. Occasionally, I admit, his slowness, his heavy silences, his melancholy, and his sighs made me a little impatient, but his kindness was apparent, and at eighteen or twenty I experienced still as in my childhood a sense of security to see him in our midst. The image of a huge oak tree came to mind. We lived in the protecting shade of this tree. Truth forces me to say that his death caused me less pain than sadness, but a sadness which lasted a long time.

What strikes me when I think about him is that he never showed the least opposition to my projects, nor to the lifestyle I adopted when I returned from America. No question on my goings and comings in Paris, even when I returned late, or, even as happened once or twice, when I slept out. I was free. The most he did was recommend prudence. "Be careful: if you can't be good, be careful." That is the advice given to boys in the U.S. With all that I saw the role of Oedipus reduced to zero because if I was Adrienne Mesurat, I didn't have, as she did, substantial reasons to push my father down the stairwell. His confidence in me was apparently limitless. He was unaware that, like so many boys my age, I threw myself into the streets every night in search of sensual pleasure.

That some autobiography had slipped into *Adrienne Mesurat* would be only natural. The trip to Dreux and Montfort-l'Amaury is true in its smallest details. In 1925 in an hour of moral distress that would recur often, I decided to leave Paris just to go anywhere else. At the Gare Montparnasse the name of Montfort-l'Amaury caught my eye. For the next forty-eight hours I took my anguish there and to Dreux. In describing the anxieties of my heroine, I only had to remember my own. If the motivation was different, the intensity wasn't, and I persuaded myself that Marivaux wasn't exaggerating when he claimed that, limited in everything, we are limited but little when it comes to pain.

Many other personal experiences served for unconscious borrowing. The stairway where Adrienne spent the night after the death of her father and which was transformed into a place of horror—how would I not find again the stairway of our 1908 villa where I shivered with excitement, seated on a step with a wavering candle and a collection of La Fontaine's fables? Childhood terrors have an indescribable quality. What a little boy of eight can see in masses of shadow which move at the slightest breath of air, only a novelist can imagine, but he doesn't imagine: he remembers. He is eight years old all over again.

I should never finish if I listed every detail life furnished me when I wrote. My error was, no doubt, in believing that I invented, but if I hadn't believed I was inventing everything, perhaps I wouldn't have written anything. In *Adrienne Mesurat* I certainly recognize the obsessed creature who pushes her arm through a window in an impulse to reach the inaccessible. The author himself was satisfied with separating the curtains and pressing his martyr's forehead against the glass. Other images come back to me, numerous and perfectly readable. A young man can hardly pick up his pen without telling about himself. Who thinks he can fool anyone by putting a mask over his face? Eyes tell the truth, but he doesn't know about that; he does not see his own glance. At least age will teach him the meaning of that disguise. Yet it doesn't. The trickery continues on the plane of fiction where all is allowed in a kind of higher game.

I have never really been a reader of my work. Once printed, a book remains closed to me, keeping the secret of its defects, but how could I not discover the blood kinship between Adrienne and the violent loners of my other narratives? If the young Frenchwoman is smothered by the invisible walls of her moral prison, Karin the Danish girl paces as if in a jail in the heart of a city which pretends not to see her. Nor should we exclude Joseph in *Moira,* enclosed in his seamless virtue from which he can escape only through crime. All became like that line in Milton, their own dungeons, not by a penchant for misfortune but from the effects of inexorable determinism. The *fatum* of the ancients has been mentioned in this connection. A relationship may exist between this rigorous way of viewing human fate and the fatalistic mentality prior to our era. Christianity came to obstruct the terrible mechanism of destiny, but the traces of that liberation don't appear until late in my novels. How does that happen? Psychoanalysis is there, as always, on the job and full of answers. I have not retained them because in my eyes at least they do not dissipate the mystery. Behind the explanations of psychoanalysis, there is, in my opinion, an eternal "why."

If ever a novelist has worked in the night of literary creation, it is certainly the person writing these lines. However, I am not the only one, and that in itself would justify my attempts at clarification. The list would be long of writers famous and obscure who in telling their stories have simply told their own story, the story of the person they do not know, who held the pen and guided the hand.

What does all this mean? Is there really in us writers someone who hides and who tries nevertheless to be expressed in our books through the figurative language of the novel? Where does this mysterious host come from? From our childhood? Is it therefore the child who speaks and acts, intoxicated by the immense freedom of fiction? Doesn't Dickens ever remove himself from his pots of blacking on which his hand, trembling with rage, pastes labels? Will Dostoevski leave the nightmare where he sees his father castrated and killed by the mujiks? We can wonder whether Stendhal himself completely escaped the charm of Uncle Gagnon. Now Dickens's revenge on society is almost total. He makes it over from top to bottom. Sometimes he shakes it with a burst of laughter, sometimes he walks over it, knife in hand, because there is in him an adolescent of the most disturbing type, a "terror." Dostoevski's soul is universal. He is Karamazov, a pig, but also running from one pole of childhood to the other, he is Alyosha. He is all the decadents, all the killers, all the *startsi,* all the victims and saints of his creation. As for the tender and violent Stendhal, we will find him in the features of those handsome young men, all closer to the irresistible Gagnon than the forty-year-old with sideburns who doesn't like his own looks. As soon as he writes, everything fails, he suffers and causes suffering the way a millionaire spends his fortune. And did Balzac need hundreds of characters to fulfill himself? Did Flaubert need an entire province backed by a Carthage and deserts full of Anchorites beset by hallucinations? A boar and a unicorn? But the child has such demands. Imagination has taken charge.

(Translated by Marilyn Gaddis Rose)

Adrienne Mesurat

figurative language of the novel? Where does this mysterious host come from? From our childhood? Is it therefore the child who speaks and acts, intoxicated by the immense freedom of fiction? Doesn't Dickens ever remove himself from his pots of blacking on which his hand, trembling with rage, pastes labels? Will Dostoevski leave the nightmare where he sees his father castrated and killed by the mujiks? We can wonder whether Stendhal himself completely escaped the charm of Uncle Gagnon. Now Dickens's revenge on society is almost total. He makes it over from top to bottom. Sometimes he shakes it with a burst of laughter, sometimes he walks over it, knife in hand, because there is in him an adolescent of the most disturbing type, a "terror." Dostoevski's soul is universal. He is Karamazov, a pig, but also running from one pole of childhood to the other, he is Alyosha. He is all the decadents, all the killers, all the *startsi,* all the victims and saints of his creation. As for the tender and violent Stendhal, we will find him in the features of those handsome young men, all closer to the irresistible Gagnon than the forty-year-old with sideburns who doesn't like his own looks. As soon as he writes, everything fails, he suffers and causes suffering the way a millionaire spends his fortune. And did Balzac need hundreds of characters to fulfill himself? Did Flaubert need an entire province backed by a Carthage and deserts full of Anchorites beset by hallucinations? A boar and a unicorn? But the child has such demands. Imagination has taken charge.

(Translated by Marilyn Gaddis Rose)

Part One

Chapter I

Drawn up to her full height and with her hands behind her back, Adrienne stood looking at "the graveyard."

This was the name given in the Mesurat family to a group of a dozen portraits hanging above a sideboard in the dining room, so close together that they almost covered one side of the wall. There were seven Mesurats, three Serres, and two Lecuyers, the latter families connected with them by marriage, all dead. With the exception of one painting about which we shall have something to say later, they were photographs such as were common twenty-five years ago, frank and harsh, in which the face appeared against a white backdrop without any indulgent shadow softening its defects, and where truth is suffered to speak its own harsh language.

It was easy to tell the Mesurats from the Serres and the Lecuyers at a glance. With their low foreheads, their strongly marked features, and an indefinable air of decision in their faces, it was a common saying that the former family looked like leaders. Men and women alike, they gazed at you straight between the eyes with the almost aggressive authority a good conscience confers. "What about you?" they seemed to be saying. "Do you know what it means to have a tranquil heart, whose beats are always steady, which knows neither fear nor anxiety, which receives its joys and portions out its suffering with composure, and all because it has nothing to reproach itself for?"

There were old faces and young faces. This girl wearing the veil over her head must have died before thirty, a nun in some active order. She had the same flat cheeks, the same strongly molded jaw as the white-haired man in a frock coat. The old woman beside her, with an avaricious mouth and steady eyes that seemed to be adding up an account, was quite evidently her mother.

In contrast to the Mesurats, whom no one could possibly confuse with any other family, the Serres and Lecuyers were much alike and might well have sprung from the same stock. You guessed that they had been born, grown to maturity, and disappeared like so many plants, content with life and no less resigned to death. Their aggregate appearance conveyed nothing, unless perhaps that vacant, wandering and good-natured expression that one catches at times in the eyes of a crowd. It was a common saying that only their money explained their alliance with the Mesurats, and the same people who described these latter as leaders would add that they had swooped upon the Lecuyers and Serres like falcons on lambs.

Strong and weak alike, Mesurats, Serres or Lecuyers, all paled into insignificance before old Antoinette Mesurat, who ruled like a queen even the proudest members of this sturdy stock, and her portrait in oils, painted by an artist of the literal school, dominated this rugged stock, and attracted attention from the first. Possibly fifty years old at the time her picture was painted, she was one of those women for whom age does not exist, and whose face—as though nature, satisfied with its work, had decided against any modification—rapidly acquires the characteristics it will carry to the grave. The grizzling hair, drawn tightly back, revealed a short, round skull where there was little room for ideas and still less for change once the preconceived ideas had acquired their place. Studying the massive forehead, unfurrowed by a single wrinkle, you would inevitably conjure up the image of a wall. In the black eyes there was nothing of the rather vacant look of the Serres and Lecuyers, which appeared to be fixed on some object in space. These were the watchful, wide-open eyes of a self-possessed woman who looks facts in the face and measures obstacles to her will without the flicker of an eyelid. Her deep bust and powerful shoulders were covered with a silk bodice, whose sheen the skill of the artist had sought to reproduce. But no futile grace of brushwork could soften in the slightest degree the energy and stubbornness that inhered in every line of the powerful and martial physique

Adrienne remained motionless a few moments before these portraits. As her eye wandered from one to another her head fell a little to one side. She sighed.

"Is that you, Adrienne?" said a woman's voice from an adjoining room. "What are you doing?"

With a mechanical gesture, Adrienne began to pass a duster over the marble top of the sideboard.

"Nothing," she replied. "The glass of these photographs is so dirty you can hardly see what's underneath."

"You should wash them with a little alcohol and then rub them with a dry cloth," answered the voice after a moment's pause.

There was a brief silence.

"They'll be just as ugly afterward," said Adrienne, as if talking to herself.

Taking a seat upon one of the velvet-covered chairs ranged against the wall, she began to stare at two rectangles of sunlight that lay upon the carpet beneath the windows.

She bowed her head from boredom as someone else might from fatigue. But her shoulders stayed square, and her back did not bend. At first glance, with her hair covered by a big handkerchief and a blue apron tied over her skirt, you might have taken her for a servant. But she had a commanding look which would have quickly corrected that impression. She was a true Mesurat, and despite her extreme youth (she was no more than eighteen), her face already revealed the passion for authority whose full expansion could be studied in the portrait of Antoinette Mesurat, her grandmother. Between the two women, indeed, there was a resemblance so marked as to be almost ludicrous. But the eyes of the younger woman were intact with youth. Her full mouth and pursed lips betrayed a healthiness that was to be sought vainly in the pale face of her older sister. Her cheeks were still rounded and retained a childish bloom which lent an air of innocence to a face where an unwavering mind was so evident. It was only after looking at her for some time that you realized she was beautiful.

She got up and, after shaking her duster out the window, leaned against the bar and looked from end to end of the street. The great heat was keeping everyone indoors, and only at rare intervals did anyone pass by, hugging the meager shadow at the foot of the walls. The girl's eyes rested for a moment upon a few stunted lime trees in the garden opposite and passed almost immediately to a house known as the Villa Louise, a house which formed the angle of the street. The shutters were closed. It was a pretentious little affair, built of flint divided into compartments by thin courses of brick, with a little turret at one corner and a roof of patterned tiles. Another house, entirely white and covered with a slate roof, stood away from it on the other side of the street. Adrienne by turning her head a little was able to see that its shutters, too, were closed. A step sounded on the pavement. Instinctively the girl snatched off the kerchief that covered her hair. Lowering her head, she recognized a neighbor, who was walking with her eyes fixed on the ground and a string bag over one arm. She drew quickly back, as though she dreaded being seen, and remained motionless, braced against the window-frame, until the footsteps died away.

The voice called again. Adrienne threw the handkerchief over her hair and knotted the two ends behind her neck. Then she went into the parlor.

With a slow deliberate glance she assured herself that everything here was in good order. The armchairs and chairs, arranged in a circle in the middle of the carpet, gave a somewhat ceremonious air to this part of the house. The walls were hung in a reddish paper, decorated with a design of something that looked like violet-colored thistles. There were a few inferior pictures—blackened landscapes and portraits carefully protected by glass. The dark wood furniture was of the Regency style, modified by the taste for comfort which prevailed at the period of the Second Empire. Backs were ample, legs solid, the plush of the upholstery had a rich pile. It all invited rest and inspired confidence.

A long couch had been drawn as near the window as possible, in such a manner that nothing of the figure stretched on it could be seen except the drawn-up knees and one thin little hand that lay upon them. It was the woman who had just spoken to Adrienne.

"You ought to change the water in the flowers," she said, turning at the sound of Adrienne's footsteps.

"I will, later on. Isn't Désirée somewhere around?"

"She's gone to market."

Adrienne walked over to the mantelpiece and frowned as she studied a pair of bronze candlesticks that stood upon it.

"Tell me," she asked, presently, "do you know when the new people are coming who have rented the Villa Louise?"

"The new tenants of the Villa Louise? June or the beginning of July, I suppose. They didn't think of writing to tell me. In any case, it is high time they clipped their lime trees and painted their shutters."

There was a brief pause and the voice began again.

"Anyway, this year it isn't 'the tenants,' it's 'the tenant.' A Madame Legras, all by herself, it appears."

Adrienne turned her head toward the window.

"I know. We've heard plenty about that from papa."

She took up a glass vase full of geraniums and walked toward the door.

"Where are you going?" asked the voice.

"To change the water in these flowers."

The door opened and closed. A deep silence descended upon the parlor, the silence that seems as much a part of hot summer days as the light itself. On the hardwood floor, waxed and polished to excess, and between two crimson-red rugs, a ray of sunshine lay like a wide stripe of burnished metal. By the window a few flies were circling lazily in the close air. There was the distant gurgle of water rising in a vase. The door opened again.

"Do you remember what time they came last year?" asked Adrienne as she came into the room.

"Who? Are you still talking about the people opposite?"

"Yes, of course."

The answer came only after another pause.

". . . End of May."

Adrienne wiped the vase on her apron. She set it down in the center of a small round table and drew near the couch.

"How do you feel today?" she asked, still gazing out the window.

"All right," answered the voice with a slight inflexion of surprise. "The same as usual."

"Oh!" said Adrienne.

An expression that was pensive and embarrassed at the same time came over her face. She put her hands on her hips and threw her head back, her eyes still fixed on the Legras villa.

7

"You'd have more sun across the street," she said, suddenly.

"We have sun here all the morning."

"There you'd have it in the morning, and afternoon too"—she stopped a moment and then went on to explain herself, a little impatiently—"because the house faces west and south. At this very moment if Madame Legras was there she'd have the rue du Président Carnot full of sun."

She had said this with a mixture of sadness and indignation that she had trouble controlling.

Although no one could see her, she motioned with her hand toward the street she was talking about.

There was silence for a few moments.

"You're quite right," said the voice. "Well—she isn't there to enjoy it. . . . Will you help me get up, Adrienne? If you would just pull the sofa toward you—"

Without a word, Adrienne put her hand on the back of the lounge and pulled it away from the wall—quite easily, for she was strong. The woman who had been lying under the window got to her feet and took a few steps, steadying herself on one piece of furniture after another. Her age seemed uncertain because illness had made her old before her time; and you would have hesitated to give her thirty-five years. Her tall body was stooped like that of an old man who didn't seem able to hold himself up, and she kept her right hand extended as she walked, in a fashion that suggested blindess. Constant fear of stumbling had accentuated her naturally timid expression. Her eyebrows, perpetually drawn together by suffering anxiety, had ended by carving two deep parallel lines on her forehead. She had a prominent nose, which gave a false sense of assurance to her features, and her hollow cheeks were completedly etched with minute wrinkles.

As Adrienne stepped aside to let her pass, she fell back into an armchair with her mouth half open, breathing quickly as she let her eyes wander around the room. The younger woman, her arms still akimbo, looked at her silently, with hard eyes that nothing seemed to soften.

"What is it?" she asked at last, abruptly,. "Are you tired, Germaine?"

The sick woman raised her head.

"No," she said. "What's the matter? Do I look bad?"

Her eyes opened wider as a sudden fear welled up in them.

"Why don't you answer? Do I look bad?" she repeated, seeing that Adrienne wasn't going to open her mouth.

Adrienne shrugged her shoulders.

"I didn't say you looked bad," she said quickly.

"I slept five hours last night," Germaine insisted with the effusiveness of those who are making out a good case for themselves. "I feel quite well; just the same as yesterday and the day before."

But Adrienne was looking out the window and wasn't listening.

Chapter II

The house in which the Mesurats lived was called Villa des Charmes, because there were two hornbeam trees which grew in the narrow garden between it and the roadway. M. Mesurat had bought it at the time he retired and made up his mind to live in the country. It pleased him just as much as though it had been built to his design. But among his neighbors it was a common comment that it usurped precious space where a really fine house might have been built, and that it was unworthy of such an important street as the rue Thiers. To tell the truth, it was a rather poor effort. Possibly because its architect had been required to fit the largest possible number of rooms into the space assigned him, or for some other reason, it had one unpardonable defect. Its front windows (there were two on each side of the door, four on the first story and four on the story above) were so close together that their frames practically touched, leaving hardly anything of the façade visible. In view of the material that had been used for it, this was, perhaps, just as well. The builder had chosen a coarse stone, streaked with minute fissures, whose color inevitably recalls a certain kind of brown nougat. Hundreds of similar houses are to be found in the outer suburbs of Paris, with the same balustraded flight of front steps, the identical shell-shaped penthouse above their doors. It must have been the ideal of an entire class of French society to have been so eagerly and uniformly reproduced.

However, M. Mesurat was not blind to the imperfections of his villa. He judged it, indeed, with the extra severity that we sometimes keep for those we love. Perhaps it was so he wouldn't have to blush for it. Whenever he spoke about it to his neighbors, it was in the tone with which reference is made to some poor but honest relative. But he would have liked it to be as generally admired as he admired it himself. Sometimes, late in the afternoon, when he had finished the perusal of his newspaper and had nothing to occupy his mind till dinner, he regretted that he had no friends whom he could invite inside, if only that they might realize the many advantages of his beloved villa, the size of its rooms, the splendid view their windows afforded upon the gardens of the Villa Louise. . . . Who was to guess from its exterior alone how perfectly his villa was planned and built? Who would dare to say, after a visit to the interior, that a Mesurat had made a bad bargain?

But this man, so jovial and tyrannical at home, was as timid as a child, once he had shut the gate of the Villa des Charmes behind him. Up to now the stationmaster at La Tour l'Evêque was the only person with whom he had any sort of acquaintance. The friendship had grown up as the result of a thousand petty incidents, not the least of which was the purchase of his newspaper, morning and evening, at the station bookstall. No doubt there had been company at the Villa des Charmes in the past. But for some time, and for reasons which the reader will learn presently, their visits had completely ceased.

The complacency so noticeable in Antoine Mesurat as concerned his property appeared ridiculous to his daughters, who found plenty of room for improvement in Villa des Charmes. Nevertheless, by virtue of a dispensation that is common after a certain age has been reached, he perceived nothing to wound his feelings or to make him change his conduct in the slightest.

This old man was serenity itself. He was short, thickset, with a big chest that he was fond of thumping with his fist as though to display its solidity. He had the tranquil and stubborn face of men who do not suffer life to disturb them, and who cling to their peace of mind as a miser clings to his treasure. No emotion of any sort was to be read in his eyes, striking in their empty expression, and of so lively a blue that they seemed to diffuse a sort of light over the forehead, temples and sanguine cheeks. A dull blond beard, white around the edges, hid his chin and reached almost to his tie. Whenever anyone looked at him, he had a funny way of wrinkling his fleshy nose and blinking his eyes. But this was a tic with no ironic intent. Usually he talked and smiled a lot.

Most assuredly, he was happy. His life was the simplest. But it was made up of certain habits which he had acquired one by one, as someone might gather flowers or rare stones in the course of a long walk, and he cherished each and every one with all his heart. His daily stroll across the town, the arrival of the evening paper, the hour of dinner—all were so many felicitous moments for this man, who seemed destined to live forever, so much joy and energy did he put into the mere act of keeping his place among the living.

He had been a writing master at a large school in Paris, and in the year 1908, at which time this story opens, had reached the age of sixty. Fifteen years earlier he had lost his wife—whose maiden name, Lecuyer, was commonplace enough—of whom he spoke little and regretted not at all. Afterward, he had won a considerable sum in a lottery, which allowed him to retire a few years earlier than would otherwise have been possible, and to live at his ease, a simple matter for him because his tastes were very modest. Perfect regularity reigned inside Villa des Charmes. There were three bedrooms, and three occupants for them—himself, Germaine and Adrienne, his two daughters. "What more could one ask?" he used to say, stroking his beard with the back of his thumb, his mouth open.

That evening Germaine failed to appear at the table. M. Mesurat frowned. Departures from rule did not please him.

"Isn't she coming to dinner?" he asked as he took his seat.

Adrienne was on her feet. She was occupied in pulling down an enormous hanging lamp with a ground-glass globe until it reached the tips of the flowers which decorated the center of the table. The rise and fall of this heavy affair was operated by a counter-weight and a series of chains.

"Is Germaine not coming to dinner?" M. Mesurat asked again.

Adrienne mumbled a response which was lost in the noise of the chains. She sat down and unfolded her napkin.

"Well?" said the old man, impatiently. "Did you hear me speak?"

The young woman looked him straight in the eyes.

"I answered you," she said, shortly. "Germaine is not feeling very well."

"Then she is not having any dinner?"

"No."

He shook his head and crumbled a piece of bread into his soup without further questions. Adrienne ate in silence.

When his soup plate was empty, he wiped his mouth and smoothed his beard.

"I took my walk this afternoon," he said, reaching out for the wine decanter. "There's quite a lot of building going on behind the presbytery."

"Is there?"

"Yes, the big house. You know the one I mean."

Adrienne nodded.

"They are at the third story. The flag will be up before July."

He filled his glass and strummed on the tablecloth, stretching out his fingers like a pianist.

"Do you know when the tenants opposite are to arrive?" asked Adrienne after a moment's silence.

He stopped strumming and looked at his daughter.

"No. Why do you want to know?"

"No particular reason."

M. Mesurat inclined his head to one side and half-closed his eyes.

"Last year—"

"Ah!" exclaimed Adrienne in spite of herself.

"—it seems to me the people who had it came in June. Are you anxious to know Madame Legras?"

"I? No indeed. We're much quieter without her."

She pushed back her plate and crossed her arms on the table.

"Have you finished?" asked her father.

"Yes."

He rang the bell and resumed his strumming with a satisfied air. During the rest of the meal he entertained his daughter with the changes he had noted since he first came to La Tour l'Evêque. But she was not listening. From time to time she patted her hair as though to assure herself it was tidy, and although she sometimes shook her head in her father's direction, her eyes were vacant, and it was quite evident that she was following a train of thought foreign to the long dissertations of M. Mesurat. The milky light from the lamp fell full upon her and gave to her face a pallor that accentuated its somewhat impassive character. A shadow emphasized the straight line of her brows and the rather heavy contour of the lower lip, very much as a portraitist stresses certain features whose significance he wishes to throw into relief.

As soon as dinner was over, she left her father settled for his evening in the parlor and went out, her head covered with a scarf. The air was mild. She followed the rue Thiers, left the Villa Louise behind, and stopped at the corner of the rue du Président Carnot, which ran straight to the main highway. For a moment she hesitated, listening attentively to a murmur of voices which seemed to come from a neighboring garden but it was dark and she had no fear of being seen. She stood with her back against the wall, and raised her eyes. A few yards away, at the corner of the road, a small square building was visible. Its roof was lost in the darkness, but its whitewashed walls stood out, as though faintly luminous. Two black oblongs, one above the other, indicated the place of shuttered windows.

Minute after minute passed. The sound of footsteps fell upon her ears. Someone was coming down the street from the direction of the state highway. She left her place reluctantly and, turning the angle of the Villa Legras, followed the rue Thiers as far as another street, which crossed it at right angles. Here she waited, unable to make up her mind to go in. From the crest of a wall just over her head bunches of wistaria exhaled the heavy odor of flowers which have wilted in the heat of too warm a day. She looked at the two lighted windows in her own house. The lower one belonged to the parlor, the other, two stories higher, to her sister's bedroom. Still listening carefully to the footsteps which were slowly approaching down the rue du Président Carnot, she tried to pass the time away by imagining the two indoors. First, Antoine Mesurat, in his armchair, his legs stretched out before him, the collar of his waistcoat up under his ears, dozing, with a newspaper in his hand; then Germaine, sitting up in bed with a pile of pillows behind her head, her face flushed with the fever which gripped her every night, her eyes upon a book which she was holding before her, but her thoughts far away.

The feet came nearer; they crossed the rue Thiers and continued down the rue du Président Carnot. Adrienne thrilled with pleasure. In her haste to return along the way which she had just traversed, she began to run on tiptoe. She stopped, breathless, at the gate of the Villa Louise, and gripped one of its bars. Something that was almost happiness dawned upon her face. Her eyes shone with emotion and she seemed to be counting the quick breaths that came from between her open lips. As soon as the footsteps died away she resumed her walk and arrived at the spot she had just left.

Once more she leaned her back against the wall of Villa Louise. This time she could distinguish the entire silhouette of the square building, even to the stone quoins at its angles, which stood out darkly against the whitewashed walls. From time to time a ray of moonlight broke through the clouds with which the sky was covered and fell upon the slate roof. The young woman strained her eyes to catch the play of this fugitive gleam. All at once the moon rose. An entire side of the street leaped into view and stood out in the brilliance of this clear light. It was all so unexpected that Adrienne could not refrain from a start of surprise. She advanced to the middle of the road. The slate roof glistened now like a sheet of water struck by a ray of light. Between the high chimneys the black top of a tree swayed to and fro. From the recesses of some garden far away two dogs began to bark in chorus.

She listened, looked again, seemed to be waiting for something. Finally, as the street darkened anew, she drew the cool air deep into her lungs, threw a last glance at the house, which seemed to be foundering in the gloom, lowered her head, and returned home.

As she entered the parlor to seek a book, the noise of her footsteps awoke her father, who was sound asleep in his armchair. He stretched his arms toward the ceiling and yawned.

"Have you been out?" he asked.

"No," she answered, looking at him steadily. "You've been asleep."

"So I have. What time is it now?"

"I don't know."

She took up a book that was lying on a desk, and left the room.

It was not her custom to delay going to bed. But tonight she waited an appreciable time in the corridor outside her own door, hearkening to the noises of the house. Downstairs, old Mesurat was seeing to the bolts upon door and windows. The rafters trembled as his heavy tread passed from room to room. He coughed. Soon she heard the two strong puffs with which he extinguished the lamps in dining-room and parlor, and almost immediately he began to hum a march from some popular opera. She knew that presently he would be coming upstairs. She entered her bedroom, closed its door stealthily, and stood awhile, still listening, in the dark. Mesurat had begun to climb the staircase. His hand fell heavily upon the wooden hand-rail; the banisters creaked with a noise that Adrienne knew well. Passing his daughter's door, he rapped upon the panel with his fist, and cried, "Good night."

Adrienne started, but did not reply. Expected as it was, the mere sound of her father's voice was so disagreeable to her mood that it reached her like a blow. She uttered an "Ah!" that was part exclamation, part sigh, and lit her lamp. The feet climbed on. They stopped at the upper landing, where M. Mesurat had his own bedroom.

Chapter III

Now, the house was absolutely still. Not a sound came from the street. It was a moment especially distasteful to Adrienne. She would have liked to hear a door close, to catch the murmur of a voice. She hoped that her father had forgotten his newspaper or pipe and would go downstairs again to fetch it. She even found herself listening for, as something suddenly grown desirable, the dismal sound of her sister's cough, which she hated to hear during the day. But she was well aware that Germaine put her head under the bedclothes at night to smother the sound.

She undressed slowly, herself taking pains, so tyrannical a thing is complete silence, to make no noise, and got into bed without blowing out the lamp on her bedside table. She knew she would not fall asleep for hours, and she was unwilling to lie awake in the dark. The air was heavy and the lighted lamp increased the heat. She lowered its wick. For a few moments she tried to become interested in the yellow-covered novel which she had brought up with her. But in face of the hundreds of pages to come, boredom overtook her. She slipped the volume beneath her pillow, put one bare arm under her head, and waited, motionless, in an attitude that had become habitual with her.

The silence around her seemed to be full of a vague and continuous buzz, like that of some tiny insect; the sound was only in her own ears. Her eyes wandered from side to side of the room, striving to discover some new aspect in its familiar furnishings which might have escaped her till now. She detested her room, especially at night, during the empty hours that passed before sleep. The flowered wallpaper which her father himself had chosen, and of which he was so proud; the wardrobe, bought in one of the big stores and given her as a present on her sixteenth birthday; the iron bedstead on which she lay—how many memories they all represented, how many insupportable years, how many restless nights similar to this!

She never looked back upon her childhood without a feeling of lassitude, so arid did these epochs of her existence seem to her. When had she ever been happy? Where were those moments of happiness of which childhood is supposed to be composed? Where were her holidays? Brought up by a father who lived only for his comfort, and by a sister who thought of nothing except her illness, she had early become callous. Before the puckered eyebrows of Germaine she had learned to laugh rarely and to speak little. She had grown up in a positive apprehension of displeasing old Mesurat, who had patience with neither sulks nor tears. In such a school the will matures early. Everything in her that was morose and disdainful—the Mesurat side of her character, in a word—had developed at the expense of the Lecuyer. A precocious severity tightened her lips, lowered the straight line of the brows, and gave her face the expression of concentration and firmness which was the characteristic of her family upon the paternal side.

By the time she reached sixteen she seemed to have already acquired the moral and physical physiognomy that she would bear to the end of her life. Without friends, and without any apparent desire to make them, she followed the classes at Ste.-Cécile, where her sister sent her, answered her schoolmistress when questioned upon her lessons, and came back home to wander in the garden alone or to shut herself up in her room. Nothing seemed to influence her. She feared nothing, desired nothing. Boredom and a sort of sullen resignation alone could be read upon her face.

Two years had glided by in a profound monotony. Existence at the Villa des Charmes followed the rhythm that Germaine and M. Mesurat imposed upon it. Life became a series of habits—of fixed gestures accomplished at fixed moments. Change of any sort would have had an aspect of anarchy. Distractions were out of the question, and Adrienne, little by little, as though obeying some unwritten rule, had come to dispose of her time in as precise a mode and as rigorous a fashion as in a convent. She, too, knew the necessity of accomplishing each task at a given moment. But, by a singular contradiction in her nature, the necessity displeased her, and she resembled a nun who has lost her faith yet who keeps a sort of irritable attachment for her rule, because it is the rule which she once chose for herself.

Adrienne had reached her eighteenth year without any event, good or bad, modifying the current of her life. Her father had often made her come down when some caller was being entertained. He would keep her with him a few moments, regarding her complacently, for he was proud of her and thought her beautiful. Then, as soon as he judged that the visitor had been sufficiently edified as to the good appearance of his daughter, he would dismiss her as though she were a child. It is a fact frequently observed that the world and humanity cease to change or develop in the eyes of old people. At a certain point in their lives everything becomes static. Adrienne was fifteen years old the year M. Mesurat reached fifty-seven and was never to appear a year older in her father's imagination.

It may be thought surprising that no question of Adrienne's marriage had ever arisen. But, in addition to the fact that M. Mesurat desired nothing so little as to hear it raised, and that Germaine gave the matter no thought, the girl herself seemed indifferent. Wasn't life going on well enough? What need to complicate matters?

Suitors had presented themselves, for the Mesurats were not without property. But the young men bore the small-town stamp too evidently upon them. Sons of notaries or tradesmen, they had all alike appeared impossible, and their proposals as strange as though made by so many idiots. Adrienne failed to conceive what life would be like in the company of any one of them. The very notion made her laugh. Mesurat, too, and in no uncertain fashion, repelled the idea of letting go a daughter to whose company he had grown accustomed. He joined in the merriment as though some enormity, too palpable to be taken seriously, had been proposed. Germaine kept silent. It was from this date that visits from outside became rare events. Confronted by the almost hostile attitude of Mesurat, they gradually ceased completely.

19

Nevertheless, under the façade of this uniform existence, Adrienne concealed a restlessness that no one would have suspected. Her life had made her cunning, and the face which she presented to the eyes of father and sister was one upon which neither one nor the other, even if they had taken the trouble to seek it, would have read the least emotion. At night in her room, or by day during her walks abroad, she entertained a host of thoughts which she would not have avowed to a living creature and of which she herself felt a little ashamed. It is only at the cost of infinite precautions that the proud timidity of those who have grown used to withdrawing into themselves and repelling the outer world can ever be penetrated. Adrienne herself would have had difficulty in finding words to express her feelings. It is even likely that the word "feeling" would have struck her as bizarre. All that memory could offer her was a series of images with which neither joy nor sorrow was associated, but whose force was so great that they prevented her from thinking of anything else.

She saw herself, especially, two weeks earlier. It was on a road near the surburbs of La Tour l'Evêque. She was wearing a blue percale dress and her arms were full of field flowers. It was a hot, still day. Somewhere up in the sky a lark was uttering a strident note that seemed the very voice of the heat and glare. Shadows had dwindled to a black thread at the foot of each tree and post. Adrienne could feel little warm pearls of sweat trickle slowly down her temples and arms. Suddenly she perceived a carriage coming toward her from the direction of the town. It was one of those hired hacks which seem never to have been anything but shabby, with squeaky springs and dusty cushions. The driver wore an alpaca jacket and had put his handkerchief under his straw hat. Without her knowing why, the spectacle of the advancing carriage seemed full of interest to the girl. She stepped aside into the long grass at the edge of the road to see it pass. As it came nearer she recognized the man who was sitting in the carriage. It was a Dr. Maurecourt, who had established a practice at La Tour l'Evêque some months earlier. M. Mesurat had never dreamed of inviting him to his house, although they were neighbors and the older man felt a very lively curiosity where the doctor was concerned. But Mesurat's timidity prevented him from making any overture. Moreover, he had heard that the doctor never accepted invitations, declining them on the plea that he was very busy. Busy? With what? The town was small; his practice could not be very extensive. All the same, it was quite true that the doctor made none but professional visits. No one ever saw him strolling in the public park or chatting at the garden gates during a walk, as was the habit of his fellow townsmen. On the contrary, he walked quickly, head down.

The carriage passed close to Adrienne. Possibly the doctor became conscious of the searching glance that the girl sent in his direction. He raised his eyes from the book he was reading and turned his head toward the spot on which she stood. He was a small, slight man, of middle age, but with a pallor that added to his years. In his sallow face Adrienne noted a pair of dark eyes which rested upon her with a certain curiosity. He seemed to hesitate, then touched his hat with a shy and almost furtive gesture. It was only a second before the carriage rolled by.

The incident left a very strong impression upon Adrienne's mind. It was a little like one of those dreams which stick in the memory by reason of their extraordinary character. Indeed, the impression that the whole walk that day left upon her mind was of a waking dream. When she had stepped aside from the road and stood in the grass, it was with a firm persuasion that the moment was an important one for her and that she would often think of it subsequently. But is this not often the case with those to whom life at the moment offers nothing and who place a foolish and superstitious hope in the immediate future? How many times before had she not had the same certitude? How many prisoners have thrilled each morning with joyous anticipation at the jangle of their jailers' keys?

Through a habit which Adrienne immediately contracted, the road beside which she had stood to see Maurecourt pass became her regular and favorite walk. Moreover, as on the first occasion, she never failed to fill her arms with a bouquet of daisies and meadow-sweet, reckoning, no doubt, with the obscure reasoning of a mind at its wits' end from monotony, that like circumstances produce like effects. And, though the doctor never reappeared on the road, she armed herself with all the obstinacy inherited from her father and covered the same ground every day for a week.

However, this Maurecourt, so little in evidence and whom none could flatter themselves they knew, lived not far from the Villa des Charmes. Some time elapsed before Adrienne learned this fact. As a rule she lent only a distracted ear to the chit-chat which her father retailed each evening. But from the day on which she saw the doctor she became more curious. Without asking any questions, she listened. It was by this means she learned (M. Mesurat being one of those for whom a piece of news keeps its freshness after weeks of comment) that Dr. Maurecourt had leased the square house opposite the Villa Louise. At first she was reluctant to believe it, as one is reluctant to believe in the reality of any event that is personally disastrous or advantageous, and she watched her father keenly before admitting to herself that he spoke the truth. The old man was cutting his meat into small pieces with the concentration of people whose ultimate passion is consumption, and noticed nothing of the anxiety that his daughter was doing her best to conceal.

"Papa," said she, after a moment's pause, and in a toneless voice, "what a good thing that will be for Germaine!"

Germaine had finished her own dinner and was stretched out in the parlor. M. Mesurat drew his eyebrows together.

"What has it got to do with Germaine? She's not sick, is she?"

"No," said Adrienne, resuming her customary caution. "But if she fell ill—"

"Why, then, of course," assented old Mesurat grudgingly. "It's a handy thing for everybody to have a doctor nearby."

"Yes, indeed," said Adrienne.

She hurried to her room as soon as possible, to hide her shining eyes and the cheeks which she felt were glowing with excitement. She leaned out the window and perceived the top of the square house and the corner of a shutter. Had she known of this house before? How was it she had never noticed it? It seemed to her now that the little building, of which she could just make out an angle, must have risen from the ground, at the corner of the street, like a palace in the *Arabian Nights*. She feasted her eyes with the sight of it. She gazed at the plumed head of a young tree which trembled between its red brick chimneys, and at the regular design of the dark stone quoins.

Suddenly an idea entered her head. She left her room, and stood for a moment upon the staircase, leaning against the banisters. Scraps of conversation reached her from the parlor. She could distinguish Germaine's voice questioning her father. She mounted noiselessly to the landing above, entered her sister's room, and walked to the open window. Again she leaned out eagerly. At her feet the street was now visible in its entire length; there was nothing here to impede her vision as on the floor below. Her eye could survey the whole of the Villa Louise garden from wall to

2 2

wall. But it was not this which interested her. She was examining the white house. How well she saw it all from here—from the ridge of its slate roof to the little barred window of the cellar! The two windows were open. She could distinguish a red tablecloth and the corner of a piece of furniture—a writing-desk, perhaps. She drew her head in, her heart beating wildly, and sat down upon the window seat. With a lingering glance, charged with sudden longing and sadness, her eyes devoured the room in which she found herself, but which belonged to another.

Henceforth, her thoughts ran on nothing save Germaine's bedroom. To say that she thought about it all day is an inadequate phrase. Temperate expressions are out of place when it is a question of certain souls whom loneliness has marked for its own, and who pass without transition from an empty existence to a species of interior frenzy which subverts their reason. The desire to possess this room as her own dominated the young girl abruptly and exclusively. By an absurdity only possible with a heart that had grown to maturity amid boredom and was suddenly overcome by folly, her desire obsessed her to such an extent that she often forgot what was her real motive in coveting the room and passed whole days without thinking of Maurecourt at all.

She went about with a head full of confused and unrelated schemes. She never spoke of them. Her prudence increased as her monomania grew upon her. Nevertheless, a little observation would have shown her father and sister that all her words now were directed to a single end. A complicated project had taken shape in her brain. Naturally, Germaine required the sunniest room in the villa—that from which the white house was so easily and completely visible. On the other hand, the Villa Louise was more exposed to the sun than the Villa des Charmes, since it looked out on two streets. Why should not Germaine go to lodge with Madame Legras as soon as she arrived? Her room would then be free and Adrienne could move into it. The absurdity of this solution will be apparent when it is remembered that neither Adrienne, her father, nor her sister, had the slightest idea who this Madame Legras might be, beyond the bare fact that she was a married woman and was coming to live by herself. Would she entertain such a bizarre proposal even for a moment? Nevertheless, Adrienne persisted, insinuating that her sister would be much better off on the left side of the rue Thiers than on the right.

In face of the natural resistance of Germaine, who was quite in the dark, the first scheme was quickly replaced by another in the young girl's mind. Why should she herself not go to live with Madame Legras? If she could have a bedroom on the rue du Président Carnot, the view of the white house to be had from its windows would be incomparably better than that from Germaine's room. But the prospect of living with a stranger, so natural when Germaine was concerned, took on a very different aspect when applied to herself. She was naturally timid, and the very notion of bargaining with a person whom she did not know made her pause. She perceived how crazy was her delusion. And a sudden hatred rose in her against the future tenant of this villa, which defied her covetous longings and from which she could not withdraw her eyes. All her resentment was transferred to the new tenant. She detested her with the unreasoning hatred of a child. She wanted something disagreeable to happen to avenge her—she hoped bad weather would spoil Madame Legras's holidays.

One morning when she was leaning out the window of the dining-room, she saw a man on the pavement opposite. Though it was a hot day, he was dressed in black from head to foot, wearing a badly cut frock coat and a silk hat. He was walking quickly. She followed the figure with an indifferent eye. She saw it cross the rue du Président Carnot and keep straight on along the garden wall of the white house. It stopped at a door, opened it, and disappeared. Adrienne pressed her hand on her mouth to stifle a cry. She had seen Maurecourt!

A terrible week followed. As though fascinated by the glance which this man had thrown her way as she stood on the edge of the road, she felt that she must see him again at any cost. She said to herself that even if he passed once more before the house while she was at the window, it would be enough. After that her mind would be at rest. But when did he go out? Very early, surely—or very late. Perhaps during mealtime. How was it possible she had not recognized him at once when he passed? She managed to be at the window now twenty times a day. But she did not see him again.

She seized another chance to slip out of the Villa des Charmes after dinner and to prowl around the white house. She ran no risk of being seen. People at La Tour l'Evêque seldom go out after sunset, but what could she be hoping for? She saw a light in a window of the first floor, and walked to and fro in the street until it went out. Without knowing why, she felt a keen satisfaction when the light was extinguished. She returned home quite worn out but full of confidence. The next day she was looking forward to night with such impatience and glee that she could hardly hold herself in in front of her father and sister. As soon as it was possible to slip out without attracting attention she was back at her street corner. In face of the little white house and its lighted window she felt truly happy. "He is there," she thought to herself, "and I know it!" In some inexplicable fashion, this certainty became as much a pledge for the future as a promise that Maurecourt would have given himself.

Now the new habit was fixed, taking the place of the walk through the country in the hope of seeing a carriage appear on the road. From morning to night the young girl thought only of the moment when she would be able once more to stand with her back to the garden wall of Villa Louise. She kept a close watch on the sky, fearful that clouds would come up and spoil the weather, thus depriving her of the one precious hour, renewed from day to day, which had become her sole reason for living.

Chapter IV

Twice a week during the summer Adrienne went into the garden to cut flowers under the attentive eyes of her father, who watched her from the top of the steps, and her sister, stretched out upon the sofa. She walked slowly down the brick-bordered paths, stopping every now and then to pull up little weeds which left a milky juice upon her fingers, and moving the blades of her shears menacingly before any blossoms which had wilted in the sun. When her round of inspection was over, she cut five or six stalks of red geraniums, the only flowers which would grow in that penurious soil, and reentered the villa to put them in water. For the rest of the day, her duties were confined to going over the house, seeing that the maid had used her mop and duster to make sure that everything was in perfect order. Formerly she had acquitted herself of these petty tasks willingly enough, thankful for them because they eased the boredom of the long hours between meals. But now they had become irksome. She would have preferred complete idleness, in order to abandon herself entirely to her daydreams and to the pleasure of pursuing every trivial train of thought which entered her head. Sometimes she sat down in a big armchair in the parlor, her head turned toward the window, her hands crossed upon her knees, and remained there an hour at a time, as though absorbed by something she could perceive in the sky. She revelled in this inaction, natural enough in the hot season, and sank into a condition very much like torpor, where everything in her head was jumbled in a sort of pleasant confusion.

This was far from being in accord with her natural character. On the contrary, she was an active woman. But that sort of pastime which consists in no longer exercising control over thought, and permitting it to coil and uncoil at will around some prospect or memory, seemed useful to her because it kept her from falling into melancholy, and allowed her to wait for the end of the day without undue suffering.

The slightest noise from the street always brought her to her senses and drew her nearer the window. Instinctively she turned her head to the left, in the direction of the little white house, whose shutters were closed at eight in the morning and not reopened until six in the evening, when the air was freshening a little. Adrienne knew this moment well. She watched for it with an anxiety which she would have been hard put to define as pleasure or pain. She did not dare to walk yet in the rue du Président Carnot for fear of being seen, or perhaps of seeing the person she was dying to see. But at half past five every evening, restlessness began to overtake her. At a quarter to six she stole quietly upstairs to the bedroom on the third floor where Germaine never came before night, and took her post at the window. She sat down upon the window sill and, to get a better view, gathered the curtain in one hand, supported herself against the gutter with the other, and leaned out above the garden.

She waited thus minute after minute, drawing back when the cramped position tired her or when she feared that Germaine, who was strolling round the lawn below, might raise her head and surprise her. In the silence of these late afternoons the faintest noises reached her ears. She heard the creak of the basket chair in which her father sat upon the terrace, opening and folding back the big, thick pages of his *Temps*—the grating of the pebbles under her sister's measured tread. These familiar sounds were torture to her nerves. They recalled to her the monotony of her daily existence. They were like so many malicious voices, repeating to her that she would never escape from the charmed circle which Germaine and M. Mesurat were tracing around her. She would willingly have stuffed her fingers in her ears. But she was awaiting another sound, feebler because farther away, which would reach her in time from the end of the street.

Sometimes, unable to look and listen a moment longer, she was seized with a sudden desire to scream aloud. Malaise would overcome her those last seconds of waiting. It seemed to her then that the sky was darkening and that the roof of the little house was standing out in white against a background that had suddenly turned black. She asked herself whether she could last it out and if she would not be forced to draw her head in and sit down just as the moment she so longed for was reached. But it was always at this crisis of her weakness that the clock in the dining room downstairs struck six. A few seconds passed. Then she heard the noise of two shutters being pushed outward and striking the wall one after another. She saw a middle-aged woman, probably a servant, lean for a moment against the bar of a window on the second story and look from one side of the street to the other. Adrienne, who had drawn her head back to keep from being seen, resumed her position, her hand upon the gutter. It was at this moment that she distinguished the crimson tablecloth and the polished corner of a table covered with papers. The blood rushed to her cheeks and hummed in her ears. The whole weight of her body seemed to be pressing down upon one wrist. She had the singular fancy that she was about to be launched into space and borne toward the room which suddenly seemed so near her. At last, she would straighten up, her hand quite numb; she would turn away from the window and, going back into the room, fall dizzily into an armchair.

One day, just as she had closed the door and begun to descend the staircase, she found herself face to face with her sister, who was coming up. Germaine looked at her inquisitively and suspiciously.

"Whatever are you doing up here?" she asked.

Adrienne blushed scarlet.

"Nothing," she answered. "Why are you coming up?" she went on, stupidly.

"I?" repeated Germaine in the complacent voice of a person satisfied in advance with what she is going to say. "I am going to my room to rest awhile."

Two steps more brought her to Adrienne's side. The young girl felt her sister's breath upon her face and drew away. There was a moment of silence while the two women looked into each other's eyes. Adrienne shrugged her shoulders brusquely and, passing in front of her sister, ran downstairs.

She entered her own room and slammed the door violently. A sudden rush of anger made her stamp the floor with her foot. She flung herself upon the bed and hid her blazing cheeks in her pillow. She was ashamed of herself! To be surprised by Germaine, by that sickly and malevolent old maid! She raised herself on one elbow and rained blow after blow upon the pillow, repeating, under her breath but furiously: "Idiot! Idiot!"

For the first time she wondered what her father and sister would think of her if they could look into her heart. Then she shrugged her shoulders. "What does it matter?" she said, after a moment's reflection. She felt superior to both, as though in a flash she realized how futile and ineffectual their existence was, and how much that was fresh and important had come into her own.

That evening she dined alone with M. Mesurat. Germaine, as often happened, was not well enough to come downstairs. Adrienne was glad. She had no wish to see her so soon after having blushed in front of her; moreover she was afraid that malice might prompt the elder sister to ask her what she had been doing that afternoon upstairs and in a room that was not her own. She could imagine the astonishment on her father's face and the questions that would be multiplied. "Up there, at six o'clock? Why, at six o'clock you always read in your own bedroom! What's got into you?" As though some ritual ordained that she should be in a certain place at a certain hour! The mere idea filled her with fury and impatience.

No doubt the evil moment was only deferred until tomorrow. But between now and tomorrow, what a delicious hour was to intervene! Hardly had her father settled in his armchair than she was outside. Pleasure made her tremble. Setting her fingertips in the scarf that covered her shoulders, she ran lightly to the corner of the rue du Président Carnot.

It was still light enough for her to see every detail of the little white house. Day by day it was taking on a clearer and clearer significance in her mind. At first she had looked at it with a sort of uneasy curiosity. Now she hurried toward it as to a refuge. Was she going mad? What pleasure could she find in the mere contemplation of the ordinary little building? If the person who lived inside it could come to her help! But "the person" did not even know her. And what was she thinking of? Come to her help? Help—against whom. . . ?

She put her hand to her head, positively dazed by the thoughts that rose suddenly in her mind. She was annoyed with herself for spoiling her pleasure with all these stupid reflections. Was it not enough to be here—at the corner of the street, alone, in front of the house, where she had longed to be from the moment she rose from bed? Why, then, didn't it make her happy? What was the matter with her? Her eyes filled with tears. Suddenly she felt herself dominated—challenged—by something beyond her understanding. She ran across the street and pressed her lips on the garden wall of the little white house.

Almost immediately, she came to her senses and looked sharply around her, but the street was empty. She stifled a queer little laugh and murmured, "Even if someone had seen me, they would not have understood." Her cheeks were burning. She began to walk back up the rue du Président Carnot, as quickly as she could, as if she were being followed. Presently she found herself upon the national highway and stopped. The night was warm and still. She was panting, out of breath. Above, however, the tops of the trees were swaying gently in some breeze that she could not feel. On the further side of the road, as far as the eye could reach, the dark fields stretched away, under a somber sky that was spangled with little trembling points of light. She discovered that she was crying. Surrounded by the immense loneliness of night, her tears struck her as childish. She took a few steps along the road. The stones crunched under her feet. She listened to the noise they made with the feverish attention of a child who is suffering and believes he has found a distraction. If she went on walking, she knew that she would finally arrive at Longpré, on the waterside, then at Coures. . . . Thousands of people of every sort had followed this road. Why not she? Why should she not go where she pleased? She began to run a little, but her skirts hampered her and she had to stop, her heart pounding.

She sat down upon a low stone wall and began to hum. It seemed to her that she had passed beyond herself and was shaking herself free of something, little by little. It was as though, suddenly, a thousand memories fell from her, and she became a new person.

She must have sat several minutes at the roadside, plunged in a reverie so deep that it resembled sleep, when a gust of wind sweeping along the ground made her shiver. She got up and began to walk along the road, first in one direction, then in another, her hands clasped behind her back, her eyes on the ground, humming an air under her breath. But she realized almost immediately it was a tune M. Mesurat was fond of whistling, and she stopped.

Her eyebrows drawn together, she was walking now in the direction of rue du Président Carnot, and quickening her pace a little. As she left the highway she was suddenly cold and put hands upon her bare arms. Her skin was quite cool. Then, as though this contact had awakened an imperious idea, she stopped suddenly and, holding her arms before her, looked at them steadily in the dim light that came from the sky. They were round and white; they had that undefinable odor of fruit that comes from healthy flesh; their sinuous line went from shoulder to wrist like a master draughtsman's. She looked at them a moment with a glance in which pleasure was mixed with sadness, and let them fall despairingly at her side.

No one had ever told Adrienne she was beautiful, but she knew it. She could recall a night, only a week ago, when she was in her own room, the prey to one of those accesses of melancholy which often came upon her without any apparent reason. She was sitting before her dressing-table, her arms upon its marble top, looking at her reflection in the mirror by the light of a lamp. The black hair which fell in long tresses down her cheeks and covered her shoulders lent an air of majesty and sadness to her face. Nevertheless, her eyes were shining; the blood coursed swiftly under her skin. She looked at herself a long time, admiring the faultless features which the glass showed her, the straight self-willed eyebrows, the blue eyes, the full lips never parted. Their seriousness surprised her. She tried to smile, but she involuntarily closed her eyes before the fictitious expression of joy that resulted, as though before something shameful. At the end of a moment's space she opened them again and this time recoiled before the afflicted face that met her vision. Submerged suddenly by a wave of mute despair, she had let her head fall upon the marble tabletop. Her disordered tresses covered the brushes, flasks, and little boxes that littered it.

The mere memory of this night sobered her now. What good did it do her to be beautiful? What happiness did her thick hair—her clear complexion—bring her? The conviction that she was ridiculous at the very moments she was suffering most saddened her. A desire took hold of her to get back home, to go to bed and sleep.

In retracing her steps, she did not, this time, stop before the little white house. She could not help noting, however, that the light in the second story had been extinguished. Once more, despite her agitation, she felt that strange, uneasy satisfaction which was a nightly experience and which she spent her life awaiting.

A few minutes later she was back at the villa. She was surprised to find how long she had been absent. Her father had gone to bed and she was forced to find her way in the dark. She was tiptoeing to her own room when a door on the third floor opened, with a creak of hinges that seemed to rend the silence.

"Is that you, Adrienne?" said Germaine's sharp voice.

The young girl stopped on the threshold of her room, her heart fluttering with surprise and anger.

"What do you want?" she asked in a thick voice.

"You go out after dinner every night now," pursued Germaine. "Do you know that you've been gone an hour and a half?"

"That's none of your business," answered Adrienne.

She flung open her door and entered her bedroom, but not before she had heard Germaine cry, in a shrill and furious voice:

"Yes, it is!"

This was quite enough to drive Adrienne beside herself with rage. She shut her door hard and turned the key twice loudly and openly in the lock. Then she put her ear to the crack. But silence had descended anew on the house. For a few minutes she waited in the dark, listening to her agitated breathing, until she heard her sister's door close softly. The stealthy sound made her start. She had an impression that it was a symbol of things in Germaine's character of which she had had no idea till now. She wondered how long she had been spied upon by the sick woman.

"Well," she concluded in a tired voice, "so much the worse—so much the worse!"

She took two or three steps toward the table where her lamp stood, but changed her mind quickly and proceeded to undress in the dark. She had no desire of repeating the experience of a few nights ago and of sitting in tears before her mirror. She preferred to get to bed and to sleep as quickly as possible. She tore off her clothing with feverish hands, let down her hair, and slipped in between the sheets. But her thoughts precluded any idea of sleep. She was hot. The blood was pulsing in the arteries of her neck. She tossed from side to side without finding a comfortable position. She flung off the cover, whose weight put her on edge, and then the sheet, whose contact exasperated her.

For an appreciable time she lay motionless, hoping that sleep would come to her if she did not stir. But each time she closed her eyes, bright spots dancing in their orbits compelled her to open them. Her arms and legs ached and forced her to turn over on her side again. Finally she got up and sat at the foot of the bed. All sorts of thoughts came into her head, as though in mockery: she remembered, for instance, how she had sung just now at the side of the road. She saw herself again, pressing her lips to the wall of the little white house, and could feel herself blushing at the mere thought of the things of which she was capable.

After a quarter of an hour had passed she lay down again, her arms stretched along her sides, her head heavy. As always happened at the moments she was most unhappy, memories of her childhood returned to her mind. She repeated in a low voice the names of several schoolmates whom she had quite forgotten. She began to think of the Cours Ste.-Cécile; especially of a mistress of literature who had harassed her incessantly, a spinster, invariably dressed in a stiffly starched white blouse and a blue skirt whose darned patches glistened in the sunshine. The poor woman must have led a hard life indeed to make her so mean! Adrienne could see and hear her giving out the lessons, book in hand, watching for the mistakes of her pupils with a bitter smile. She heard the voice, pitifully shrill and triumphant, as it cried: "Three mistakes! You will learn twenty additional verses. . . ."

Suddenly she seemed to be falling, and holding herself back. She wanted to move, but her hands were crossed behind her neck and she could not unclasp her fingers. She had a brief sensation of struggling—and dropped off to sleep.

At the end of a few hours she awoke, as abruptly as she had fallen asleep. She looked around her, but the darkness was complete. She could not even distinguish the dim whiteness of her bolster. A line that she had once learned darted into her head and its words came to her lips:

"C'était pendant l'horreur d'une profonde nuit."

She had never before thought of what the words actually meant. But now that her memory recalled them after years of forgetfulness, they seemed to her stamped with a fresh and awful beauty that terrified her. There is, as a matter of fact, something calm and reassuring in the first hours of darkness. But as the night advances and the noises of the earth are stilled one by one, obscurity and silence take on a different character. A sort of supernatural immobility weighs upon everything. There is no word truer or more eloquent than "horror" to describe the hour or so which precedes dawn.

Adrienne drew back the blanket over her legs and turned to the wall, which she could touch with her hands. She heard her own breathing, and for a moment took it for that of someone bending over her. But this superstitious terror evaporated as she woke completely. She had been having a nightmare. What had it been about? She could not remember. She wondered whether she had cried or said something out loud and whether the sound of her own voice had been the thing that woke her up. The idea of having spoken out alone, in the middle of the night, frightened her. She feared silence, but she feared even more to break it. By exhaling and inhaling through the mouth alone she tried to muffle the sound of her breath.

She was dozing once more when an idea crossed her brain. No doubt, the Legras woman would be coming soon. Perhaps she would be able to help her. To help her?

She fell asleep.

Chapter V

At breakfast next morning, no reference was made to the scene which Adrienne had had with her sister the night before, and as soon as she had swallowed her black coffee, Germaine settled herself, on the couch in front of the parlor window, as usual. However, when Mesurat left the house for his walk, the old maid raised herself up from the cushions and looked toward Adrienne, who was straightening the slipcover on a chair.

"Will you kindly tell me now," said she, "what you were doing out-of-doors last night?"

Adrienne looked around quickly. Her face turned scarlet under the white handkerchief that covered her hair.

"Did you speak to papa?" she asked.

"You wouldn't like that?"

Adrienne turned her back and affected to be busy with a vase of flowers.

"Well, Adrienne . . .?" said Germaine, laying her arm along the back of the sofa. She had the decisive and restrained air of people who relish in advance the quarrel they mean to provoke.

"What do you want?" asked her sister.

"I want an answer," said Germaine. "For some time you have not been the same. You go out at night. What do you do? I insist on knowing."

Adrienne turned around and took a few steps toward the couch.

"Why?" she asked. "You're not my mother."

She felt she was losing patience and regretted what she was about to say. Then, as her anger swept over her, she abandoned herself to the sheer pleasure of giving vent to it—and of wounding.

"Is it because you're seventeen years older?"

The blood leaped to Germaine's pale cheeks. For a moment her face wore an expression of surprise; she appeared to doubt for a second there was any insolence in her sister's words. Then her features contracted.

"I am here in your mother's place," she replied, in a voice tremulous with hatred. "Luckily there is someone to watch over you, and it is I. You are in duty bound to answer me. I want to know what you were doing last night."

Adrienne shook her head vigorously.

"Do you hear me?" went on Germaine, keeping her eyes steadfastly upon her sister. "Either you tell me, or I speak to Father."

"You're not going to know," said the young girl, hoarsely.

Germaine lay back upon the cushions and crossed her hands.

"As you wish," she said in a menacing voice.

Adrienne drew away from her and resumed her tasks. There was a brief silence. Then Germaine began again, with that obstinacy often noticeable in weak people, who will not accept defeat and are always ready to resume the battle.

"I suppose," said she, "because you are left so much to yourself you think I don't know what's going on. Your face tells the whole story."

Adrienne was dusting the mantelpiece. She looked at her reflection in the mirror and said in a toneless voice:

"What story does my face tell?"

"That you don't sleep at night and are running about the streets," said the old maid, brutally.

Adrienne went on passing her duster over the mirror with a mechanical gesture. From the astonished expression in her clear eyes, she seemed to be seeking some meaning in the words her sister had just uttered.

"Running about the streets?" she repeated at last. "That isn't a crime. And if I can't sleep, is that my fault?"

Germaine bit her lips. It was impossible to misinterpret such an answer. She felt herself ridiculous and coarse.

"You know well enough what I mean," she said, in a flurried voice. "I am going to speak to your father about your conduct unless you tell me what you were doing last night."

And confronting Adrienne's contemptuous silence, her curiosity became envenomed and changed suddenly into fury. She got up abruptly and knelt on the sofa, supporting her body on one trembling knee.

"You're going to tell me," she cried, pointing her finger at her sister. "I'll find a way to make you speak."

The girl did not answer. This sudden explosion of anger put the finishing touch to her consternation.

"First of all," Germaine went on, raising her voice as though to convince herself of what she was saying, "if you are doing no harm, why do you make such a secret of it? Why do you wait till it's dark to slip out of the house?"

Before the mute regard of her sister, her rage burst all bounds.

"You understand me quite well," she continued. "You may as well give up playing the innocent. That won't work with me, and you know it. Do you think I'm a fool? Do you think I don't see you going up the street every evening at nine?"

Adrienne's face blanched.

"Why are you trying to make me unhappy?" she stammered.

"Unhappy!" echoed Germaine. "What about me? Do you think I have not been unhappy?"

After a strange convulsive gesture, she went on:

"I have suffered in every possible way, suffered horribly—do you understand? And one such experience is enough. I will see you never commit the mistakes that I did."

"What mistakes—?"

"There is no need you should know. It is solely for your own good that I am questioning you. It is out of pity for you."

She put her handkerchief to her lips.

"Are you going to answer me?" she asked again.

Adrienne shook her head.

"No!"

Germaine looked at her for a moment, then shrugged her shoulders, and stretched out on the sofa again.

"You mean it is just as though I had never spoken?"

"Yes," said Adrienne.

She took up a vase and carried it to the bathroom. The scene she had just been through so astounded her that she forgot the anger which she had felt toward her sister at its start. She placed the vase of geraniums in the basin and turned the tap on full. The pressure was high and the jet roared in the basin with a deafening din. Bent over her flowers, the girl watched the water mount until the vase began to wobble on its base. When she had filled the vase, she turned off the tap. She was sorry to hear the noise of the water stop. It had helped to prevent her thinking for a few moments.

Then she sat down on a chair, absolutely stupefied by what her sister had just told her. Up to now she never had had any conversation with Germaine. Everything the woman did irritated her, and even her gestures were a source of annoyance. She also felt an instinctive repugnance for the disease from which her sister suffered and disliked her coming too close. All these things served to create a distance between the two which increased with time. Then suddenly she seemed to be in the presence of a stranger: it was when Germaine spoke about her suffering.

She rose, took up her vase, wiped it pensively on her apron, and returned to the parlor. For a moment she stood in the middle of the room, her eyes fixed on the garnet rug. Just between two armchairs, the sun cast a long rectangular spot in the same place.

Adrienne was amazed at her sister's silence. She took a few steps, put the flowers on a small round table, rearranged some books upon the writing desk.

"Tell me—" she began, then stopped.

Germaine made no reply. Adrienne walked to the sofa and looked closely at her sister. The old maid had not moved, but her eyes were red, tears trembled along the edge of their lids and trickled down on both sides of her long aquiline nose.

"What are you looking at me for?" she said in a choked voice.

And, as Adrienne made no answer, but continued to gaze at her, she averted her face.

"Go away," she said. "I detest you."

That evening, as Désirée placed the *cafetière* before M. Mesurat, the old man turned toward Adrienne.

"I have an idea," he said. "We're too dull after dinner. Suppose we play cards together. Let us have a game of *trente-et-un*."

The younger daughter was folding her napkin. She let it fall from her hands and raised her eyes toward her sister's. Germaine's face was impassive.

"Well, what about it?" went on Mesurat, stroking his beard with the back of his thumb.

He stopped, as though embarrassed by the surprise which he read on his daughter's face.

"Papa," said Adrienne, breathlessly, "I don't know how to play any card games."

"I'll teach you," said Mesurat with a jovial air. "Two minutes is enough. Germaine will play with us, won't you, Germaine?"

Germaine nodded her head.

"The fact is," went on the old man, "we have got into the habit of doing nothing all evening. I read my paper, your sister goes upstairs to rest. What we all need is a little distraction. Why—what's the matter?"

Adrienne was on her feet and was pressing her hand against her side. The blood had left her cheeks; she rested one hand on the back of her chair as though afraid of falling.

"What's the matter?" repeated Mesurat in an imperious voice. "Eh, Adrienne?"

"I want to lie down in the next room," she murmured.

"Sit down," commanded Mesurat.

Seizing her by the wrist, he forced her into her chair. She closed her eyes; her brows drew together.

"What a strange faintness—all of a sudden," remarked Germaine in icy tones.

She shook her head, pushed away the cup of camomile tea which was steaming under her nose, crossed her arms upon the table, and looked steadily at her young sister.

"It's the heat of the room," said Mesurat. "This lamp is hanging too low. Push it up, Germaine."

Germaine reached out a hand to the hanging lamp and pushed it up slightly. Under its light Adrienne's face appeared almost ghastly. M. Mesurat frowned as he looked at her.

"You are going to drink a little coffee," he said, filling a cup.

"I don't care for any, papa," said Adrienne.

The old man hesitated for a moment. With a glance, he consulted Germaine, who shrugged her shoulders.

"Just as you like," said he.

He emptied his cup in two gulps, and got up. At this moment Adrienne opened her eyes. Seeing that her father was leaving the table, she believed for a moment that the idea of cards had been given up, and her face lightened. But Mesurat slapped his palm on the back of his chair and said, with a good humor that rang false:

"Up with you. We'll all feel better in the parlor."

She obeyed without another word. As she passed before her father, he laughed and gave her a little tap on the shoulder. She took a few more steps, entered the parlor, and stood for a moment in the center of the darkened room. Everything in her head was confused, as though after a sudden fainting spell. One dominant thought, however, kept recurring, and threw her into an agitation which increased from one moment to the next. The hour was near at hand when, ordinarily, she should be at her street corner. It was a fine night. Through the window the sky was still pale with that afterglow which is like a prolongation of daylight in darkness. There was not a cloud in the sky. A sort of exaltation took hold of her, closely akin to what she had felt in her sister's room, when she leaned out the window feeling suddenly that the little white house had drawn nearer and that she could reach it now in one bound. She clasped her hands. She heard her father stumbling against an armchair, then the sound of a match struck and restruck lightly against a box. Presently lamplight flooded the room.

"Draw up a chair," said Mesurat, settling himself before the little round table.

She made an effort, took a chair, and seated herself between her father and Germaine, who was shuffling the pack. She noted that the lamp was smoking, but did not think of speaking about it. Everything had the air of a nightmare—the old maid shuffling the cards; the old man breathing noisily; herself seated at the round table instead of being out-of-doors near the little white house. The line from Racine returned to her memory. What night could equal in horror the scene which she had before her eyes? And abruptly she bowed her head and put her fists against her forehead.

"Come on!" cried the father. "What is it this time?"

He took hold of Adrienne's hands and pulled them away from her face.

"You are going to tell me what is wrong," he said, in a voice full of rising anger.

"Nothing—nothing, I tell you," protested Adrienne, desperately, putting her hands on her lap.

"Papa, please explain the game to her and let us begin," said Germaine, impatiently.

Mesurat recovered his composure. He took the pack which Germaine had just laid down, and began dealing it without a word. Adrienne kept her eyes fixed upon the table. She watched the little pile of cards which fell before her noiselessly, one on top of the other. A sort of languor came over her. She took the hand which had been dealt her, put the suits together mechanically, and was beginning to shuffle them again when a cry from her father made her jump in her seat.

"Not yet," he cried. "Wait till I explain."

He showed her the rules of the game, accompanying his words with little precise gestures, raising his forefinger, showing her the cards, which he had arranged fanwise in his hand. She nodded her head from time to time.

"Now, begin!" he said when he had finished.

She played a card at random, which Germaine covered quickly with one of hers. M. Mesurat put down a card in turn, explaining the reason for his play.

"And now," he went on, "be careful what you lead."

Adrienne frowned and looked over the hand which she held fanwise as directed by her father. She had not paid any attention to his explanations, and as he watched closely to see what card she would play, she had a moment of sheer bewilderment, like some pupil asked too difficult a question by his teacher. Kings, queens, and knaves danced before her eyes. She picked an ace of spades, changed her mind, took a ten of diamonds.

Suddenly she noticed her hand was shaking like a leaf. Neither her father nor her sister took their eyes off her for a moment. She put her cards against her breast as though to hide her hand.

"I don't know what to play," she said.

"Didn't you understand what I told you?" cried Mesurat, furiously.

"Play something, no matter what," said the sister, peevishly, rapping her skinny knuckles on the marble top of the table.

"All right," said Adrienne, who was rapidly losing her head. She examined her hand again, and drew out a card which she threw upon the table.

"No! no!" cried Mesurat. "You can't play that yet. Listen to me."

With his face close to hers he began the lesson all over again, in a slow, deliberate voice that grew higher in pitch as he proceeded. She failed utterly to follow him. So many things were conflicting in her mind that the words conveyed no meaning. All she caught were so many vocables, hoarse with impatience. The breath of the old man was warm on her cheek. She closed her eyes, overtaken with sudden disgust, and tried to gather her wits. One word alone rang through her brain, with the disordered resonance of a cracked bell: suffer—suffer! This was suffering. With a catch at her heart she remembered that the hour had now gone by at which she always reached the corner of the street. A superstitious feeling overwhelmed her. For the first time she would fail to keep her old rendezvous. It meant bad luck. Perhaps at this very moment the doctor was leaning over the window ledge! . . . With a bound she was on her feet and flung down her hand.

"I won't play," she said.

"What?" roared Mesurat.

"I don't want to play."

She felt her sister's bony fingers round her wrist and tried to break away.

"Sit down!" said the old maid in a commanding voice. "Sit down!"

M. Mesurat had begun to beat upon the table with the palms of his hands.

"You are going to obey!" he snarled. "You are going to tell me what has come over you."

"Sit down!" bayed the old maid again.

Adrienne struggled feebly. Her strength had left her and she could not free herself. She could only hold her sister away, crying:

"Let me alone! Let me alone!"

"Stop shouting," exclaimed M. Mesurat. "You are going to alarm all the neighbors."

"Wait a moment," said Germaine.

Letting go her sister's arm, she rose and, dragging herself as quickly as she could, closed the window.

"Now shout," said she, supporting herself against the wall.

M. Mesurat rose in turn. The blood had rushed to his face and neck, but he made a point of speaking in a measured tone, like a man who is in control.

"There's no use in shouting," said he. "Adrienne is going to explain what all this nonsense is about."

He took his daughter by the arm. She was deathly pale and had to lean on the back of her chair.

"What do you want me to do, papa?"

"To speak to us. To tell us what is the matter with you."

"There is nothing the matter."

"Very well, then," said Germaine. "Let us go on with the game."

Adrienne did not answer. It seemed to her that something unknown was stealing into the room she knew so well. An indefinable change had taken place. It was like one of those dreams where those places you know you've never been appear familiar. To her first feeling of curiosity, fright had succeeded—then terror at feeling herself unable to fly, paralyzed and a prisoner. She wondered, as she threw a glance around, whether she were not going mad. The things she saw struck her now, not in their familiar aspect, but by their strange and remote character. As in some nightmare, she experienced all the horror of not being able to move, of being retained by some invisible force between this armchair and this table. Her eyes encountered the lamp. She noticed that it was no longer smoking and by this petty detail measured the whole extent of the turmoil that had been filling her mind since she sat down before the card table, since someone had lowered the wick and she had not noticed it. M. Mesurat's voice brought her back to herself.

"If you won't speak I am going to speak for you," he said, bending toward her. "You say nothing is the matter with you. But you're dreaming, you're distracted, you refuse to play. Well, I can tell you something about the reason."

Germaine stirred uneasily. Mesurat glanced in her direction and went on.

"It has come to my knowledge, by way of someone whom I won't name, that for some time past you have been slipping out every night. You stay out for an hour, for two hours, perhaps longer. Eh? Can you deny it?"

He leaned closer to Adrienne. Within a few inches of her own face she saw his swollen eyelids, the fleshy nose intersected with little blue veins. The words she wanted to utter stuck in her throat.

"And that is not all," the father proceeded. "You think yourself so smart. You imagine that none of us are aware of what is going on. . . ."

He stopped a moment, and continued:

"Every afternoon, between half past five and six, you go up to Germaine's room, you stick your head out the window and begin to watch—"

"That isn't true," said the girl, breathlessly.

"Germaine . . ." said Mesurat.

Germaine blushed deeply, but did not open her mouth. The old man banged his fist on the table.

"In any case, I've had quite enough of all this. Do you understand me? I intend to know. You are hiding something. Will you speak or not?"

He seized her arm and shook her.

"You are meeting someone, eh? Own up!"

Adrienne cried aloud with pain and tried to break away, but the old man was strong.

"No," cried he, "I won't let you go. You are going to answer me. You are in love with someone, aren't you?"

He shook her so violently that she could hardly stay on her feet. She saw terror on her sister's face and felt herself in the grip of a sort of wild panic.

"Yes!" she screamed, in a voice whose shrillness surprised herself.

"Huh! Who?" he demanded. There was a moment of silence while the old man caught his breath after his violent exertion.

"Who?" he repeated.

"I don't know his name," the girl stammered.

Mesurat loosened his grip a little.

"You don't know his name!" roared Mesurat, transferring his grip to her shoulders. "You dare to tell me that! Do you dare treat me like an idiot!"

Overpowered by a rage that he could no longer control, he shook her backward and forward with all his strength. Adrienne heard her teeth clashing together at each shock and uttered smothered cries. Speechless with terror, Germaine did not budge from her seat. Suddenly Adrienne slumped against her father's chest and fell at his feet in an inert mass. She had fainted.

Chapter VI

When she opened her eyes she was in her own bedroom. She could hear footsteps dying away down the passage, the noise of a door being closed, and the murmur of voices behind it. Then suddenly complete silence fell upon the house. She was lying, fully dressed, on her bed. The air was hot and close. A few tiny flies were circling around the lighted lamp, buzzing faintly. She sighed deeply, raised herself upon her forearms, and sat on the edge of the bed, looking around her. Her eyes fell upon the wardrobe that her father had given her for her eighteenth birthday. There was something in the association so grotesque and so cruel that she could not stifle an exclamation of disgust. She looked in its mirror and saw that her hair had fallen down and was lying upon her shoulders. Though the sight of its disorder gave her a shock, she made no attempt to remedy it, but kept her eyes riveted on her reflection. Her cheeks were ashy pale. She looked so devastated she didn't recognize herself. Her mouth hung open. She was looking at herself grown suddenly older, but she kept on gazing steadily. Had she really suffered a transformation? She noticed that the lamp threw a shadow under her eyelids and gave her a disagreeable expression. "I look like I'm dead," she said to herself.

Presently, by dint of hard staring, a sort of dark outline trembled above her head upon the mirrored surface. It overtook her face and her shoulders. A second image hesitated a moment and rose slowly above the first. Her eyes ached with the strain of watching them draw apart, but she could not close her lids. She went on watching those two people in the looking-glass who wavered to and fro without moving a muscle. Then all thought ceased in her brain. She fell back upon her pillow as though she had received a blow upon the head, and slept.

It was broad daylight when she opened her eyes, but she hated the thought of getting up and lay some minutes awake on the bed. In half an hour she would have to be downstairs as usual. She would have to listen to her father as he read the headlines of his newspaper aloud. She would have to watch her sister examine the bottom of her cup and wipe it with an end of her napkin, as she did every morning before pouring out her coffee. Life would go on the same as before in spite of the horrible scene of last night, while, within her, everything seemed changed.

When she came downstairs to the dining-room, she saw M. Mesurat holding his journal before him at arm's length. As the day gave every promise of being very hot, he had taken off his black alpaca coat and hung it over the back of a chair. In his ruddy face, concentration hollowed little wrinkles around his nose and eyes. Because he was far-sighted, he could read only by grimacing. He saw Adrienne as she came in the door, and looked at her from out the corner of one eye.

"Good morning," said he, cheerfully.

"Good morning, Adrienne," repeated Germaine in turn. She was stirring the sugar in her cup.

"Good morning," the girl replied.

She sat down. It was as she had foreseen. Nothing had changed. She looked at the red squares of the tablecloth and the cups of colored porcelain with a kind of wonder. In the polished metal of the silver coffeepot she saw the distorted reflection of her own face that used to amuse her so when she was a little girl. After a moment's reflection she poured out her coffee and, as though yielding to the force of some enchantment, heard her own voice asking, just as if this morning were like any other:

"What's the temperature for today, papa?"

There was a brief silence while the old man turned to the top of the third page for the answer. Behind the big sheets, still smelling of fresh ink, his voice was heard:

"Forecast for the twentieth, eighty degrees, with slight rise probable."

Adrienne felt herself beaten. She raised her eyes furtively and caught a glance that passed between her father and Germaine. This tacit congratulation between the pair filled her with horror, and she averted her eyes. The sky outside was almost white—full of potent and limitless light that the eyes could scarcely bear. From her seat she could see the Villa Louise behind its stunted lime trees. Why wasn't she the daughter of this Madame Legras? She was sure she would be less unhappy. She felt that her father and her sister were stealthily observing her and their silence became insupportable.

"When do the people opposite arrive?" she asked, in order to break it.

Mesurat put down his paper and looked straight before him through his reading-glasses.

"Let me see," said he, "last year—"

"The beginning of June," supplied Germaine, breaking her roll. "But that's no reason Madame Legras should come the same time."

"You're right," said the old man, with a convinced air.

He threw a last glance over his journal and dipped half of his croissant in his coffee.

"Why do you want to know?" said Germaine, in a voice which affected indifference.

"I don't particularly want to know. I merely said—"

"You asked, all the same," Germaine went on.

Adrienne shrugged her shoulders and did not answer. Mesurat propped his paper against the *cafetière* and said, with his mouth full:

"The ministry is going to fall; it's certain."

Over the top of his newspaper he looked stealthily at his two daughters. Adrienne had lowered her head and was making up her mind to drink her coffee. Germaine's eyes were still upon her sister's face.

A few minutes after breakfast was over, Adrienne took up her shears from a drawer in the kitchen and made as if to leave the house. Her father had put on his panama hat. But, contrary to habit, he made no move to go on his walk. Instead he sat down in his favorite armchair at the head of the garden steps. As Adrienne came toward him along the corridor, he spoke:

"Where are you going?"

"Into the garden, to cut some flowers."

"This isn't the day," said a voice.

The girl turned round and saw her sister watching her from the sofa through a window of the parlor.

"Did you hear?" said Mesurat.

"The geraniums are faded," said Adrienne. "We ought to have some others."

She had turned red and grasped her shears tightly in her right hand. Mesurat stretched his legs before him as though to bar her way.

He spoke again.

"Did you hear what your sister just said?"

Adrienne supported herself against the door jamb and looked at her father. Under the tilted panama his eyes seemed two dark cavities. But the brim allowed the light to fall full upon his fleshy nose and upon the massive jaws which lost themselves in his tawny beard. His cheeks wrinkled. He let a satisfied laugh escape him.

"Why are you looking at me?" he asked after a few moments.

"I want to go out," she said in a smothered voice.

"Well, you—won't—go—out!" said Mesurat, emphasizing each word with a flourish of his newspaper.

"Why not?" she asked in a faint voice.

He did not answer at once, but looked her straight in the eyes. She saw the paper trembling in his hand, and, taking fright suddenly, stepped back into the corridor. He jumped to his feet and followed her. She retreated along the passage, keeping close to the wall, the palm of her left hand touching the warm paneling. A nervous desire to cry aloud possessed her, but she could not unclench her teeth. She saw her father advancing upon her. He slammed the door noisily behind him, and shouted out:

"You want to know why, do you?"

The furious voice made her tremble from head to foot. In the parlor to her left she heard her sister rise and close the window as on the previous night. Her heart fluttered terribly in her chest. She dropped her shears and made a mute "No!" with her head.

"I'm going to tell you, all the same," said Mesurat slowly but raising his voice as he proceeded. "I don't want you to go into the garden, I don't intend to let you leave the house, until you tell me the name of that man. Do you understand?"

"Yes," said the girl in a voice that was little more than a whisper. Her knees shook. She would have fallen had she not had the molding of the wainscot under her hand.

"All right, then," said the parent. "Find yourself something to do about the house."

He opened the door, went out, and sat down again in his armchair. Through the grating she saw him take up his newspaper and shake its pages loose. She closed her eyes a moment, then picked up her shears and went into the parlor. Her sister was on her feet, with concern written upon her face. She had one hand upon the mantelpiece and was watching the girl in the mirror which reflected the door. There was an appreciable interval of silence. Adrienne put her shears on the little marble-topped table and looked at the geraniums which were in a vase at its center. She picked off a few petals which the heat had wilted. When she had done this, she stood motionless. Behind her she heard Germaine walk to the sofa and try to open the window. After a few futile efforts her sister spoke:

"Will you help me open this window?"

Her voice was weak and eloquent of fatigue. She let herself fall upon the couch without waiting for an answer from her young sister.

"How did you manage to close it?" asked Adrienne, stolidly.

"I don't know; perhaps it shuts easier."

Adrienne hesitated a moment, then walked to the window and opened it. She even straightened the sofa which Germaine had dragged out a little from the wall. Finally, she sat down in an armchair in the middle of the room. Emotion had stupefied her and she was hardly conscious of what she did. She noticed that her breathing was short, but that it gradually became more regular. The sun reached her feet and covered the bottom of her skirt with a long rectangular streak. She looked at it until her eyes smarted. Then she raised her head. Fleecy clouds were passing across the sky. They seemed to dissolve in the blinding light. The heat grew more intense. Not a sound reached her ears from out-of-doors; the very birds were silent. She could no longer even catch the rustle of her father's newspaper and guessed that he had fallen asleep.

Chapter VII

A few days later she was seated at the dining-room window, looking into the street. She had just come back from a walk on which her father had made her accompany him, and had not yet taken off her hat. Every day, now, M. Mesurat took her out to walk with him. They went together to the other end of the town, to see the house that was being built behind the presbytery. The framework of the roof was already in place, and that very afternoon, to the great joy of Mesurat, who had clapped his hands at the sight, they had seen the green branch and the tri-colored flag attached in triumph to the highest point of what would later be the roof itself.

It was nearly six o'clock, but the sky was as clear as at noon. Adrienne thought to herself that these changes in the sky were the only changes which she could now notice in the scene which lay before her eyes. The lime trees in the Legras garden were just about the same. The scarlet and pink geraniums still grew placidly, with their coarse fibrous leaves and the downy stalks. She turned her head and looked at the slender tree whose top branches swayed gently above the roof of the little white house. Her heart sank. Nothing was changing in her life. Several times, when sitting at table, she had felt tempted to cry aloud: "Well, then, here you are! I am in love with Maurecourt, the doctor in rue Carnot!" If only to see what would happen. But she never could bring herself to pronounce the words. She fancied more than once that, just as she seemed upon the verge of doing so, Germaine or her father would start a conversation, as though they guessed her thought and had made up their minds to prevent her making her confession. This coincidence struck her; she attributed a sort of mysterious origin to it, and came to see in it a sign that she was not meant to speak of her love, but must keep it a secret. In the loneliness of her bedroom, when her father and sister were asleep, she acquired a habit of saying the name "Maurecourt" out loud, being first careful to cover her mouth with her hands so that no one should hear her. She ended by repeating the name, which the violence of neither Germaine nor M. Mesurat could tear from her, ten and twenty times, with a cruel joy that made her suffer acutely. Finally it seemed to her that this habit was all that saved her from actual suffocation. She never wept; but at certain times, when discouragement and melancholy took the place of anxiety and delusive hopes, she felt her throat swell, and the blood, flying to her head, beat in a dismal rhythm against her temples.

She took off her hat now and plunged her hand into her hair as though to diminish its weight by lifting it from her scalp. Her clothes kept her warm. She rose and leaned upon the balustrade, her knees pressed against the bottom of the window frame. Far away a carriage was passing along the highway, but the distant noise receded rapidly. Further off still, some dogs were barking. She listened greedily to these signs of life. The silence of the street had become insupportable. It almost seemed that passers-by avoided this quarter of the town for fear of disturbing the immobility which weighed upon it.

Mournfully she was thinking how close it was to the hour when she had formerly slipped upstairs to Germaine's bedroom. Now the door was kept locked. Still, by leaning out of other windows, she could see her little white house, but far less clearly.

A light breeze was rising. Closing her eyes, she took in a long, deep breath. Suddenly she heard footsteps mounting the street and turned her head quickly in the direction of the little white house. Her heart gave a jump and stood still. The little man who was walking close to the wall was Maurecourt. For a moment she doubted the evidence of her eyes, and recoiled instinctively, dreading to be seen and yet desiring it with all her might. He was walking briskly, his eyes on the ground. In another instant he would have disappeared from sight. She lost her wits—made a gesture toward him which she repressed instantly, and pressed her hand upon her mouth as though to a stifle a cry. Now he was opposite her; now he was passing right in front of the house, along the wall of the Villa Louise! She gripped the balustrade and leaned toward the street as though to call him back. She even raised her arm. But by this time he could not see her and continued his rapid walk until only his back was visible. There was nothing to do now but to cry aloud. Then he would turn around. She turned away. She couldn't do it. She was in the grip of one of those nightmares where you are incapable of moving a muscle or of uttering a cry. It seemed to her that she was filled with some power but could not use it. She heard his footsteps dying away and abruptly he had left rue Thiers, and was following another street. Ah, she might wave her arms now if she chose! She racked her wits like some woman at bay. To see him—to call him! But how? A sudden idea crossed her mind. If she were ill, he would come. If she were ill—ill or hurt. Hurt! She shut the lower sash of the window and, shutting her eyes tight, thrust her two naked arms through the pane.

The noise of the breaking glass startled her. She saw her arms streaked with red; a few seconds more and the blood was pouring down them. Although not in actual pain, she moaned, then began to cry. The tears did her good. But fear took hold of her as she saw her dress covered with blood and she rushed toward the door, her arms stretched out in front of her.

Her father ran in, followed by Germaine, quite out of breath. A change came over their angry faces as they saw the blood and they exclaimed "*Ah!*" in the same breath. The old man recoiled and looked at Germaine aghast.

"How did you do that?" cried Germaine between gasps. "You must be mad! Quick!" she continued, addressing her father. "Bring some tincture of iodine and a roll of lint. You'll find them in a drawer in my room."

Mesurat disappeared. While waiting, Germaine took a napkin from the sideboard and wrapped it around her sister's arms. But the contact of the stiff linen with her raw wounds made Adrienne cry aloud and she sought to tear off this improvised dressing. The sight of her blood drove her beside herself. She had the feeling that her reason was leaving her. She sank into a chair.

"Will you let me take care of this?" said Germaine, picking up the bloody napkin from the floor.

"Call the doctor!"

"Be quiet and keep your arms raised," commanded Germaine.

Adrienne obeyed. She was deadly pale and asked herself confusedly what all this blood could mean. Had she hoped that a doctor would be called in for a few cuts on the arms? Where had her wits been to believe such a thing for a second? It would have been so easy to have waved her hand as the doctor passed. She could have stopped halfway in the gesture—then pretended to be taken with some sort of seizure—carried her hand to her head, and uttered a cry—

Mesurat reappeared. He was carrying a small bottle and a roll of something white.

"Quick!" said Germaine.

She took the phial from his hand and with the little brush attached to the cork swabbed the wounds. Adrienne screamed from the smart. At the end of a few moments the blood ceased to flow and Germaine wound the roll of gauze around her sister's arms. Mesurat looked on with an expression that was at once confused and curious. Now and then he made as though to help, but his elder daughter, with an authority she rarely showed, waved him aside. This woman, whose whole life had been the slow development of one disease, found herself, so to speak, in her element when it was a question of bandages or drugs. At such moments she manifested a surprising activity. It was always she who cured Mesurat's colds or Adrienne's headaches. Everything necessary for first-aid treatment was to be found in a cupboard in her bedroom. Indolent by habit, she seemed to rally as soon as the health of her father and sister was endangered. She measured drops with a steady hand, never lost her head in any petty emergency—dosed and nursed, in short, with rare competence and presence of mind. It was certainly not through any goodness of heart that she acted so, but rather because the instinct which makes people who are hopelessly ill hate sickness in all its forms, drove her to combat it in others and so in some way avenge herself for her powerlessness in her own case. She exercised her healing function with a jealous fervor. It was quite understood that she was not to be resisted nor contradicted nor helped. As for calling in a doctor from outside, the idea never entered any head at the

Villa des Charmes. Call a doctor when Germaine was there! M. Mesurat would never have even considered such a wild notion. Neither would Adrienne herself, and it was having believed Maurecourt's intervention possible that showed how far her madness had led her.

"I must love him a great deal." she said to herself.

And the mere admission seemed a revelation to her.

Within two days she was almost well again. She was able to take off the bandages; the edges of the wounds had begun to join. But she kept a deep impression of what she had done. She didn't recognize herself in the violent act, and thought, with a sort of added respect mingled with fear, of what had driven her to it.

May was coming to an end. Already a good many people from Paris had descended upon La Tour l'Evêque, and the Harmonic Society had resumed its concerts in a kiosk in the middle of the Public Gardens. In the streets toward the center of the town a certain animation was to be remarked. But the quarter in which the Mesurats had their home preserved all the tranquillity of winter and spring. You could hear more often the sound of carriages on the national highway, and that was all.

One morning Adrienne was cutting geraniums under the eyes of her father and sister. Although she had not yet answered their questions, she had been permitted to resume this old occupation. The real reason was that Germaine was by now too weak to walk around the garden and M. Mesurat judged picking flowers beneath his dignity. The girl was stooping over the beds when she heard the sound of a carriage, and lifted her head. Her father had lowered his newspaper and was looking attentively straight ahead.

"What's the matter?" asked Germaine.

"Don't you hear it?" said Adrienne.

She walked to the gate and stood there motionless, her face pressed between the bars. A warm wind was whirling the dust along the road with an imperceptible sough. The noise of wheels drew nearer.

"I hear it now," said Germaine.

"It's coming from the highway," added the father.

This little dialogue, by the way, in which hardly a word varied, took place several times a day. Some moments passed. Suddenly Adrienne grasped the bars with all her strength. A carriage was descending the rue du Président Carnot. Between the "clop! clop!" of the horses' feet could be heard the grinding of the brake as the driver tightened it for the steep descent.

"Madame Legras?" thought the girl, and her heart began to beat rapidly.

At last she was going to see the woman whose arrival she did not know whether to desire or dread. M. Mesurat got up.

"Well!" he exclaimed in a tone of surprise.

The carriage turned into the rue Thiers. It was not Madame Legras, after all. Adrienne could not stifle a little cry of disappointment. But her curiosity redoubled when the driver reined in his horse and pulled up at the very door of the Villa Louise.

A little woman descended from the carriage. She was very short. Her threadbare black clothes sufficiently announced her station in life. Quite evidently she was a servant. She had the timid and serious air of all good domestics, and insisted on lifting out the black cloth bag which the driver had placed beside him. But the man jumped from his seat and shouldered it. The little woman drew out a key from her handbag, opened the gate, and entered the garden, followed by the coachman.

The entire scene was observed by the inhabitants of the Villa des Charmes with passionate curiosity. Germaine had sat down again. Mesurat, on his feet and with his mouth wide open, stared at the Legras garden as though an abyss had suddenly opened before his eyes.

Adrienne felt her heart leap in her breast. Anything that even resembled novelty in her life moved her so deeply as to make her suffer physically. Confused thoughts swarmed through her brain. She gripped the bars so tightly that she hurt her hands. She could see only a very small section of the roadway, but by a feat of imagination she could follow the street until it reached the country and linked itself to the main roads that ran between fields. A sudden project entered her head that filled her with joy and fear. She would open the gate and reach the street, run straight before her—to the woods—the fields, no matter where, so she might be free for an hour. She could hear her father behind her back talking to Germaine; she guessed that the eyes of the pair were no longer upon her. She lowered her right arm; her hand closed gently upon the handle of the gate. A second passed. She pulled it gently toward her, biting her lips. It refused to yield. Finally she seized and tugged at it vigorously, regardless of noise she might be making. The gate was locked.

A week passed slowly without bringing any change into Adrienne's existence. The windows of the Legras house stood open all day, and in the morning sheets and blankets were hung out to air in the sun. The old servant could be seen going from room to room, broom or mop in hand. Then, a gardener came to clip the lime trees in the garden. This lasted two whole afternoons. It can well be imagined that none of this was lost on M. Mesurat, who even suspended his afternoon walks to pursue this activity in all its aspects. Germaine evinced no less interest in what was going on across the street. Stretched out upon her sofa, she was in an excellent position for making observations.

Adrienne alone seemed indifferent. After having desired, feared, waited for the arrival of Madame Legras, she suddenly lost interest in her at the very moment the great event was about to take place. A strange languor had descended on her. The moment she was free to go upstairs, she sought her own room and stretched herself upon her bed—either to sleep or, when sleep refused to come, to set herself adrift on a flood of reverie. It seemed to her that the ultimate depth of her despair had been touched when she perceived that her father locked the garden gate every morning. It was now a question of physical superiority. He was stronger than she. How was she to get possession of the key? By a singular contradiction, a sort of resignation reached her when she realized how powerless she was. Suppose she had found herself free? What would she have done? Prowled around the little white house, as before, or, as once before, carried her grief and woe along the rue Carnot and on to the highway, hoping against hope that she might meet the doctor once again? Now she was locked up—kept under the family eye. Perhaps, after all, it was better to be plunged in unrelieved boredom rather than to pass feverishly from a moment of anxious joy to the lowest depth of affliction. She was tired.

Every evening she joined in the game of cards that her father had had so much trouble teaching her. The day she had flung down her hand on the table in an access of anguish, declaring that she would not play, seemed quite far away. She took her place after dinner between her father and her sister without any display of bad temper. One would have thought that this girl, with the stubborn face and eyes, had definitely chosen her part and was conforming to the rule of the house in every petty detail as the only way to escape tedium on the one hand, and a brutal and terrorizing constraint on the other. After all, it was no worse to be playing cards than crying and yawning in her own room or braving the fury of a tyrannical old man and an embittered invalid.

"I must try to be like them," she used to say to herself. "It is the only way to have peace."

M. Mesurat noticed the change and congratulated himself on it when he and Germaine were alone together. His peace of mind was being respected. What more did he ask? But Germaine had no real faith in Adrienne's submission. Far more subtle than her father, she suspected her sister of all manner of underhand projects, while her more inquisitive soul could not forgive the girl for not having revealed the name of the man she loved. How priceless this spectacle would have been for some observer of this nightly game of cards! These three persons brought together around the lamp—how many motives divided them, how many hostile thoughts in their heads? A father, concerned only for his own habits and for having peace in his house. Two daughters, one tortured by love, the other by jealousy and curiosity. The situation even seemed to be typified in a concrete manner by a game, the essence of which is to ward off your opponent's attack, to bring his strategy to nothing, and to triumph over him in the end. The cards fell on the marble table when a voice proclaimed a point gained or lost, or uttered some brief comment. Nearly always it was M. Mesurat, trained by long practice, who won, despite the acrid concentration of Germaine, and all the efforts of Adrienne, who sometimes became quite involved in the game.

You have to have lived entirely away from Paris to appreciate the tyranny of custom. It is not too much to say that the habit of suffering had grown upon Adrienne all the more easily because everything around her bore the stamp of a life regulated by long observance, where the unexpected was out of the question. The trick of cultivating memory had taken up residence with her and was never to leave her. It was as though the one look the doctor had bestowed upon her followed her everywhere and forced her to think of none other. Nothing so resembles a creature bewitched as a woman in love. Will ceases to count, her very thoughts are preempted. She is as nothing without the one human being who can impel her to action. Separated from him, she falls into a kind of stupor and keeps from life only the consciousness of her loneliness and unhappiness.

There is something truly appalling in these provincial existences, where nothing changes outwardly—where everything preserves the same external aspect quite irrespective of the profoundest moral and spiritual modifications. Seen from without, nothing betrays the anguish, hope, and love that reigns within, and the heart may maintain its mysterious functions till death stills it forever without anyone daring to cut geraniums on Friday instead of Saturday, or walk through the town at eleven in the morning rather than at five in the afternoon.

Chapter VIII

Contrary to Mr. Mesurat's prediction, Mme. Legras did not settle into her villa until ten days after the arrival of the servant. By a strange coincidence, Adrienne alone witnessed her arrival. For some days Mesurat had relaxed the vigilant watch maintained over his younger daughter, resuming his morning walk to the railroad station and back, and it was during his absence that the great event took place. As for Germaine, worried when she saw the sky clouding and the sun going under, she had stayed in bed as she always did at the least threat of bad weather. Vainly she cried out to her sister to tell her what was causing the noise of carriage wheels. Adrienne revenged herself upon all the spinster had made her suffer by not talking to her anymore.

She stationed herself at the dining-room window and looked into the street quite openly. A month ago, she would probably have hidden herself behind the curtain, a prey to emotion. She would have said then that she detested the newcomers, that she was jealous of her, even though in some inexplicable fashion her jealousy was mingled with respect and sympathy. This was probably because Mme. Legras owned a villa directly opposite the little white house. What a privilege to be the doctor's immediate neighbor and to be able, at leisure, to see all that went on behind his windows! It seemed to the young girl that Mme. Legras derived a kind of reflected glory from this special situation.

However, for a week or two, these impressions had become vaguer. One might have thought them effaced, since the girl appeared so calm as she watched Mme. Legras descend at last from her carriage. She was surprised herself at her tranquillity. "So this is Madame Legras!" she repeated, as though to stimulate a waning curiosity. And she added, by conjunction of thought quite natural under the circumstances, "So I don't love Maurecourt anymore?"

Mme. Legras was short and thickset. She was dressed in black, but with luxurious silk and lace suggesting considerable vanity. A large hat adorned with trailing sprays hid her face, but heavy shoulders and a plump neck gave away her age. She jumped out of the carriage lightly and called her servant in a shrill voice. All her gestures were rapid; she affected the annoyance of a person who does not know which way to turn without assistance, and, obtaining no answer from within, began a series of orders to the driver. The man took up her luggage, and the two entered the garden of the villa, with a yellow basset trotting at their heels. Adrienne listened to the sound of their feet upon the gravelled walks and to the voice of Mme. Legras, asking the coachman what the weather had been like at La Tour l'Evêque. She watched them mount the steps and disappear into the interior of the villa.

A few moments passed. The horse kept tossing his head to shake off the flies which clustered on his nose. His head was crowned by a straw hat, with two openings through which his quivering ears protruded. His coat glistened with sweat. Suddenly the girl gripped the window bar and leaned out farther. A sort of shining haze made her open her eyes wider, and she recognized the carriage at which she had been staring for a few seconds. She had already seen those yellow wheels and the faded blue cloth of those cushions. Abruptly her memory carried her back two months. She was at the side of a country road, her arms full of wildflowers. A carriage was passing close to her. In the carriage a man sat reading. Lifting his head, he threw her a glance, at once abstracted and profound. It was Maurecourt. The whole scene rose before her with a clarity, a profusion of detail, that staggered her. Her knees gave way. The pungent smell of the wildflowers invaded her senses as if they were still in her arms, and she asked herself if, this time, she were not really going mad. She sat down upon the window seat, quite unable to take her eyes off the vehicle which recalled so painfully and almost ironically, the mysterious moment when she sensed that her whole life was about to change. What happiness had she not hoped for? She dared not even think of it now. Tender and merciless at the same time, these memories that recalled her ephemeral joy tore at her heart and she marvelled that under the impact of a suffering so violent and full she did not break down. Her eyes were dry; she sat still, with no more motion than a statue, her mouth hanging open, holding her breath so as not to interrupt the full course of the thoughts ravaging her.

A few minutes later the coachman reappeared, swung himself to his seat, and cracked his whip above the horse's head. The wheels turned. In three seconds the carriage had disappeared and the curious nightmare which was holding Adrienne in its hallucination began to ebb. The girl rose. She mechanically took a few steps in the room. She had the impression that her feet were leading her where they pleased and that she was no longer their mistress. As she passed a table she let herself fall into a chair and gave way suddenly, weeping, with her face laid upon her outstretched arms.

Presently she heard Germaine calling her. Her first impulse was not to answer, but there was a note of anguish in her sister's voice which surprised her. She dried her eyes, still uncertain what to do. Germaine called again. She rose and went to the foot of the staircase.

"What do you want?" she cried.

Without waiting for an answer, she mounted the stairs and entered Germaine's room. The window was shut and an odor of eucalyptus made her wince. In a saucer near the head of the bed a medicated cigarette was still smoldering.

"What do you want?" said Adrienne again, standing in the doorway.

Germaine was sitting up in bed, her shoulders covered with a woolen shawl. She looked at her sister anxiously. She seemed even thinner than usual, and her cheeks were flushed.

"Shut the door," she said.

Adrienne hesitated before obeying. She disliked being shut up in a room with the invalid. Finally she closed the door behind her and walked rapidly to the window.

"Don't open it," said Germaine in a frightened voice.

Adrienne turned round.

"What is the matter with you?" she asked.

Germaine lifted her wasted hand and let it drop on the bed as though its weight were too much for her strength. A horrible lassitude was stamped on her face.

"This fever takes it out of one," she said.

"Have you a temperature?"

"I can't get it down," said Germaine. "Usually it rises toward evening and falls in the morning. It's the changeable weather, no doubt."

"It isn't cold today."

The sick woman shook her head and closed her eyes. There was a moment of silence.

"Do you want anything?" asked Adrienne. "Aspirin? . . ."

"No," said Germaine. "I don't want anything at all."

Turning her head toward her sister, she added, "Sit down."

Adrienne did not move. She was divided between a desire to escape from the room and surprise at hearing herself spoken to in such a tone.

"Sit down," repeated the sick woman in an imploring voice. "Can't you see that I'm not well?"

It was the first time that such an admission had left her lips. Adrienne sat down in the center of the room.

"I can't bear being alone," continued Germaine.

"Why not? What are you afraid of?"

Germaine looked at her young sister in bewilderment.

"I'm not afraid," she said at last. "What makes you say that?"

"I don't know," Adrienne said impatiently. "I didn't say you were afraid."

Neither spoke. Adrienne had crossed her hands across her apron and sat quite still. Disgusted with the sick-room air around her, she was trying to breathe as lightly as possible.

"Adrienne," said the older woman at the end of an appreciable silence, "you don't believe I am really sick, do you?"

"No."

"But you didn't say anything when I told you."

"What did you want me to say?"

"Aren't you anxious about me?"

"No," replied Adrienne.

Her stomach turned. She felt she was being invaded by something vaguely sinister. It was as though in some mysterious fashion Germaine's own dismal thoughts were infecting her and poisoning her blood. Before her sister's penetrating glance she turned her face away.

"Listen," said Germaine at last. "I have something to tell you."

She stopped as though to collect her thoughts, and closed her eyes. Against the white pillow her face seemed to be burning away with some hidden fire. Her hair, already turning gray, fell on each side of her face in a short braid tied with a blue ribbon. She looked so little like herself that Adrienne had a moment of panic. She was on the point of getting up, when Germaine once more opened her eyes and looked at her.

"Listen to me, Adrienne," she said, gently. "I think I'm going to die."

Adrienne got up and took a step toward her sister. Sheer stupefaction prevented her from saying anything for a moment.

"You are mad, Germaine," she said at last.

Her anger rose suddenly against this woman who was trying to frighten her.

"Yes," she repeated, "mad! You have nothing but a little fever."

Germaine shook her head.

"I have been sick twelve years."

"Nonsense," said Adrienne. "If that were true we should have known of it."

"You know it perfectly well," her sister said calmly. "You are afraid for your life to come near me. And your face—your expression whenever I come near you! Do you think I don't notice that? Even now—"

Adrienne cast down her eyes. She was perfectly conscious of the disgust written on her face. A few seconds passed.

"It's nothing contagious," said Germaine.

"Why don't you see a doctor?" said Adrienne, her cheeks reddening as she spoke.

A strange light came into Germaine's eyes at the words.

"What doctor?" she asked.

"Any doctor you want," stammered Adrienne. "There are plenty in the town."

"The doctor in the rue Carnot—eh?"

"He, or some other."

"But rather he," persisted the spinster, "than another."

"What do you mean?" said Adrienne, who felt all her old rancor toward her sister rising in her breast. "What makes you say that?"

Germaine raised her hand and let it fall just as she had a few moments ago.

"I guessed," she said.

Adrienne looked at her without a word. She tried to read her sister's thought in her eyes, but the older woman sighed deeply and turned her head away from the scrutiny. Something gripped at Adrienne's heart. For the first time she felt ashamed of her love. How ridiculous it must seem! She felt a horror of this sick creature who had nothing better to do than to spy on others, and, at the same time, a horror of herself and of the secret passion that was devouring her as might some sickness of her own.

"It's not true," she said at last.

"Yes, it is," said Germaine. "You cut your arms on purpose."

"What do you know about it?" said Adrienne in a smothered voice.

"Haven't I eyes to see?"

"And what affair is it of yours?" said the girl, stamping her foot. "You are only making me wretched."

At these words Germaine made a motion of her head, as though to hear better.

"How?" she asked.

"How?" repeated Adrienne, no longer able to contain herself. "I can't go out when I want to any longer. I am forced to play cards with you two every night. I have to make the tour of the town with papa every afternoon. I am not free any longer. I am not even allowed to look out of the window."

She checked herself as she saw the effect her words were having upon her sister. A slow smile creased the sick woman's cheeks as she listened. Her lips parted and she made no attempt to conceal the joy in her eyes. Adrienne gazed at her a moment. Her own thoughts were in such disorder that she staggered a few paces toward the door and leaned against the head of the bed. Twenty different ideas swarmed in her brain. And all at once, before the smile which lingered upon the haggard face of the older woman, she had an intuition of the truth.

"So now you're happy!" she exclaimed.

She wanted to say more, but the words would not come out of her throat. She shrugged her shoulders furiously and left precipitously, slamming the door behind her. On the landing she stood listening. Not a sound from her sister's room! She thrust her hands into the pockets of her apron and breathed hard. And suddenly, lifting her head with an air of bravado, she muttered these words:

"Die, then! Die! . . ."

She heard Mme. Legras's dog barking. Someone pushed in the gate of Villa des Charmes. It was her father, back from his walk. She went downstairs and found him in the parlor. In her confusion of mind she began to walk from one end of the room to the other, her eyes on the carpet and her hands still in the pockets of her apron.

"What's the matter with you?" asked the old man.

She stopped instantly.

"With me? Nothing."

Why, indeed, had she come down to the parlor? She turned toward the door, but her father stopped her.

"What a face! What were you doing upstairs?"

"Upstairs?"

"Yes, upstairs," shouted Mesurat. "Don't repeat every word I say after me. I want to know what you were doing upstairs."

Adrienne shook her head.

"Nothing."

"What do you mean?" cried the old man, exasperated beyond measure. "Here you are, your cheeks all red and your hair a mess."

She glanced quickly at the mirror and noticed that her hair was indeed falling over her forehead. There was something wild in her face that surprised herself. She stepped back quickly and leaned against the head of the sofa.

"She's going to die," she exclaimed, abruptly.

Mesurat stood stockstill in the middle of the room. His hat, which he had not yet removed, hid his eyes.

"She?" he repeated. "Who?"

Adrienne breathed heavily.

"Germaine!" she answered in a little flat voice.

"Germaine!" exclaimed Mesurat furiously. "You must be crazy. She's not even sick."

"Yes, she is sick." As she said the words Adrienne felt the blood leaving her cheeks.

The old man brought his hand down on the back of an armchair.

"Hold your tongue," he commanded, "If she were sick she would have said so."

"She told me."

"It's a lie. She's perfectly well."

Adrienne looked at her father without answering. He was crimson with fury.

"Get out!" he shouted suddenly.

She left the room and closed the door behind her as though she was walking in her sleep. Across the street, Mme. Legras's dog was filling the garden with his shrill yapping.

Chapter IX

The weather had changed and it rained in torrents the whole week. Neither Adrienne nor her father was able to leave the house. As for Germaine, there was never any question of such a thing, even in the mildest weather, with the difference that now she kept to her room and did not appear at any of the meals. At first old Mesurat pretended not to notice her absence. While detesting any change in the habits of the household, he refrained from mentioning the matter to Adrienne, for fear of lending importance to something he had made up his mind to ignore. "The less we say about it," he was thinking, "the more quickly a problem goes away."

Nevertheless, his bad temper showed that he was disturbed. It was all very well to say that Adrienne had lied and that Germaine was no more sick than he was, but something aroused his suspicions. Not wanting to lend credence to these thoughts, as though to encourage himself in his skepticism, he made a point of asking Adrienne, every time they sat down at the table, why Germaine was so late in getting down.

"You know why," the girl would say, wearily.

"No, I don't," cried Mesurat, furiously. When Adrienne told him once again that Germaine was sick, he banged his fist on the table and ordered her to hold her tongue.

"I forbid you to speak of that," he said. "Germaine is perfectly well. Anyhow," he added one day after a moment's reflection, "we shall see."

And he passed the back of his thumb over his blond beard with the air of a man whose mind is quite made up.

One morning, as breakfast was announced, he climbed the stairs to the landing outside Germaine's room, and began to shout, "Aren't you ready, Germaine?"

After a moment's silence, he called her again, this time rapping upon her door with his kunckles.

"I'm not coming down," said a voice from the room.

"Oh yes, you are," said the old man with an air of authority.

He glued his ear to the panel, and seized the handle of the door. The blood rushed to his cheeks and made his eyes look bluer than ever. He was stooping as though to listen, and his arched back made one think of some powerful beast crouching before it springs on its prey.

"Do you hear me?" he repeated. "I am going to make you come downstairs."

At the sound of his angry voice, Adrienne had mounted the stairs softly. She stood on a step halfway to the upper landing, her back against the wall, half frightened and half curious as she listened to her father's growling voice.

"Germaine," went on M. Mesurat, "I warn you I am coming in and that I will make you come downstairs."

As though to give force to his threat, he turned the handle of the door backward and forward. A cry of alarm came from inside the room.

"No, no, papa," said Germaine's voice. "Go away!"

She was silent a moment, then went on:

"Go away, I am going to dress."

"Are you coming down?" insisted Mesurat.

After a few seconds, a voice seemed to answer, "Yes," but so feebly that Adrienne could not catch it. She only guessed what her sister's answer had been from the exclamation of triumph uttered by her father.

"Good!" said the old man. "I thought you would."

He released the handle and began to run down the stairs. As he passed Adrienne, he gripped her hand and shook it violently.

"As for you," he cried, his eyes challenging her to reply, "if you ever tell me again that she is sick—"

He didn't finish. Shrugging his shoulders, he released her hand and continued down.

A quarter of an hour later, Adrienne and M. Mesurat were still at the table and had finished drinking their *café au lait*. More than once the old man seemed on the point of going to see why his elder daughter had not yet appeared. But he contented himself with first resting his fists on the table and bending forward as though ready at a moment's notice to push his chair behind him and to leap to his feet, and then changing his mind, grumbling under his beard. Adrienne watched this pantomime out of a corner of her eye and kept silent. During the last few days she had felt a sentiment, until then unknown, creeping into her heart. At first it had shocked her, but only to yield her, later, a strange secret joy. She despised her father. For many years she had respected him, perhaps even imagined she loved him with that tepid love which is distributed among the different members of a single family. But from the day when he had shaken her in order to force her to play at cards, she had realized that fear was the basis of her respect, and that daughterly affection played no part in it. She feared him still. She dreaded the strength of that hairy wrist and of those cruel fingers which could leave such red marks upon her bruised arms. Only a moment ago her heart had fluttered at feeling him seize her hand to crush it in his own. Meantime, she was becoming accustomed to these displays of violence and suffered less from them. It seemed to her that from the moment she had felt herself free to take note of the ridiculous attitudes of her father, she experienced a sense of liberation and breathed more freely. It was like a revenge taken upon him of which he was at the same time the instrument and the victim. Could it really be she who was forcing him to make these absurd gestures, to walk in that heavy-footed fashion, his mouth open, to eat so repellently? No! But it might have been thought that he was doing all these things to degrade himself further in the eyes of the daughter, who kept an eye upon him that was at once curious and disgusted. Perhaps the greatest consolation of the oppressed is to feel themselves superior to the oppressor, and this compensation can be carried to such a point that it is hard to say whether the oppressed do not get more satisfaction out of feeling themselves better than their tyrants than the tyrants get out of their persecution. There were times when Adrienne was positively transported with a strange joy, and for a second or two managed to forget Maurecourt. As, for instance, when her father, yielding to an inveterate habit, counted the flies on the long band of adhesive paper which hung from the chandelier in the parlor and, then, raising his forefinger, and with a triumphant look in his eye, cried out: "Fifteen in an hour!" Or when, having some letter to answer, he began tracing parallel lines on a sheet of notepaper, an old professional trick which clung to him, and inscribed a splendid "Monsieur" with scrolls and flourishes which cost him deep sighs and groans.

Toward her sister, Adrienne entertained sentiments of a different order. She knew Germaine to be of a hateful disposition, jealous of others' health and happiness. But she would easily have pardoned this if the revulsion which she had for her malady had not stifled in her every sentiment of pity. She never passed Germaine without holding her breath so as not to absorb the air which it was her conviction the spinster poisoned with her sick respiration. At the table she suffered intensely from having her at her elbow, and rejoiced secretly each time weakness kept her sister to her own room. Sometimes, it is true, she tried to conquer her feelings and forced herself to speak to Germaine more gently than was natural to her. But Germaine maid never seemed to appreciate these attempts at kindness and remained plunged in her sullen temper and irremediable despair. Moreover, deep within herself Adrienne experienced a disgust which no consideration could overcome. She detested her sister as one detests a nest of vipers, with the instinctive horror of the healthy for whatever can shorten life or pollute its sources.

Between these two beings—one sick, the other senile—she had a very clear consciousness of her own strength and health. But the joy she drew from it was never more than fleeting. What good, indeed, did it do her to be only eighteen? Was she happy? She dreamed of running away—of throwing herself at the feet of Maurecourt, in whom she placed all her hope, and begging him to make her his wife. Between the Villa des Charmes and the little white house there were only a few steps, but these few steps separated two worlds, and she saw her situation only in antitheses. On the one side, home, unhappiness—on the other, Maurecourt, happiness. Here life in decay—death prowling about the house. There a calm existence, free of care, full of an equable joy which each day would renew. She drew for herself an ideal portrait of this Maurecourt, whom she had only glimpsed but who, in her imagination, assumed the physiognomy of a symbolic being. With the mysticism of naïve souls, the more she suffered from the circumstances of her present life, the closer she felt to him, and she sometimes discovered a strange sweetness mixed in with the abuses that she was forced to endure. "If I did not love him," she said to herself, "I would not be suffering so much." This thought comforted her a little, as though, through some mysterious dispensation, the doctor benefitted from her troubles. All these chimeras ranged incessantly through Adrienne's brain and completed her distraction.

A sudden exclamation on Mesurat's part made her jump. Turning her eyes toward the door, she saw her sister enter the room. The old maid walked painfully, her eyes nearly closed like those of a person overtaken with vertigo. But Adrienne was surprised to note how little she was changed. She had expected a face still more ravaged, and the weakness of a woman at the point of death. Germaine was horribly wasted, and helped herself to walk with a stick. But there was enough color in her cheeks to lend the illusion of health.

"Now, you see," said Mesurat, jubilantly. "I told you you could come downstairs. It is only a question of a little good will."

He passed the back of his thumb rapidly over his beard and looked across at Adrienne as though expecting some sign of approbation. But the girl affected not to see his glance.

"Come," said he, vexed at this passive attitude, "pour some coffee for your sister. Ring for more bread."

Reaching his leg under the table, he gave a vigorous push to the chair which the sick woman was trying to draw toward her.

"Sit down, Germaine," said he in a cheery voice, delighted to see her in front of him in her habitual place.

She let herself fall upon a chair. Sitting sideways, her head hanging down and her forearms on the table, she panted slightly and seemed quite worn out. Without a word, Adrienne filled a cup with black coffee and put it before her sister. She looked at her attentively, unable to hide that avid and cruel curiosity that we can espy in young children when they assist at some punishment inflicted upon a little companion.

"Drink it!" commanded Mesurat.

Germaine lowered her head and brought the cup near her lips. But she put it down almost at once. She shivered.

"Close the window," she said.

At this moment the maid entered, carrying a plate of bread. Mesurat shrugged his shoulders.

"Shut the window, Désirée," he said, exasperated.

Désirée laid down the bread, closed the window, and left the room. There was a moment of silence.

"Come," said the old man, seeing that Germaine made no move, "drink your coffee."

Germaine raised her head. Beneath her red, fluttery eyelids her eyes were fixed on Adrienne.

"Bring me my aspirin," she said.

Mesurat seemed to have been waiting for something of the sort.

"What for?" he exclaimed. "What are you going to do with your aspirin?"

The older woman turned toward her father. Her parted lips, her head which trembled slightly, betrayed a violent emotion.

"To bring down my fever."

"Your fever!" the old man cried. "Go and look at yourself in the mirror in the parlor. You have no more fever than I have. I never saw you look better."

He went on, carried away by the sound of his own voice, which rang through the room.

"I know what fever is. I had it myself, in 'eighty-six. When people have fever they stay in bed. They lie flat on their backs for two weeks without being able to move."

And, as Germaine opened her lips to speak:

"Hold your tongue!" he cried. "In the first place, this is not the climate for fever. There is no such thing as fever in Seine-et-Oise. Mind what I say. You're not sick. No one has ever been sick here."

His voice grew louder and louder. He punctuated his bellows with blows of his fist upon the table.

"Now, understand me once and for all. I've had quite enough of this. I want peace. I want to be left alone. You understand, Adrienne? I'm saying this quite as much for you. The first one who speaks to me about sickness will hear something she won't like."

He got to his feet and laid down his napkin in the middle of the table, among the plates and coffee service. His daughters stared at him without daring to answer. He was breathing heavily, but seemed to enjoy the sensation his words had created.

"Now, that's understood—eh?" he cried after a moment of silence.

Shrugging his shoulders four or five times in rapid succession, he plunged his hands into his coat pockets and stalked out into the parlor. Adrienne and Germaine heard him sit down heavily in an armchair, with a weary sigh.

Chapter X

A few minutes later, obedient to the mania of her father, who insisted that everything should be as usual in the house, Germaine was lying on the parlor sofa beneath the window, although there was no sun and the clouds promised rain.

As soon as the old man had left the house to buy his newspaper at the railroad station, she called her sister to her side. Adrienne, who was carrying out her daily inspection of the furniture, obeyed reluctantly. At first she had frankly enjoyed her father's cruelty in insisting on the invalid's quitting her bed. Recalling all the ill turns that Germaine had done her, she had mentally applauded what she told herself was a just revenge. But the violence of old Mesurat had gone beyond anything she looked for. She had the vague feeling of shame toward her sister that one always feels in the presence of those who have been humiliated out of all proportion to their wrongdoing.

"Well?" said she. "What is it?"

"Adrienne," said Germaine, so steadily as to surprise her young sister, "I have made up my mind to leave this house."

"Leave the house? You can't mean it!"

"I have no intention of discussing it with you," replied Germaine in a harsh and uneven voice. "You must see that I can't go on living here at my age, under the control of a man who will not even allow me to stay in bed when I like and when it is necessary. Besides, the climate here is bad, execrable. Look how cold it is this morning, after all these roasting days. It is enough to kill anyone. What I need is warmth and sunshine and an even temperature. And I need also to feel free. Papa is growing terribly old. He is a tyrant—yes, a tyrant! You saw that this morning. . . . This ridiculous, hateful scene! I've thought of going away for years. But I've been prevented by all sorts of difficulties, which really don't amount to much. This morning I feel strong enough to go, and I can't wait a moment longer. You will have to help me—you simply will have to. Do you understand? I'm not afraid of your crying for me."

And she laughed bitterly.

"My health," she went on, "my happiness—yes, my happiness—everything depends on what I'm going to do. I loathe this house—my room that turns as cold as ice when the sun goes down. I refuse to pass another winter here. I've had enough of it."

Adrienne's heart leaped. She thought immediately of her sister's room. It would be free now! She thought of the window at which she would be able to sit all day. She took a step toward the sofa.

"But what about papa?" she said in a hurried voice. "What will you tell him?"

"Papa is not going to know anything about it till I've gone."

"And then—the money, Germaine? Where are you going to find money for the journey?"

"Money—money!" repeated Germaine, with a nervous movement. "Don't bother about that. I'll find it. The question is, will you help me—help me to go away?"

Adrienne repressed the cry that rose to her lips.

"If you think I can help you—" she began.

She stopped suddenly, seized with a sort of shame which prevented her from betraying her joy. Germaine began to laugh.

"What are you laughing at?" asked Adrienne.

"Oh, nothing," said Germaine. "Now, will you write a letter I dictate? You can put it in the mailbox when you go out with papa. Look in the desk and you'll find some notepaper."

Without another word, Adrienne obeyed. She took paper, pen and ink, and sat down before the card-table.

"Are you ready?" asked Germaine, and began to dictate the following letter:

> MADAME: I am desirous of staying with you for a week while seeking some spot where the climate is suitable for my state of health. I accept in advance your rates for board and lodging. I regret being unable to send you the letter of introduction usual in such cases, and which circumstances, that I am sure you will appreciate, have prevented me from securing. I will arrive tomorrrow, Tuesday, by an evening train.
>
> > Believe me, Madame. . . .

She stopped. "Do you say 'Madame' to a nun?"

"I don't know," said Adrienne. "I believe not."

"I can't help that," said Germaine. "I have no time to bother about such things. Go on: "'—very sincerely yours.' . . . Sign it, and address the envelope,

"'The Mother Superior, Saint-Blaise Hospital.' . . . What department is Saint-Blaise in?"

"I don't know."

"Look it up in Larousse. But hurry. It's going to rain and papa will be coming back."

Adrienne took one of the books from the shelf at the back of the writing-desk, and began to look through it. As she turned over its pages, her fingers trembling from haste, Germaine, raised upon one elbow, was watching the garden gate. Her face was set, but a strange, intent look in her eyes betrayed her anxiety. Mechanically she drew a corner of her shawl across her chest.

"Well?" she said impatiently, rapping the arm of the sofa with her hand.

Adrienne closed the dictionary and completed the address.

"Côte-d'Or," she replied. "I'm writing it down."

"Very good! Now seal the envelope. You will find a stamp in the small drawer. This afternoon when you go out with papa, you will slip this letter in the box."

She stopped and seemed to be racking her brain.

"Wait," she continued in a hurried voice. "There was something else. . . . Oh yes! Put the book back. You must write to the livery stable to send a carriage tomorrow morning and tell the man to stop at the corner of rue Carnot, at half past six."

"Half past six!" exclaimed Adrienne.

"I want to go before papa is up. Tell the cab people to have it there on time—say, a quarter past six—and that I'll be outside with my baggage."

"Suppose it's raining—"

Germaine gave a frightened start. It was clear she had not thought of such a contingency. But she recovered her composure.

"So much the worse," said she. "I'll be there in any case. I can take an umbrella. It will be all right. . . . Ah, the key to the gate! You'll find it in papa's waistcoat pocket!"

"Papa's waistcoat pocket! But—when, Germaine?"

"Oh, I don't know—this evening. Here comes the rain!"

Adrienne got up and went over to the sofa. The headlong rush in which Germaine had spoken ended by making her as nervous as the invalid herself.

"How do you expect I'm going to get at the key?" she asked.

Germaine looked at her with a face twisted by anguish.

"Wait till late tonight. Go into his room. He keeps the key in his right-hand waistcoat pocket. Take it; open the gate with it; then go in again and put it back. Will you—or won't you?"

Adrienne hesitated.

"Will you do it?" said Germaine, desperately. "Say 'yes.' Oh, I implore you! If I could only do it myself! What are you afraid of? That he'll wake up?"

Her face seemed to clear. She lifted herself on her elbow and said, lowering her voice as she spoke:

"I swear to you he won't wake up. Isn't he always saying he never moves at night and that a clap of thunder would not rouse him? Do you hear? I swear it."

"All right," said Adrienne.

Suddenly she herself was seized with a sort of enthusiasm for the plot.

"Of course he won't wake up!" she cried. "How absurd! I'll write to the livery stable. How long are you going to be away?"

"I don't know. Don't forget—quarter past six."

The gate at the bottom of the garden opened. They saw Mesurat hurrying up the central path. Adrienne slipped the letter inside her bodice, and put the pen and ink back on the writing-desk. As her father entered the parlor she was busy dusting the brass candelabra on the mantelpiece. Germaine's eyes were closed. She seemed to be sleeping.

All that afternoon Mesurat and his daughters watched the sky with an anxiety that was the same for all three and differed only in degrees of intensity. Would it clear? Three pairs of eyes ransacked the clouds for some promise of fair weather. But the annoyance the old man felt at seeing a threat to his daily constitutional was as nothing compared with Adrienne's concern and the sheer terror which gripped Germaine's heart. If they had been at all religious, the two women would have been praying. At each gust of rain they exchanged a look charged with terrible dismay. Looking at them, one would have imagined that their lives depended on the state of the weather between four and five. To understand fully such a state of mind, it may be well to recall for a moment the kind of existence shared by the two sisters. It may even seem surprising that after having lived for such a long time under circumstances of insufferable monotony, they had not discovered in themselves sufficient patience to endure just a little longer and to wait for a favorable day to put their project into execution. If it rained between four and five, Adrienne could not go out, and as a consequence could not mail her letter in time for it to reach the carriage depot before night. But if Germaine was unable to go away the following day, what would prevent her from postponing her journey until the next day, or even the next week if necessary?

But the human heart is made that way. It is capable of letting years elapse without once dreaming of rebellion against its lot. Finally a day arrives when, at one stroke, endurance reaches its limit. The remedy must be instant or it is useless. To defer, for a single day longer, an enterprise which the victim had not the remotest idea about the day before, means losing everything. On the sofa where she had passed so many hours immobile as a statue, Germaine now tossed from side to side, the prey to an anguish which forced her to press her hands upon her breast, or to hide her face to smother a moan, listening to the clock strike every quarter, imploring the sky for that clear patch of blue which the capricious wind alternately promised and refused.

The afternoon dragged on interminably. After lunch the rain stopped. The sky assumed a whitish pallor which it seemed fated to keep until the end of the day. Germaine's miserable restlessness had by now infected Adrienne. She ended by coming to sit near the sofa, so she could speak to Germaine the moment a chance presented itself and to settle upon the last detail of their conspiracy.

If Mesurat had been informed of what was going on he could not have clung more steadfastly to the parlor. Seated in his armchair, he was perusing the advertisement columns of his newspaper with the close attention of the aimless reader. Every now and then he looked up to yawn or to ask some trivial question which further strained the nerves of his daughters. Adrienne had taken up a book and pretended not to hear what her father said. It was Germaine who replied in monosyllables. Two hours passed.

At last the old man got up, left the room, and stationed himself at the head of the garden steps.

"Adrienne, the stamps!" said Germaine in a hoarse whisper. "You will find them in the little drawer on the right side of the desk. And see if there is any money in the bottom drawer."

The girl tiptoed to the secretary. She opened and closed the drawer stealthily. She came back to the sofa.

"I've got the stamps," she said under her breath.

"And the money?"

"I had no time to look. He's coming back."

Germaine made an angry gesture.

"He's not! He hasn't moved. I can see him from here. I'll let you know if he does. Quick!"

She pushed her away toward the desk. Adrienne returned and opened the drawer of which her sister had spoken. It was stuffed with papers. But on a pile of receipts she spied a portfolio and seized it. She was going to open it when she heard Mesurat shutting the outer door behind him. She closed the drawer and barely had time to throw the portfolio on her sister's knees before the old man came in.

"Aren't you reading anymore?" he asked, seeing her in the middle of the room.

"No," she answered, turning away to hide her flushed cheeks.

"It's going to clear up," said the father, sitting down again in his armchair. "We shall be able to go out in an hour."

She sat down and took up her book again. Her heart was beating fast and she feared her father would catch the sound of her heavy breathing. But he was humming a tune, wagging his head from side to side. At the end of a few minutes he fell asleep.

"Well," said Adrienne, leaning toward her sister.

"It's empty," said Germaine. "Look again."

"I can't do it," said the girl, emphatically.

"That means you don't want me to go?"

Adrienne bit her lips. In her mind's eye she saw the little white house and the interior of the room with its red tablecloth that could be seen so well from the third-story window. It seemed to her that good luck in her love affair depended now on her sister's departure. Germaine guessed the thoughts that were flitting through the girl's head and went on:

"I can't go away without money. Look again!"

Adrienne bowed her head and seemed to be thinking hard.

"How much do you want?" she asked.

"Four hundred francs for the journey alone," said Germaine, promptly.

"And afterward—?"

Germaine waved her hand as though to imply that only the immediate future was worrying her.

"I have my jewels," she said at last. "I can get on somehow."

And she added, impatiently:

"The great thing is to get away, isn't it? I must have money for that."

Adrienne's eyes plainly showed her perplexity. She clasped her hands across her knees.

"I can lend you that much," she said, as though by an effort.

Germaine looked at her coldly.

"Out of your savings?"

"Yes."

"All right. Lend me five hundred francs."

Adrienne rose and stole out of the room. Once outside, she sighed deeply. It was painful for her to part with the money that her father had been making her set aside for seven years. But she told herself that she would willingly give twice as much to have her sister out of the house. She went up to her room, took a little olive-wood box out of her wardrobe, and opened it with a copper key. Inside were more than three hundred gold coins in little paper rolls. They were Christmas and Easter gifts, and birthday presents from Mesurat and an old cousin who had died recently. She took a roll of twenty-five coins, put back the box, and locked the wardrobe. For a moment she stood motionless in the middle of her room. Was it joy or regret that pierced her heart? She went to the window and looked at the little white house on the street corner. The sight restored her courage. She remembered the two letters that she had to mail, took them from her bodice, sealed the envelopes, and affixed the stamps. Then she went downstairs.

Her father still slept. Her sister's face wore an expression of intense anxiety. The spinster beckoned her to come closer.

"Have you got the money?" she whispered.

Adrienne gave her the roll. Without a word Germaine assured herself that the paper was firmly fastened, and slipped it inside her dress. Then she fell back on the cushions.

"What were you doing up there all the time?" she asked, fretfully. "He might have heard you walking about. Are the stamps on the envelopes?"

Adrienne nodded, and sat down in an armchair. There was nothing to do now but wait.

Chapter XI

Four o'clock struck at last. Mesurat rose from his seat to go out with his daughter. Adrienne was already dressed for the street. She had put on a short blue jacket with sleeves puffed at the shoulders, and a black straw hat, tilted forward a little to leave room for the heavy masses of her hair. She wore string gloves and held an umbrella whose metal collar she was nervously clicking up and down.

"Come on," said her father, noticing her impatience, but little guessing its cause. "You're going to go out."

He added with a glance at the sky, "If the weather stays fine there will be a concert in the public gardens."

They started at once. Although the girl knew every step of the route they would follow, she was nonetheless extremely nervous. She told herself that if her father should decide to cross the street just a few yards beyond the usual spot, she would be unable to mail the letters. This accident, however, failed to occur, and Adrienne took care of her letters exactly as she intended. Keeping close to the wall, she slipped the letters into the slot with a rapid movement which did not arouse the slightest suspicion. Her success filled her with such joy that she could not keep herself from seizing her father's arm and leaning toward him as though impelled by a sudden impulse of affection.

"What's the matter?" asked the old man, in surprise.

Adrienne blushed and let go of his arm.

"I felt a little tired," she stammered.

"Tired? How absurd! You have not walked fifty yards."

They went on in silence. A few moments later the trees of the little square, which the municipality had deeded to the town, came into sight. The town-hall clock was striking quarter past four. Several groups of pedestrians were making for the center of the park, not without casting frequent looks of anxiety toward the sky. After passing the central gate Adrienne and her father followed the main alley toward the bandstand, whose red corrugated iron roof and slim columns were visible a long way off above the trees. Around this edifice, designed with an evident attempt to imitate Chinese architecture, a large number of folding chairs were arranged, many of them already occupied, but a custom of more than eight years' standing assigned to M. Mesurat and his daughter two good places below the spot where the leader of the orchestra took up his stand. As they made their way there between the outer seats the young girl touched her father's elbow.

"Papa," she said, "someone has taken my seat."

This was indeed the case. A stout woman, dressed in brown, was sitting on Adrienne's chair.

"What a nuisance!" said M. Mesurat, the most timid of men once his foot was beyond his own doorstep. "Explain to the lady."

And he hung back a little while his daughter went toward the offender.

She stood opposite her, and said, "Madame, I'm very sorry—"

Her protest died away on her lips. She was speaking to Mme. Legras!

"What are you sorry about, mademoiselle?" said Mme. Legras, raising her head. She had a voice that was at once level and ironic, and a quizzical expression in her eyes. Although she did not seem more than forty, she was already marked by age. Her face was oval, a little too full, but with something pleasant in the regularity of its lines. Her aquiline nose, her thick lips, suggested a sensuality quite in harmony with the majestic air which good features assume when fat begins to invade them. She wore a serge jacket with revers of taffeta. It was half open and showed a jabot of heavy lace that fell over the front of her shirtwaist. A veil that drooped from her hat hid her hair, but one guessed it was abundant. She exuded a strong odor of talcum powder.

"I hope you are not going to tell me that I have your chair," she went on. "It will make the third time I have been disturbed. I am not budging."

And then, as if there were a connection between the two facts:

"Besides, I know you. You are my neighbor at Villa des Charmes."

Adrienne nodded. She stood rooted to the spot, divided between resentment at seeing this woman occupy her place, and surprise at finding herself suddenly in the presence of Mme. Legras.

"It doesn't matter," she managed to murmur at last. "We'll sit somewhere else."

"Sit down beside me. Who is with you?"

M. Mesurat had come forward, listening with a hang-dog air. Adrienne introduced him awkwardly and both sat down, the girl between Mme. Legras and her father. Without realizing it, she was ashamed of the old man, and turned her face to Mme. Legras as though to prevent her from seeing him. But Mme. Legras, inquisitive, moved her own head back and forth and examined the old man out of the corner of her eye. He turned away slightly, uneasy by this attention and furious, moreover, at not occupying his usual place. A pretty figure he would cut if someone should come up and claim the chair on which he was sitting!

"Your father seems very nice," whispered Mme. Legras in Adrienne's ear. "Shy, isn't he?"

"Yes, madame."

"I thought so. A fine head. I'll wager he's a retired officer."

Adrienne turned red. Not for worlds, it seemed to her, would she admit what her father's profession had been.

"He did his military service at Bourges," she stammered.

And she added quickly, opening her handbag:

"I must buy a program for the concert."

"I have one," said Mme. Legras.

She passed the folded sheet she held in her hand. Adrienne examined it a moment. But the letters swam before her eyes and she could not read a word. At this moment Mme. Legras leaned forward and spoke across her to M. Mesurat.

"I see you are musical, monsieur."

The amiable and trifling question made the old man blush. He passed his thumbnail down his beard and answered shortly that he always attended the concerts of the Harmonic Society. Mme. Legras nodded approvingly and smiled. She had long even teeth and seemed quite proud of them.

"You were telling me he was an officer at Bourges," she murmured in Adrienne's ear. "Have you been at La Tour l'Evêque a long time?"

The girl was opening her mouth to reply when exclamations that broke out all around saved her the trouble. The band had arrived. People who had been drifting around the bandstand without making up their minds where to sit, rushed toward the free seats and took noisy possession of them. An instant later the instruments began to tune up. The orchestra broke into a brilliant overture.

Adrienne had been attending these concerts too long a time to take very much pleasure in them now. Without being a musician, she judged rightly that these soldiers played only moderately well and that the quality of their instruments corresponded poorly with the intentions of the composer. Today, however, she experienced a singular emotion that began with the first bars. No doubt the recent events in her life had rendered her susceptible. She listened to a long phrase that rose in languid tempo and passed by a sudden effort into a rhythm that became more and more rapid. She melted at once, as if a sudden voice had spoken to her in a language she alone could understand. Between herself and the orchestra that mysterious correspondence set in, that secret conversation, so to speak, which is music's most potent charm and which explains why it has so great a grasp on the human heart. She listened. As theme after theme followed, in which joy seemed to invoke sorrow, and sorrow joy, the melody tore at her heart even while it was bringing tears of pleasure to her eyes. In the different rhythms, which seemed to be the pulsations of her own heart, she recognized herself. She recalled her suffering, her loneliness, and those wild outbursts of laughter on the highway that were sadder than any sighs. A feeling of suffocation overcame her. It seemed to her as though, in a moment, she lived through all that she had suffered for months, and these sufferings appeared all the more true and sharp for being uttered by a voice that was not hers. For the first time she heard the tale of her sorrows, and they seemed dreadful. It was possible, she thought, that she might have become resigned to them in time, as one becomes resigned to a wound that will not heal. But this music explained everything, showed her only too clearly the reason for her suffering. She had a feeling of humiliation, and looked at Mme. Legras askance, as though she feared her neighbor might have recognized her in this narrative of wretchedness. But the stout lady seemed quite insensible to the beauties which stirred Adrienne so profoundly. She was casting her eyes around with an interested and complacent air.

The overture ended amid a salvo of applause which made Adrienne start in her chair. She became conscious of a hand that was pressing her own kindly but firmly. Turning her head, she met the eyes of Mme. Legras, who was looking at her closely.

"Come," said the new acquaintance, "is it the music that is making you cry?"

"I didn't know I was crying," answered Adrienne, forcing a smile. She would have liked to free her hand, but Mme. Legras held it so tightly that she could not do so without seeming ungracious.

"What was the name of the last piece?" she asked.

"I don't know," said Mme. Legras. "'Dame Blanche'—or something of the sort. You know you are coming back to have something at my house," she went on in a tone that was at once playful but determined. "We are neighbors and will have to get acquainted."

Adrienne blushed with pleasure. She had a sudden conviction that the overture just heard was really the magnificent prelude to a new life. Otherwise why would it have moved her so deeply? This woman, practically a stranger, had asked her the first time they met to the house she had been longing to enter. Wasn't that a sign? She was on the point of asking her whether she could see the rooms that opened on the rue Carnot, and was turning her eyes, shining with gratitude, upon Mme. Legras, quite ready to accept her invitation, when she thought of her sister. Perhaps she ought to see that everything was in order for her departure. The least mistake might prove fatal.

"I'm afraid I can't today," she said.

"Why not?"

Her new friend's air was suspicious, as though the mere fact of having known Adrienne for five minutes gave her a right to share her secrets. The girl shook her head.

"Some other day, madame, with pleasure."

8 7

"Come tomorrow."

"Yes, tomorrow."

The thought struck her that her father might raise objections and even forbid her going to Mme. Legras after Germaine decamped, but she didn't have the courage to dwell on that thought. For the moment, she was calm, almost happy. Shouldn't that suffice? Trouble would come soon enough, so to speak, without her going out to find it. She was only afraid her father had heard her conversation with Mme. Legras. Suppose he made trouble, prevented her from going to Mme. Legras's tomorrow? But he was reading a program which he had picked up from the grass, and did not seem to have heard. Adrienne leaned closer to her neighbor.

"Don't say anything about it to my father," she murmured in her ear, adding, as Mme. Legras's face showed her surprise, "I will explain later."

A blare of brass instruments cut the conversation short. The musicians were tuning up. After a brief silence the orchestra broke into a noisy and pompous march. Adrienne recognized, with indescribable disgust, the tune her father was so fond of humming and which he was accompanying now with furtive little nods. Seized with sudden irritation, she clenched the hasp of her handbag between her fingers with all her might. This was her life today, this dull ugly march that was making so many eyes sparkle round her. She could hear Mesurat blowing out the lamp and his heavy tread as he mounted the stairs, whistling into his mustache. She was horrified at herself and turned cold as though seized by nausea.

Amid the tumult of applause she heard the level voice of her new friend saying:

"What wretched music!"

She would have liked to shake her hand for the words, but did not dare. Drops of rain began to patter overhead. A few people opened their umbrellas. Others got up, hesitated, and turned their eyes toward the musicians, who stood consulting among themselves. The shower grew heavier and there was a general rush for shelter. Some climbed the steps of the bandstand; others made for the trees. Mesurat took his daughter by the arm.

"Come on," said he.

"Good-bye," cried Mme. Legras, who had opened a tiny blue silk umbrella. "I'm going to take shelter here." As Adrienne looked back at her, she gave a wink of connivance, and disappeared in the crowd.

Chapter XII

As the gate of the Villa des Charmes closed behind her, Adrienne felt she was reentering a prison. From her conversation with Mme. Legras she brought back a sort of nostalgia for liberty which was very painful. The mere thought of this woman, able to come and go just as she pleased. . . ! She crossed the little garden, picking her way among the puddles, and ran up the steps, which were being pelted by the raindrops. In the hall she stamped her feet once or twice, wiped her shoes, and went into the parlor.

It was quite gloomy there, for the Villa des Charmes was a dark house once its windows were closed. A moment later Mesurat entered in his turn, slightly out of breath.

"They hadn't time to play the whole program," he explained to Germaine, who was in her accustomed place on the sofa. "Just an overture and then a march. You know the one—"

He hummed the opening bars.

As Adrienne passed behind him she shrugged her shoulders and threw up her eyes.

"Many people there?" asked Germaine.

"Not one empty place," said Mesurat. "A big success."

"We met Madame Legras," said Adrienne, who was unable to refrain from speaking of her new friend. The very sound of the name seemed to abate the sadness and boredom which weighed upon the room. She took off her hat, peeled off her gloves, which were sticking to her hands from the rain, and put them on the marble-topped table.

"Yes," said the old man, turning to his younger daughter. "A rather pretentious woman—eh?"

Adrienne turned red.

"Because she's well dressed? I don't think so at all."

"Possibly," said the old man, nettled at even a hint of contradiction. "I think so, anyhow." And he sat down in an armchair.

"No one knows anything about her husband," he continued. "He comes down for weekends, sometimes. I've heard they are rich."

"Rich?" said Germaine, echoing him.

"Yes," said Mesurat, raising his forefinger impressively. "But no one seems to know how they made their money."

Adrienne picked up her hat and gloves and left the room. This gossip was not to her taste and she was sorry she had mentioned the name of her new friend in front of her father and sister. As she left the parlor she experienced an almost physical relief. She felt inclined to dance and jump like a child, and ran upstairs to take a look at the villa which she was going to visit the next day. Suddenly she felt happy. She thanked her stars that she at least had a room of her own where she could take refuge—where she could shut the door, amuse herself with her plans and hopes for the future, and hide the inexplicable burst of happiness which had taken such sudden possession of her.

She closed the door, sat down at a window, and drew back the curtains. It was pouring harder than ever. The sky was growing darker. The paving stones glistened, and yellow water was pouring down the gutters. The monotonous drumming of the rain filled the street.

At the end of a few minutes Adrienne heard the wheels of a carriage coming from the town. Presently she perceived a cab turn into the street and pull up before the Villa Legras. The leather hood, streaming with rain, was down, and the girl merely got a glimpse of her new friend as she jumped out and turned hurriedly to the gate, after calling out something to the coachman which Adrienne could not catch. The gate opened and clanged too noisily. Mme. Legras ran across the garden, climbed the steps as fast as her stout legs would allow her, and kept ringing impatiently at the door. There was barking coming from inside the house. The door opened and Mme. Legras disappeared within.

The incident had lasted only a few instants. Already the carriage had turned and taken its way back to the town. Adrienne let go of the curtain, which she held in her fingers, letting it fall back into place. She buried herself anew in her reflections. What independence her neighbor enjoyed! Fancy being able to take a cab—to do what one liked. She got up and glued her forehead to the windowpane. Through the mesh of the curtains she saw in the gathering dusk the white walls of the little house where Maurecourt lived. Above the black slate roof the top of the young tree drooped motionless beneath the rain. Downstairs Mesurat was talking to Germaine. The confused hum of his voice reached her ears. She grew sad again, just as suddenly as, a few moments ago, she had felt happy. Her gaiety left as abruptly as it had come.

After dinner it was so cold that Germaine asked for a brushwood fire in the grate. Otherwise, she said, she could not stay in the room. Her father at first demurred, indignant at the idea of a fire in early June. Eventually he agreed that it was not warm, and offered to lay the green branches at the back of the hearth himself. What he dreaded above all was the loss of his card game. Of course a fire in summer was extraordinary—ridiculous! But he consented to violate custom rather than sacrifice a habit that was growing more and more precious to him. His game of *trente-et-un* had become the crown upon his evening. After it was over, he could blow out the lamp and, telling himself he had had a busy day, could go to sleep.

While he crouched before the fireplace, Adrienne shuffled the pack silently, her arms upon the table. Beside her, her elder sister reclined rather than sat in an armchair, following her father's every movement with an absorbed and feverish eye. She was wearing a sort of knitted sweater. Over her shoulders she had thrown a serge jacket, whose sleeves hung below the arms of her chair. Her contorted face told of the conflict that was raging within. As Mesurat raised and lowered the iron shutter with a great clatter, she profited by his absorption to lean toward Adrienne.

"Did the letters go out?" she asked in a low voice.

The girl nodded. Germaine closed her eyes with an air of immense relief. A moment passed. Mesurat rose to his feet and with a thrust of his slippered foot pushed up the trap. The whole parlor was illuminated by a rosy light that danced over walls and ceiling. The branches writhed and crackled in the flame. Germaine opened her eyes. Her eyes met those of the old man. He was looking at her closely, a little red from his efforts, and dusting his hands against one another.

"Well! Now are you satisfied?" he asked.

She murmured a "yes" and sat up straighter. Her wasted hands took up the cards as her sister dealt them before her one by one.

Mesurat, who kept looking at the fire, was seized with a sudden idea.

"Adrienne," said he, "where have you put your shoes?"

"In the kitchen with yours," answered the girl. "They dry quicker there."

He left the room. Germaine's eyes followed him out the door. She turned to her sister.

"Adrienne," she said, quickly.

"What do you want, Germaine?" asked the girl.

She was struck by the strange expression on her sister's face. She seemed to be smiling. There was a look in her eyes Adrienne had never seen before.

"What do you want, Germaine?" she repeated.

Germaine put out a hand toward her, but she did not take it.

"I'm going away, Adrienne," said the woman in a strangled voice. "I shall never come back."

She passed her handkerchief across her lips and added, as her head drooped lower:

"Never. It's all finished and done with. All over—finished—"

Suddenly she fell forward, her face on the outspread cards, and began to sob convulsively. Adrienne got up.

"What is the matter, Germaine?" she faltered.

Gingerly, and with the tips of her fingers, she touched her sister's shoulder, which quivered from time to time as the result of a sort of hiccough. But Germaine could not control her emotion.

"Be quiet! Be quiet!" pleaded the girl. "Papa will be here in a minute."

The father's footsteps, in fact, were to be heard in the passage leading from the kitchen. Germaine sat up. Putting her handkerchief, rolled into a ball, between her teeth, she contrived to stifle her tears. Finally the fear of arousing her father's suspicions restored her to calm. Adrienne sat down and continued to deal.

"Look here!" said Mesurat, entering the room. "They were soaked through. They would never have got dry in the kitchen."

He was holding, one in each hand, a pair of shoes, which he proceeded to put before the fire, carefully and with the toes outward. Adrienne and Germaine looked at him, the same expression of curiosity and disgust on their faces. He squatted on his haunches before the blaze, recalling in a fashion that was hateful, through sheer ridiculousness, a little urchin making mud pies. Adrienne felt her face flush with shame and lowered her lids. But Germaine did not turn away her head.

"Come, papa," said Adrienne, tapping on the table with her cards. "They're all right now. Come and play."

Putting one hand upon the carpet, he shambled to his feet and drew his armchair to the table.

"Who leads?" said he.

He sat down, took up his hand, and examined it.

"I do," said Adrienne.

She threw a card to the center of the table. Germaine covered it with one of hers. Mesurat let a third fall upon the pair. No one broke the silence until the end of the game.

Although she was overcome with fatigue, Adrienne slept badly. She had managed to slip into her father's room and take the key from his waistcoat pocket. The task was not a difficult one, for the old man fell asleep quickly and slept heavily. But her terror of waking him, of stumbling against a chair, of hearing him cry out, and of being discovered, made the sweat run down the girl's face. She regained her own room trembling in every limb, and prey to an agitation that robbed her of all her strength. She undressed in the dark and threw herself upon her bed.

She had been asleep only a few minutes when she woke up as suddenly as though someone had touched her on the shoulder, saying, "Come, open your eyes, think—think!" She tossed from side to side, seeking some spot on her bolster which the weight of her head had not yet hollowed. But it was in vain that she sought to escape from the obsession of her thoughts. Her restless sleep did not last.

The events which were imminent compelled her to think over the past few weeks. She tried to connect the past with the future, imagining, by some mysterious logic, that she would most likely succeed in guessing what the future reserved for her by recalling all the good and bad that had happened to her in the recent past. What place did her love occupy in her life? Had it effected any change at all? At first she was tempted to answer "No" to this question. Immediately afterward she reflected that she would not have shown such zeal in seconding Germaine's flight if she had not coveted her sister's room. Why did she want this room so? Then she thought of Mme. Legras. She had blushed before this stout commonplace woman like a little girl; she had spoken to her with all the affability of which she was capable. Tomorrow she was going to call upon her. Why? What did she hope for? She did not dare even to name it to herself. But here, too, she perceived the great fact of her love.

Her thoughts reverted to the object of her passion itself, the man who without willing it or even being conscious of what he was doing, was making her unhappy. It seemed to her that, for some time, her suffering had been less. Perhaps this was because she had not laid eyes on him since the day she cut her arms. Then why was she striving to see him again? Why did she keep a watch on the road for the greater part of the day? Was it not possible that, if she never saw him again, she might be entirely cured of her obsession? Yet the very thought filled her eyes with tears. Wiping them on the edge of the sheet, she said to herself: "Some people are sick, and I am in love. There's nothing to be done about it."

And while crying, she fell asleep again.

Early next morning she was awakened by someone rapping softly at her door. She jumped out of bed and opened it. Germaine stood outside. Her hollow cheeks were frightful. Dark circles were round her eyes and it was evident she had not slept.

"You're really going, then?" asked Adrienne.

"Really going," answered Germaine in a determined voice. "Give me the key."

She was dressed in black and had all she could do to carry a little bulging valise. Her hat was too big for her face and made her look grotesque. She caught Adrienne's glance and said:

"Yes, I took one of your hats. Mine were too old."

Something was troubling her. She set down her valise and leaned against the door frame while Adrienne was getting the key.

"Thank you," said Germaine as she took it. "It's only half past five. I'll wait downstairs."

Adrienne assented mutely. She did not care for the way her sister looked at her—so seriously and so uneasily. Suddenly Germaine spoke.

"*Au revoir,* Adrienne," she faltered.

"*Au revoir.*"

Yet Germaine lingered. She looked at Adrienne's set face with a look of despair on her own.

"Will you write me?" she asked.

The girl shrugged her shoulders. With a sudden gesture Germaine reached out her arms; her lips were quivering and tears stood in her eyes. But Adrienne, terrified, stepped back into her room. Without another word Germaine picked up her valise and descended the stairs softly, her hand against the wall.

Adrienne went back to bed. With her head upon the bolster again, she could hear her sister open the dining-room door and shut it quietly behind her. It was raining. The drops pattered on the window with an almost imperceptible noise. The girl drew up the bedclothes to her chin, and with her eyes fixed upon the ceiling gave way to reflection. She regretted not having kissed Germaine, or, rather, not having been able to kiss her; for the moment she had seen her stretch out her arms a feeling of invincible horror had made her recoil. Perhaps one kiss would have been enough to give her the illness which her sister suffered. Germaine had assured her that her disease was not contagious. But wasn't that what all sick people said?

Adrienne was wide awake by now. Her fears returned. Suppose her father got up a little earlier, went downstairs to the dining-room, and found his daughter dressed and ready to go out! But this was impossible! The only thing to be feared was that he might hear the wheels of the cab as it stopped at the street corner. And, even so—what could he do? She rid her head of such thoughts and replaced them with plans for the day which was already dawning. In the morning she would go up to her sister's room. In the afternoon she would go to see Mme. Legras.

Six o'clock struck. Once again she began to wonder how M. Mesurat would take the disappearance of his elder daughter. After a moment's reflection she determined to pretend ignorance and let him discover everything for himself. She could not repress a laugh as she pictured to herself the stupefaction of the old man, and hid her face under the clothes as though afraid her merriment would be overheard.

Suddenly she caught the sound of a door being opened stealthily. Germaine was leaving the dining room. She crossed the parlor and went down the passage. "The idiot!" said the girl to herself. "She is dragging her feet!" At the end of a few seconds another door opened and shut. Now Adrienne could hear her sister's feet on the gravel walk. Her heart began to thump. She could not resist the temptation of getting up and going to the window. Germaine had reached the end of the path. She was standing in front of the gate and bending down. Her valise and her open umbrella were at her feet, crushing a pink geranium. Now she was stooping lower; her arched back, her black dress, made her look like some big insect. Her arms were moving. Adrienne heard the screech of the key as it turned in the lock. Instinctively she stuffed her fingers in her ears. How could her father not hear? But Germaine opened the gate, picked up her valise, then her umbrella, and disappered.

Adrienne went back to bed. From under her pillow she pulled a little gold watch which she wore in her belt by day. It was five minutes past six. Why had Germaine left the house so early? The rain would chill her to the bone. She shut her eyes and snuggled down under the blankets, in the middle of the mattress. She longed to fall asleep and not to be forced to live through the moments that crawled so slowly. There was a moment when she thought she heard her father's feet descending the staircase, and flung back the bedclothes, seized with sudden panic. But her ears had deceived her. Nothing broke the silence except the rustle of the rain against the windows.

Lying still soon became unbearable. She got up and threw on a dressing gown. Why on earth didn't the cab come? Why didn't the clock strike six-fifteen? Without reflecting that of these two questions, the second answered the first, she began to pace between the bed and the window, in the grip of a terror she could not master.

She heard her sister coughing in the street outside. The bell of a church a long way off rang once. Watch in hand, she sat down near the window. From here she could see, if not her sister, at least her sister's valise. Her eyes went back and forth from the face of the little watch in her palm to the worn leather of the shabby suitcase. The water was pouring down the side of the street with a peculiar undulation given it by the shape of the cobblestones, which made the gutter resemble a large braid of hair. Even in her impatience she noted this detail, glad of any distraction that helped pass the time.

At last she heard wheels coming down a street nearby. This must be the cab! It was by now twenty minutes past six. She got to her feet, waving her hands like a child. The cab appeared. Adrienne stuck her fingers in her ears. The noise wouldn't wake her father! But her fear was short-lived. The carriage had stopped at the corner of the street. Germaine had closed her umbrella. She threw it, together with her valise, under the enormous leather hood. She gripped the little iron rail of the coachman's seat, and hoisted herself, as best she might, into the carriage. Adrienne had the impression that she fell as she tried to sit down.

A few moments later the street was as empty and as silent as before. Above the roof of the little white house the dark leaves of the tall young tree were trembling in the morning breeze.

Chapter XIII

That morning, as she entered the dining room, she could not keep the blood from rising to her cheeks. She dreaded the moment when her father would ask her where Germaine was. To her great surprise, she found him reading his paper at the table, where only two places were set at the table. Her confusion grew when the old man said "Good morning" to her from behind his newspaper, in a voice that did not seem in any way changed. As though in a dream, she sat down. With a shaking hand she poured out her coffee and broke a roll into two pieces. Her heart was pounding in her bosom and she could not keep her eyes from her father. But the thick red fingers of old Mesurat were holding his journal without a tremor, and its pages hid his face completely.

She began to eat. Suddenly he let his paper fall to the ground and drew in his chair.

"What's the matter this morning?" said he. "You don't ask me for the weather forecast."

Without waiting for answer, he pulled a crumpled scrap of paper from his pocket and threw it under his daughter's eyes.

"Read that!"

It was a note of four lines written in pencil. Adrienne recognized Germaine's writing and read:

> I am going away, papa. Don't try to find me. No one knows my address. I have taken what belonged to me from mamma's jewel case. Good-bye.

"Where did you find that?" the girl stammered.

There was no answer. The father put the note back in his pocket and filled his cup. His face bore the set expression of a man whose fury has been cut short by utter surprise and who devours his anger in silence. He finished his coffee without raising his eyes. As soon as breakfast was over he got up and left the house.

Adrienne was alone. For the first time in her life she had the villa to herself. She reflected on this with a mixture of joy and anxiety, as though the situation were replete with some great mystery. She was free to go where she pleased. She could go up to Germaine's room; she could leave the house—the garden; she could even run away, as one day she had had a mind to do. Instead she sat stockstill, her eyes upon the cup of coffee which she could not bring herself to finish. Something stopped her from getting up, a sudden inexplicable inertia. She didn't get up. In a few minutes her father would be back and her brief independence over. Once more she would be the daughter—the slave of Antoine Mesurat. She experienced an agreeable feeling in abandoning herself to her fate, in letting things take their own course. Long ago—very long ago, it seemed to her now—she had tried to be happy. Now she wouldn't try anymore. She would go on living from day to day, bowing her head beneath the wrath of old Mesurat. She felt drowsy. Dropping her head on her arms, she fell asleep.

The clock, striking nine o'clock, woke her. She was surprised to find her father had not yet returned. Generally he went straight to the station, bought his paper, and was back within a quarter of an hour. Where could he be? She made up her mind not to bother about him, got up at last, and fixed her hair.

She thought of going up to her sister's room, but the old horror of contagion made her hesitate. Since Germaine had confided that she was dying, Adrienne could not bear the thought of even touching a garment she had worn. And yet—didn't she encourage her to leave so that she could have her room? It seemed absurd to give up the fruit of her victory for a mere hygienic scruple. Besides, she told herself, to stimulate her courage, if one room was contaminated, the whole house was, also.

After a moment's reflection she decided on her course of action. Going to the kitchen, she took a saucer, which she filled with sulphur. Then she went up to the top floor. "I ought to be feeling happy," she said to herself. "I am going to lean out that window for the first time in a month. Do I no longer love Maurecourt?" The very question brought the blood to her cheeks.

She pushed the door open and entered the room resolutely, but holding her breath. The window was closed. She opened it and inhaled the air deeply that entered with a few drops of rain. For several minutes she looked at the little white house. The tile roof shone like polished metal under the rain streaming over it. The window on the first story was half open, and she could perceive a corner of the red rug which she had almost forgotten. She felt that her eyes were filling with tears which she could not hold back. "How unhappy I am!" she murmured to herself.

Almost immediately, in a pensive tone strangely mingled with bitterness, she added:

"Because of him."

She shut the window sharply as though she had had enough of a spectacle which only wrung her heart. She took a match, struck it under the marble chimneypiece and set fire to the little heap of sulphur. Clouds of acrid smoke rose from it. She ran out of the room.

Mesurat did not return till lunchtime, and did not address a word to his daughter. He even seemed to avoid meeting her eyes. During the meal he read his newspaper, or pretended to read it. Adrienne often caught his eyes, raised above his glasses, and fixed upon space in a meditation which he interrupted only to carry food to his mouth. She was well pleased with a silence that accorded so little with what she had feared, and began to congratulate herself on having escaped with so little trouble.

Immediately after his luncheon was over, Mesurat took his hat and went out again, without asking his daughter to accompany him. Such a reversal of his habits first delighted Adrienne and then made her uneasy. She had lived too long under an inflexible rule which provided for each hour of her day not to have caught something of her father's own mania for system, and this sudden upset in the schedule of his comings and goings seemed strange. Without admitting it to herself, it shocked her almost as some irregularity of conduct might have done.

These vague misgivings were soon driven out of her head by reflections of a different order. She remembered how elegantly Mme. Legras had been dressed when they made her acquaintance yesterday, and determined not to call upon her without giving the most scrupulous attention to her own toilette. She went to her room and passed her wardrobe in review. Although her choice was limited, the examination took a long time. She had three summer skirts—one of thin serge, the other two of white cotton. It was still raining. Her cotton outfits would be covered with mud. She never had any luck. And besides, she hated the outfits. On the other hand, she imagined that the serge made her look older. She tried on all three, and finally put an end to indecision by settling on one of her winter dresses. She chose a costume of heavy brown material with a pleated blouse, starched at the collar and wrists, and a rather modest jabot of lace.

By half past three she was ready. She had let down her hair and put it up again three times. Now she was sure that there was nothing more to change and that she looked as pretty as it was possible for her to look. She passed back and forth in front of her wardrobe mirror, closing her eyes and then opening them suddenly, the better to judge the effect she would create. "If I were going to see Maurecourt," she said to herself, "could I have dressed myself better?' She shook her head and sat down. All her joy died in her heart at the thought that she was about to see, not him, but another, and that it made no difference whether she looked well or badly dressed—pretty or plain. To think of having spent two hours before her mirror simply to go and take tea with Mme. Legras. What unavowed hope had been in her heart? She shrugged her shoulders and resolved to go and call upon her neighbor before her father could prevent it.

A maid took her umbrella and showed her into the parlor. The room appeared small; and though it was cluttered up with all sorts of objects, it gave an impression of unappealing poverty. The furniture was neither well made nor of good quality. It had been in use so long, and had passed through so many hands, that it had ended by taking on that almost impersonal character noticeable in furnished lodgings. The profusion and diversity of the chairs in particular was positively amazing. They were of all kinds and descriptions, ranged semicircle-wise at angles of the room, or drawn forward near tables that were loaded with lamps and nicknacks. Yet there was not one that tempted a caller to sit down. A vast rubber plant extended its dropsical leaves over an upright piano. Nearby a bureau protruded its belly, as though it would call attention to the beauty of the handles on its bulging drawers. Draped window curtains bordered with heavy ball fringe dimmed the light.

Adrienne sat down on one of the cushioned seats of a small tête-à-tête sofa and waited. She felt nervous and bashful. A mirror heavily framed in fly-blown gilding showed her a young girl with red cheeks that were growing redder. She was half sorry she had come, and asked herself what she would say and how she would explain calling so soon. A clock crowned by a pair of cupids wrestling amorously rang out half past three. Little by little she recovered her poise. She leaned back on the sofa and looked around her with more assurance, hardly yet able to realize that she was actually calling upon Madame Legras in the house her imagination had been busied with for so long. Through the window she could see the Villa des Charmes. This seemed so funny to her that she could not help smiling. She wondered from what part of this villa there was the best view of the little white house. Would she dare to ask?

The door opened briskly and Mme. Legras entered, preceded by a strongly built, yellow basset which began to sniff Adrienne's shoes, growling a little.

"Welcome!" cried Mme. Legras, gaily, reaching out both hands to her young visitor.

She wore a white blouse with a deep ruching of lace, and a skirt of gray taffeta, fitting tightly at the hips and flaring around the legs in a series of folds that rustled noisily as she walked. Her hair, still black and fairly thick, was styled low on her forehead and almost hid her eyebrows. As she entered, the room became filled with a strong odor of mignonette.

"Let's not stay here," she said as she took both of Adrienne's hands in her own. "We'll be cozier in my own room."

She drew the girl from the parlor and ascended the stairs, her arm round her young friend's waist, and talking away with joyful volubility.

"So that's how we get the better of papa!" she said, with a little playful pressure of her fingertips. "You'll have to tell me why he's mean. I'm going to keep you all the afternoon. I was thrilled to meet you at the concert. I'm bored to death in La Tour l'Evêque."

She explained that she came to the town for a rest.

"I'm not your age any longer, you know," she went on with a sidelong glance. "Here we are. Come in!"

She pushed her companion into a small bedroom upholstered in red and old rose. The same tawdry luxury reigned here as in the parlor below. A bedstead of light-colored wood, whose shape attempted to reproduce the more capricious forms of the eighteenth century, came unmistakably from one of those big drygoods stores in Paris for which such things are turned out by the thousand. Two armchairs in the same style, but painted white, stood to either side of one of those tiny round tables topped with marble which seem made on purpose to be upset. Thick carpet, stained, muffled their footsteps.

"Oh, how pretty!" cried Adrienne.

"Isn't it rather sweet?" said Mme. Legras. "Pure eighteenth century. Take off your hat. Yes, yes—I insist! You'll find a looking-glass over there."

Adrienne stooped down before a mirror and took off her hat. She was annoyed with herself to find she was blushing again. Why should she feel so bashful with a woman who seemed so amiable? She had an insane desire to laugh out loud. There was something about this room, this mystery, her flight from her own house, all of this, so appealing and unexpected, enchanted her. Suddenly she turned toward the window and looked out through its café curtains. But she could see only the Villa des Charmes.

"What's wrong?" asked Mme. Legras, who was watching her, and read disappointment on her face.

"Nothing," Adrienne answered. "It's still raining."

"Sit down," said Mme. Legras, pushing her toward a couch. "We'll have tea in an hour. And now let us begin to make one another's acquaintance."

She sat down and packed a number of cushions behind her shoulders. The dog sprawled on a hassock at her feet.

"First of all," said she, "myself! Then I shall feel more at ease. Brief biography of Madame Legras. A good enough woman—neither old nor young. Yes, yes," she went on as though Adrienne had protested, "neither old nor young and somewhat on the shady side at that. A rather lively temper—I warn you—but here"—she put her hand on her bosom—"here, a real woman's heart. Mother, sister, wife, all at once and—a firm friend!" She raised one finger as she spoke the last two words. "Queer tastes—lots of whims, even. But all the gayer for that. So much for her character. On the other hand, a quiet life, with no great events and no great sorrows; no dreams at all; a husband who's a good fellow; no particular ambitions. In a word, *bourgeoise, bourgeoise, bourgeoise!* Now, how does that suit you?"

Adrienne made a violent effort at control. She felt that the moment had come to shake off her shyness and to say something amiable.

"I understand," she said, reddening a little. "I'm just as *bourgeoise* as you, myself."

"Dear child!" exclaimed Mme. Legras, extending her hand above the table to press the girl's arm. She began to laugh. "Come, let us strike a bargain. What do you say? I live here all by myself, except from time to time when my husband comes down. But his business keeps him so busy. Anyhow, I'm often quite alone. You are, too, aren't you?"

"Yes, madame."

"'Yes, Léontine,'" corrected Mme. Legras. "Well, then, every time one of us feels bored, she'll go to see the other."

She stopped at Adrienne's terrified expression, and then went on, briskly:

"—and we'll take walks together. Now let's speak of you. You'll let me call you by your Christian name—Adrienne, isn't it?"

"Yes."

"Please—*please* say 'Léontine.' Nothing does so much for friendship and confidence. Imagine that I've known you for six years and see how easy it becomes. Won't you take off your jacket?"

Adrienne loosened two buttons of her coat and smiled as she laid her arm along the back of the chair.

"My dear," said Mme. Legras, "how old are you? Come! You're not of an age when there's anything to hide. Nineteen?"

"Eighteen."

"Eighteen!" The woman turned her full face to Adrienne and clasped her hands upon the table. Her brown eyes seemed to lighten to yellow, and they rested on the girl with a curious expression. The corners of her mouth lifted a little.

"Eighteen years old!" she repeated, with a knowing tone. "Lucky Adrienne! And with a face like yours!"

She gave a queer, deep laugh.

"Don't hang your head," she went on in a still deeper voice. "People with eyes like yours needn't be afraid to look the whole world in the face."

There was something in the way she spoke, so insinuating and at the same time so confidential, that made a strange impression on Adrienne. These intimacies of language disconcerted her and she felt that all her pleasure in coming to see this woman was evaporating as she listened to her speak. Perhaps Mme. Legras guessed what was passing through her mind.

"Come!" said she in her normal voice. She raised herself a little from her cushions and smiled. "The prettiest girls are the ones who don't know it. But let me tell you that you are wasting yourself. Would you like me to read your hand?"

Adrienne raised her head; her eyes shone.

"Can you tell fortunes?"

"You shall see," said Mme. Legras. "Here—!"

Adrienne offered her right hand.

"The other one, too."

Mme. Legras took both hands and, as they rested on the table, turned them over so as to see the palms distinctly. She pinched the flesh below the thumb.

"Ah! ah!" she said, looking slyly at Adrienne. "You are going to have an interesting life—"

She bent over and added, after a moment's consideration,

"—and a long one. A few little illnesses. Nothing of any consequence."

She continued her examination of Adrienne's hands. The girl could feel her breath on their skin.

"Am I going to be happy?" she asked, after a moment of silence.

"What do you mean by 'happy'?" asked the woman, without raising her head.

Adrienne shrugged her shoulders.

"I don't know," said she.

She hesitated, and said, at last:

"Can you see a marriage?"

Mme. Legras pressed the girl's hands, as though to make the lines stand out more clearly. Her head sank lower. Adrienne could see the big comb, ornamented with gold knobs, that she wore thrust through her chignon. Silence reigned.

"Yes, a marriage," said Mme. Legras thoughtfully.

She raised her eyes and looked at the girl's attentive face as though to question her. But Adrienne lowered her lids.

"When is it coming, this marriage?" she asked, with ill-concealed impatience.

"Quite soon. But everything depends on you."

A violent emotion took possession of Adrienne. Her hands seemed to hurt her and she tried to draw them back.

"On me?" she repeated.

"On the skill with which you play your part in the game. You're pretty, but that's not enough. Men are animals that don't let themselves be captured unless you stun them with the first blow. Awkwardness at the start is never made up for later. Are you rich?"

"Well off enough."

Mme. Legras looked at her, her lips slightly parted.

"How much?" she asked, brusquely.

Adrienne made a gesture of ignorance.

"My father has saved money."

"Just set your mind at rest, child," said Mme. Legras, slapping the table with her hands. "I'd bet on your succeeding if you looked like a scullerymaid. Instead of which—"

She lifted one finger, as though to count.

"—you are young, you are good-looking, and you are rich! And now, a word of advice. You have a pretty neck; don't hide it! Your hair is superb; show it!"

On seeing the confusion and joy which the girl's face betrayed, she regained her former tone of command.

"Don't look so serious; you frown too much. An air of reserve— good! But no more. And look after your toilette. Your clothes should fit you better. No more cotton gloves—*hein*? All these things count. You want to please? Very well, then, believe me that men never notice pretty things, but anything unbecoming hits them in the eye. It may sound strange, but it's true. Ask them what color were the pretty suede gloves that you were wearing that very morning; they won't be able to tell you. But put on cotton gloves and watch their faces!"

She crossed her hands upon the table and narrowed her eyes. Her voice sank to a murmur.

"And now," said she, "tell me whether I'm right or not. Your father keeps you a prisoner. He spies on you. I'll wager that you've come to me this afternoon without telling him a word."

Adrienne started in her chair. She recalled the few words she had said the day before, and was amazed to find how well Mme. Legras had guessed that her father was to be kept in the dark. She felt a keen distrust and at the same time a violent desire to tell everything.

"My father does not like me to go out alone," she faltered.

She stopped. Something inside her warned her not to let this woman into her secrets.

"He doesn't like you to go out alone because he does not want you to see your—this gentleman. What's he like—your friend?"

Adrienne turned scarlet. These questions made her head spin. She felt as though someone were dragging off her clothes, piece by piece. To hear her love spoken of in this offhand fashion, and by a stranger, seemed monstrous. She reconciled herself to it only by the thought that Mme. Legras might be useful to her.

"He has black eyes. . ." she began in a dolorous voice.

Then she stopped. She reflected that this was absolutely all she could remember of the face she had seen.

"Young?"

"Yes," Adrienne, after a brief hesitation.

"Go on!" said Mme. Legras impatiently. "Is he a tall man?"

Adrienne could not answer her. She now perceived that she had paid no attention to these details, and suddenly they assumed major importance in her eyes. Had she never looked at Dr. Maurecourt? Yes, she had seen him the day he had walked up the street and she had thrust her arms through the glass. Why hadn't she looked at him more closely? Now, when she wanted to, she was unable to describe him. The discovery overwhelmed her. She asked herself if she were not crazy to suffer for a man whom she would probably not recognize if she passed him on the street. Her ears began to buzz. She gripped the back of the couch. She shivered, although the room was close and hot.

"What's the matter?" said Mme. Legras, jumping to her feet and running round the table. "How funny you are, my dear!"

Her voice was anxious. She took Adrienne's hands in her own and chafed them.

"What's wrong?" she asked again. "It wasn't anything I said, was it? Was it anything I said?"

Adrienne made a quick movement of protest with her hand.

"My head aches," she said. "I feel dizzy," she added almost immediately.

"Dizzy!" repeated Mme. Legras. "My dear child, you must lie down, then."

She made the girl rise, and, passing her arm around her shoulders led her toward the bed. Adrienne sat down on it. An onset of vertigo forced her to close her eyes. She gripped a rail of the bedstead in one hand. "Lie out quite straight," insisted Mme. Legras in a rather alarmed voice. She repeated the words until the girl obeyed her.

"It's not going to be anything," she said, after a moment's silence.

She stood for a while in the middle of the room, undecided how to act.

"Stay quiet just one minute," she said finally as though struck by a sudden idea. "I'm going to get you a cordial that will put you back on your feet."

She glided swiftly across the room and closed the door behind her. Adrienne kept her eyes closed and seemed to be sleeping.

Chapter XIV

It was nearly dark when Adrienne came home, worn out and despondent. Mme. Legras had made her drink a glass of port wine which had given her a violent headache, and her legs shook under her at every step.

As she pushed open the gate of her own villa, she almost felt nauseated. Never before in her life had she felt so sick or so unhappy. She loathed the sound of the gate as it closed behind her. The rain was still falling, and the little rivulets of muddy water which flowed round the lawn were fuller than ever. Nothing can be imagined more dismal than this garden, sodden and streaming, disappearing into the dusk.

She went straight to her room and, after taking off her damp clothes, flung herself on the bed and hid her face in the pillow. Everything had eternally to be started over. She seemed doomed to traverse a sort of endless cycle, where hope gave way to despair and joy to fear. She had expected such great things from this visit to Mme. Legras. And here she was back again without having even asked to see which room overlooked rue Carnot. Worse still, she had refused to confide in the woman, who seemed so ready to help her. But indeed, as regards Mme. Legras, she felt an unconquerable disgust whose motive she could not figure out. "She's such a ridiculous woman," she told herself. "I could never bring myself to tell her who I'm in love with." The idea that those thick lips could come together and part to pronounce the name "Maurecourt" was intolerable. It seemed to her she would prefer to keep her secret, even if it meant suffering all her life.

She pleased herself by imagining an ideal confidante, someone to whom she could speak of her misery without shame or regret and of whom she could ask advice. Didn't she know anyone? Her sister? She had to suppress a cry as she remembered that the old maid had been aware of everything going on in her mind, and that she had, no doubt, told her father what she knew. The memory of her conversations with Germaine on the subject humiliated her profoundly. She took her head in her hands as though to stop the thoughts that were tearing her apart. A sort of madness took possession of her. She could never confide in anyone. She was alone. She told herself that if the world were suddenly depopulated, and she were the sole survivor, her inner life would be no different. Just as she could not be more silent if her tongue were cut out.

All at once, an idea occurred to her. She sat up and supported herself on one elbow, thrilled to the utmost fibers of her being. She would go to Maurecourt and consult him for some imaginary illness. During the course of their conversation she would tell her own story as though it concerned one of her friends. She would tell him the whole story of this miserable woman. Perhaps he would be touched; in any case, the ground would be prepared and it would be an opportunity to see him. She would knock at the door of the white house. She would penetrate within the study which she could see from Germaine's room; she would touch the red rug. Her imagination took fire. What was to prevent her going at once? Why should she not go? If she were really ill, she would not hesitate. In a quarter of an hour she might be sitting tête-à-tête with Maurecourt. She only had to dress herself and cross the street. The mere thought made her head spin. But she put off the visit through sheer faint-heartedness. It was too late today. Tomorrow she would certainly go.

She was still buried in thought when the garden gate opened and closed. She recognized the tread of her father as he came up the central path and mounted the steps. As she heard him cross the threshold, terror seized her. She even thought of locking her door. During that eventful day she had hardly given the old man a thought. She had no idea what he was doing. But she augured nothing but evil from his absence and dreaded the hour when she would have to go downstairs and confront him. For the first time it occurred to her that she had to pass a whole night alone in the house with a man whose violence could come very close to madness. Adrienne found herself half-regretting Germaine's departure. The maid did not sleep at the Villa des Charmes. She was married and had her own room in the town.

She dressed and waited. More than a quarter of an hour elapsed. She heard her father calling her to dinner, as he did every night. At once she found herself less nervous, almost reassured, and answered in a voice that resembled a shout. Her heart swelled with hope. She allowed herself to form a wish that there would be no further question of Germaine's absence between her father and herself. Perhaps he would act as though nothing had happened. It seemed to her that another scene would kill her. Again emotion mastered her, and her weakness was such that she had to grip the hand-rail as she went downstairs.

Her father was reading his evening paper and eating his soup. She dared not look at him. She sat down silently in her place and began her dinner. But her terror and headache took away all appetite for food. She swallowed a few spoonsful of consommé, but had to let her plate be taken away half full. The meal dragged to a close. Behind his newspaper Mesurat went on eating without paying any attention to his daughter. He got up the moment dessert was finished.

Without a word he went into the parlor, lit the lamp, and seated himself in his armchair. For the twentieth time he unfolded the *Temps* and resumed his meticulous perusal of its columns. Adrienne had followed him and sat at another side of the room. She was beginning to hope that a little later she could quit the parlor for her bedroom, when she noticed that her father was observing her steadily out of a corner of his eye. What was he waiting for? She soon knew.

No sooner had Désirée left the house than he got up, went out, and locked both the garden gate and the hall door. There was nothing out of the ordinary in these precautions. They were consecrated by the habit of fifteen years. Nevertheless, the girl's heart sank. She shuddered at the noise of the keys in the locks. She thought of calling on Mme. Legras for help, but her common sense triumphed over the impulse. Suppose the woman came, what could she say?

She rose and took a few steps in the parlor, her heart palpitating, but without reasoning over this sudden panic. Her father was coming back along the corridor. She still had time to fly and to lock herself in her room. But the impossibility of finding any justification for doing so, to say nothing of her fear of appearing ridiculous, held her back.

When Mesurat reappeared she was surprised to see how tired he looked. He even gave her the impression of being smaller than usual. Possibly this was because he slouched a little and because his shoulders were stooped. He crossed the parlor and stood in front of her. She noticed that there were dark circles around his eyes and that his forehead was scored with deep wrinkles. He grasped the lapels of his coat in his hands and looked her straight in the face. The girl averted her head.

"Did you go out this afternoon?" he demanded.

"Yes."

"Where did you go?"

She reached behind her for the little table, and faltered:

"To see a friend."

"Who was it?"

She had not the strength to lie, and answered at once:

"Madame Legras."

He shrugged his shoulders.

"Do you know the kind of woman she is?"

Her face grew white, but she did not reply.

"Go upstairs to your room!"

Adrienne left the parlor. Her father followed, holding the lamp a little above his head. The two mounted the stairs. As is usually the case in a small house whose architect has been forced to take advantage of every foot of space, they were steep and awkward to climb. Adrienne stopped halfway to the landing and leaned against the banisters. It seemed to her that her knees were giving way under her. She wondered if a fall on the marble of the corridor would kill her. "Not high enough," she thought.

"Go on," said Mesurat, almost as though he guessed the project that lay in his daughter's head and was willing to second it.

She continued to climb the stairs, still leaning on the hand-rail. At the threshold of her room she stopped and looked round at her father.

"Good night," she said, hoping against hope that he was going to leave her.

"Go inside," said Mesurat, motioning with his finger.

"Aren't you going to bed?" she asked in a shaky voice.

Without answering, he pushed her slightly to one side, opened the door, and entered the room. He put the lamp down on the table and stood with his hands upon his hips.

"I'm waiting," he said.

She came in, but remained near the door.

"Give me the key to your wardrobe," said Mesurat.

Adrienne began to shake from head to foot. She hesitated a moment, then, glancing at her father's face, rummaged in the drawer of the little table that stood by her bed and found the key. He snatched it from her and opened the wardrobe door. In the silence the door swung on its hinges with a heavy sound, and the mirror threw the reflection of the lamp across the room like a flash of lightning. Mesurat thrust his hands into a pile of linen until they came upon the little olive-wood box.

"Open it for me," he commanded.

"Why, papa?" asked the girl in an imploring voice.

She put the back of her hand against her forehead. A sudden impulse came over her to throw herself at her father's feet. She felt so weak, so cowardly, that the exact degree of abasement to which terror might lead her became a matter of indifference. She clutched to the foot of the bed for support.

"How much did you give your sister?" asked Mesurat.

"Five hundred francs."

"Five hundred francs!"

He repeated the sum twice, as though he could scarcely believe his ears, opened his mouth to say something, but changed his mind.

"Unlock that box," he said, instead.

Adrienne drew her watch from her belt and detached a tiny key. When the box was open, Mesurat glanced inside and assured himself that it was half empty. He turned to the girl.

"It's true, then," said he. "You little fool!" he cried, sharply. "You'll never see that money again. Never! Do you understand? How do you expect your sister is ever going to pay you back?"

He stopped, struck with a sudden idea.

"Well, it's so much off your dowry. You think yourself rich, eh? You think people get married without money."

Adrienne recoiled as he advanced upon her. Something was turning round and round in her head. In confused fashion she recalled Mme. Legras's words about money and marriage. A terrible fatality seemed to be forcing one event upon another, like the details of an evil dream. She could almost bring herself to believe that Mesurat and that woman were in league to fill her heart with despair. She could not utter a word. Powerless to turn away, her gaze remained glued to her father's face. Those eyeballs, in which the blood made a tiny red network, fascinated her. She walked back step by step until her open palms met the wall. It seemed to her distracted mind that someone was driving nails through them.

"You helped her to go away," said her father, in a husky voice. "It was a plot between the pair of you to fool old Mesurat. Isn't that so?"

Adrienne shook her head. The old man took a piece of paper from his pocket.

"What's the meaning of this, then?"

She recognized, with horror, the letter she had written to the livery stable. Mesurat replaced the note in his pocket and stepped back a little.

"Now," said he, "you see how useless it is to lie. Would you like to know how I spent the day?"

He began to walk up and down the room, affecting a calm that was more repulsive than his anger, so perfectly was it evident that he was enjoying the situation.

"Listen! I went first of all to the livery stable. You're not very smart if you believe that I didn't know just where to start my inquiries. Because I wasn't such a fool as to imagine that your sister, with her lazy habits, was going to walk to the station. Just so! What do I find? That you ordered a carriage to be here at quarter past six. . . . Finally, they showed me the letter—your letter, you imbecile! Next step—the railroad. Do you think I have no friends at the station, after going there twice a day, and talking with everyone? What am I told? Why, that Mademoiselle Mesurat took the six-fifty-five for Paris. *Hein?*"

He stopped and looked at his daughter, swelling with triumph, and with his hands clasped behind his back. She did not stir.

"And that's not all," he cried, all his anger returning. "I come back and find you gone out!

"*Out!*" he repeated with an emphasis that under any other circumstances would have been comical. "You think you're free to do as you like.

114

You go over the road to see that—that Legras woman. Ah! I know all about her, too—your Léontine Legras. We'll come to that later. Anyhow, I go up to Germaine's room. I find it reeking with sulphur. I see the whole game. You want that room for yourself. You fumigate it. You chuckle at the thought that you can lean out of the window now all day long. That's where you make your mistake. Germaine told me all about you and your window."

Still Adrienne did not move. He glared at her furiously, and continued his tirade.

"You won't have that room. It's closed from today on. As for the key"—he struck his chest over a top waistcoat pocket—"the key is there. Try to steal it from me like the last time. I've had one lesson and I know now just how far I have to be on my guard."

The words were accompanied by a bitter laugh. It was easy to see that he had rehearsed this whole scene carefully behind his newspaper, with all the proper cries and gestures. But by now his anger was mastering him, and he let his malice have full vent with a fury that carried away any desire to produce an effect.

"From now on I'm going to show you!" he cried, suddenly. "You've been bent on upsetting everything in this house and you're going to be the first to suffer. I'm going to lock you into this room for so many hours every day. When you go out, it will be with me. I'm going to make you do what I choose until you're of age."

Then followed a phrase which was a relic of his old profession and which he used from time to time. "I'm going to make you respect the regulations in their utmost rigor."

He puffed and struck the table a blow with his fist that made the lamp tremble.

"So if you have any idea of running about as you've been doing, put it out of your head. No more walks at night. *Hein?* Germaine told me about them. I'm going to bring back your sister and have her watch you."

Suddenly he shouted, "Give me her address!"

Adrienne did not answer.

"Give me her address or I'll kill you!" howled the old man, turning scarlet. The girl only shook her head. He took a few steps toward her. She held her breath and clenched her teeth; her heart was beating so hard that she could hear the sound of it just as though someone were tapping the floor with a heel. He looked at her and shrugged his shoulders twice.

"Fool!" said he in a thick voice. "You want to be free here. You want to meet *him* when you like—to go and see him every evening as before. Well, you reckon without me. What wouldn't you give to have me out of the way, eh? Don't be afraid; I'm pretty solid."

He thumped his chest twice. Then, without any warning, he struck her. She did not move. The mark of his blow showed red on her pale cheek. Her fixed eyes, wide open with horror, her look of impotent hatred, seemed to exasperate him. He struck her again, with all his might. She tottered and gave a sigh that was like a death rattle.

He drew back and, trembling with fury, cried:

"Wait a bit! I'm going to see your doctor. I'll teach him to touch a Mesurat. As it's your money he's after, I'll begin by disinheriting you. You shan't have a sou. You shan't marry at all. All my money's going to the state. You'll see! I'll go tomorrow morning—to him first and then to my lawyer. You've had enough fun at my expense, both of you. One runs off with my jewels—another disgraces my name with a cad who only wants her money, while I—poor blockhead—poor old fool—am supposed to be sitting by with wool over my eyes!"

He checked himself and, seeing her still motionless, cried out:

"Perhaps you don't believe me? Well, then, I'm going to settle with your Maurecourt tonight."

He bounded from the room and reached the staircase in a single stride. Adrienne followed him with her eyes. Then, suddenly, her whole being seemed to expand and swell. She dashed out of the room in turn, slamming the door behind her with all her might. In the darkness she could hear her father pronouncing her name—but in a changed voice. A moment passed. She thought she saw a light swaying above his head. Panic seized her and, without knowing what she did and as though hurled by some irresistible force into the darkness, she rushed toward the staircase. Her weight came full upon her father's shoulders. He lost his balance and fell forward, while she clutched the rail. She heard him cry "Oh!" as though someone had choked off his breath. He must have fallen at full length, his forehead striking a stair, and rebounded to the bottom in two great somersaults, his feet rattling against the banisters in his descent. She felt the rail tremble under her hand—then the sound of a second fall, duller than the first.

She bent over the landing as far into space as she dared, with the hand-rail cutting into her stomach. Beads of sweat from her eyebrows ran down the sides of her face. In a low voice she called:

"Papa!"

Then she sat down on the step nearest the landing and waited.

Chapter XV

Some time passed. She asked herself whether she had been asleep and what hour it could be. The pain in her body forced her to crouch forward. She made one or two attempts to rise, but an abominable fatigue weighed her down and she remained where she was, the small of her back pressed against the balustrade. Her teeth chattered; her head seemed empty and light. For a moment she thought that she was in bed, dreaming; the dream was that she was sitting on the staircase and remembering a scene she had just had with her father. The illusion afforded her a sort of relative tranquillity. She was quite willing to go to sleep, but the thread of light which shone under the door of her room kept her awake. She had the impression at one moment that the narrow ray, drawn across the darkness as though by a ruler, was holding up her heavy eyelids. At another, she believed herself still asleep and dreaming.

She found a little rest in this state of torpor, but finally realized she was awake. The consciousness of what had just happened returned little by little, but she refused to credit it. In that case what was she doing here? "Perhaps I walk in my sleep," she said to herself. She laughed under her breath and, gripping the banisters, pulled herself to her feet. She noticed that she was dressed; the noise of her heels on the polished wood brought her to her full senses, and she hurried into her room.

The window was closed and there was a terrible smell of kerosene. The lamp must have been burning a very long time. She looked at her watch. Two o'clock! She had slept, then. But not in her bed. The bed-clothes were not disturbed.

As she was putting her watch in the drawer of the little table by the bed, she thought she heard her father, shouting as he had shouted just now. She turned round, but saw nothing. Her head buzzed. "How can he be shouting?" she asked herself. "He has gone to bed." She took off her shirtwaist and let down her hair. She noticed her fingers were trembling, and was frightened. "I'm going up to papa's room," she said, aloud, in a steady voice.

She took the lamp in both hands and left her room, her eyes fixed upon the staircase which ascended to the next floor. It seemed to her that an interminable time elapsed and that she was walking unsteadily. She reached the staircase and managed to climb three steps. Then she sighed deeply and stopped. "I can hear him snoring," she said to herself, but she knew she heard nothing. She gripped the rail with her right hand and held the lamp a little above her head. Then she began to mount the stairs again, one at a time like a child, and reached the landing of the upper story.

Her father's room was just over her own. To the right was Germaine's. She never went into her father's. The old man used to say that he didn't like people "rummaging around him." She walked to the door and listened. Then she turned the handle very slowly and carefully. But the door was locked. She leaned against the wall and waited.

Terror lent a theatrical air to her face.

Then she began to move slowly. She made a few steps as though against her will, murmuring: "No! No!" all the time. Reaching the rail of the landing, she leaned over the well of the staircase. She looked down-ward into the darkness. But the light was so bad that she could see noth-ing. Holding the lamp almost at arm's length, she finally made out a body at the foot of the stairs. Her fist trembled. There is a way of lying on the ground without motion which speaks for itself—which resembles neither sleep nor a stroke. Death is never counterfeited. She could make out the head, lying in a sort of dark patch, the arms extended haphazardly above the skull. The knees were bent and the two feet rested side by side on the last stair. When she drew back her arm the vision disappeared.

She went downstairs again, one hand against the wall, with a measured step that creaked in the silence and to whose monotonous sound she appeared to be listening attentively. She was so absorbed in thought that if someone had passed her at that moment it is probable she would not have noticed. One foot followed the other, with that strange precision which the most mechanical gestures unconsciously assume when some imperious subject of meditation has taken possession of the soul and absorbs its faculties. Her eyes stared straight before her. But at the bottom of their vacant look something lurked that resembled a positive paroxysm of surprise and spread a look of horrible stupidity over the rest of her face.

When she was in her room again, with the door closed behind her, she set her lamp upon the table and looked in the wardrobe. The olive-wood box lay half open upon a pile of linen, just as M. Mesurat had left it when he had flung it back, telling his daughter that she had broken into her own dowry. She counted the money over, put each roll of coins back in its place, closed the cover, and gave a turn to the little key which was still in the lock. Then she shut the wardrobe door and began to undress leisurely.

The room was stuffy. She opened the window and stood for a moment inhaling the fresh air, which tickled her bare shoulders like cold fingertips. Dogs were barking from the direction of the highway. There were two of them who seemed to be answering and trying to outbay one another. The moon was shining softly. A breeze was chasing the clouds out of the sky and the young tree above the little white house swayed gently. How calm everything seemed! She chafed her shoulders with the palms of her hands and jumped into bed, shivering pleasantly. Everything she was doing now—these familiar gestures, which she was repeating once again—afforded her a sort of animal joy, unreasoning enough, but which she could have explained in something like these words: "Things must be going on perfectly well. Nothing can have changed, since I am going to bed as usual, since I open my window—chafe my shoulders." She blew out the lamp and snuggled into the covers.

In the darkness she closed her eyes and yawned. But a continuous buzzing prevented her sleeping. The sound appeared to be now very near and now a long way off. The slightest noise made it cease. She thought of humming, but stopped at the first bar, recognizing her father's favorite march. The buzzing began again. She clapped her hands, and the noise they made scared her. She stopped her ears, and they were filled immediately with a low roar—like a torrent flowing very fast.

With a violent kick she threw the quilt far from her body and got up. It was then that terror took full possession of her. She was aghast at finding herself out of bed. Since she was on her feet, something must have happened. What had she got up to do? To find the lamp, of course, and light it because she was afraid. "How stupid of me! How stupid of me!" she kept stammering. Her lower jaw fell and she had trouble closing her mouth. She found the matches, struck one which went out—then another whose flame flickered in the draught from the open window. Finally she relit the lamp.

She gave a sigh of relief. In the light she wasn't afraid. Nobody is afraid so long as they can see. She would get back into bed without blowing out the light. The church clock struck three. She counted the strokes one by one, aloud, then lay down again.

When she closed her eyes now, she could see a red haze through the fine skin of her eyelids. She resigned herself to lying awake indefinitely and, crossing her hands upon the coverlet, lay quite still, looking straight before her. The buzzing began again, but with the lamp lit she did not mind it so much. She forced herself to think of her childhood, recalling its most precise details—the way her schoolmates dressed themselves, their names, their faces. In the silence of the night it seemed to her that all this little world came to life again with its chatter and laughter. But she took no pleasure in such memories. They tired her; moreover, these souvenirs which she more or less dragged out of her past imposed a choice upon her. There were certain faces which she refused to remember. She wanted to confine her recollections solely to school life. She did not care to see herself again in the rue Thiers, coming home from her classes, shutting the gate behind her, following the corridor, mounting the staircase to her room, to this very room—in this very house.

Something oppressed her horribly. It was as though poison had been mixed with the air she had to breathe. She put her hands upon her chest. She needed all of her will power to master the terror that arose in her. In the chaotic turmoil that was going on in her brain, she remembered the admonition given a classmate at Ste.-Cécile: "Whenever anyone is in danger, he must say the words: 'Jesus, Mary, Joseph!'" But she could not unclench her teeth, and had to content herself with wiping away with her hair the drops of sweat that stood on her temples.

Suddenly she opened her mouth and uttered a cry. She heard herself plainly, but had much ado to recognize her own voice. It was the shrill cry of fear. She leaped out of bed and ran to the window in the hope that she would see someone passing, or, at any rate, hear a sound from the distance which would prove to her that there were human beings not far away. But the silence of the dawn lay upon all the neighboring villas and their deserted gardens. She felt as though she were being tracked down, as though she stood at bay in this corner of her room and could not even get back to bed. Her imagination liberated itself with a kind of fury, and took belated revenge upon the restraint it had been made to suffer. She reached to the back of the chair where she had flung her dressing gown, put it around her shoulders, and sat down on the window seat. For a moment her new position reassured her. She would only have to call for help now and someone would come. Then she reflected that she could not sit there till daylight. It was not yet four, and the sky was still quite black. She was afraid of catching cold—of falling ill like her sister. On the other hand, the idea of closing the window and putting those four panes of glass between herself and the world to stifle her cries was just as intolerable.

The buzzing had begun again. She listened for a long time to its strange ebb and flow in her head. For a moment she had the impression that it came from outside, from another corner of the room, and that it was growing louder. At times the noise was almost imperceptible, and yet, by some inexplicable quality, had the character of a loud and continuous roar. She felt she was growing feverish. Perhaps she would eventually fall into delirium. What would she do then? What was to stop her, for instance, from throwing herself out the window? A thousand fears besieged her. The lamp was flickering and she would soon be alone in the dark. She might catch cold, get pneumonia. She was going to go mad. She took a step toward the table and took the lamp in her hand. Its light and warmth were a reassurance, and besides, it was a weapon: she could throw it at the head of anyone who attacked her. At whose head? She looked toward her door and regretted that she had not turned the key in the lock. Now it was too late. She could never get across the carpet to it. Her strength was leaving her. In a sort of dédoublement she saw herself, half dressed, leaning against the frame of a window, lamp in hand. What was she doing there? What was she waiting for? Suddenly she was penetrated with a formless terror. It was not, as just now, the horror of something prowling about her, the feeling of being hunted: it was an ignoble horror of herself, of her slightest gestures, of her shadow, even of her thoughts, in which she believed she perceived the premonitory symptoms of lunacy! Against her will, a cry broke from her—then another. This relieved her. She began to shout, "Help!" The volume of her voice surprised herself. She was astonished to find how easily she could shout, and little by little her anguish abated.

Here and there, dogs began barking nearby. She stopped a moment, pleased with the racket she was causing. Then she began again, in a shriller and steadier voice, and, as none answered, gathered all her strength and cried: "Madame Legras!"

Several moments elapsed. She heard nothing except the desperate barking of the dogs and the rattle of the chains against which the frantic animals were straining. By now she was feeling better. Her strength came back; she put down her lamp on the table and, crossing her chamber in a few strides, locked the door.

Seated on her bed, she watched the sky paling slowly. The stars seemed to be receding far, far away and disappearing. She sat a long time without moving, then shivered and yawned. Almost without her knowing how, her head fell back on the bolster. Drawing the covers over her, she went to sleep, curled into a ball at the bottom of the bed.

Chapter XVI

She was awakened three hours later by the sound of loud voices from the ground floor. Immediately she recalled everything that had happened last night, and sat up, listening intently. She recognized the voice of Désirée and that of a neighbor, but could not understand a word they said. Her heart began to beat quickly. She got up, turned the key, so as to be able to open the door at once, shut the window, and waited. Downstairs two women were exchanging conjectures, punctuated with cries. Suddenly she heard them calling her. But she did not answer and remained standing in the middle of the room. For the first time her thoughts ran upon an inquest—the police! What attitude was she to adopt? What was she to say? Would she be believed if she described it as an accident? Had anyone heard her cry aloud during the night? But, compared with the terrors which she had felt, her present anxiety was nothing. In broad daylight she felt more sure of herself. "What proofs have they?" she asked herself.

At this moment the two voices called again. She answered, "Yes!" rather faintly, and half-opened her door. Downstairs Désirée was crying: "Mademoiselle! Oh, mademoiselle—a terrible thing—"

"What has happened?" called Adrienne in an impatient voice.

"Monsieur has fallen down the staircase."

"'Monsieur'?" repeated the girl. "Where is he?"

Désirée did not answer at once. "Alas, mademoiselle!" she cried, presently. Then—silence!

Adrienne fought down the terrible emotion which once more was gaining on her. She crossed the landing and stood near the stairs, but could not bring herself to look down. She heard the woman to whom Désirée had been speaking moaning with fright. It was an old herbseller, on her way to market, who had come in soon after Désirée to offer her wares for sale. Adrienne lost patience.

"Will you tell me what's the matter?" she cried harshly.

A sudden and monstrous curiosity impelled her to lower her eyes. She recognized the figure she had seen once before by the uncertain light of the lamp. Against the pale colors of the mosaic floor the corpse was clearly defined. The black shadow around the head seemed smaller. She looked at it a long time and could not realize that this was her father at all. She had believed it for an instant last night, when she leaned over the landing on the second story and held the lamp out until she made its rays fall on the flags of the foyer. Now that the terrible silence of midnight was over and the darkness which filled the whole house with horror had departed, she refused to credit it. It was as though someone had substituted a mannequin stuffed with sawdust for the corpse which she had seen. She felt that Désirée and the old peddler were watching her face narrowly for signs of emotion, and the blood left her cheeks.

"How did it happen?" she stammered.

"Did mademoiselle hear nothing?" asked the *bonne,* a little dark woman, dressed in a camisole and a gray skirt.

Adrienne shook her head. Leaving the stairhead, she walked unsteadily toward her room. A sudden idea struck her.

"Call Madame Legras!" she cried down the staircase, and closed the door.

From her room she could hear the two women leave the house and cross the garden.

More than a quarter of an hour passed. She waited, sitting on the bed and trying to decide what line of conduct she must follow. What surprised her most was that she was so little upset. It was as though the previous night had consumed all the terror of which she was capable. Nothing had happened just the way she had expected. Perhaps she should have appeared more agitated before those two women just now. She resolved to feign a silent sorrow and not to budge from her room.

The gate swung open and four or five people crossed the garden. She heard what sounded like a man's voice and felt the blood rush to her heart. Was it the police commissary? She forgot her resolution of a moment ago and started to her feet. But she could not screw up courage to go to the window. The wardrobe mirror showed her a woman with rings round her haggard eyes, livid cheeks, and loose hair floating over the shoulders of a pink dressing gown. Her hands were like ice.

A moment later she heard the footsteps and the exclamations she so dreaded in the hall. Cries arose. She could clearly distinguish the voice of Mme. Legras and was struck by its vulgar and powerful quality. Perhaps it was this that she had mistaken just now for a man's. Her first instinct was to turn the key in her lock, but she reflected that this would be very unwise. She did the exact opposite, and opened the door.

"My poor child!" said Mme. Legras from the bottom of the staircase. "Are you there? No, don't come down. I'm coming up."

Turning to a group of servants who stood round her, she gave an order that made Adrienne gasp.

"Go and fetch the doctor—for the permit."[1]

The doctor! Maurecourt! Not for an instant had Adrienne dreamed of this eventuality. At last she was going to see this man—in her own home! Doubtless she would have to speak to him. All her plans of yesterday were being realized. A savage joy invaded her heart. It seemed that things were coming to pass in spite of herself. She reflected that she would feel much easier talking to him now because he would account for her trouble by the accident that had happened at Villa des Charmes. In her bewilderment she found herself saying, "I hope papa speaks politely to him," and stopped, aghast at the thought.

A moment later Mme. Legras was with her. She wore a wide brown travelling cloak over a dressing gown whose hem came below it and whose ruching of white crépon swished round her heels. A black veil fell from

---

[1] French law, in case of sudden death, does not permit the body to be touched until a doctor has given the necessary authority [trans. note].

her hat and concealed her face.

"This is frightful," she said, closing the door behind her. "How did it happen?"

Adrienne shrugged her shoulders and lowered her head.

"Poor child!" repeated Mme. Legras. "And you all alone!"

She sat down on the bed beside the girl and took her hand.

"Never forget that I am here. *Hein?*"

A moment passed. Mme. Legras kept her eyes on the girl.

"My poor child," she repeated.

And then, as though speaking to herself:

"Poor gentleman! He was going downstairs in the dark. Not wise at all at his age. Yet there was the hand-rail. Didn't you think of holding a light for him?"

"I didn't hear him go down," said Adrienne, shortly.

"Ah!" sighed Mme. Legras. "You were sound asleep, then?"

Adrienne longed for the woman to go and regretted having called her. She disliked the way in which Mme. Legras chose to probe the details of the accident.

"And he died without a cry, I suppose," the new friend went on. "Terrible! I'm afraid the police will want an inquest."

Adrienne started.

"Don't you like the idea?" asked Mme. Legras. "My child, it's a pure formality."

Someone knocked at the door.

"Come in!" said Mme. Legras without letting go of the girl's hand.

It was Désirée.

"The doctor will be here in ten minutes," she said in a low voice. "It seems," she added, "that cries were heard in the night."

"If so, I would have known it," Mme. Legras answered, quickly. "I sleep very lightly. The slightest sound awakens me."

She made a gesture as though to dismiss the maid. But Désirée seemed disinclined to take the hint.

"Does mademoiselle require anything?" she asked.

Adrienne shook her head.

Désirée looked round her. Suddenly her eyes fell upon the lamp. Adrienne followed them and trembled. All the oil was burned up.

"Look," said Désirée, in a still lower voice. "Mademoiselle's lamp is empty. And I filled it the day before yesterday."

Passing quickly in front of Adrienne and Mme. Legras, she took up the lamp and examined it with a critical air. Having done so, she tiptoed out as though she were leaving a sick-room.

Mme. Legras pressed Adrienne's hand.

"What do you think of that woman?" she asked.

Adrienne looked at her with frightened eyes.

"Why do you ask?" said she in a voice that died away in her throat.

"Because she seemed to me to speak very strangely," said Mme. Legras. "I could have sworn that she is keeping something to herself. That lamp, for instance. What is there so extraordinary in its being empty?"

She put up her veil round her hat brim and looked straight into Adrienne's eyes.

"You spent the night wide awake, that's all. Didn't you? The same thing with those cries they speak of. Suppose we say you had a nightmare and called for help in your sleep."

Adrienne did not move. Like those animals caught in a snare which stand stiff and motionless for a moment before fighting for their lives, she did not dare to say a word or make a movement. She felt the fingers of her new friend twining themselves between her own, as though to hold her the more securely.

"My little Adrienne," said Mme. Legras, gently, "would you like me to see the doctor and the police commissary for you?"

The room grew dark around the young girl. Without a word she let her head fall on the bosom of the woman she hated, who went on stroking her hair with delicate fingers and murmuring words she did not understand.

Part Two

Chapter I

"You see how smoothly everything went off, just as I said it would. Why should they raise any difficulties over burying him at once—the poor gentleman! Doctor Maurecourt was simply splendid. Such perfect breeding! You should make his acquaintance. You ought to see a few people, and not stay all alone as you do. It's very bad for you. Do you know, though, what shocked me a little—just a very little, dear? You don't mind my saying so? Not having the funeral at church. Oh, I know you will say that everyone is free to think as he likes. All the same, just a touch of ceremony at the end does no harm. I am a believer myself. Don't imagine I'm a devotee, far less a mystic. But I was brought up in the principles of thirty years ago. I am *bourgeoise*. I go to Mass. Didn't your poor father have any religion at all?"

Mme. Legras was speaking. Dressed in a lilac gown and with an enormous straw hat on her head, she sat under one of the trees in the garden, embroidering a handkerchief. From time to time she raised her eyes from her needlework and shot a glance under the hat brim in Adrienne's direction. The girl was seated at her side, listening in silence. She was in mourning. She shook her head.

"No," she answered.

The continual chatter of her friend was not pleasing to her. In certain of Mme. Legras's phrases she thought she detected a treacherous significance which gave ample food for thought. But she never refused to lend an ear to the unending stream which came from her lips. Every morning, since her father's funeral, she went over to see Mme. Legras and stayed until lunchtime. In the afternoon the two very often took a walk or drive together. Once or twice they dined tête-à-tête. Adrienne had not changed her opinion of her new friend one bit. On the contrary, she detested her more than ever. But some tie seemed to exist between her and this woman so strong that she was powerless to break it or to rid herself of a companion who had now grown odious. She was quite sure Mme. Legras realized there was a mystery connected with her father's sudden death. This alone might have warned her to keep so dangerous an acquaintance at arm's length. On the contrary, whenever she was not with her neighbor, Adrienne was overtaken with an inexplicable anxiety. She missed her chit-chat. That garrulous and indiscreet tongue, forever running on Mesurat's tragic end, had become necessary to her. In listening to it she managed to experience at one and the same time a positive repugnance and a relative relief. Without offering a word in reply, she would sit with her hands crossed on her knee, hearkening to the trite babble mingled with suggestions that made her blood run cold. Sometimes the name of Maurecourt was dragged into this monologue, and the girl felt as though a blow were being aimed at him. She managed to conceal these mingled emotions behind an impassive face and answered Mme. Legras's questions as briefly as possible.

"You gave me to understand that he forbade your leaving the house," the older woman went on, as she drew her needle through one of a number of little leaves that she was embroidering in a corner of her handkerchief. "Poor gentleman! And he had such a gentle, timid air. Didn't you tell me yourself that he was timid?"

"Yes."

"Well, here you are now, quite free," went on Mme. Legras, smoothly. "What are you going to do with all your time?"

Adrienne shrugged her shoulders, as though to express indifference.

"The first thing to do is to make up your mind to forget," went on the voice. "Good Heavens! a woman as young as you, with all her life before her . . .! Weren't you surprised to hear how rich you were when the lawyer read your father's will?"

"I'm not so very rich," said Adrienne.

"Nonsense! You have his entire fortune."

"First of all, I divide everything with my sister—then, I don't get my own share until I come of age."

Mme. Legras sighed deeply. She was quite aware of Germaine's critical condition.

"Let us pray God spares her!" she said, piously.

Both women were silent. It was a radiant summer day and the garden was filled with the scent of flowers. Masses of lilac exhaled their sad and oppressive odor. On the lawn, which lay between the two women and the house, the yellow basset was chasing butterflies, yapping shrilly as he dashed round and round in circles. Birds were calling to one another in the lime trees.

"There," said Mme. Legras, drawing off her thimble. "Enough for today!"

She rolled scissors, thimble, and thread in a handkerchief. Adrienne was familiar with the signal which let her know every day when Mme. Legras had had enough of her company. It humiliated her to such an extent that she was always vowing not to come back, or to leave half an hour earlier, knowing well that she would be unable to do either. She drew out her watch and affected surprise.

"Quarter to twelve!" she exclaimed.

"You're not thinking of going!" Mme. Legras never failed in this remark.

"I have to think of lunch," said Adrienne.

"Well, then—" said Mme. Legras, with a smile. The two women rose and said good-bye.

"Come back soon," called Mme. Legras after her, as she left the garden.

Once in her own house, Adrienne always waited in the parlor until lunch was served, and passed the time as best she might. Often, as before, she put on an apron above her black serge dress and wiped the furniture, over which she felt quite sure Désirée's duster never passed. Or else she amused herself by taking the books out of their shelves, brushing their backs with a clothes brush, and putting them back in order of size. It never occurred to her to read one. Like many women whose childhood has been dull and who have nothing but unpleasant memories of their school days, reading for any length of time was as repugnant to her as though it were still a question of homework to prepare for the next day.

Very seldom indeed did she go to her own room now before bedtime. She felt less lonely in the ground-floor rooms, if only because the dining-room communicated with the kitchen by a narrow passage. Solitude was what she most dreaded. One day as she heard Pyramus, the basset, barking across the road, the idea occurred to her of buying a dog for herself. But she did not care much for dogs. Cats suggested spinsterhood, so she wanted none of them.

If Mme. Legras had invited her to come and live at Villa Louise, she would have accepted gladly in spite of the pain which association with the woman gave her. One day, on thinking the matter over, she reached the conclusion that Mme. Legras was not only the person whose conversation distracted her most effectually, but the sole human creature in whose company she cared to be.

Strange as it may seem, she could not imagine herself taking part in the simplest conversation with the doctor. She tried to think of him as lit-tle as possible, dismayed by the sadness that always descended on her when she did. The idea that he had once been in the house seemed strange and even terrible to her. Instead of bringing him nearer, it made him seem still more remote. She had not dared to confront him when he came, and she could never make herself believe that he had actually sat down in the parlor where she spent every day. It shocked her like a sacrilege to think that he should have entered a house so unworthy to receive him. She hardly ever looked out the window now. Far from feeling free to act as she chose, she had the impression that something irreparable had come about, that it was too late now to turn her eyes toward the little white house or abandon herself to dreams about it. If it ever happened that she yielded to temptation and looked at the blue roof beneath a trembling treetop, she repented her impulse so bitterly that the momentary pleasure she gave her-self and the suffering which was its inevitable result were out of all propor-tion.

The important thing in her life now was to listen to Mme. Legras talking. "She's a good woman at heart," the girl often told herself, as though to excuse her continual need of these trite and perfidious monologues. But she knew her words were false as she uttered them. She feared Mme. Legras, she dreaded her smile, her lingering handshake, and above all that loose tongue which let slip so many strange conjectures. Sometimes she was on the point of fainting when Mme. Legras referred to her father's death. What alarmed her most was the placid and matter-of-fact tone the woman used in expressing the most disturbing opinions. On one occasion, for instance, she had remarked, without even raising her head: "Do you know, I should not be at all surprised if someone told me your poor father had been murdered." Adrienne did not answer. But the tips of the fingers that she held twined in her lap turned icy cold. She had a sudden impulse to leap to her feet, to run to the railroad station, to take the train as Germaine had taken it, and to be gone. Instead, she remained motionless upon her chair, her eyes fixed on the skillful needle of Mme. Legras as it filled in the outline of a cluster of rosebuds in the corner of a handkerchief. Nothing could induce the girl to withdraw before half past eleven had struck. She sat still, awaiting the painful moment when Mme. Legras would roll up her work—when she herself would draw her watch from her belt with an astonished face. And she went away then with a quite indescribable regret, made desperate by the thought that she would be alone in the Villa des Charmes, which she detested more each day. She went so far sometimes as to stuff her fingers in her ears as she slammed the gate behind her. She could not bear to hear a noise which she knew so well and which recalled so many things to her mind.

One day she did not return home at once, and the idea entered her head of going into the town for lunch. But the fear that it would be known and seem strange held her back. What would Désirée say if she failed to come in at her usual hour? She was sure, in spite of what Mme. Legras appeared to believe, that the maid suspected nothing. But she was resolved to do nothing which would give anyone the slightest excuse for speaking of her. For a similar reason, she never went out at night. She might meet someone. Far better to stay at home—after dinner she would sit down below a lamp in the big parlor and look over old photograph albums. With her elbows on the card table, she listened to the noise of dishes and pots and pans which reached her from the kitchen as she turned over the pages languidly. But as soon as she heard Désirée leave the back of the house and pass through the corridor on her way home, she began to feel nervous. She listened intently to the noise of the door opening and shutting, to the footsteps along the path, to the hateful creaking of the gate, whose hinges were stiff and which had to be slammed. It seemed to her then that silence spread about her like a great shadow, and that in back of this silence was a strange murmur, made up of a multitude of voices. At such a time it became an effort to turn the pages of her album; even the sound of her breathing disturbed her. By a strange mental twist she found herself at last almost regretting the time when two persons, seated at this very table, forced her to play cards with them.

Chapter II

M. Mesurat had been dead now for three weeks. Germaine, hastily alerted, had not returned to La Tour-l'Evêque for her father's interment, given the critical state of her health. However, she had had a copy of his will sent to her and had dispatched to La Tour l'Evêque a notary from Saint-Blaise to represent her interests. When the old man's will was read, it transpired that the modest fortune left by him was divided equally between his two daughters. It also appeared that the deceased had not foreseen the possibility of dying before his younger daughter attained her majority, and it had been necessary to appoint a trustee. The sole relatives of M. Mesurat were an elderly unmarried woman at Rennes and a bachelor cousin who resided in Paris. Both had quarrelled with their cousin Antoine many years before, and were well aware that they had nothing to expect from him. Notices of the death were sent them in vain: neither one nor the other was willing to undertake a useless journey. In the absence of a family council, and in face of the refusal of Adrienne's relatives to concern themselves with her, the district judge of La Tour l'Evêque designated Maître Biraud, notary-at-law, as trustee for Mlle. Adrienne Mesurat until her majority was reached. Germaine Mesurat retained a power of attorney and was authorized to propose to Maître Biraud whatever modifications she considered fitting in the management of Adrienne's fortune. It was arranged that Adrienne should receive certain sums agreed upon by the lawyer and her elder sister, month by month, said sums to be deducted from her share in the estate. Germaine, being of age, might draw her money as she pleased. The settlement was concluded in three weeks.

As time passed, Adrienne gradually became inured to the circumstances of her new life, to loneliness and the sadness which never left her. She seemed to be suffering less. On waking in the morning, she no longer had that sorrowful feeling of surprise once hers at the thought that the day which was beginning would bring her nothing. Now, on the contrary, this very certainty seemed a good thing, and the very absence of any hope her best assurance against misfortune. What could possibly happen now to dismay her? Had she not by now exhausted the very sources of her melancholy? Suppose Maurecourt were to die, for example? How would her life be changed, since she no longer kept the slightest illusion in regard to him?

To pass the time away until she could set out for a walk with Mme. Legras, or go to watch her sewing in her garden, she looked for some occupation, and put into execution certain plans which she had been entertaining a long time. It was a question of changing the arrangement of every room in the house. She had already moved the furniture about in the parlor, breaking up the symmetrical arrangement of the armchairs, placing them against the wall instead of keeping them ranged in the middle of the carpet, and leaving a clear space that increased the apparent size of the room. She changed the hanging of several pictures. Germaine's old sofa was pushed into a corner between the two doors. She took off the panther skin and draped the sofa with a Breton shawl. These petty changes so altered the aspect of the room that Adrienne affected not to recognize it, and smiled at the effect of her work.

One morning she took a notion to climb to the third floor and examine Germaine's bedroom. Up to now various considerations had restrained her. First the fear of possible infection. Désirée had been instructed to clean the room thoroughly and to open the windows every day, while all that remained of Germaine's wardrobe had long ago been given away to the poor. It seemed to the girl that the longer she waited, the more worthwhile the visit would be when it was made. Hadn't she all her life to go upstairs? Besides, since she no longer wished to think of the doctor, it would be futile to stand at the only window from which she had a chance of seeing him. This morning, however, she felt stronger than usual—indifferent, even. "Perhaps I love him less already," she said to herself with feigned cheerfulness. She congratulated herself as on a victory. She might yet be happy, perhaps, once she succeeded in stifling this love for good and all.

She went upstairs. Her hand trembled a little as she opened the door, and an indefinable scruple delayed her on its threshold. The last time she had seen her sister here was the day Germaine had called her up to tell her she was going to die. There was danger in the room, greater even than the risk of contagion. There was the memory of a woman marked for death, who had passed long years of wasted suffering within its four walls. The bed, the chairs, the little medicine cabinet—everything spoke its own terrible and eloquent language. The idea seized Adrienne that perhaps merely being in the room brought bad luck. For a moment she thought she would close the door without entering. But her hesitation did not last. Something drew her irresistibly toward the window, now stripped of its curtains and blinds. She held her breath and took the width of the room in a few long strides. Her heart was palpitating; probably she had run upstairs too fast. When she had thrown the window open, she took in deep breaths of the outside air, leaned over the gutter and looked straight before her. Between the lime trees at the Villa Louise she could see Mme. Legras walking along her flower beds, shears in hand. A little behind her was the basset, his sharp nose against the ground, sniffing the stone. Adrienne would have liked to hail her neighbor. But she controlled the impulse and contented herself with watching the stout lady pass from one plant to another, her face entirely hidden by a big straw hat.

Suddenly Adrienne turned her head to the right. As before, she gripped the edge of the gutter and leaned out as far as she possibly could, the better to see the little white house. This was the real reason she had come upstairs! She admitted it now, and felt a sudden transport at the thought of savoring a joy which she had denied herself for so many weeks. She gazed with a sort of greedy relish. The sun was on the slate roof. The blaze reflected from it was what struck her first. Then her eyes sought the lower story and the window, which, as usual, was open. As she saw the window, Adrienne had the impression of being carried back a month. It was a positive shock to her to see how little everything had changed, as though she had had a right to expect some transformation. Simultaneously she recognized the languor which she had experienced a month ago in the same place—the positive suspension of life in her inmost being. Her wrists hurt. She kept looking out until she could make out the interior of the room that so intrigued her and which she always assumed to be the doctor's consulting-room. A ray of sunshine lit up the crimson rug and the angle of the desk.

All of a sudden, she drew back and pressed her hands against her mouth. Someone had appeared at the window. Certainly it was not the doctor; even her momentary glance showed her that. She stood upright a moment, her face turned away from the little white house, the back of her head against the window frame. A kind of moan broke from her. She kept murmuring: "Who can it be? Who can it be?" but dared not turn her head to find out. It seemed to her that her destiny depended on that moment—that she was on the point of finding out something dreadful yet essential which would mean happiness or unhappiness. A profound silence weighed on the street. The very birds were mute. Sound or motion had ceased as though by the spell of some enchantment. At last she could bear it no longer. She put her trembling hand on the gutter once more. The window was empty.

She drew back quickly and sighed. "It was a mistake," she told herself. "There was no one there at all."

She ran out of the room.

That afternoon, as she was leaving the house to go to Mme. Legras, the postman handed her a letter. She opened and read it in the street. It was from the superior of the hospital where Germaine had taken refuge.

MADEMOISELLE: We beg to join most sincerely in the profound sorrow which must be yours at this time, and trust that the thought of Divine Providence is sustaining you during these difficult days. We were somewhat concerned, as doubtless you were yourself, for the bad effect which the sad news might produce upon your sister in her precarious condition. But she appears resigned to all the trials which are our lot on earth. Please do not be too anxious on her account. One might even dare to say that she is better. The air alone of this region—

Adrienne skipped ten lines and went on till her eyes fell on the bottom of the letter:

—weak to write you herself, begs you to deposit 500 francs at the St.-
Blaise bank in her name and to renew the deposit monthly—

She tore the letter into bits and threw them into the gutter. She had not written to her sister once—it was Mme. Legras who had taken care of sending word of M. Mesurat's death—and only thought of her by accident and in the vaguest fashion. The idea of forming any new ties with the sick woman could only exasperate Adrienne. Even more having to do any kind of commission for her. It was not that she begrudged Germaine her share in the paternal inheritance. It was the obligation of having to think of her once every month that annoyed her—going to see the lawyer, mailing a letter, pronouncing her name! She laid it all to the hatred which she had always felt for her elder sister, but it was really due to something far stronger which she could not make up her mind to admit even to herself. Two things had taken a preponderant place in her existence. She must think of the doctor—or make up her mind never to think of him, which was only another way of letting him occupy her mind. She must listen to Mme. Legras as she talked about her father's death, and slyly accused her of having murdered him. Anything which distracted her from her ill-resisted love and from her unavowed remorse was unbearable.

As she crossed the street she was regretting that she had not had her gloves on when she handled the letter from the hospital, which the sick woman had certainly read over and perhaps breathed upon.

"Why is she still alive?" she asked herself, callously. "What does she have to fill her life?"

A moment later she was in the garden of the Villa Louise. Mme. Legras was just leaving the house. She came down the garden steps, brandishing a blue pole which she was holding in her left hand, while with her right she pressed a brown package against her bust.

"What's that?" asked the girl.

"You'll see in a minute," said Mme. Legras.

She reached the rod to her as though it were her hand, and sat down under one of the lime trees. Adrienne took a seat beside her.

"My dear girl," began the elder woman as she busied herself untying

141

the string around her parcel, "I have a little piece of news that I hope is not going to upset you."

"News—"

"I'm going away—"

She placed her plump hands on the package and looked at the girl as though to judge the effect of her words. Adrienne only lowered her eyes.

"—and I'll return in three days," added Mme. Legras, bursting into laughter. "My husband needs me," she added, with a demure air. "Oh, nothing very serious; but his business keeps him so tied down that he cannot get away. So, you understand—Did I ever tell you what his business is?"

Adrienne shook her head.

"Textiles—wool, cotton, silk," quoted Mme. Legras. "Oh, I'm a regular little *bourgeoise*. And not a bit ashamed of it, either. Here's one proof the more—"

She opened her package. It seemed to contain a length of bright blue stuff. Mme. Legras rose, unrolled the material completely with a certain solemnity, and held it out at arm's length. It was a tri-color flag, about the size of a large table napkin.

"I see," commented Adrienne.

The white, powdered face above the flag looked so droll that she could hardly keep from laughing.

"My husband sends me this for the Fourteenth," Mme. Legras explained. "The other one we had was too faded. I've kept the staff for this one. First-quality silk. Feel!"

Adrienne took it between her fingers.

"Two days after tomorrow is the Fourteenth," went on Mme. Legras as she sat down. "I must sew this flag to the rod. Do you know it rather thrills me? I was brought up on the principles of thirty years ago, being a good Frenchwoman, a good Christian. I don't say that on your account, my dear. But I was talking of my husband. You must really meet him . . . . Do you mind holding the rod for me while I sew? . . . Unhappily, his business has been going none too well for some time. The competition from abroad is terrible, especially in England. . . . Do you mind holding the rod steadier, my dear? . . . Consequently, all sorts of worry—about money, naturally. You should thank Heaven for having saved you from such things. You had a good father who did everything to insure you a happy future."

She bent over the rod and began to sew.

"I was speaking of him only the other day," she went on, with an abstracted air.

"Of whom, madame?" asked the girl, after a moment's pause.

"Why, of your father! You don't go into the town, my dear child. I'll wager you have no idea what these country towns are like. You have to be a Parisian, as I am, to realize the difference. Chatter, chatter, chatter! I confine myself to listening. But yesterday a woman called Grand—You know her, don't you?"

"The woman that keeps the draper's shop," said Adrienne. Her cheeks turned pale.

"That's who I mean. I was buying a spool of blue cotton for this very flag. Mademoiselle Grand waited on me, and as she wrapped up the spool—do you know what she said?"

"No, madame."

"Please hold the thing firmer, my dear, or I'll prick my fingers. . . . She said: 'You live opposite the Villa des Charmes, don't you? You must know Mademoiselle Mesurat. Her father died very tragically. There's something unnatural about the whole affair.' You understand, my dear, that I'm just quoting Mademoiselle Grand?"

"Yes," said Adrienne, with a catch in her breath.

"Of course," said Mme. Legras, without raising her eyes from her sewing, "I have no opinion either way. But since you called me on the day of the accident, I can say what I think to you, however close I keep my mouth shut to other people. Well, I do think it all rather strange. I often wonder about it. And then, I have a certain instinct in these things that doesn't deceive me. My dear, your father must have had a light when he went downstairs."

There was a brief silence.

"So I just said to Mademoiselle Grand, 'Yes, it does seem a little unnatural.' Naturally I wasn't going to discuss you with that woman. You would not have liked me to, would you?"

"No."

"I was sure of it, my dear," said Mme. Legras, very gently.

She finished her seam without another word. With her hands clasping the rod, Adrienne looked at the white, robust neck under the straw hat, at the head bent over the needle. Her heart was invaded by a sort of dumb fury. It seemed eminently unjust to her that Mme. Legras should be at liberty to nourish whatever plans she pleased—to carry the most villainous thoughts in her head, of which she, Adrienne, the object of all these criminal meditations, knew nothing. She would have liked to strike the woman, to have upset her chair, to have done anything to prevent her thinking. "What right has she to cross-examine me?" she asked herself. "Probably she wants to make me talk and use whatever I say against me. I shan't answer her anymore."

"There we are," said Mme. Legras, making a knot in her cotton thread. "It's done. Let go—let go, please!"

She almost tore the staff from Adrienne's hands, which were clasped tightly on the wood and did not release it at once.

"Of course you're going to put out a flag," said Mme. Legras, admiring her tri-color at arm's length.

"Of course," said Adrienne.

"You seem a little sad and *distraite*. Is it what I just said?"

"No."

Mme. Legras put her head on one side.

"Is it your boyfriend?" she asked in a low voice. "You never speak of him, and that's wrong. I have more experience than you. I understand these things."

"I'm not seeing anyone," said Adrienne, in a hoarse voice.

"Then you're making a mistake," Mme. Legras retorted, spreading the flag across her knees. "A pretty girl like you!"

Adrienne shrugged her shoulders.

"Being pretty doesn't help much," she murmured. "I'm none the happier for it."

"It doesn't help when you have no money," said Mme. Legras.

The girl was going to answer, but checked herself. She was sorry for having said anything at all. She loathed hearing this woman refer to her love affair. The window that she had seen open that morning, and the face that had come to it, flashed into her mind. How could she persuade Mme. Legras to ask her inside her villa? There must be rooms in it with a full view of the little white house. But did she really want to see the window again? Did she really want to see the unknown person who had been looking out of it a moment ago? She spoke at random.

"How long ago did you buy this villa?"

"You must be dreaming!" answered the older woman. "You know quite well that I was not here last year. Besides, I haven't bought the villa at all; I have only leased it. My husband leased it."

She clasped her hand across the outspread ensign and added, in a rather chilly voice:

"If you think what I said just now was indiscreet, perhaps you had best not expose yourself to such accidents in the future."

"It never occurred to me that you were indiscreet," said Adrienne, blushing deeply.

"Very well then," replied Mme. Legras, rolling up her flag. "Don't let us fall out about nothing. You value your secrets, and it's natural you should."

She added almost immediately:

"I have no secrets, and that's the simplest way of all. Please let us not refer to it again—"

She made a gesture of her hand as though to efface something she saw before her, and rose.

"Will you excuse me, dear? I have to pack. After lunch I have to go to the veterinarian. I've left my dog there. I think he's scratching a bit too much. Do you want to come with me?"

"Thank you very much," said Adrienne, "but I can't."

"*Au revoir*, then. No hard feelings?"

"Why should there be?"

The two women shook hands and Adrienne returned to her own house.

Chapter III

Early next morning the girl was drawn to the window by the noise of wheels stopping at the gate of Villa Louise. She saw Mme. Legras leave the house and settle herself in a carriage, which drove off quickly. Her heart sank at the sight. For a long time after its customary stillness had fallen on the quarter she remained motionless, her eyes fixed upon the spot where she had seen her neighbor get into the cab, as if something irreparable had just happened, leaving her incredulous of the extent of her misfortune. Within her was a strange sense of emptiness. It took Mme. Legras's departure to make her realize how necessary the company of this odious woman had now become to her. She did not even attempt to explain such a monstrous paradox. She simply endured it as one endures something too overwhelmingly strong to be resisted. How much better off would she be if she understood the origin and nature of her slavery? How would it help her to be able to give a name to the thing that was forcing her to pay her daily visit to Villa Louise? She preferred not to question the hideous fact. The strange fear of herself which she had felt the night her father died— her horror at what she was capable of thinking and doing—still was part of her. Only by some kind of magic, which had a principle she didn't understand, she needed the perfidious gossip of Mme. Legras to give her even a semblance of interior peace. How was she to go on living if that woman went away? Yet she had gone. Three days had to be spent somehow before she came back—three days of insupportable loneliness, three silent days of which her old terrors would take full advantage, and against which she would have to battle incessantly until the monotonous and rapid voice of her neighbor returned to break the evil spell.

She dressed herself quickly, resolved to go out. There had been a violent storm during the night and the weather was cool. The gray and threatening sky seemed to touch the treetops. It was not yet eight o'clock. She took the first umbrella she could find and went out without waiting for the *bonne* to serve her morning coffee.

Once in the street, she turned her back resolutely upon the little white house. She wouldn't go in that direction—that wasn't what she wanted to think about. She wanted to tire herself out physically— to walk until her legs ached, to think of nothing, remember nothing—just to keep going through the town and into the country—then come home and sleep. She walked up a side street, turned to the left, skirted the wall where the wistaria shed so sweet an odor, and went straight on. In three minutes' time she was in the marketplace of the little town. A few people bowed or nodded to her. She returned their greetings awkwardly and quickened her steps. It mattered little to her where she went. The essential was to keep moving. Nevertheless, she decided to leave the market, where everybody must recognize her. She turned down a narrow side street which led to the church, and stopped under a house porch to recover her breath. Her skin was moist. It had become too hot to wear her gloves. She took them off and mopped her nose and cheeks with her handkerchief. After a few minutes she resumed her walk and gained the principal thoroughfare of the town. It was quiet enough here at that early hour. A few prentices taking down the shop shutters stared at this lady who was walking so fast. She noticed it, turned back, was seized by an unreasoning panic, and changed her direction. Everything grew confused. This girl, who was usually so composed, had lost her head. She would have started to run if she had not been afraid of looking suspicious. At the bottom of her heart the fear always reigned of doing something which would appear "strange." As she was crossing a street, a cart which she had not heard, and which was coming from the right, all but ran over her. She leaped back and nearly fell.

In her nervousness she kept to the left of the pavement farthest from the roadway and nearest the wall. Suddenly she lifted her eyes. Upon the glazed door of a shop she read the name: Ernestine Grand.

She stopped at once. The shop front was painted black. In its badly dressed window, knitted garments in pale-colored wools, stockings and slippers, were piled together pell-mell. Long red and blue aprons hung from hooks. Adrienne recalled the draper's shop Mme. Legras had spoken about. This must surely be it. It seemed to her that, in some inexplicable fashion, and almost as though the whole incident were a dream, she was going to find her neighbor inside. Besides, here was a handy means of escaping the curious eyes which she felt sure were fixed on her. She walked into the shop.

The tinkle of a cracked bell announced her entry, but it was some time before anyone came out to serve her. The little shop was poorly lighted. A long counter took up the greater part of it. Green drawers with brass handles occupied the entire side of one wall. A vague smell of cloth and mildew assailed the nostrils. Every sound from outside was muffled and changed in character, and the street, from which the shop was only separated by a single thickness of glass, might have been miles away.

Adrienne took a chair and pulled off her gloves. In the profound stillness of the shop she could hear the sound of her own breathing. A confused hum was in her ears, as always happened when she found herself in a close room. But her heart beat less fast than in the street outside and she grew calmer.

At last a door at the back of the shop opened and a woman entered who seemed displeased to find a customer so early. She threw a furtive look over the counter to be sure that nothing had been left exposed. She was a tall thin woman, and walked without making any sound except the rustle of her black dress. She said "good day" and placed herself behind the counter, in front of Adrienne.

"Mademoiselle?"

"I want a spool of white thread," said Adrienne, quickly.

She took off her gloves once more in order to appear at ease, and with her eyes followed the movements of the woman, who began to pull out a drawer without further words. To give herself courage, she clasped her hands tightly on the counter. She would have liked to say something which would be an excuse for Mlle. Grand to talk about Mme. Legras, but could think of nothing. Suddenly she heard the following sentence issue from between her own lips:

"Did Madame Legras come here yesterday?"

Then she was silent. A deathly moment passed before the woman closed the drawer and answered as she turned around:

"The day before yesterday—to buy some thread."

Mlle. Grand had pinched features and the flesh of her face appeared dead, like that of nuns who never go out and breathe the same impure air all day. She laid the tray containing spools of different colors on the counter, and leaned forward a little. Adrienne watched her blanched eyelids and the parting in the center of her grizzled hair, which she wore in two bandeaux.

"Will mademoiselle kindly choose?" the woman said in an even voice. Without altering its level tone in the slightest, she added:

"She said she knew you very well."

"That is so," said Adrienne, with a sort of vivacity which she checked at once.

With the tips of her fingers she lifted several reels, but made no choice.

"She left yesterday for a few days," she went on, with an absorbed air. "I saw her yesterday afternoon. She had a flag to sew, and I helped her."

"Mademoiselle has had a hard time," said the woman, after a few moments. "That was what I was saying to Madame Legras—'"

Adrienne raised her eyes slightly and saw both hands of the speaker on the counter. They were long hard hands, their discolored skin wrinkled at the knuckles. She sighed, and took up one spool which she inspected more closely.

"Madame Legras's husband is in business, isn't he?" she inquired suddenly, setting down the reel.

"'M. Legras?'" echoed the draper.

She gave way to a little noiseless laugh. Adrienne looked at her.

"Isn't he in the silk and cotton business?" the girl asked, with uneasiness in her voice.

Mlle. Grand shrugged her shoulders slightly and smiled.

"I don't know the gentleman," she said.

"But she was speaking of him yesterday; she told me he was in the silk and cotton industry."

"Mind you, I am not saying she does not know someone in the trade—"

Adrienne gave way to a nervous little laugh.

"Then—her husband—"

The woman dropped her head on one side, and rubbed the tip of one finger up and down the edge of the tray.

"I don't want to say anything indiscreet—" she began at last.

"There's no question of that," said the girl, leaning across the counter. "Anything you say is between ourselves. I give you my word for that."

For the first time since she had entered the shop, Mlle. Grand now raised her lids and fixed her pale eyes on Adrienne. The two women looked at one another a moment.

"The gentleman seems to be rather generous with her," said the woman, again lowering her eyelids.

"Did she say so herself?"

"Yes," said Mlle. Grand in an almost inaudible voice.

One would have thought she was confessing a sin of her own.

"Mind you, she has never said the gentleman wasn't her husband, as you may well believe. But the thing is no secret here, however much she may think it is. Everybody knows it."

Adrienne was aghast. She remembered what her father had hinted about Mme. Legras. A hundred petty details whose significance had escaped her recurred to her now: the cosmetics her friend used so lavishly, her free and easy manner the very first time they had spoken, her voice! Everything that had disgusted her was explained by what she had just heard. How was it that she had not understood before? But could anyone credit the impudence of these creatures—not scrupling to appear in public—at the Sunday concerts! For Adrienne did not hesitate to place Mme. Legras in the most abject category of fallen women. Her forehead and cheeks blazed. Never had her pride received such a blow! To think she had made friends with a street-walker! Something thrilled in her. She was suddenly conscious of being a Mesurat—a Mesurat, but how dishonored, how soiled, almost! She put down her veil, picked up her gloves and the spool, and left the shop without another word.

As soon as she got outside the door she drew the spool out of her handbag and dropped it in the gutter.

A fine rain was falling noiselessly. It was not much more than a mist, but she opened her umbrella and began to run. She didn't care now who saw her. The great thing was to get home as quickly as possible.

When she was indoors she did not go to the trouble of taking off her hat and jacket. She sat down in a corner of the parlor, her lead bowed and her arms on her knees—the attitude of a woman in despair. What tore at her heart more than anything else was the feeling that she had been duped. It seemed to her that the humiliation would kill her. Doubtless Mme. Legras had gossiped around the town. Women of her sort always did. She must have exaggerated the intimacy between herself and Adrienne, and repeated a hundred things which the girl had had the unpardonable naïveté to confide. How everybody must be laughing and making fun of her!

She recalled Mme. Legras telling her fortune—Mme. Legras questioning her on her father's income. All these things corresponded so faithfully with the idea she entertained of women of Léontine's calling that she asked herself whether she had not been crazy not to understand earlier. And each fresh memory drew forth a groan of indignation.

Presently more serious considerations recurred to her which heightened her agitation. It was not likely that Mme. Legras had refrained from gossiping about M. Mesurat's death. What had she said about it? What part had she made the daughter play in her stories?

Adrienne rose and took several paces up and down the room.

Then, the suspicious manners of Mme. Legras—those ambiguous phrases of which she was so fond. What did all this mean—what did it really mean? To be sure, she had thought of these things before. But up to now she had gone no further than saying to herself, vaguely: "This is a treacherous woman: she's playing a double game," forbidding herself to follow the train of thought further, for fear of perceiving that she must deprive herself absolutely of the woman's company. Now she had come to herself at last. This had to end! Otherwise this woman would bring the whole town on her back—and have her arrested as a criminal. She said the word out loud, in an emphatic voice: "A criminal! Me!" The idea could not have shocked her more if it had been the first time she had given it a thought. Doubtless, she had heard Mme. Legras insinuate all manner of infamies, and had felt afraid of her. But had she ever really believed that this woman suspected her of murder? Surely not! If so, would she have gone every day to see her? Would she not sooner have taken to flight? Well, all doubt was over now. Mme. Legras was a woman of ill-fame, thus a creature capable of the most atrocious designs. What was she to do?

She leaned against the mantelpiece and put her hands over her eyes. Through the darkness she made for herself red flashes kept coming and going. It was raining harder. She heard the drops patter on the sill of the half-opened window. After a while her body grew too weak to support her upright and she sat down at the marble-topped card table. She had an impression of having lived alone in this house, not for a month, but for years. Do what she would, the image of her father appeared persistently before her eyes. She kept thinking: "Since my father's death—my father's death—" and it was as though the unspoken words flung a veil over the tragedy which prevented her from looking it in the face. The trite expression satisfied her because of the everyday aspect it gave to Mesurat's terrible end, repressing the sinister reality in her memory.

To keep it at an even greater distance, she let her thoughts run upon the doctor. From where she sat she saw the little white house, and gave herself up to the contemplation of a stretch of wall and an angle of its roof with the languid and somber joy of someone who has long fought temptation but has yielded at last. Behind these walls a man was living who had the power by a single word to make her happy forever. She summoned his image to her imagination. Why did she not go to see him—speak to him face to face? Why? Because she had waited too long and the right moment had passed. She said to herself, with the superstition of a soul whom loneliness has robbed of all hope, that the problems of her life were each predestined in advance by some occult power, and that there was only one right moment for each action. There had been some one hour, some one minute in the past, when she should have put on her hat, crossed the street, and rung the doorbell of the little white house. . . . Now, nothing was left her but to live on as best she might, with her useless regrets and the love which she had not known how to have triumph.

She made no fight. She suffered the memory of her former hopes to return and tear her apart. It even seemed to her that she was sinking toward the ultimate recesses of her unhappiness as toward a refuge. Once she had touched these, nothing more could reach her.

Moved by a sudden resolution, she got up and went to Germaine's old room. By going and sitting there at the window she would prove her strength—would show that she was now resigned and that the incertitude, born of a hope and of an apprehension that were both alike sad, had passed from her.

She entered the room, opened the window, and leaned out, her hands gripping the zinc gutter. Drops of rain fell on her neck. Her heart began to beat with the precipitous movement she had come to know so well, and whose repercussion seemed to shake her entire being. She looked at the little white house. As invariably happened, her glance travelled from the slate roof, glistening in the rain, to the treetop, which the lightest breeze caused to quiver. She would not look at the window yet. She reserved this as something that would be at once a supreme joy and a supreme test. She even forced herself not to see it.

Today there was someone at the window. Even while she was looking at the roof and the tree, she knew this, and knew, too, that her heart was beating faster for no other reason. This time, however, she did not draw in her head. She waited a few seconds, then lowered her gaze.

A child—a little boy twelve or thirteen years old—was leaning over the window bar and trying to reach the edge of the gutter with a toy whip. She held her breath and followed his movements. The child reached out his arm, grasping the whip handle in both hands. She could see only his head, but noticed he had black hair. His face was kept low, his mouth was probably against the bar. He was dressed in a blue-checked smock. A deep white collar that fell over it at the neck contrasted vividly with his black hair.

She waited motionless till the child left the window, then drew back and took a few steps into the room. The door was ajar; she shut it. Then she shut the window, too, and sat down upon a chair. She fulfilled every gesture, slowly, as though following some ritual. And suddenly, in the stifling silence of the little room, she abandoned herself to every sad thought she had struggled with, and tears streamed down her cheeks.

Chapter IV

A few minutes later she hurried downstairs. She had made up her mind that she would no longer stay in this house. The sight of these walls—of this furniture—of these mute witnesses, which recalled and revived her suffering incessantly, was making her too unbearably unhappy. She went into her own room, filled a little valise at random with a few necessities for travel, took a hundred francs from the olive-wood casket, and left the Villa des Charmes. Before leaving the house, she told Désirée that she would be away for a day or two.

She congratulated herself on her sudden act. Only five minutes ago she had been weeping in a stuffy room. Suddenly she had perceived that she was a fool to be weeping, a fool to let life overwhelm her without an effort to defend herself. And now she was on her way to the station, with a firm and rapid pace that exhilarated her, her bag in one hand, her open umbrella in another. It was still raining. As she walked she could hear the drops drumming on the tightly stretched silk, and tried to weave some kind of rhythm into the sound they made. It seemed to her that her attention to such petty things was a proof of her new freedom of spirit, and lifted her, in some queer fashion, above herself. Perhaps her fit of weeping had done her good. It had made her feel ashamed of herself, yet somehow stronger.

When she came in sight of the station she had to ask herself where she was headed. The train for Paris was not due for two and a half hours. In any case she did not want to go to Paris. She had been there several times and had brought back nothing but a disagreeable sensation of confusion and feverishness. In the waiting-room she looked over a timetable. In a quarter of an hour there would be a train for Montfort-l'Amaury. Something in the look of the name, and of a colored poster advertising the historic interest of the little town, pleased her. She bought a second-class ticket, and began to walk back and forth in the waiting-room and on the platform. A sudden animation took hold of her, and, as soon as she was quite alone, she began to utter sentences without finishing them. Anyone overhearing her would have thought them addressed to some weak companion who had to be encouraged and made to move.

"Let us be off," she said, half aloud, "quickly!" . . . She looked about her furtively and went on: "This has got to end. I won't stay here. I can't stay here."

Fearing she had spoken the last few words too loudly, she covered them with a cough. But there was no one near enough to hear. This made her laugh. She was stifling the sound with her handkerchief when the train was announced.

The few travellers who were waiting for it on the platform all got in third class, and she had no trouble in finding an empty compartment. As soon as she was seated on the blue cloth cushions and felt the train begin to move, first slowly, than faster and faster, she felt inclined to get up and burst into song. It was the first time she had ever travelled alone, and for the first time she felt she was really free. The inexplicable constraint which she suffered at Villa des Charmes was lifted from her shoulders. She would no longer have to fight with herself, no longer have to think of certain matters. As she watched the trees, the houses, all the odious landscape of La Tour l'Evêque fade away in the distance, a fullness rose in her throat. But it was something quite different from the anguish of a few minutes ago.

Her hat was pressing into her forehead. She took it off, and opened both windows to air the stuffy compartment. The wind blew through her hair. She threw her head back, listening to the regular vibrations of the train. The noise was not disagreeable to her. There seemed to be a hidden meaning in the dull rhythmic clang of the wheels, which found an echo within her like some sonorous phrase, continually repeated in order to fasten it in the memory forever. Finally she dropped off to sleep.

The train was entering the station at Montfort when she awoke, roused from her sleep by the halt and sudden quiet. She threw on her hat, clutched her umbrella and bag, and jumped out on the platform. A porter who noticed her looking about with a flurried and timid air showed her the exit.

She found herself on a square, surrounded by trees and sodden with rain. A white road whose end she could not see led straight toward the country, between woods and open fields. She went back into the station and asked a railwayman the way to the town. The man waved his arm in its direction and further informed her that it was half an hour's walk away, but that she could take a cab. Two or three were parked before the station doors.

She hesitated. The rain was still falling and showed no signs of ceasing before night. On the other hand, Adrienne's training made her look upon a carriage as a form of luxury. She calculated the cost rapidly. After all, the fare would come out of her savings and not out of the sum she drew month by month. This argument decided her. She made her way toward a *fiacre* in the rank and installed herself under its capacious leather hood, after directing the driver to take her to the town.

As far as the first houses of Montfort-l'Amaury the road is paved and bordered with trees. To right and left stretches the same open country, dull and melancholy beyond words upon a rainy afternoon. All that Adrienne could make out, by leaning forward on her seat, was an uninterrupted expanse of fields covered with green crops creased and tossed into furrows by the wind and rain. The horizon was bounded by an irregular screen of trees which seemed engaged in a fruitless effort to get together and make a wood. A colorless sky added its pallor to the desolation of the landscape.

She leaned back on the cushions and ceased to take notice of her surroundings. Presently, she perceived, by the slackened pace of the horse, that the carriage had turned into some sort of street. She leaned forward again, and saw a few children, attracted by the noise, who were peeping out from the doorways and following the carriage with eyes in which she thought she read distrust.

The driver reined in his horse in front of a church. After the noise of wheels and hoofs, the girl found the silence vaguely disagreeable. She got out. It was the lunch hour and the streets were deserted. As she paid her fare, she heard a cock crow from some yard nearby. Without knowing why, the ragged sound made her heart ache with sadness.

When the cab was out of sight, Adrienne remembered that she should have asked the driver to take her to some restaurant or hotel. She disliked the idea of going into a shop for the information she required and of disturbing people who were seated at a table. She turned at random into a street which descended rather steeply and which seemed to be the main artery of Montfort. The houses were so old and so still that she could not help gazing at them with a sort of half-frightened curiosity. She turned back and looked again at the church tower. Here and there its stones had assumed the very hue of the rain. It was patterned irregularly with a dark moss like seaweed. Under the rainy sky, at this silent hour when all life and motion seemed suspended, the girl had a confused impression that the old village was waiting for her and that she had been drawn to it by some secret and potent spell.

She began to walk again. A board at the intersection of two streets recommended a hotel, and a white arrow indicated that the way to reach it was to continue straight ahead. Soon Adrienne had left the farthest houses of the little town behind her, and was walking upon a country road bordered by trees and hedges.

She began to think she had made a mistake. But a second board repeated the instructions of the first, and she noticed, at a turn in the road, a long low house, rather poor in appearance, which bore between two windows at the height of the second story, the large black letters: Hotel Beauséjour.

The house had two doors. Adrienne knocked at one without obtaining any response. Through a window on the ground floor she could see a country *salle à manger* paved with red tiles. She waited a moment, then passed to the other door, and entered it without knocking. She was in a poorly lighted room. A long mirror framed in black fronted the door and cast a wan reflection upon the gloom. Leaning over a zinc counter, a workman in a blue cotton jacket was sipping a glass of wine and watching a little boy who sat drawing away busily at the far end of the room, his forearms on a marble table. Both turned their heads when they saw Adrienne.

"There's a customer!" shouted the workman to some one in the interior of the house.

Adrienne was making up her mind to go when a woman appeared in the frame of a doorway. She had gray hair, a fat white face, and was perhaps fifty years old. A blue apron covered her stomach tightly. She stood with her hands upon her hips.

"Do you want a room?" said she.

Without waiting for an answer she added, in an acid voice:

"We haven't got any left!"

"I want some lunch," said Adrienne.

"Good!" said the woman. "This way."

Adrienne followed her into the room that she had seen through the window.

"Do you want to eat now?" asked the proprietress.

"At once, please," answered Adrienne.

She sat down at a little table near the fireplace, and deposited her bag near her chair while the woman spread a cloth over the oilcloth-covered tabletop. It was cold in the empty dining room, but she was too tired to think either of complaining or of going elsewhere.

"If you really want a bedroom," said the landlady as she laid fork and spoon before the girl, "I have just one left. You have time to look at it before the soup is ready."

"Fine," assented Adrienne.

Picking up her valise, she followed the landlady. The two passed through a doorway at the end of the dining room, crossed a little courtyard, and mounted a wooden staircase between two walls painted green. As she labored up the stairs behind her guide, watching the worsted-clad ankles and the enormous heels which emerged at each swish of a gray skirt, an acute desire seized her to run away—to slip downstairs softly and take to the road again. How she would run! But she lacked strength of mind to carry out any such scheme.

On the first landing the woman pushed open a door and showed a room whose space was almost wholly taken up by an iron bedstead. She shut it again and remarked:

"That's let to some people from Paris."

She turned into a corridor as she spoke.

"That one, too," she added, with a jerk of her thumb in the direction of another door.

Arrived at a third door, she turned and looked Adrienne full in the eyes.

"I can let you have this one till tomorrow."

She opened the door. Before Adrienne's eyes was a square room containing a vast wooden bedstead. Through a little window near the ceiling could be seen a whitewashed wall and the tops of a few trees. A washbowl stood on a pine table.

"All right," said Adrienne.

She sat down her bag, lowering her eyes before the piercing gaze of the landlady.

"I'll take this room," she said.

When she came downstairs she saw the workman seated not far from the place she had chosen. He was eating and reading a newspaper. She sat down in turn and began to eat what was brought her. From time to time she could not resist casting a glance toward her neighbor. She liked having him there. It made her feel she was not altogether alone. Above a black marble mantelpiece a big almanac leaned against a mirror, which was getting discolored by time.

She ate very little, but, to warm her chilled body, drank some of the sour wine which was served her. Nothing broke the silence save the rustle of the newspaper, which the young workman continually folded and unfolded. At times he leaned over the sheet with a sort of avidity while carrying a morsel of food to his lips. He was a young man of about thirty, his face powdered with plaster, his eyes bright and inquisitive. He had a trick of brushing up his little fair mustache with the back of his hand, and he eyed Adrienne furtively from time to time. At one moment, just as the girl was assuring herself that he had not finished his meal and that he was not preparing to go, their eyes met. Realizing that he had surprised her, she blushed and turned away her head.

"Bad weather for travelling," said the man, lowering his newspaper.

Adrienne nodded.

"Probably you are not from these parts," he went on.

She bit her lips. Why on earth had she let her eyes wander? Wasn't it enough to be mixed up with a Mme. Legras, and to have drawn confidences from a woman in a draper's shop? Did she have to join in a conversation with a plasterer? A few seconds passed which seemed interminable.

The workman neither moved nor spoke. On her side she crossed her hands in her lap and sat absolutely still. Suddenly she heard her neighbor saying, in a deliberate and sarcastic voice:

"Madame is travelling?"

A short mocking little laugh followed, and a crackling of paper announced that he had shaken out his news sheet and was resuming the perusal of its columns. Adrienne straightened herself in her seat and sipped a little water.

Do what she would, she could not continue her meal. All the dishes seemed tasteless. The few mouthfuls she forced herself to swallow stuck in her throat and seemed likely to choke her. The stringy meat, the purée of potatoes mashed in water, disgusted her. Only the wine, with its acid tang, pleased her palate. She drank a glass of it.

She had been cold when she came in and now she was hot—almost too hot. She raised herself a little on her seat and in the dull looking-glass saw that her face was red. The blood mounted to her head and beat in her temples. She sat back. A sudden desire to weep took possession of her, but her eyes remained dry. It was not sadness that made her want to cry, but rage, and rage against herself. What was she doing in this restaurant? Was she any happier here than in the Villa des Charmes? Something seemed to be pressing her forehead just above the eyebrows. If she could only get her eyes to water, she was sure it would soothe her. But these vain attempts to give way to tears fatigued her. She leaned her elbow on the table, supported one burning cheek in her open hand, and closed her eyes. She had the impression that everything around her was being shifted like scenery. The noise made by the young workman every time he touched his plate with his fork reached the girl like some strange sound which the buzzing in her head prevented her identifying. This lasted a few moments. When she reopened her eyes they fell upon the menu, scrawled in violet ink. She looked at it without being able to decipher a word. Suddenly an idea flashed across her brain. She had noticed a pencil upon the mantelpiece just now. She reached for it, turned the menu over and began to write upon the back:

"Monsieur . . ."

She drew her pencil through the word slowly, as though thinking of something else, then crossed it out vigorously until it was quite obliterated, and wrote these words hastily:

Here, at Montfort, on the 11th of July, 1908, I was more unhappy than I have ever been in my life. I was unhappy on your account. Will you never have pity on me?

By now tears were running down her face. She folded the paper and put it in her corsage. The words which she had just written were in some way a release, and she felt a little better. She heaved a sigh and blew her nose.

When the landlady entered, carrying a morsel of cheese and a plate of fruit, Adrienne told her, in quite a firm voice, that she had changed her mind and would not stay for the night. The weather, she added, was too bad. Without touching her dessert, she paid her bill and went upstairs to get her valise.

As she looked at the whitewashed walls of the little room, she had a thrill of joy, as of escaping a danger. She enjoyed thinking how horrible it would all look when she was far away. Night would come slowly through that window, whose panes, so high up on the wall, allowed only a view of a long wall and a few trees, glistening in the rain. What hours would have been hers, under the red quilt, in that room at the back of a solitary house, already so gloomy under the lowering sky! She caught up her luggage and ran out.

As she crossed the dining room afresh on her way to the door, the landlady was talking to the young workman as she served him his coffee. She did not look at them, but knew that their eyes were following her with hostile curiosity. She caught a few words uttered by the woman:

"I was sure of it—that girl—!"

Chapter V

She opened her umbrella and, despite her fatigue, began to run. She was surprised at finding herself able to go so fast and to take such long strides. It was for all the world as though she were being carried along by a motivating force of which she was no longer mistress, as though she were flying before someone whose footsteps she could hear at her back. In a few minutes she reached the church, and looked at it hastily under the drenched silk of her umbrella. Those green stones over which a deluge seemed to have passed, that pavement pelted by the rain, suddenly seemed things so strange and remote from herself that she received an actual shock. All at once she received an impression unexperienced till now—a sense of the complete indifference of all these things to the drama that was being enacted within her, the indifference of that church and square to her suffering, the indifference of millions of human creatures to her fate. Her heart sank at the thought of her solitude. She crossed the square and entered a café just to find someone to speak to.

There was no one, and she would have been surprised had there been. This cold, mean town, as though reluctant to let its people be seen, hid them in the recesses of its houses. She called aloud, and after a brief interval a man appeared. He had jumped up from the table and was wiping his mouth as he entered. Resentment at having been disturbed was visible in his face.

"What can I do for you?"

"Where can I hire a cab?"

"Are you going to the station? Wait till four o'clock. They all go to meet the train from Dreux."

"I want one now," said Adrienne. "Where can I find it?"

The man rested his fist on the marble top of a table.

"I hire out the cabs," said he, in an impatient voice. "There is no train for Paris before four."

"I'm not going to Paris," said Adrienne, who was growing impatient herself. "I'm going to Dreux."

She had made the decision on the spur of the moment, and added, "There is a train for Dreux at two o'clock."

The man looked at her for a moment, shrugged his shoulders, and turned his back upon her.

"A trip like that isn't worthwhile," he grumbled as he disappeared through the door. "I should want my return fare paid."

She picked up her bag, which she had put upon a table nearby, and down whose leather sides water was trickling. Anguish took her by the throat. The long road which she had to travel by foot seemed too rough an ordeal, yet one that she would have to accept. The quicker the better! She left the café and almost ran across the square. She had noticed that the faster she went the less she felt her fatigue.

The rain stopped as Adrienne left the village and entered upon the state road. A fresh breeze was blowing, but the wheat, its ears now heavy with rain, hardly stirred. Along the ditches, however, the short grass blew this way and that, like hair through which invisible fingers were being passed. Profound silence lay upon the deserted country. The girl walked on, keeping her head down for fear the length of the road might discourage her, and resolved not to raise her eyes till she was in front of the station. To occupy her mind she counted each click of her heels on the paved road. Sometimes she shifted her bag from one hand to another. But soon her reflections robbed her of all sense of motion or fatigue, and she arrived at the station much more quickly than she had expected.

There was no train to Dreux till three o'clock, and she had to wait in a *buvette* outside the station. It was a little house, newly built, where nothing had had time to get dirty. The billiard table smelled of varnish. The marble tops of the tables had not lost their polish. On one of these was a rack of postcards that squeaked on its axis as she pushed it around with her finger. Adrienne sat down near these postcards, after ordering a cup of coffee and taking off her hat, which she shook free of rain underneath the table as soon as she was alone. The pain in her head beat against her temples and forehead by turns, like some trapped and terrified bird. Her drenched clothing clung to her body and she shivered occasionally. To pass the time away she began to examine the postcards, and could not help noticing what a false idea they gave of Montfort. What could be gayer than these old streets lined with leafy trees? And this church—which she had seen livid and sinister under the rainy sky—how innocent it all seemed! She chose a postcard of the church. Without hesitating a moment, and as though she were accomplishing a natural and half-conscious gesture, she turned it over and wrote the doctor's address on it. It was the first time she had ever written his name, and when she had finished the address she stopped, dumbfounded at what lay beneath her eyes.

The idea then struck her to write to the doctor—to send him this postcard without any signature. In this way she could tell him everything, no matter what. He would never know who sent it. Why had she not thought of it before? She might tell him she loved him—liberate herself from the weight stifling her.

When the waitress brought her her coffee, she asked for an envelope and began to write as follows:

"I love you. You have no idea of it, but if you knew all I have suffered on your account, I know you would pity me."

Here she stopped. The words expressed very imperfectly what she felt. She had not thought that it would be difficult, at the very start, to give adequate utterance to an emotion she felt so strongly.

"I am so unhappy that this alone should make you love me."

But this phrase rang false to her the moment she had written it down, and she murmured, "Why?"

"What does it matter?" she asked herself. "He will never know who wrote him the card."

"I love you," she wrote on; "that is all I can write. But my heart is full of you. I am thinking of you always, and crying my eyes out."

As she wrote these last words she began to cry in real earnest.

She took the envelope the girl brought her, and wrote the address, a second time, upon it. Then she drank her coffee and awaited the arrival of her train.

Dreux is a small town, but in it are held the most important markets of the district. When Adrienne had walked down the street from the station and reached the town hall, she had to pick her way between a number of carts which blocked the street and filled an entire corner of the square. Drovers dressed in smocks were talking together in groups around calves and pigs whose fates were being sealed in interminable discussions. The sidewalks were crowded with peasant women, who offered their chickens for the inspection of the passers-by. In spite of the mud and puddles of brown water which the saturated ground could no longer absorb, the center of the square was given over to stalls loaded with vegetables and dry goods. An indifferent crowd strolled between the displays, invited to buy by monotonous cries which they gave no sign of hearing.

Adrienne took her time in crossing the square. She liked the sensation of being jostled by people whom she had never seen before and who forced her to follow the stream and to trudge with them through the mud. It was for all the world as though she were taking part in a procession in which she lost her identity, forgot her cares and everything else that marked her out from the rest of the world, to become like these men and women with clenched faces. She even felt that her own face had assumed the expression, dull and suspicious at the same time, which she saw on every hand. Without her knowing why, this state of mind was an inexpressible relief.

Imperceptively she had drifted toward a squat building, decorated with statues, which she assumed to be a church. Beside it a street opened off. She followed this, still dazed by the tumult of the market, casting her eyes to right and left with a mechanical interest which made her say to herself, "Look! here is a jeweler's, there's a bakery," as though she felt in conscience bound to utilize her excursion and miss no source of information.

In that late and sunless afternoon, the houses of the main street, their window blinds pulled up to the top so as to lose no single gleam of a light which cost nothing, had a desolate air. On nearly every door a little brass plate bore some name or other in thin script and seemed to be guarding the threshold from any intrusion by a stranger. The steep pitched roofs came down low over the windows of the upper stories, like a hat pulled over the eyes to avoid recognition. The same expression of mistrust seemed to rest upon the house fronts that Adrienne had just noticed upon the faces in the market square. She felt it and quickened her pace. Not for anything in the world would she have asked to be directed to a hotel. She preferred to seek it unguided, even if this meant enduring the mute, almost hostile glances of the passers-by, who saw she was a stranger.

At the top of the street she found what she was looking for. It was a house larger but meaner than its neighbors, which an open door robbed of all character. She threw a glance over its façade. A name in letters of an exaggerated size proclaimed it a hotel, and rows of narrow windows crowded closely together lent an air of fragility to the entire edifice. She entered. In the vestibule a bluish gas jet was making darkness visible. She followed a long corridor and came to a desk where a fat woman sat reading, holding her newspaper close to a lamp. It seemed to the girl that she was now fairly committed to a labyrinth from which there could be no return. Through a half-open door she perceived a long dining room. It was full of the gathering dusk but her eyes made out a number of little tables, spread with white tablecloths and grouped around an immense oval table reserved for transient guests. It was as though something said in her ear: "There's a place for you!" She asked for a room.

The fat lady threw her a number and held out a key to an attendant, who took Adrienne's valise and turned up a staircase. Adrienne followed him. They climbed two flights, following another passage, and stopped before a door which the boy opened.

"There you are," said he, setting down the bag at the foot of a bed.

Adrienne had a violent struggle with herself before she could enter. The narrow room, carpeted in dull red, seemed frightful to her. As she stepped over the threshold, she recalled, without any apparent reason, the child's face, pale and almost chalk-white, which she had seen at the doctor's window. She had an indefinable impression that the boy was coming into the room with her.

When the boy had shut the door behind him, she walked to the end of the room and stood erect, her hand upon a little table just under the window. All she could see were the roofs of the houses opposite and a livid sky which was growing darker momentarily. Her heart sank; she felt tears fill her eyes, but mastered her emotion. "I mustn't let myself go," she murmured. Her fingertips sank into the plush cover of the table; she did not like the sensation and withdrew her hands, holding them in the air as though seeking something pleasanter on which to rest them. She sat down in an armchair with a stuffed back and looked around her at the furniture. The greater part of the room was taken up by an iron bedstead, painted black and covered with a red eiderdown quilt. In another corner, nearer the door, was a small wardrobe—the kind that big furniture factories turn out by tens of thousands. A mirror in its door reflected the squalid image of a wall papered in red and pink stripes and a washbowl on a sort of iron tripod. And this was all. A dusty smell came from the carpet and curtains.

Adrienne rose to her feet. She was unwilling to let herself be overcome by the sordid melancholy of the room. She was tired out now and did not have the strength to look for anything better. It was already past five. After a few moments' thought she opened the window slightly, took off her shoes, and stretched herself on the bed to rest.

She drew the eiderdown quilt over her and tried hard to sleep. But her head ached. For some minutes an idea she had had more or less all the afternoon had been refusing to leave her head. Why did she feel so warm? Was it fever? Her cheeks were burning. Just now, in the street, she had been shivering. But the open air was cold. Why was she still shivering, under this heavy quilt, stuffed with feathers?

"Oh, come—come!" she repeated to herself, as though to drive away the thought which was haunting her. But she could not rid herself of it. The harder she tried, the more she felt herself invaded by an abject and growing terror. She shut her eyes, crossed her hands upon her breast under the quilt, and tried to force herself to think of something else. But her imagination refused to obey her will and dragged her to the thoughts she most feared. Suddenly the girl pressed her face into the pillow and covered her ears with her hands. Too many memories besieged her, stifled her. She would have given anything to fall into a deep sleep, to lose consciousness for hours—no, for days, if only she could have escaped from a vision which had pursued her since her lunch and which had her at last completely in its grip.

She recalled her sister the morning of her flight from home. Under the ill-fitting hat, which wobbled about on her head, she saw Germaine's hectic face, flushed with fever. The eyes, rimmed with black, looked as if they had been filled with tears. But you could see they were quite dry.

Were they, though? Had there not been a moment when Germaine was on the point of hanging her head to one side, of stretching out her arms and bursting into tears? And Adrienne had shrunk away rather than let that sick woman touch her or breathe near her face.

All of a sudden, the words which she had been keeping out of her consciousness flew to her lips and escaped in a groan: "I've caught Germaine's disease." She twisted and writhed on the bed, arching her back and carrying her clenched fists to her mouth. Her head wagged from side to side upon the pillow in a gesture of obstinate resistance. Little cries broke from her which she tried vainly to smother with her handkerchief.

She jumped from the bed and ran to the wardrobe. Her cheeks were flushed and the disorder of her rumpled hair added to her air of consternation. Tears were trembling on the points of her eyelashes. For a moment she looked at herself in the mirror and then walked to the window. It had grown much darker, but not a shop-front was lighted up as yet. Groups of people were coming back from market without exchanging a word between them. An echo in the street redoubled the monotonous sound of their hobnailed shoes on the cobblestones. She pushed up the window to its full height and leaned out. An abominable melancholy seemed to weigh on the whole place. Nevertheless, she could not run away now. She was caught. She must stay in Dreux, pass a whole long night in this town! Why had she ever left La Tour l'Evêque? But—no! It seemed to her that she had made the journey in spite of herself and that some all-powerful force had coerced her.

As she let one hand fall down at her side, she realized that her clothing was damp. In her confusion she had never thought of this. The sleeves and shoulders of her jacket, which she had not yet taken off, were wet through. She moved her feet. They were icy cold. The idea crossed her mind of taking off every stitch of clothing, rubbing herself down with a towel, and getting into bed. But the prospect of remaining shut up in that room till morning was too terrible. She resolved to go out, and to buy some medicine at a drugstore. She grew calmer after reaching this decision. At least she would be able to talk to someone and relieve her mind a little.

She folded some paper and slipped it inside her shoes before putting them on again, for they were soaked through. Then she went out.

It was not as cold as she had imagined, and the pavement was already dry. After following the main street a few yards she found a pharmacy and pushed open the door resolutely. The desire to be reassured, to be cured if it were possible, overcame her timidity. There was not a moment to be lost. But as soon as she stood in the presence of the pharmacist, who was an old man, she could not think of anything to say. How could she explain her fears to him? He would send her to see a doctor. Finally she told the man she had a cold. She regretted the words the moment they were out of her mouth. Why had she not told the truth? Perhaps this lie would seal her fate.

"Do you think it's serious?" she asked, her head buzzing as she spoke.

The old man looked at her as though she were demented.

"Serious?" he repeated. "How long have you had it?"

She explained that she had had a temperature since midday. He lowered his head and disappeared behind a great cabinet covered with boxes and bottles. For a minute or so she heard the sound of drawers being opened and the clink of weights in scales. The druggist was a frail man, stooped with age, and with an irritating precision in his every movement. She sat down—then got up and looked at him between the bottles. On a slip of paper he had put a little white powder and was letting it fall into one side of his scales slowly and carefully.

"I suppose it's nothing," the girl said. Her voice shook slightly from anxiety.

He did not answer immediately.

"I am going to give you a syrup," he said at length when he had finished weighing his powder.

A few moments passed. He made up the packet, sealed it, wrote some directions on it in an illegible hand, then took down a bottle filled with gooseberry-colored liquid and examined its label.

"You don't think it will last, then?" said Adrienne, with an effort to appear indifferent.

He laid one hand on the bottle and looked at her suspiciously, almost as though he feared she might change her mind and buy nothing.

"That will depend on how well you look after yourself," he said. "These things have to be stopped at the beginning."

"But I am taking it in time," answered Adrienne, laughing, as though to apologize for an anxiety that must have seemed so childish.

"Are you afraid it's something more than a cold? Have you been to see a doctor?"

She shook her head.

"Oh, I'm not so sick as all that!" she said.

The phrase sounded in her ears like a passing bell. How often she had heard it on Germaine's lips! She took the bottle from the druggist's hand and asked how much she was to pay.

"Four francs," said the man, adding, as Adrienne could not altogether conceal her surprise: "The most serious illness has a small beginning. What you spend at one end, you save at the other. With the syrup and the powder I've given you, you can be quite easy in your mind."

This was what she wanted to be told. She paid for her medicine and left the shop.

She was still sitting at the little table, where she had been put, near a window, though it was some time since she had finished dinner. She could not yet make up her mind to get up and go to her room along all those narrow corridors. Even before dinner she had felt too weak, and had passed an hour in a badly lighted dining room, watching the guests come in one by one, look at her inquisitively, and take their places, after having turned over a pile of magazines which were strewn upon a table of imitation ebony.

She had taken her syrup and powder and felt better. The druggist's words had somewhat calmed her fears. But her nerves were on edge from the loneliness in which she had spent the day since morning. Over and over again, the same question kept forming in her mind. Why was she here? What had she gained by flying from La Tour l'Evêque?

The guests left the room one after another. One young man wearing an eyeglass nodded slightly as he passed her. She bowed in return. She would have been glad to speak to anyone—even to the man who waited on her, and who looked across the room at her now and then as though to hint that it was late and high time she went away—even to the young workman from Montfort, if he had been here now.

She got up at last, and as she walked toward the door the idea entered her mind to go out again. It had not been raining for some hours and her clothes were dry. At least this would defer the dreadful hour when she would have to go back to her bedroom. She put on her gloves, deposited the bottle and packet of powder at the desk, and left the hotel.

Once outside, she congratulated herself on her idea of taking a walk. It was not nine yet, and a splendid night. The street was steeped in that strange light which a full moon gives, so white as to be almost green. Not a cloud was in the sky, and as though out of respect for the magnificent spectacle, the town was plunged in silence.

Adrienne walked down the street without meeting a soul. When she reached the market she stopped, amazed at the change which had come over a place which had seemed to her so ugly and dismal before. The vegetable and dry goods stalls had been taken away, and the carts had vanished. The entire square was empty, covered with pools in which the reflected moon seemed to be slowly swimming. Toward the north the square was bounded by a modern building; elsewhere small houses and trees made a sort of girdle around it as far as the building that Adrienne, on account of the statues which decorated it, had taken for a church, but which was really the remains of an old town hall. It strongly resembled the keep of a castle crowned with a pointed turret, and, under the moonlight, had a romantic air which struck the girl's imagination.

The beauty of the scene took hold of her and gave her momentary peace, during which she forgot her cares. For a few seconds she stood stockstill, unwilling to mar the magic silence of the night with her footsteps. By a sudden trick of memory, the thought of certain days in her childhood came back to her. Yes, there had been days when she tasted happiness. She had not known it at the time. She had been destined to wait for this hour of her life to realize it. It had needed this ruined tower bathed in moonlight to recall a hundred forgotten things to her memory—walks she had taken in the country through the fields, or talks that she had had with her schoolmates in the garden of the *cours* Ste.-Cécile. These memories came back to her in no particular order, but so vividly that each one gave her a pang. This evening she was so weak that even very little sufficed to affect her. Why did she know nothing now of the happiness given so lavishly to others? A sort of sorrowful impulse turned her desires toward that boon which was no longer hers and which memory rendered still more beautiful and more desirable.

She heaved a sigh and took a few steps on the sidewalk which surrounded the square. The clock on the town hall sounded ten strokes, followed immediately afterward by a bell above the church. Dogs began to bark from afar. She stopped and raised her eyes to the stars. There were so many that even when she chose one little portion of the sky, she lost count of them. The myriad points of light trembled before her eyes like the petals of so many white blossoms on the surface of a black lake. She remembered a song they used to sing in class:

. . . le ciel semé d'étoiles. . . .

She remembered how the voice had to be raised when she came to the word "*é-toi-les,*" and from the three notes that followed, so difficult to hold and so distant today, expressed a poignant nostalgia that tore her heart as she recalled them. She put her hands to her face and wept.

A few moments afterward she began to walk again. She took a curve which gave upon the square, and which she concluded must be the main street. But she quickly perceived she had made a mistake. The street which she was following led out of the town. She turned back and took another street, at the end of which she could see the outline of the big tower. In order to be quite sure, she resolved to return to the square. From there it would be easier to find her way back.

As she walked on slowly, and not at all anxious to return to her room, she passed in front of a café. A workman was just coming out. He was quite young. She had just time to see his face in the flare of coarse light. His cheeks were beardless and rather thin; the whites of his eyes glistened. He stopped when he saw her and stood looking at her, his hands in his pockets. She crossed the road at once and was quickening her pace when she realized he was following her. He walked quickly, and his feet, shod in espadrilles, made hardly any noise on the stones. He did not say a word, and this terrified her all the more. It seemed to her that she would have been less frightened had the man shouted out some insult or some threat. For a moment she had the idea of calling for help, but the fear of ridicule restrained her. For the same reason she did not dare break into a run. Perhaps this would only make the man more enterprising. She hurried on, taking longer and longer strides, and instead of keeping straight toward the square, took to an alley, the first she found on her right.

It was here her pursuer caught up with her. She turned on her heel, her back to the wall, and spoke breathlessly.

"Go away!"

But he remained standing in front of her. His cap was on one side of his head, and showed a lock of black hair which shone like metal. He had strongly marked features; his eyes, as far as she could make them out, were black. A red handkerchief, knotted negligently round his throat, accentuated the whiteness of his skin. He gave a smothered laugh.

"What are you afraid of?" he asked.

Adrienne clenched her hand on the handle of her umbrella.

"Leave me alone, or I'll shout!"

The young man looked at her for a moment, then shrugged his shoulders.

"I didn't want to hurt you," he said.

With that he took himself off. She heard him walk away farther and farther. He was whistling a popular waltz. At first she congratulated herself on having got off so well. But suddenly an immense regret invaded her heart. Out of the loneliness someone had come to her, and she had driven him away! Just because he wore a jumper and had spoken to her without knowing her! How could she have done such a thing? She recalled his voice, so grave and a little tender, as something irremediably lost that she would never find again. If the man should come back she would certainly speak to him. But would he come back? Had she not discouraged him once and for all?

She followed the alley in the direction he had taken. But when she arrived at its end she found herself facing two streets that branched off in different directions. She listened, but could not hear a sound. He was no longer whistling. She took one of the branches more or less at random and walked more quickly. Her heart began to palpitate. "If I come across him again," she said to herself, "he will speak to me and I'll answer him." By a detour she had not foreseen the street brought her back to the square. A glance around her showed her that no one was in sight. He must have taken the other direction. Perhaps if she ran back she might still find him. Run back! The thought brought her to a sense of what she was about. It seemed to her that Germaine's suspicious eyes rested on her. Panting a little, she leaned against the iron bars of a butcher's shop. Now she was actually doing what her father and sister had once falsely accused her of. She was running after a man! It seemed to her that her action had some mysterious connection with the squalor of the scene she had endured when the old man and the sick woman cross-examined her, tortured her, and when, at the bottom of their eyes, she had divined the filthy thoughts which their lips did not dare express. Suddenly, another thought swept away all her scruples. She saw herself in a solitude to which no words could do justice, deprived of the most innocent friendships. She had had no wish to do wrong—merely to speak and to hear the sound of a voice answering hers—merely not to be forced to return to her hotel without having broken the silence of a whole day save with *"merci"* and *"bonjour."* The very thought of the room where she would have to spend the night seemed sufficient excuse for what she had been about to do.

She ceased examining her conscience and continued her pursuit, choosing a street which she judged would bring her nearer to her cavalier. She broke into a run and found it saved her from thinking. In the silence of the night her steps rang out with a sound that frightened her, and she tried to keep upon her toes. Moment by moment, fatigue grew upon her. Soon she had lost her way and realized she was going altogether at random and that it was useless to keep on. Nevertheless, she did not stop. She followed the street she was walking on to its end, took another, and found herself upon a sort of walk planted with plane trees whose thick foliage diffused the fresh cool smell of the rain. She stopped at the sight of the drenched soil, full of puddles, and sat down on a bench.

Her heart was beating painfully, with great thuds that shook her body from head to foot. She could feel its violence in her stomach and in the arteries of her neck. "I ran too quickly," she panted. She bent over double, joined her two hands upon the handle of her umbrella, whose ferrule she had planted in the soft ground, and leaned forward like a worn-out old woman. She looked stupidly at the mud on her boots and at the hem of her black serge dress, all splashed and draggled. The breath escaped from her parted lips like a moan; her tongue was dry and rough. She remained so for some minutes, incapable of getting up despite the chill on her body and the cold air which was drying the drops of sweat as they trickled down from face to neck. A horrible fatigue bent her shoulders. It was as though someone had driven the point of a sharpened stake into each shoulder blade. Her head was empty.

She got up at last and, without knowing how she did it, found the way back to the hotel.

She asked for her bottle and her powder at the desk, and climbed slowly to her room. Putting down her medicine on the first spot that came under her hand, she flung herself upon the bed without even troubling to light the gas. Never had she so longed for sleep. Although the least movement cost her an effort, she blessed her physical weariness, thanks to which there was a comforting confusion in her brain. She was absolutely incapable of uttering an intelligible sentence.

Almost at once she fell into a deep sleep. She had thrown herself upon the eiderdown quilt, and under the weight of her body it puffed out all about her in a sort of series of rounded and motionless waves. As she laid her head upon the pillow, her hat had fallen back. She had pulled her legs up under her. Her arms were stretched out straight and one hand rested upon another. Everything in her posture was eloquent of complete exhaustion. She breathed heavily, her face half buried in the pillow, but from time to time her bosom heaved as if her lungs were making a futile effort to fill with air.

The shutters had not been closed and the moonlight entered the room freely. It lay upon the floor at the bottom of the bed in a long rectangle and gave the carpet that strange hue which seems to be compounded of several dead colors. Not a sound reached to where she slept, either from outside or from the interior of the house.

Adrienne had been asleep half an hour when she saw Germaine enter the room. She had not heard the door open, but she quite clearly saw her sister pass near her bed. Germaine did not look at her, but walked with a measured tread toward the mantelpiece where Adrienne had laid down her medicine, took up the bottle and examined it closely. She was dressed in black, as usual, and her head was bare. On her face was an indefinable expression somewhat resembling a smile, but was more the look of someone who recognizes a familiar object. She took the bottle of syrup in both hands and seemed either to be trying to decipher the label or to make out the color of the liquid. After a few moments she shook her head and, for the first time, looked in Adrienne's direction. She stood with her back to the light and the girl could not clearly see the face turned toward her. A few moments passed. The woman did not move. She continued holding up the bottle so that the light passed through and showed how much had been drunk. At last she put it back on the mantelpiece very carefully and as though she feared breaking the silence of the night. For the packet of powder at its side she scarcely spared a glance.

Then she passed to the window and assured herself that it was closed.

She stood directly between the brown plush curtains, and her shadow did not move, stretched out on the long rectangle like a corpse in a coffin, much taller than Germaine, who seemed quite small. She seemed absorbed in her contemplation of the black sky, whose every star was visible through the net casement curtains. The moonlight shone on her shoulders and on her hair, carefully combed. Some time passed without her making a movement, though Adrienne could hear the sound she made as she rubbed one hand stealthily against the other, without moving her elbows in the slightest.

She had all the air of waiting for something or someone. Suddenly she turned around sharply as though the door had opened behind her, and walked with a rapid step toward the part of the room where Adrienne lay, like someone going to meet a new arrival. It was at this moment that Adrienne made out her face. It was ghastly pale and she walked with her eyes closed. Earth clung to her hair and was sprinkled on the bosom of her dress. At every step she took some of it fell on the carpet, but always came back as though an invisible and insulting hand were throwing it in her face. She stopped a moment close to the young girl. Her hands were clasped and she made no movement of any sort with them.

Two or three minutes passed. The door had not opened, but Adrienne knew quite well that someone else had come in. She realized it from her sister's lips, which moved in speech without a sound being audible. Then she knew that this someone had passed between Germaine and the bed, and saw her sister walk over to the wardrobe. She remained in front of it quite a long time, speaking, explaining something to the invisible being who was standing at her side, and who the girl felt could only be her father. At this moment Adrienne struggled so hard that she awoke.

She sat up in bed and looked around her. Cries rose in her throat, but nothing came out except a kind of rattling noise. She was amazed to see no difference between this real room and the room of her dream. Her eyes roamed around her, seeking Germaine in the wardrobe mirror, looking for her shadow in the rectangle of moonlight upon the carpet. When she was thoroughly awake and her anguish a little less, she jumped from her bed and lit the gas. It was barely eleven o'clock. She filled the washbowl with water and bathed her face. The mirror frightened her. She opened the door of the wardrobe and hung the shawl which she was wearing over it, hiding the glass which terrified her.

"I was too hot," she said to herself. "I should not have lain down without taking off my clothes. What a nightmare!"

She began to laugh. The window had not been opened for five or six hours and the air in the room was close. She was still breathing hard, as in her dream. Suddenly she coughed. She jumped up and looked at herself in the glass over the mantelpiece. The blood had left her face. In the gas-light her cheeks looked blue-green. She coughed again, watching her reflection as she did so, and the sight filled her with unutterable terror.

"It's begun," she said under her breath. "The first coughing spell!"

She thought a moment, then seized the bottle of syrup which stood in front of her and put it to her lips. The thick liquid sickened her, but she swallowed a little, then looked at the label with an air of infinite disgust. As she put the bottle back on the mantelpiece, she glanced toward the mirror and saw that the door of the wardrobe had swung wide open. She was not prepared for this and uttered a cry, but smothered it instantly with her hand. What would people think who heard her? The thought that she had neighbors comforted her a little. But almost instantly the certitude that she had none entered her mind.

"I'm all alone on this floor," she said to herself.

She listened a moment to the roar the gas-jet was making as it burned on in a ground-glass globe at the end of a chandelier that hung from the ceiling, then began to undress quickly. As she raised her hands to unfasten the hooks at the back of her blouse, she had an impression that she had already made exactly the same gesture, in circumstances absolutely similar, and stood before the mirror, rooted to the spot by a memory whose origin she could not recall and which for that very reason terrified her even more. The crude yellow gaslight fell on her face and gave it a theatrical aspect. Her mouth hung open. She remained this way for several seconds, with her elbows raised above her head, fearing now to make the least movement. The gas-jet flared on with a sort of busy and continuous drone that filled the silence and in some inexplicable fashion seemed to be a part of it.

She took down her hair and made an effort to shake off the torpor which was invading her brain. There must surely have been opium in the medicine she had drunk! It seemed to her that, even if she stayed awake, the nightmare she had just had would begin afresh. On the other hand, if she went to sleep, the vision that had just terrified her would be waiting for her. The thought made her tremble. She asked herself desperately how she was going to get through the night.

Little by little she felt a fear creeping over her against which her own will was powerless. Everything in the room around her sickened her or frightened her; the wardrobe, whether opened or shut, was horrible to her for the memories it aroused. She tried not to look at the little armchair against whose upholstered back Germaine's skirt had brushed just now. The mere idea of going back to the bed where she had almost fainted from terror was unthinkable. The farther she got from her dream, the more actual it seemed. She lived over every moment of it. She knew that she would need only to close her eyes to have her sister's face next to hers and to feel the presence of that other being whom Germaine had come here to meet.

Her heart beat violently. Suddenly she put her back to the wall and turned her face to the room. Now no one could possibly pass behind her. But, no sooner had she done this than she understood her mistake. Far from abating her terror, it only carried it to a new extremity. She should not have admitted to herself that she was afraid. For a moment she stood there, the palms of her hands pressed against the wall, listening to the remotest stir, and nearly out of her senses. The sound of her own breathing disturbed her; she thought she could recognize in it the sound of someone else breathing thickly and hoarsely.

A clock somewhere in the town chimed half past eleven. Five hours at least to wait till dawn! Why had she not spent the night on her bench, under the plane trees? The idea even entered her head of dressing, packing her bag, and leaving the hotel. She could always say at the desk that the bed was not clean. But courage to do this failed her. An unconquerable desire to sleep made her head nod. Each time it fell forward on her breast, she felt that her whole body was following it—and falling! Each time this happened she pulled herself together and shook her hair from side to side with a frantic gesture.

Finally she decided to put on a wrap and to open the window. The cold air on her face revived her. She took a railroad guide from her bag and turned its pages over without being able to find the place she wanted. All sorts of images floated through her brain, until she even forgot what she was looking for in the little book, whose flimsy leaves slipped between her trembling fingers. The face of the doctor came back to her, as he had

178

looked at her from the seat of the carriage. But it would not stay in her head. It was as though the fear within her kept her from dwelling on the sole thought in which she found a little comfort.

"That's the real trouble!" she said to herself.

She felt her knees tremble, and sought to recall the face of the young workman who had followed her. How moist his lips were! She remembered how they moved as he spoke, showing the white uneven teeth. Then something quite different and far stronger than these confused memories that she was trying to evoke rose tumultuously within her. Her pulse beat against her temples with blow after blow that rang through her head. She believed she was about to fall, and caught hold of the bedstead. Now she was quite sure there was someone behind her! As once before, she could hear a respiration much too strong to be hers just over her shoulder. The railway guide slipped from her; she let it fall upon the carpet and buried her face in her hands.

Part Three

Chapter I

It was early in the morning when Adrienne reached home. Désirée had not yet arrived. She entered the parlor and opened the windows. She sighed as her eye fell upon the trees in the Legras garden. Was it twenty-four hours ago—or a month—since she had last looked on them? How little everything was changed!

There was a postcard from Mme. Legras on the little marble-topped table. She read it at once:

> My dear [said her old friend], you are going to celebrate the 14th with me. I shall be back tomorrow, the 12th. M. Legras's business is going better than I thought. Love. Léontine.

She tore the card into little pieces and flung them into the grate. There was another letter on the table. She recognized the writing and put on her gloves again before opening the envelope.

> Mademoiselle [the letter began. It was from the superior of the hospital where her sister was being nursed. Adrienne stopped at the first

words and recalled her dream. Her hands trembled with emotion, but she went on reading]: Happily I have no bad news to give you of your sister's health; but that is all I can say. We still hope that the air here will give her a little strength and that her appetite will come back. It is something to be able to say that she is no worse.

She begs me to let you know that she has changed her mind in regard to money matters, and that you need not forward her the money she asked you to send. She has written to the lawyer, who will forward her whatever sums she needs. So this trouble is off your hands. She adds, very reasonably as it seems to me, if I am permitted to express an opinion in the matter, that the sum which has been assigned to you seems larger than your circumstances demand, and she has written Maître Biraud to this effect. Do not be surprised, therefore, if this month you receive a hundred francs less than last.

Adrienne did not go on with the letter. She laid it on the table and bit her lips. She wore a harassed air. Little dark circles around her eyes made them seem brighter, but the rest of her face expressed a profound bitterness. She dropped her head and remained motionless for a few seconds, looking intently at a ray of sunshine which was lengthening along the carpet. Then she heaved a sigh and began to pace back and forth in the room.

It was cool, but the sun promised a fine hot day. A blackbird was trilling in one of the low trees in the garden. Sometimes he stopped as if to think of a new tune. But whenever he began again, it was always with the same joyous scale, lingering on the final note with a sort of rapturous vanity. The girl stood for a moment before the window, attracted vaguely by the song, which recalled many things to her mind. Since her father's death she had fallen into the habit of continually returning to the past—her childhood especially. She would sink into a profound reverie, letting her mind wander wherever memory chose to carry it. Blackbirds came into the garden nearly every summer, early in the morning when there was nobody about. They made themselves quite at home and waddled about the paths, sleek and fat, like so many well-nourished priests. At least, that was always the comparison Mesurat chose when he wished to describe them.

She noticed that the geraniums were growing well; the rain had given them new life. The grass needed cutting badly. She went back to the table in the center of the room, took up the letter again, and read the last page, holding the paper between the very tips of her thumb and forefinger. The sister did not add anything of importance, and ended with pious good wishes which Adrienne did not take the trouble to peruse. When she reached the end, she tore up the missive and threw the pieces on top of the postcard from Mme. Legras. She took off her gloves, sat down at the writing-desk, and, after a few moments' reflection, wrote as follows:

MY DEAR GERMAINE:

I propose that, through the intermediary of Maître Biraud, we fix upon a definite sum which I shall receive every month. This will spare you all annoyance until the day when I come of age and can dispose of my property as I see fit. I hope the air at St.-Blaise is doing you good and that you will soon be well and strong.

Your sister,
ADRIENNE.

She read the letter over and, not seeing any blotting paper, waved it for a moment to dry the ink. But just as she was folding it to put it into an envelope, she changed her mind and tore it across, slowly, into four pieces. She crossed her hands on the desk and, raising her eyes, fixed them on the lime trees of the Villa Louise, which she could see from where she sat. A little wrinkle came between her brows, as though she were concentrating deeply on what was before her.

A sort of ebb and flow of memory was going on within her which filled her with anguish. Without any warning, and without her knowing why, words that she had heard long ago returned to her mind— insignificant remarks exchanged between Germaine and her father. Do what she would to drive these voices from her head, the strength to disregard them was absolutely lacking. Up to this moment a sort of nervous energy had kept her going. But within the last few minutes the effects of her long sleepless night began to make themselves felt. Not that she had any desire to sleep. It seemed to her that a numbness was stealing over her limbs, and that her head was too weary to act. She was the prey of every thought or dream that cared to fasten on her. Her stupor had become a positive enchantment of the will. It was growing to be a painful matter for her to avert her eyes from any object on which they had once become fixed.

After a few moments she made a violent effort and pulled herself together. The strange torpor that was creeping over her alarmed her. She got up and began to pace back and forth again.

"It's all the same to me," she murmured. "It's all the same now."

As she came near the window she stopped to look out, and she could just make out an angle of the little white house. This contemplation took up a few minutes; then she resumed her pacing back and forth, which took her from the door that led into the dining room to the door that led into the hall. She had not broken her fast and her head felt light. All of a sudden faintness seized her and her legs gave way. She fell on her knees by the sofa that had taken the place of Germaine's old couch, and gave way to a fit of weeping which shook her from head to foot. She hid her face in her arms and repeated, mournfully:

"All the same. Yes, everything!"

Two hours later she was sitting in her bedroom. She had unpacked her valise, put away all her things, and life had begun again, that lonely life which she had made for herself and which nothing, it seemed to her, would ever change. What had she gained from her trip? Had she not been forced to come back? If she had even returned with a calmer mind and a stouter heart! On the contrary, she had only bruised herself afresh, only sunk into a deeper melancholy.

"I can't—I can't go on living this way," she said over and over again, striking her knee with her clenched fist. But, instead of rousing her to action, the words sounded merely like the statement of an irremediable fact. Nevertheless, sheer boredom and disgust for the thoughts that were obsessing her forced her to seek some distraction, or at least something to occupy her hands.

She opened her wardrobe and took out an old hatbox where she kept every letter she had ever received. Most of them were tied up in little bundles of ten or twenty and testified to the care with which Adrienne had preserved them. A strip of white paper was slipped under the ribbon which tied each packet, and upon this paper, in ornate figures such as M. Mesurat once taught his pupils, was written the year of receipt. There were five or six packets, letters from classmates, written during vacations; or letters from relations. These last were rare, for the Mesurats had very few relatives and took no trouble to keep up a sustained correspondence with those they had. In this section of Adrienne's correspondence with her cousins in Paris or at Rennes there was little except requests for trifling services. Finally there were ten or twelve letters, never opened, lying scattered at the bottom of the box.

It was these last that Adrienne began to read. One came from Paris, three from La Tour l'Evêque itself, another from Rennes. They were all letters of condolence, written after the death of M. Mesurat. Up to now Adrienne had never been able to make up her mind to read them. But her habit of keeping all her letters was so ingrained that she had put them aside with the others. She did not touch the family letters, but those which came from La Tour l'Evêque intrigued her, because she did not recognize the handwriting. She opened one envelope with a hairpin and drew out a little gilt-edged card slightly perfumed. It was from Mme. Legras. The girl drew her eyebrows together as her eyes fell on the words "terrible calamity . . . devoted friend." After a moment's hesitation, she tore the card across. The sight and smell of it filled her with horror.

The second letter was from the stationmaster, who had known M. Mesurat well and had the right to consider himself one of his friends.

The third was in small, hurried handwriting, difficult to read. It was signed: Denis Maurecourt. Adrienne uttered a cry as she read the name, and blushed furiously. Her hands trembled and for some time she could not make out the words under her eyes. The mere thought that this man had taken notice of her, had gone to the trouble of using a pen, ink, and paper to write to Adrienne Mesurat, moved her to such a degree that she could not tell whether she was made happy or unhappy by it.

She repeated, "Imagine that! Imagine that!" over and over again in a tone of the most extreme surprise, then wiped the tears that were running down her cheeks and read the letter. It was short, a little formal, but Adrienne discovered a delicacy in it that enraptured her. The sense of several phrases escaped her altogether; she read them without the slightest idea what they were about, without the words even appearing to have any connection one with another. It was the stereotyped ending that attracted her most. She thought she could never tire of reading it over, "Yours respectfully"! To each of the words she attached a deep and individual significance.

When she was in a condition to read the letter more intelligently, she began to cry violently. To her it appeared an act of charity, so to speak, whose merit was incalculable. In a transport of gratitude, she carried the paper to her lips and pressed them on the spot where the doctor's hand must have rested as he wrote. Suddenly she remembered the postcard which she had sent him from Montfort-l'Amaury. What would he think of it? She felt quite confused at the idea that perhaps he had laughed at it, and congratulated herself on having left it without any signature. Then, after a moment's thought, she regretted not having signed her name at the bottom of the card. Some solution might have come of it. As for an anonymous card—what end would it serve except to make the situation still more confused and difficult?

"No! I would never have dared to sign it," she murmured to herself.

She reread Maurecourt's letter, and slipped it into the bosom of her dress.

All that afternoon she walked in the country. It was a warm day, and she hoped that the fresh air and exercise would cure her of a strange oppression that she was beginning to feel in her chest. At times short fits of coughing relieved it, but these frightened her still more, as being premonitory symptoms of what she most feared. She did everything possible to suppress them, imagining that by this means she might cure their cause. Beyond everything else, she wished to profit from the peace of mind which the reading of Maurecourt's old letter had left behind. Possibly the word "joy" is too strong to describe what was passing within her. There was too much fear, too much apprehension for the future, in her heart for joy to reach it. But she felt calmer.

When she got back to Villa des Charmes, she learned that a lady had called while she was out. At first she thought this must have been Mme. Legras. But a glance across the road assured her that the shutters of Villa Louise were still closed. The visitor had not given her name, but had promised to call again in the afternoon.

Adrienne did not have long to wait. She had scarcely taken off her hat when the doorbell rang. She snatched up a book at random and sat down on the sofa, her heart beating fast. She judged it best to be found in this attitude. In lives as circumscribed as hers, receiving a visitor is no commonplace event. To meet such extraordinary cases an amount of ceremonial is called for that may seem absurd to a Parisian, but is nonetheless quite indispensable in the judgment of an inhabitant of La Tour l'Evêque. Adrienne, then, took up a position, not exactly lounging, but in harmony with the leisure of her occupation—that is to say, with her head bent and one finger to her cheek, the other hand holding the book, whose lines danced and swam before her eyes.

At the end of a few seconds the parlor door opened, giving entrance to a lady, dressed in black, who advanced briskly but silently toward the center of the room. Adrienne rose at once, laid her book aside, and bowed.

"I have not the honor of knowing you, mademoiselle," said the stranger, "but I live not very far away."

She stopped, as though willing to mystify Adrienne a little longer, and smiled. She might easily have been forty years old and there was no sign of any pains taken by her to conceal her age. Her thin face was covered with wrinkles. Around the mouth and eyes they fell into a design that gave the effect of a fixed smile. Only her eyes had remained young. They were black and their pupils slid from left to right as though moved by perpetual curiosity. As she spoke to Adrienne, the girl was certain she was numbering the pieces of furniture in the room and drawing up a mental catalogue of them all. Her voice was mild, with an even warmth of tone that was far from disagreeable.

"Will you be seated, madame?" said Adrienne.

They sat down on the lounge, both alike on the extreme edge, and drawn up very straight.

"In order not to puzzle you any longer," said the visitor, "I will tell you that my name is Marie Maurecourt, and that I am the sister of your physician. Till recently I have resided in Paris, but a few days ago I came to live with my brother."

Her eyes wandered once more around the room as she spoke, from door to windows, and rested upon Adrienne at the end as though by chance. The girl did not say a word.

"Are you surprised that I should come to see you, mademoiselle?" went on the stranger.

Adrienne twisted her hands together till her knuckles almost cracked, made an effort, and then said, quickly:

"I hardly expected it, as a matter of fact."

"And yet—what more natural? We are close neighbors. You are alone. I judge that you are not very happy. That is easily understood, mademoiselle."

Her eyes shifted to the garden. There was a brief silence. Adrienne still waited.

"My brother and I both thought," said Marie Maurecourt, presently, "that we could be of service to you. When I say 'my brother and I,' I use a figure of speech that may mislead you. We did not consult together. My brother does not even know that I am paying you this visit. But yesterday we happened to be speaking of you and he seemed to think that it was almost a duty—a duty—. How am I to say it? Please help me."

"I don't know," said Adrienne, almost under her breath.

"—well, a duty not to leave you so much alone—a duty to let you have our company as much as possible. Therefore, since I thought the same, I have come to see you. I should tell you that my brother is a very busy man. He has very little time to himself. His health is none too good; every visit that is not absolutely necessary or any fatigue beyond his work is absolutely forbidden him."

She spoke the last sentence in a rapid voice and without looking at Adrienne.

"Now then," she went on, gently, "I want you to feel that you are not alone, that you can count on me if you ever feel too sad. It's a very simple matter; you only have to write me and I will come."

She got up abruptly and stretched out her right hand to the girl, who rose in her turn.

"By the way," said Marie Maurecourt, suddenly, "you do not happen to have written us recently?"

Adrienne held her breath. Under her lids she examined the shifty eyes which were avoiding hers, but read nothing in them.

"No," she answered, after a slight pause.

A sudden anger against this woman invaded her heart. Had she come to play the spy, too, like Germaine, like Mme. Legras? The idea that her postcard might have fallen into these hands was insupportable. She recalled the words: "If you knew how unhappy I am—" and she blushed.

"No," she repeated in a more resolute voice. "It was not I."

For the first time, Marie Maurecourt's eyes rested full upon Adrienne's. They were black, with a sort of yellow flame in the iris which gave them an expression that was slightly wild and almost malevolent. She shrugged her shoulders almost imperceptibly.

"Some silly mistake—" she murmured.

She went on, in a more distinct voice:

"I hope you don't mind my visiting you. I wanted so to see you."

"Why, the very idea!" protested Adrienne.

Both women moved toward the door.

"I understand you have been travelling," said Marie Maurecourt, turning to Adrienne, who was following a little behind her.

The girl did not answer. Both were at the top of the steps which led to the garden. Adrienne held herself very straight and did not proffer a word. Suddenly her visitor reached out a hand for the door frame as though overtaken by sudden weakness.

"Did you have a pleasant journey?" she asked.

Her eyes had lost the harshness of a moment ago. Something almost imploring was in them now, a humbler expression, almost as of one begging for an answer—begging to be told the truth.

"Yes, thank you," said Adrienne, dryly.

Marie Maurecourt sighed. After a second handshake the two women separated.

Chapter II

Shortly before lunch on the following day, the *bonne* announced Mme. Legras.

"Say that I'm out," said Adrienne, who was passing her duster over the furniture in the dining-room.

But, almost as she spoke, Mme. Legras came in. She had heard Adrienne's words from the parlor.

"Out!" she exclaimed. "Do you send a message like that to me?"

She was wearing a lilac frock and a hat covered with white flowers. Adrienne looked at her without a word. Mme. Legras turned toward Désirée, who was looking on at the scene.

"You can go," she said in an impatient tone. "I don't think mademoiselle has any need of you."

When the two were alone, Adrienne sat down. Her face was livid.

"I don't want to see you," she said.

"So I notice," remarked her old friend between her teeth.

She stood in front of the girl, her arms akimbo.

"Will you have the kindness to explain why?" Her eyes flashed as she spoke.

"I prefer to live absolutely alone," said Adrienne, "and to see no one."

She felt the contemptuous look her neighbor gave her like a lash, and got to her feet.

"No one," she repeated, with a gesture of her hand.

"That is not an answer."

Adrienne shrugged her shoulders.

"It will have to serve," she said.

Mme. Legras turned purple. She seized the girl's wrist.

"Come," said she in a smothered voice, her face close to Adrienne's. "You don't mean what you say. You have something or other against me?"

The young girl shook her off unceremoniously.

"I owe you no explanation," she said. "Please leave me."

Mme. Legras was silent a moment. Then she burst into laughter and sat down on a chair.

"My poor child!" she said, in her normal voice. "What has got into you? If it's a joke, please have done with it. It is quite impossible you should speak this way to your best friend."

She seemed to have settled upon her attitude, and shifted to a note of the utmost surprise, as though the full enormity of the incident had only just struck her.

"Come, Adrienne," she went on, "you can't seriously mean to take this tone with me. Have you lost your wits? Come back to common sense. Let us pretend nothing has happened—"

Anger caught Adrienne's breath as she answered:

"I don't know how to tell you more plainly that I no longer wish to see you, madame."

"And I," said Mme. Legras, "do not know how to tell you more plainly that you are a little fool. If there is one person in the world whom you should love and respect—yes, respect—it is me."

"No, no!" said Adrienne, in a strangled voice. "Respect! For a woman like you. You aren't trying to make me laugh, are you?"

"What do you mean by that, Adrienne?"

"You know what I mean quite well."

"I know nothing. I insist upon an explanation."

Adrienne looked at the woman with sovereign contempt in her eyes.

"Very well, then," she replied. "You may as well know that a Mesurat does not shake hands with a—with a—"

"Well, go on. With a what?" said Mme. Legras, tapping the waxed floor impatiently with the tip of her shoe.

"With a lost woman," Adrienne said in a firm voice.

Adrienne, trembling all over, leaned back against the sideboard which she had been dusting when her unwelcome visitor forced her way in. Behind her the eight Mesurats, men and women, contemplated the scene like members of some tribunal. At this moment she resembled them all. Her head was thrown back, her eyes unwavering. A few seconds passed before Mme. Legras could find voice enough to answer her. It was clear that up to the last moment she had not believed that such words could issue from Adrienne's mouth, and an overwhelming surprise could be read on her face. Around the circles of rouge on her cheeks her skin turned livid. At last she shrugged her shoulders with a furious gesture.

"What slander are you repeating?" she asked. "Do you even know the meaning of what you have just said?"

A smile twisted the corners of her mouth. This semblance of calm disconcerted the girl, who had looked for an explosion of insults, and she did not answer the question.

"I see," resumed Mme. Legras in an even voice, "that neither politeness nor gratitude is going to close your mouth, young woman. So be it, then! You come to see me every day, you accept invitations (which you never dream of returning, by the way), and all this to tell me one fine morning that I am a 'lost woman'—'lost'!" She repeated the word "lost" as though she spat it out of her mouth. "And why—may I ask? Because I put powder on my face? That isn't done at La Tour l'Evêque, eh? The Mesurats don't hesitate at jumping to conclusions, do they?"

Suddenly she seemed to lose all self-control. Leaping to her feet, she planted herself before Adrienne, who leaned back, avoiding her eyes.

"Little fool!" said Mme. Legras, almost in her ear. "I know enough about you to send you to the assizes!"

As she heard the words the girl turned toward her enemy a face from which every drop of blood had fled. She tried to speak but could not open her mouth. Fear made her lean back so much further that she touched the corner of the sideboard and felt the wall against her hand. She could not take her eyes off Mme. Legras, who was visibly enjoying her triumph.

"Aha!" said the older woman, after a moment. "Your memory's coming back, is it? You forget the services done you very easily, mademoiselle.

Do you know that I pulled you out of a very ugly hole? Do you know it? Yes or no?"

"I don't understand what you're trying to say," faltered Adrienne.

"You understand so well that, if I were to sit down at that table to write to the authorities all I know about your father's death, you'd be on your knees—at my feet, Mademoiselle Mesurat."

She pointed an imperious finger toward the big table as she uttered the words. Adrienne gripped the sideboard. Words far different from those she would have liked to utter forced themselves between her lips.

"How am I responsible?" she asked in a broken voice.

"Oh, stop that!" said Mme. Legras. "I'm not a judge. You don't have to excuse yourself to me. Only—mind this! If I ever hear that you're loosing your tongue on me in La Tour l'Evêque, I'm going to tell what I know. Do you understand *that?*"

She nodded emphatically and left.

Adrienne heard her slam the garden gate violently and, a few seconds later, that of Villa Louise. She stood listening to these noises and to the barking of the yellow basset as he greeted his mistress. At last silence settled down again—the heavy, profound silence she knew so well. She let herself fall upon a chair and sat quite still. A cold sweat was trickling slowly from the roots of her hair down her forehead and temples. Something felt dead in her. She knew she had no strength to fight, and for the first time in weeks felt the full horror of that silent house. Despite her state, she was unable to move. She would have liked to rise, to walk, but a dreadful lassitude weighed her down. She tried vainly to stand up.

She remembered the day she had squeezed her face between the bars and, as the idea of flight came to her, had turned the handle, only to find that her father's forethought had locked the gate. Today she had the impression that the same thing had somehow happened, and that, if she tried to escape from the house, obstacles deadlier still would rise in her path.

Now she understood the real meaning of her disastrous trip two days ago. It was as though the little towns which she visited had cast her out, one after another. She had said to herself that she could not go on living at the Villa des Charmes. On the contrary, it was here she must live and here only. First of all, it was quite impossible for her to change the material circumstances of her case. She was a minor. Her fortune was not under her own control. Even if it were, she could not conceive the idea of selling this house and buying another. From her father she had inherited a sort of habitual veneration which kept her inside these walls, surrounded by objects every one of which recalled a melancholy childhood and sorrowful adolescence. Doubtless she could modify their arrangement, put chairs and armchairs in one another's place. But she needed to see them around her.

She was afraid. In the kind of stupor into which she was plunged, ideas followed one another after a confused fashion that rendered them all the more redoubtable. She asked herself at one moment whether she had not perhaps been prey to an hallucination, and whether Mme. Legras had really come to see her that morning. But she still seemed to hear the clang of the two gates, opening and shutting. That could not have been a dream. Consequently, neither could the rest. The words of her neighbor came back to her, but with a changed intonation they had not had when she heard them. There was no hatred in them now; they resembled rather a cry of alarm, a "save yourself!" which rang in the silence around her. Her strength came back to her all of a sudden and she got to her feet.

Her first impulse was to write to Marie Maurecourt and tell her she wanted to see her. She went into the parlor and dashed off a note of four lines, which she slipped into an envelope.

"What's the sense of all this?" she said aloud when she had written the address.

She checked herself and went on, under her breath:

"I don't suppose I can tell her I killed my father."

The mere words, as they escaped between her lips, filled her with terror. She pressed her hands on her eyes.

"It isn't true," she protested.

She took away her hands with a sudden movement and repeated, as though arguing with someone:

"I tell you, it isn't true."

A wild anger filled her heart. Till now she had been too downcast and terrified to realize how insulting the attitude of Mme. Legras had been. But now her pride came back and a rush of blood turned her face scarlet. For the moment she persuaded herself that the woman had lied, and her anger grew to fury. As she looked toward Villa Louise her fists clenched and her eyes darkened.

"If I ever see you again!" she muttered. "Dirty—dirty—"

She sought a word that was bad enough and one that she had heard her father use came into her head.

"—bitch! Yes, bitch—dirty street bitch!"

She shook herself, sat up straight, and gave a sigh of relief as though the foul word had freed her of her anguish. Finally she shrugged her shoulders.

"Besides," she said to herself as though in response to some inward question, "I've got her and she knows it. After all, it only depends on me whether the town turns on her and forces her to leave. I'd only have to tell certain things to the right people and in a week all the people in this place would be pointing their fingers at her."

She let her eyes fall on the letter she had just written.

"Mademoiselle Maurecourt, for instance."

She decided to carry her note to Marie Maurecourt in person. She could not, of course, confide in the older woman. But, on the other hand, she could not stay alone here any longer. She simply had to see and speak to someone.

Pushing away her chair, she got up and began to walk back and forth. She still had her white apron on, and the handkerchief knotted around her head gave her the air of a peasant girl. As she passed before the mirror she glanced at her reflection and noticed she was looking none too well and a little thinner. Her black dress accentuated her pallor and made her face seem almost sallow. With her elbows on the mantelpiece she examined herself closely in the glass. There were dark shadows under her eyes and cheekbones. Around her eyelids she thought she could even detect wrinkles, finer than the finest hairs. She knit her eyebrows, turned away, and seemed to be buried in thought. All the upheaval that fear and anger had wrought in her was ebbing away and giving place to a melancholy that was more terrible still.

She fell into the low, wide armchair where her father used to take his afternoon nap, and sat there quite still, her back to the window. Not a sound reached her from the street or the house. Out in the garden the birds were ceasing to call to one another as the day neared its zenith.

Chapter III

Immediately after lunch she made up her mind to carry her letter to the little white house. She had no intention of ringing, fearing the doctor himself might open the door. She would content herself with simply slipping the note through the slot of the letter box. Even this, she told herself, would need courage. Suppose Maurecourt should be leaving the house at the same instant and she should find herself face to face with him!

At any other time the possibility would have seemed to her full of a fearful joy. But today such an eventuality was not to be faced. She longed to see him, but sometime when she felt calmer and did not look so tired. What impression would she produce today, worn out as she was? Possibly, if she had examined her conscience a little more closely, she would have been forced to admit that deep in her heart she wanted to take advantage of the mood of exaltation in which she found herself today, that she secretly counted on the effect her haggard face and faltering voice would have in arousing the man's pity, and that this, and nothing else, was her reason for not sending Désirée with the letter. But the time for thinking clearly was past. She must act, and it was in the very excess of her despair that she found the strength.

She put on her black straw hat and went out. As she was crossing the street she asked herself what she would say if she ever should see Maurecourt. She found no answer. Soon she had reached the door at which she had gazed so often, and whose green paint was blistered and broken by the heat of the sun. Her heart throbbed as though it would burst. She thrust the edge of the letter into the slot and stood stockstill a moment, unable to make up her mind to open her fingers and let it fall through. Inside the little white house someone was moving the chairs about—a servant, probably, setting the dining room to rights after the midday meal. Where was Maurecourt now?

Perhaps resting in the garden. She imagined him stretched out on a long cane chair, in the shade of a tree, a beech tree like the one whose top she could see from Germaine's old room. She found herself regretting she had not written to him instead of addressing the letter to his sister, and an access of tenderness came over her which made her sigh deeply.

"He's there!" she thought. "I wonder what he would say if he knew I was so near him."

She felt discouraged suddenly, and let the letter fall. The flap of the box closed with a little click. At the same time she imagined she heard someone walking along the path which bordered the garden wall, and ran off on tiptoe. Emotion caught at her breath. Yes, she had made no mistake, someone *was* walking on the other side. The steps stopped abruptly. She stopped, too, leaning against the stone wall. A few moments passed. She stole noiselessly away, reached the corner of the street, and waited afresh. Someone in the garden was waiting, too—she was sure of it. Soon the noise of footsteps reached her ear anew, a little more rapid this time. She heard a metallic sound. Someone had opened the box and closed it again carefully.

"I've been watched," she said to herself, frightened. "Someone has seen me."

She shrank further back behind the angle of the house, not daring to continue her flight. There was a moment of absolute silence, then the same hand which had opened and closed the box so quietly turned the handle of the door and pushed it outward. Adrienne dared not breathe. Four or five paces at most separated her from whoever was holding the door open and probably looking up and down the street to discover who had brought the letter. They had only to come out and walk as far as the angle of the wall and they would see her. But almost immediately Adrienne heard the door close. Footsteps passed toward the house. She waited a few seconds longer and then, after taking a short walk as far as the national highway, went home.

On the desk in the parlor she found a letter which must have been left while she was out. A glance at the writing and a whiff of the scent of mignonette it exhaled was enough to confirm her fears. The letter was from Mme. Legras.

She sat down and reflected quite a long time before opening it. She imagined the worst; her neighbor had written a letter to the authorities, denouncing her. Ah! it was high time she asked someone for advice! She ripped the envelope open and drew out a little lilac-tinted card which she had to read twice before its meaning reached her:

> MY DEAR CHILD:
> We are two fools to quarrel. I don't know where you got your ideas about me, and I don't recall the half of what I said to you this morning. Suppose we both blame the stormy weather, and, if you feel like it, come and bring a kiss to
>
> Your old friend,
> LÉONTINE LEGRAS.

Adrienne let her head drop upon the head of the sofa on which she was sitting, and made no move for a long time.

About three o'clock in the afternoon she received a call from Mlle. Marie Maurecourt. She was struck at once by the icy expression on her visitor's face.

"You asked me to come, mademoiselle."

"That is so," said Adrienne.

They sat down face to face. Mlle. Maurecourt was carefully, even ceremoniously, dressed. Her black silk bonnet was ornamented with small feather plumes of the same color. Her face was covered by a thin mesh veil; and all that could be distinguished was the sallow tint of her skin and two black, deep-set eyes. Her skirt and jacket of blue serge, although they fitted loosely, did not conceal the thinness of her body. She crossed her hands upon her knees. They were covered with black string gloves. She seemed to be awaiting an explanation.

"That is so," repeated Adrienne, with an effort. "Did you not tell me that I might call on you any day that—"

She was about to say "any day I felt unhappy." But faced with her caller's cold and distant air the words seemed ridiculous. Moreover, since she had received the letter from Mme. Legras, she no longer saw what good was to be derived from an interview with the doctor's sister, and already regretted her impulsiveness in writing her.

"What were you about to say, mademoiselle?" asked Marie Maurecourt.

Adrienne dropped her eyes and kept them fixed upon her hands, which she, too, had crossed upon her knees. There was a brief silence.

"Mademoiselle," began Marie Maurecourt, abruptly, "I have changed my mind since my last visit. I have thought over our interview. My present impression is that you can very well do without my company. All the more so because I believe, if what I hear is true, that you are not so much alone as you would lead one to believe."

"I do not quite understand what you are saying," said Adrienne, in an uncertain voice.

"Really!" Marie Maurecourt's tone was ironical. "You have some very pleasant neighbors, mademoiselle. I congratulate you on them. Léontine Legras is doubtless a very amusing companion. It is all the more to be regretted that my brother and myself do not feel at liberty to make the acquaintance of women of her class—"

She stopped and fixed the young girl with her eyes.

"—nor that of their friends."

"You are out of your mind," Adrienne cried.

"Kindly be polite, mademoiselle," replied Marie Maurecourt, in a studiously even voice. "Courtesy is necessary, even under such circumstances as bring me here this afternoon. I was merely telling you that you are quite free to choose your own friends, but that, given the character of Léontine Legras and the class to which she belongs, you should not even dream of maintaining relations with us."

Adrienne blushed.

"I don't see Madame Legras anymore," she said.

"Indeed!" retorted Marie Maurecourt, with a skeptical air. "That must be very recent. I understand that this very morning Madame Legras, as you call her, did you the honor of a visit."

"She came in spite of me, mademoiselle."

"Ah? That is possible. Nevertheless, correspondence seems to go on as before."

"You play the spy on me, mademoiselle. That I will not suffer!"

"You mean I take precautions before opening the door of an honorable family to a stranger. And now, my mind is made up."

"On what?" said Adrienne, her voice rising.

Marie Maurecourt looked at her a moment before replying.

"On the kind of girl you are, Mademoiselle Mesurat," she said dryly. "The proof is abundant."

At these words Adrienne lost all control of herself. She forgot the prudence which urged her not to burn all bridges between herself and Maurecourt, and made no attempt to restrain her anger.

"Explain yourself," she cried in a trembling voice. "I demand that you explain yourself."

Without other reply, Marie Maurecourt opened a black bag which she was holding between her hands, took out a letter and held it up.

"Did you write this?" she asked.

"Certainly, mademoiselle. It is the letter I sent you after lunch."

"Perfect! And this?"

She threw an envelope upon the girl's lap. Adrienne took it and drew out the card which she had written to Maurecourt. A cry broke from her.

"*That's* an answer there's no mistaking!" said Marie Maurecourt, closing her handbag.

Adrienne got up and put her hand to her throat.

"That card was not addressed to you," she said at last, in a strangely altered voice.

"I am happy to let you know at once that it never got to the person for whom it was intended," answered Marie Maurecourt. As she spoke she was following every movement of the girl with a contemptuous smile.

"You stole it," cried Adrienne. "That is an infamous action, mademoiselle."

Marie Maurecourt did not give way an inch.

"And what name do you give to yours?" she retorted. "Do you often write these declarations of love? The Legras woman should be able to give you some pointers, mademoiselle. Your friendship for one another no longer surprises me."

Adrienne rapped the floor with her foot.

"Leave this house!" she cried.

"Not without telling you that if I ever find one other letter of this sort in my letter box, I will denounce your conduct to the public. I will insert a letter in the *Moniteur de Seine-et-Oise*. We shall see then what honest people think of girls like you."

She jumped up and strode toward the door, her head and neck thrown back. Shrugging her shoulders, she covered the girl with a final look of contempt, and was gone.

Adrienne pressed her fingers on her lips to stifle the cry of rage which mounted in her throat, and let herself fall back upon the sofa. Her hands were trembling; she kept striking her knees with her clenched fists.

"I'm going to see him," she said after a few moments, in a voice which seemed to die away in her larynx. "God knows what that woman has told him!"

She drew her handkerchief from her bosom and wiped her mouth.

"Come, come!" she said, getting to her feet. "I'm not going to let myself be discouraged by a venomous old maid. There'd be no sense in that."

Her shirtwaist was very tight fitting and the stays of her collar were digging into her neck under the chin. She opened her bodice a little and breathed more easily.

"No," she repeated, resuming her walk, "no sense in that."

She sat down suddenly at the desk, took up a pen and began to write.

> Monsieur:
> I do not know what they are saying about me—

The sentence displeased her. She tore up the sheet of paper and began again.

> Monsieur:
> It is absolutely necessary that I should see you . . .

But this start seemed no better than the first. She tore up the second sheet, put her elbows on the desk, and laid her forehead upon her open hands.

"What am I to do? My God! What am I to do?" she said out loud, in a voice that was exasperated and weary at the same time.

She felt that, unless she pulled herself together immediately, she was going to collapse. She took a third sheet and dashed off the following letter:

> Monsieur:
> I want to see you. I should have asked your help long ago, for it is your help I need. If anyone has spoken to you of me, don't believe a word they tell you. I am terribly unhappy, I simply cannot go on suffering. Your duty is to help me, to come here and speak to me, alone. . . .

Then she stopped.

"I can't send this letter," she said to herself. Suddenly she cried out with a final air: "Well, and what if I do send it! Nothing can happen to me worse than what I have suffered today. Besides, I am sure he will understand."

She added the very words: "I am sure you will understand," and signed her name.

When she had addressed the envelope, she fastened her bodice, put on her hat, and went out. What she had now resolved to do was to put this letter in the doctor's hands, return home, and wait. In her present state of mind the plan seemed simplicity itself. After weeks of hesitation and uncertainty, she suddenly saw everything clear. It was her reward, she told herself, for all she had suffered up to now. She was amazed at not having thought of this natural solution before.

"Still, perhaps it would have been better to say it was for a consultation," she was thinking as she went up the street, adding immediately:

"So much the worse. I can't begin this letter all over again."

She feared her supply of energy might not last. She well knew that she could never demand another such effort of herself, and that if she did not profit by the strength that had served her to write her letter, the game was over once and for all. Of course she should have spoken to the doctor long ago! What difficulties she might have spared herself! She had let the precise moment to act slip from her. Now, by virtue of some mysterious chance, the moment had returned—she felt it—she was sure of it! It was her last chance. Her happiness—her life, perhaps—depended on how she spent the next three or four hours. This superstitious idea came to her like the sudden revelation of a mystery. She quickened her pace and reached the angle of the little house, the very spot where she had been standing just now, when Marie Maurecourt opened the door. She leaned against the wall.

How long would she have to wait? How did she even know he would go out this afternoon? She asked herself these questions and got no answer. She felt herself, at one and the same time, determined and indifferent. She kept her eye on the cobblestones at her feet, and something, a sort of dejection, came into her face as she waited. All the color had fled from her cheeks and even her lips were white. Her shoulders hurt her and she stooped her back as though a burden were laid on it. Nearly ten minutes passed before she lifted her head.

The noise of a carriage on the highway made her jump. She straightened her shoulders and looked around her. Silence fell again after a moment. It was too hot to go out; everyone was at home. She imagined her neighbors lolling tranquilly in their armchairs. Tomorrow vacations would begin. People from Paris would come to rest at La Tour l'Evêque; there would be tenants for the villas right and left of the Villa des Charmes. A cruel conviction of the solitude her unhappiness was creating around her came to Adrienne. In all that quarter—in all the town, perhaps, she was the only one who was suffering. Everywhere else men and women were eating, working, and sleeping, free of care. Their little troubles hardly existed. As for her—could she eat, sleep, be at peace half an hour at a time?

She had a spasm of resentment against this man who would not come, almost as if she had made an appointment to meet him and he was late. There was a moment when she was ready to detest him. Who else was responsible for all she was being made to suffer? How humiliating to think that her happiness and peace of mind were at the mercy of a man whom she had only once seen pass on the road.

And then, suddenly, she had the distinct impression that he was standing before her and that she saw him. His black eyes were looking into hers with a mixture of affection and curiosity. All she had been thinking of went out of her head. She understood that she was quite powerless, that reasoning would only make the wound sharper, and that nothing could alter the fact that she was a woman in love.

By sheer force of listening, she ended by imagining that she could hear footsteps on the garden path, coming toward the door. Her heart began to thump furiously. Suppose it was Marie Maurecourt and that she came face to face with her in the street? What should she do? "And if it is he?" she thought. Her pulse pounded in her ears. She clasped her hands and murmured: "No, no!" between her set teeth. Her strength was oozing away, she clenched her hands tight as though to prevent its escaping. Suddenly she left the sidewalk and crossed the street.

"It's of no use," she said, rapidly, under her breath. "I couldn't speak to him—I couldn't!"

As she felt the letter rustle in her bosom, tears rolled down her cheeks.

She felt she lacked courage to go home, to hear the gate close behind her. She walked up the street for a while, her throat aching as though a hand were clutching it, unable to make up her mind. Between her tears she could see a cloud sailing slowly across the sky, and the telegraph wires upon which the birds, overcome with the heat, were resting. She walked back and forth. A sob broke from her suddenly, and she was as much surprised to hear it as though the brief harsh sound had come from some passer-by.

"It's too much," she said to herself. "I shall go mad. I can't go on suffering this way."

In her anguish she let her head fall until her chin touched her breast, and twisted her hands continually. Nothing of what she had suffered till now was to be compared to the horrible moments she had been living through in the past quarter of an hour. It seemed to her that she had never known what it was to weep until this hour, that all her panics, her disappointments, even her despair of yesterday were only imaginary, and that for the first time she was encountering a frightful reality, that her pain was touching bottom. She would have liked to bend toward the earth—to shrivel up to nothingness. The idea of death crossed her mind, and made no impression on it. She remembered her terror when she believed she had caught her sister's malady. Her flesh no longer crept at the thought. She felt quite indifferent before a prospect that had filled her with horror the day before yesterday.

"Perhaps that's the way it will end," she said to herself.

Raising her eyes, she discovered that she had been passing backward and forward before the gate of Villa Louise. The scene with Mme. Legras came back to her, but in a confused fashion. Everything that had happened to her before Marie Maurecourt's visit seemed far off. Even that visit did not seem to mean anything any longer. She had a strange impression that she was drunk. Her knees were wobbling. She tugged at the bell, and without even waiting for someone to answer it, turned the handle and entered the garden. Hardly had she taken four steps along the path when she pitched forward and fell at full length on the edge of a patch of lawn.

Chapter IV

"No," said Mme. Legras, authoritatively, "don't move! Henriette is bringing you a cordial, and you're going to see if you can't stay absolutely still for an hour."

Adrienne, who had raised herself on one elbow, lay back. She was stretched out on a chaise-longue in her neighbor's bedroom, and gazed around her without any air of knowing where she was. At last her eyes rested upon Mme. Legras, who was standing by her side, in a mauve dressing-gown, and watching her attentively.

"How long have I been here?" asked Adrienne, after a moment.

Mme. Legras consulted a little hanging clock on the wall.

"Twenty minutes. Do you feel any better?"

Adrienne made no reply.

"Don't speak if it tires you," said Mme. Legras, sitting down beside her. "Just tell me when you want anything."

There was a knock at the door. Mme. Legras opened it and came over to the couch with a small glass half full of some liquid.

"Drink this," she said, putting her hand under Adrienne's neck to raise her head.

"Thank you," murmured Adrienne when she had swallowed the draught.

"My poor child!" said Mme. Legras, sitting down again. "We found you lying on the grass plot. We had to bathe your temples and flick your cheeks for five minutes. Are you better now?"

Adrienne nodded.

"A seizure like that isn't natural," Mme. Legras went on. "And I thought you were so strong. But the doctor will soon be here."

Silence fell between the two. Adrienne fixed her eyes on Mme. Legras.

"The doctor?" she repeated, in a toneless voice.

"Surely. I sent to fetch him at once."

Adrienne made an effort to raise her head and body.

"I don't want to see him," she said, with unexpected vigor. "I can't see him."

"My dear, be quiet," said Mme. Legras, in an imploring voice. "You shall see him when you want to. Now lie down again."

The young girl reached for her friend's hands.

"What doctor is it?" she asked.

"My poor child! you know very well. There's only one here. The doctor opposite, to be sure."

A cry broke from Adrienne, and she let her head fall on the hands she was holding.

"My God!" cried Mme. Legras. "She frightens me. What is the matter now? Adrienne!"

She got up and tried to pull her hands away.

"Don't leave me," pleaded the girl, throwing back her head. "I'll tell you everything."

"Everything—what?"

"Sit down," Adrienne went on. "I beg of you, sit down! I can't speak when you're standing up. You must listen to me, madame. Oh, help me!"

"Of course I will help you, poor child! Haven't I always told you to confide in me? Go on! See—I'm sitting down, I'm listening to you."

Adrienne hid her face in her hands.

"I can't see that man," she said. "Not today, in any case," she added, hastily.

"Not see the doctor? But he won't eat you. What are you afraid of?"

"You don't understand," said the girl, in a strangled voice. "I have suffered so terribly."

"Come, come!" said Mme. Legras, taking one of her hands. "Be sensible. You are alarming yourself over nothing. Didn't you tell me you suffered from headaches?"

"It isn't that. You ought to understand. I have seen this man several times. I know him."

She looked at Mme. Legras, who seemed to be turning all this over in her mind. Adrienne noted her bluish eyelids, lengthened artificially with a touch of grease pencil. "It's to a woman like this I'm talking!" she said to herself. "What do I care?" Her timidity vanished suddenly and she was on the point of saying, "I love him," when Mme. Legras, her face lit by a sudden thought, cried:

"You're not going to tell me you're smitten with Doctor Maurecourt."

And, as Adrienne assented with a mute sign of her head, she went on, making no attempt to conceal her surprise:

"My dear child, the thing's impossible! A man of his age! Why, he's forty-five, if he's a day!"

"I can't help that," cried Adrienne, breaking out into a fit of sobbing.

"Oh, my child!" said Mme. Legras. "You're dreaming. Just think—he has a son of thirteen, a little boy who came a day or two ago to spend his holidays at La Tour l'Evêque."

Adrienne uttered a cry.

"Maurecourt is married?"

"Married? No. His wife has been dead five years. But that does not alter the fact that he might be your father. And then, *mon Dieu!* age is a thing you can get over. But just look at him—thin, wizened, very delicate, they say. And with all that, not a sou. My poor dear, you don't call that a match."

"I can't help all that," said Adrienne, drying her eyes. "I don't love him because he's a good match," she went on, her voice broken with her sobs. "I love him just as he is."

Mme. Legras took a more decided air.

"Come," said she, "I refuse to encourage a simply crazy whim that will bring you nowhere. You must get over it. You are young, pretty, and not badly off. Eh? You mustn't spoil it all. It would be a shame. Just think what you have to offer. Good Lord, think of your own happiness! It's sheer lunacy to take a fancy to a man like that. I simply refuse to consider such a thing seriously."

She began to explain why Dr. Maurecourt appeared to her absolutely impossible from the matrimonial standpoint. But before the stubborn face of her young friend, who was quite evidently not listening to a word she said, she lost patience.

"We're a pair of fools," she said. "Both of us. Do you imagine he's thinking of such things as love or marriage? It's easy to see you don't know the man. He thinks of nothing but his patients."

"What do you mean?" asked the girl.

"Why, that he's not a man like other men. My poor child, I know well enough one can't always choose. But you couldn't do worse. You should have spoken to me first. I would have told you everything."

"But what—what?"

"All sorts of things. He's a man who goes to Mass every morning, as pious as an old market woman. He is shut up all day with his sick people, at some hospital here or some clinic there. Three times a week he goes to the hospital at Dreux, to give free advice. Besides, he has all sorts of theories on how to treat disease; he does nothing like anyone else. Can't you see the type?"

"What are you trying to tell me?" said Adrienne again.

She had become so pale that Mme. Legras was frightened and tried to calm her.

"My dear Adrienne, I am only telling you all this for your sake. You know I'm not a friend of this Maurecourt of yours. After all, I presume he has a heart like other men, though to judge from appearances—well—"

"If you don't know him, why do you speak so?" cried the girl. "Why shouldn't he love me?"

She got up from the sofa suddenly and fell on her knees before Mme. Legras, who rose quickly to her feet.

"Madame!" cried the girl, quite beside herself.

The words stuck in her throat; she repeated "Madame" in such an agonized voice that Léontine Legras for a moment believed she was on the point of death.

"My child," she said, taking the girl's hands, "you can't go on like this. . . . My God! what is the matter with her!"

"Help me, madame!" Adrienne went on crying between her sobs.

"Help you? But how? Come—get up! We'll find some way out. Have a little courage! I know what it is to be in trouble. Do you think you're the only one with problems?"

She made Adrienne get up and sit at her side on the lounge. She herself was shaking with emotion, and there was a note almost of anger in her voice as she said to the girl:

"How you let yourself go. You're not a little girl any longer."

"It's not my fault," protested Adrienne. "I can't stand any more. I'll be out of my mind if I go on living this way. There's no one I can speak to. I have to do everything myself, all day, and all night, too."

"Why don't you speak to him?"

"I couldn't."

"Write him, then."

"It's no use. His sister goes through all his mail before she gives it to him. She knows my writing. Look—I did write to him." Adrienne, as she spoke, pulled the letter from her bosom. "I meant to give him this myself—and then I couldn't."

"And I suppose I have to give it to him instead. I thought we should come to that at last. You don't stick to trifles, do you? Don't you understand I can't mix myself up in an affair like this? And then, I don't know the man. You can't make me your go-between. That would look awful. Get to know him, introduce me, then I'll see what I can do."

"It's out of the question. I've quarreled with his sister."

Mme. Legras lifted her hands to heaven.

"The whole thing's wrong from beginning to end," she said. "Here—give me the letter! I'm pretty near the end of my patience. Give it to me, I say!"

She snatched the letter from Adrienne's hand.

"Don't read it," pleaded Adrienne.

Mme. Legras contented herself with a contemptuous look.

"Listen to me," said she, finally. "This man is coming here. I'll see him first in the room downstairs. I'll tell him this letter fell out of your bodice as we were unlacing you. He'll read it. You can be certain of this—he won't see you immediately afterward. When he has heard what's the matter with you, he'll wait till you are calmer—unless he's an idiot. He'll answer you, you'll show me his letter, and we'll see what can be done. But no more foolishness—do you understand me?"

More than half an hour passed before the doctor came. Mme. Legras used the interval to put on a skirt and bodice of white linen. She left the room after telling Adrienne to stay quiet and to pretend to be asleep if by any chance the doctor insisted on seeing her at once. Before she had even reached the bottom of the staircase she had contrived to open the letter entrusted to her and to read its contents. She shrugged her shoulders and resealed the envelope carefully.

When Mme. Legras entered the parlor, the doctor was standing in the center of the room. She could not help making a mental note that she had been quite right about his age and that his face showed every one of his forty-five years. He was taller than she—about Adrienne's height, but so thin that he looked taller even than the girl. His hair, still black, covered his brow and his temples, and accentuated the pallor of his complexion, colored only on the cheekbones. He had his sister's eyes but without their perpetual restlessness; on the contrary, he rested his eyes on people and things with a sort of deliberate mildness and seemed to take them off with regret. His eyebrows, black and well-arched, helped to give him a certain Provençal cast, almost foreign, noticeable with Marie Maurecourt as well. His nose was straight and fine, with well-opened nostrils. On his thin lips and indeterminate mouth a sort of half-smile rested, which never entirely left them and which seemed to be the expression of extraordinary kindness. He had a habit of rubbing his fingers over his chin. He was dressed in black, with a waistcoat which showed its age plainly, though very carefully darned and pressed and spotlessly white.

"How do you do, Doctor!" said Mme. Legras, waving her hand toward a chair.

"Madame," said the doctor, without making any move to sit down, "I presume the case is urgent. At least that is what I was given to understand?"

"It is certainly urgent," said Mme. Legras with a consequential air. "But please take a seat, if you don't mind."

The two sat down. Mme. Legras crossed her feet and hands and began, in a somewhat solemn voice.

"It concerns Mademoiselle Mesurat, Doctor. She was coming to see me today about two o'clock, when she fell in a faint on the lawn. My maid and I had to put a wet handkerchief on her head and to flick her cheeks—"

"How long did the fainting fit last?"

"Four or five minutes. As I was undoing Mademoiselle Mesurat's dress a letter fell out. Here it is, Doctor. Your name and address are on it."

The doctor opened and read the letter. Mme. Legras coughed slightly meantime and looked at the tips of her shoes. After a few moments she raised her eyes and regarded the doctor stealthily. He was frowning deeply.

"He's taking his time," said the woman to herself. "I wonder is he learning it by heart?"

"Madame," said Maurecourt abruptly, as he folded the letter, "will you permit me one or two questions?"

Mme. Legras coughed again.

"Why certainly, Doctor," she said.

"Do you know if it is the first time Mademoiselle Mesurat has been taken ill this way?"

"The first time at my house. Elsewhere, I cannot say. She has never spoken of her health and I presumed it was good."

"Was she any better when you left her?"

"You mean just now? She had fallen asleep."

"Has she vomited?"

"No."

"Any temperature?"

"None at all."

"I'll come to see her tomorrow," said the doctor, rising as he spoke. "Will you tell her so when she wakes?"

He hesitated a little.

"Madame," said he, "there is one question which I should be wrong not to ask, for it has certainly a great deal to do with Mademoiselle Mesurat's condition."

"I am ready to answer you, Doctor," said Mme. Legras, assuming a gravity befitting the occasion.

"Do you know Mademoiselle Mesurat—I mean, know her well?"

"I see her every day."

"Has she seemed at peace—contented, lately?"

Mme. Legras had kept her hands together. She unclasped them now and inspected them as though she were expecting to find an answer written on their palms.

"I have noticed she seemed nervous and despondent."

"Do you know if her appetite is good?"

"I think not. She has been growing thinner."

With a rather dramatic accent, she added:

"She has been coughing for some days."

The doctor bowed his head and seemed to be in thought.

"Do you think she felt her father's death very keenly?"

Mme. Legras heaved a profound sigh, then raised one shoulder and one eyebrow.

"Obviously. But there must be something besides that."

The doctor took up his hat.

"Madame," said he, "I thank you. If you can prevail on her to spend the night here I think it would be as well. Often a slight change in daily habits has a good effect in a case of nerves."

Mme. Legras reflected a few moments.

"I understand," she said. "I will see she spends the night with me."

Chapter V

In the middle of the night Adrienne awoke. The moon was shining right into the small parlor where her neighbor had put her, and she realized at once that she was not at her own house. She got up from the couch on which her bed had been made, put on a pair of slippers, and went over to the window, which had been left half open. The air was close and a cloudless sky promised an even hotter day.

It seemed to Adrienne that her life now had become one of those strange existences of which a sleeper is conscious during a dream. She recalled the conversation she had had with Mme. Legras before going to bed, and how stubbornly she had resisted all attempts to discourage her, to change her heart, and to make her understand what the woman meant by a more suitable match! "A match!" the girl repeated under her breath, with a mixture of anger and weariness, "a match! What do I care about such things? Is it my fault if I love this man? I did not choose him."

She sat down on the window ledge and rested her arm on the bar. The street was all white in the moonlight, with deep black shadows at the base of the walls. A profound silence reigned—one of those silences in little provincial towns at midnight (and at midday too), which wring the heart—as though everyone had been struck by sudden death. She raised her eyes and, on the other side of the street, at the bottom of a narrow garden, saw a small house. Six graceless steps rose to a door whose upper portion was composed of a complicated pattern in forged iron. How well Adrienne knew it! How many times, as a little girl, had she not thrust her finger between its scrolls! There was something afflicting in this simple recollection. "Why am I here?" she asked herself. She lifted her eyes to the windows—twelve of them, cut in the harsh stone, tall and narrow like the house itself, with meager cornices and shutters pierced by lozenge-shaped holes.

Then the oval skylight; then the roof, almost vertical, with red tiles the weather had not managed to fade. These petty details absorbed Adrienne's whole attention. She had seen them a thousand times, but, at this hour and viewed from this place, they seemed to assume a character which she had never noticed in them before. It was as though a kind of hallucination had hold of her mind. By sheer dint of staring at Villa des Charmes from here, she almost came to believe that she had never set foot inside it—that she had never even noted the existence of the cheaply built, commonplace little house till now. And this impression did not preclude the disgust often felt for something we know only too well, and from which we suddenly turn with horror, after having borne the sight of it for years and years.

"I am dreaming," she said to herself. "I ought not to stay up this way."

But a sort of apathy kept her riveted to her place and she sat motionless, her cheek in her hand and her elbow on the window bar. And, just as she could not bring herself to get up and move away, so she was quite incapable of exercising control over her thoughts. All sorts of memories came back to her that she did not even make an effort to repel. Incoherent ideas swarmed in her head at their will. She had the strange feeling that she was in a previously unknown world, that her will had been taken away from her, that she was forced to remain absolutely passive. It was no longer a question of being sad or frightened. Absolute indifference to everything had taken the place of the despair which had thrown her to the ground a few hours before.

She felt herself, all of a sudden, a long, long way off from everything that constituted her daily existence. As she looked at Villa des Charmes, unable to realize that she had spent her whole life within its walls, she was amazed by the feelings that had made her suffer so much, and hardly recognized herself in the recollection of her pain. Something carried her out of and beyond herself; she had an uncanny consciousness of the weight of her flesh; her head, her hand, her arms—it was as though her whole body formed one mass which she herself was not strong enough to set in motion. It seemed to her that her real self was gradually escaping from this solid lump and beginning to hover just above it. And, little by little, as a delightful lightness and giddiness seized her senses, an indescribable calm descended into her heart. The villa, the trees, swung slowly to and fro before her eyes. The whole earth was rocking her to sleep.

But even as she closed her eyes, she realized the spell was breaking. Life came slowly back to her—life as she knew it, life at the mercy of memory. She saw herself at the side of the road, her arms full of a big bunch of field flowers. "That was where everything began!" she said under her breath.

And then, just as she was yielding herself up to her memories, she felt something that resembled a shock. It was as though she had been on the point of falling forward and checked herself, or rather was checked by some unknown force which dragged her back and brought her to her senses. There was a mist before her eyes, a noise rang in her ears which made her shudder. She heard the gate of Villa des Charmes clang open. There was a moment of silence. Then another sound assailed her ears which made her long to shriek aloud. Bitterly against her will she resolved it into all its elements. First a dull heavy thud, repeated at frequent and irregular intervals. A shuffling of feet followed, hesitant at first, then quicker and stronger; last, a murmur that grew and grew, a murmur of words exchanged in low, guarded tones. Dazed with terror, she was listening to the sand and little stones crunching under the wheels that turned so slowly, so slowly! Could this be she, walking near them? They were black—the wheels. The sandy road was almost white in the morning sunlight; she could see it between them at her feet. That was all she could see. She was not choosing to lift her eyes. A sole thought, enormously important, possessed her mind. "Everyone is looking at me. I mustn't walk too fast. I mustn't get any nearer to those wheels. I must keep to this pace—the same pace as the horses. Everyone is looking at me." Drowned in stupor, stifling under her crepe veil, she was following her father's funeral!

Her strength came back to her suddenly and she got up. "What's the matter with me?" she said, aloud, in a hoarse voice. "If I think of these things, I'll go mad."

She ran to the little table beside her couch, and lit a night lamp that was on it. It was not yet two o'clock. Her heart beat so violently that she pressed her fist on her bosom to slow down the pulse that was shaking her body. She sat down on the couch. "Why can't I sleep like anyone else?" she asked herself. "Is it possible I am never going to have another peaceful day, another peaceful night?"

Her hair was tumbled about her face; she put the strands back and looked around her. All this unfamiliar furniture seemed strange to her under the dim light of the oil lamp. There was too much of it, and because it had been leased to all sorts of people, it no longer had the air of being anyone's property in particular. "Why can't I go to bed and sleep in my own house?" she asked herself again. "What's the matter with me?" The question seemed to plumb the very depth of her despair, and she repeated it aloud almost impatiently: "What *is* the matter with me?"

She felt a cold draught on her bare feet and shivered. The idea of blowing out the lamp, of stretching herself on the couch again, was unthinkable. She was afraid of the dark. Too many terrible things were crouching near her, ready to leap upon her the moment the light was out; too many memories were awaiting a signal to invade her mind; there were too many scruples, too many regrets, too many phantoms against which she must go on fighting.

She looked at the lamp. It was burning under a shade of pleated and frilled muslin, whose frivolous aspect, at such an hour of night, was almost sinister. A cloud of tiny flies, awakened by the light, were circling over the chimney and dropping one after another as the flame licked their fragile wings. Around the base of the lamp were ranged a number of variously shaped shells and nicknacks in mother-of-pearl. Adrienne looked at the collection with a curiosity mingled with disgust. Do what she would, her imagination insisted on showing her the short, plump fingers of Mme. Legras, opening the little boxes or playing with the paper-cutters.

Little by little she began to get a clear idea of everything that had happened within the last forty-eight hours. She had quarreled with Léontine Legras, she had insulted her; then she had made friends with her again and now here she was sitting up in her drawing-room. She knew quite well what the Maurecourts thought of her friend—"the Legras woman," as Marie Maurecourt had called her. Between the two she had to make a choice—and what was she to do? She was staying with Mme. Legras, who had become her intermediary with the doctor. She was making a confidante of her, to the knowledge of the Maurecourts, hence to the knowledge of everyone in the town. The thought was maddening. Suddenly the idea struck her that her wishes and her thoughts were two things quite separate. There was something in her which refused to obey the orders her reason dictated. It was like some snare in which, without suspecting it, she had allowed herself to be trapped. Her flesh turned to ice at the thought.

She hesitated a moment, then leaped to her feet, snatched up her clothes, and began to dress hurriedly. Her hands trembled as she pulled on her stockings. She could not fasten her bodice nor button the top buttons of her high shoes. She put her hair in order as best she could, with her fingers. In the mirror above the clock on the mantelpiece she could see her tousled head, her panic-stricken eyes, haloed with black circles which the perverse lamp light exaggerated. A sudden horror had come over her at the sight of this disreputable furniture which had belonged to so many people in turn. She began to run to right and left, looking for her bag, which she knew she had had the day before. She saw it at last on the floor behind the couch on which she had passed so much of the night. When she had picked it up she left the room.

Groping along the wall, she followed a passage as far as the door which opened on the garden. The key was in the lock. She turned it stealthily, pushed the door open, and found herself on the steps. She crossed a path on tiptoe, then walked on the lawn, the better to muffle her footsteps. She stopped a moment when she came to a chestnut tree. It was here that she used to sit when she paid her daily visit to Mme. Legras and listened to her perfidious questions on M. Mesurat's death. For a moment the recollection of the old anguish was almost too much for her. She pulled herself together and ran as far as the gate. As good luck would have it, this was merely latched.

Now she was in the street. Under the light of the full moon the pavement could not have been whiter if it had been covered with snow. A soundless breeze was passing, and now and then the trees stirred their heads gently as though dreaming. Their restless foliage, steeped in the dead light, glistened like so much metal. She stopped a moment, through sheer weariness, but did not hesitate. With a rapid step, she crossed the street and opened her own garden gate.

She heard it clang to behind her and turned to look at it with an expression beyond the powers of words to render. Her eyes seemed to have grown much larger; she was as white as the stones in the road; her lips, open as though she were about to utter a cry, were colorless and hard to distinguish from the rest of her face. She turned toward the house and hastened up the path, the pebbles crunching under her feet.

Every movement indicated a firm resolution. She walked quickly; nevertheless, as she put her foot on the first step that led to the door, a sudden weakness descended upon her and she had all the appearance of being about to fall backward. Instead, she lowered her head, gathered up her skirts, ran up the six steps, opened the door, and disappeared into the house.

The matches were in the kitchen. Keeping her hand to the wall as she went along, she reached the bottom of the passage safely. A nameless fear was dogging her, only awaiting the moment when, overcome by the horror of darkness, she would yield to it, and a shrill cry would ring through the deserted house. At the end of the corridor she began to run, unable herself to understand how she had ever dared enter the house at this dismal hour of the night. Now she was in the kitchen, falling against chairs whose places she could not remember, feeling her anguish grow upon her, and sure it would conquer her before she could light the gas. For some seconds, half mad with fright, she groped from side to side, until her fingers fell upon a box of matches. Her hands were trembling so that it was all she could do to open it.

When she had a light at last, she looked around her wildly. She took off her hat and sat down at a deal table, under the gas, whose burner filled the silence with a queer little chirping noise. She stared at the rubbed pattern of the oilcloth tablecover, and at the circular stains made on it by the bottoms of plates and dishes.

All of a sudden, yielding to some irresistible force, she fell forward, her head on her arms, and hid her face.

More than a quarter of an hour passed before she could make up her mind to go upstairs to her room.

Chapter VI

She was standing in the middle of the parlor, a duster in her hand, looking gloomily at the furniture which a habit that was almost a nervous reaction drove her to polish day by day. As had been the case the previous night, she felt herself at certain moments invaded by a comprehensive indifference as to what the day was reserving for her. It seemed that her heart was so numbed by suffering that it had grown incapable of feeling. Her terrors, her agitation of the night before, appeared to her absurd this morning. She was quite calm, but with an ominous calm which was only the result of disgust.

While she wiped the mantelpiece she looked at herself in the mirror. Her skin had a bad color. Between her eyebrows was a line which she had noticed for some time was getting deeper—a fine vertical wrinkle that might have been etched by a fingernail. She wondered how she could make it go away or, at any rate, prevent its getting any more marked, when suddenly the vanity of her concern came home to her. "What's the use?" she asked herself. "What difference would it make?"

She continued her round of inspection, taking up each of the little knickknacks on the tables, passing her duster over the back of every chair.

"Perhaps he'll come today," she thought. "Mme. Legras said he would."

Twenty-four hours earlier the thought would have enraptured her. Now it left her almost cold. It was strange. Repeat these words as she would, summon to her memory as often as she liked the face of Denis Maurecourt—no reason to be excited, to be happy or unhappy about it all, appeared to her in her present mood. A bizarre thought occurred to her. Was it worth all this trouble? Or was Mme. Legras right, after all, and was the doctor in reality unworthy of her interest? For a few moments the conviction of a deep, bitter and abiding delusion drove everything else from her mind.

Nevertheless, the foresight of Mme. Legras proved to be justified. Soon after ten o'clock, Denis Maurecourt entered the parlor. At first the girl did not recognize him. The servant had not announced him, and he stood before her a moment without a word passing between them. She looked at him with a constriction of the heart that could not have been greater if her life were on the point of leaving her, and a cry escaped from her lips.

"What do you want?" she asked.

As she said the words she was thinking: "It's a mistake. This isn't he. He isn't so tall. He's much paler." But the conviction that there was no mistake was stronger, and she believed she was going to faint.

"I thought you were with Mme. Legras," he said. "I went there first to find out how you were. What kind of night did you have?"

Adrienne did not answer. She could not withdraw her eyes from the doctor's face. She had imagined it altogether different. She felt, at one and the same time, a deep humiliation and a bounding and tumultuous joy which prevented her from speaking. Without knowing what she did, she stepped back and sat down upon the sofa. He hesitated a moment, then sat down in turn.

"If I had known that your health was not good I should have come sooner," he said, gently. "You should have let me know, mademoiselle. Now—would you mind answering a few questions? I must know how the trouble began."

She nodded.

"Do you sleep well?"

She thought a moment, then answered, hoarsely:

"No."

"How long has this been going on?"

"I don't know," she said, adding, almost immediately: "I can't answer these questions."

"I ask them because I am trying to help you, mademoiselle," he answered, gently as before.

She sighed and hung her head.

"Oh, I know!" she said, as though speaking to herself. Suddenly her emotion became too strong for her to resist. Tears rolled down her cheeks.

He waited a moment before proceeding, then said at last:

"I understand your difficulties better than you think, mademoiselle. It is a very bad thing to live as you live—alone and without seeing a soul. You should go out—make new friends. Melancholia is a very dangerous thing."

"I don't want to go out."

He got up and seemed to be thinking. Finally he came over and stood in front of his young patient.

"Don't you want to get well?"

Immediately the thought of her cough occurred to her and she was afraid he knew something about it.

"I am not ill," she replied, quickly.

"We are playing with words, mademoiselle. You are unhappy. Don't you feel that is nearly the same as being sick?"

She raised her eyes and looked at him.

"Well," she said, "what should I do to 'get well,' as you say?"

"Will you let me ask you a question?"

She bowed her head.

"Have you any religious habits?"

Adrienne blushed deeply. She remembered what Mme. Legras had told her about the doctor, and was afraid to say she believed in nothing, for fear of displeasing him. She had a sudden desire to be like him—to resemble him in every way. After having waited a few moments for her answer, the doctor went on, as though he had not asked the question:

"You are highly nervous, mademoiselle. You are falling, little by little, into a state of despondency from which you may never be cured if you do not make an immediate effort. You must see more people; above all, trust in others more than you do. There are many things in you that have no right to be there, but which the sole fact of brooding upon them has made acute. You have certain thoughts shut up within yourself that have ended by acting on you as a poison."

Adrienne's eyes grew wide with fright.

"What do you mean?" she asked.

His voice grew more emphatic as he answered.

"I mean that you must change your manner of living. You will never be happy until you force yourself to go out and make acquaintances in the town, and find something to occupy your spare hours. What do you do here all day?"

She shrugged her shoulders slightly, but did not answer otherwise. After having looked at her for a few moments, he sat down before her, on the other side of the little table, and began to speak to her as though he had changed his mind and decided to adopt another method.

"Please be frank with me, mademoiselle. Remember that I have come to help you—I might almost say to save you—yes, to save you! Is it not true that since your father's death you have been much unhappier?"

A shudder ran through Adrienne's body.

"I know, mademoiselle," went on the doctor, "that your father was taken from you under particularly painful circumstances. It is very natural to give way at times under so great a shock. Am I right?"

The smile had left his face and his eyes were fixed on hers. She could not bear them and turned away her head. She was trembling so violently that she had to grasp the back of the sofa. The horrible sensation of being a beast caught in a trap and unable to fly took hold of her again. Little pearls of sweat broke out on her scalp and trickled slowly down her forehead. Suddenly she heard her own voice saying:

"Yes, very natural."

"And yet, mademoiselle," the voice went on, "were you so greatly attached to your father? Were there not disagreements between you at times?"

She looked into Maurecourt's steady eyes.

"Why do you ask me that?" she said, hoarsely.

"To help you tell me the truth," he answered, without moving a muscle of his face.

Adrienne locked her fingers mechanically under the table and held her breath. Her tongue felt dry and rough against her palate.

"What are you trying to say?" she stammered after a pause.

He did not answer. Then she felt something tumultuous rising in her chest. She felt all her entrails beating like her heart. Suddenly she rose, placing both hands at her throat.

"Why are you looking at me?" she said, "What are you going to do?"

Her voice was like a smothered cry. She went on, with an indefinable air of docility that made her resemble a child reciting a lesson.

"Papa fell downstairs."

"Was there no light?" asked Maurecourt, almost under his breath.

"No," she answered composedly.

She seemed to collect her thoughts and went on, speaking like a woman in a dream.

"It was pitch dark. I had shut the door of my room where the lamp was. All at once we found ourselves together in the dark, on the landing."

She stopped.

"And then—!" said Maurecourt.

"I pushed him—by his shoulders," she went on in a scarcely audible voice.

There was a long silence. During the last few minutes all her fear had gone. Everything within her was literally numb. The only impression left on her mind was that something extraordinary was happening to her. She could not see clearly—she imagined that a heavy black line outlined the head and shoulders of the doctor and that the room was growing gradually darker. It was just as though she were on the point of falling asleep. But she remained standing upright and without movement.

"Why did you kill your father?" asked Maurecourt at length.

A horrible agitation seized her. The words, uttered in a harsher and louder tone than before, aroused her from the stupor into which she had found herself slipping. A cry broke from her lips. Making a step toward the doctor, she fell on her knees at his feet. He did not stir.

"Who told you that?" she moaned. "It was that woman—it was Madame Legras."

"I have known it a long time," the doctor replied. "I have known it since the morning I wrote the death certificate."

She stifled a cry.

"Are you going to denounce me?"

"Denounce you! As though you had not been punished enough! Come, get up!"

Rising himself, he bent over her and said, in a voice that brooked no refusal:

"Get up, mademoiselle!"

The girl obeyed. A nervous tremor still agitated her hands and her head, so that she seemed to be uttering a mute, "No!" Her eyes, rimmed with black, were widened by terror. The doctor laid his hand lightly on her arm and said, in a calm but decisive voice:

"Now we are going upstairs together to your father's room."

She gave a queer twisted smile, made infinitely tragic by its contrast with her eyes.

"Don't be afraid at all," he said, deliberately. "I tell you again I have come here to help you. You are so young! You have a right to happiness. But you will never be happy till you have rid your mind of certain ideas. Now all you have to do is to obey me. Let us go up to the room."

"The door is locked," she said, casting down her eyes. "I haven't been inside the room for two months."

"Where is the key?"

Adrienne kept silence. He insisted, gently:

"Mademoiselle, I ask you for the key. Please give it to me."

As though yielding to a sudden impulse, she went to the desk, opened a drawer, and took out a key. She handed it to the doctor.

"Please show me the way, mademoiselle," said he. "Lean on my arm."

She hesitated for a moment, then put her arm under his. Everything was dancing before her eyes, and she had no idea how enough strength came to her to put one foot before another or even to hold herself upright. Against her bare arm she felt the rough serge of the man's coat, and, look-ing down, saw her white hand on Denis Maurecourt's black sleeve. Min-gled with her terror was a sort of frenzied happiness. The emotion was so new and strange that she had to bite her lips to repress a cry. Tears swam on her lashes. At the door of the parlor she let go of the doctor's arm and passed before him. But to mount the staircase she took it again. She leaned on the hand-rail so heavily with her free hand that the banisters creaked; she stumbled as she mounted from one stair to another. She did not dare look at Maurecourt, nor dare to believe that he was at her side. It was enough to hear him breathing and to see, as she looked down, his hand

and his dust-covered shoes.

When they were on the landing of the second floor, the old anguish assailed her and she stopped, letting go of the doctor's arm. He took her hand and pressed it in his.

"Have you no confidence in me?" he asked her.

Bowing her head before the steady eyes that were bent on her face, she broke into a great fit of sobbing. He let go her hand. She heard him turning the key in the lock and pushing open the door.

"Come!" said he, from the interior of the room.

Adrienne made an immense effort at self-control and followed him.

For many months she had not been inside her father's bedroom. Even during Mesurat's lifetime she had seldom gone there, and to set her foot inside it since his death would have been the last thing to occur to her. The shutters were closed and she could make out nothing. A smell of dust and mildew assailed her nostrils. She shut her eyes and leaned against the door jamb while the doctor was opening the window and throwing back the shutters.

"What is the matter?" he asked, turning round toward her. "Sit down."

He took her hand again and led her to an armchair. She sat down and looked around her. She had seen the pieces of furniture in other parts of the house so often that they no longer produced any impression on her mind, and she would have been hard put to it to describe any single object among them. She did not know whether they were handsome or ugly. It was almost as though she were not seeing them at all. For her they were *the* furniture just as for a wolf or fox the forest is *the* forest without any other conceivable description. But her father's bedroom was far less familiar. She received a distinct shock now in looking at the bedstead in pitch-pine and the straw-bottomed chairs which he had used for years. Ridiculous as it may seem, in some indefinable fashion these things looked like M. Mesurat. It was as though by sheer force of having belonged to him so long, they had absorbed something of his outward appearance. It was hard to imagine any form except his outstretched upon the mean, commonplace bed, and it would have seemed unnatural had any hand but his, with its salient veins, rested upon the back of the chairs. If any vestige of him survived on earth, it was here.

Adrienne shivered.

"Why have you brought me up to this room?" she asked.

"To teach you not to fear it anymore," answered Maurecourt. "You have kept it shut up for two months, and that was a mistake. What makes it so terrible to you is the fact that you never enter it. Just the same way, within yourself there are secret rooms which you dare not enter and whose shutters you keep closed. On the contrary, you must flood them with air and sun. Are you afraid here now—with me?"

She looked at him, with eyes so full of confidence that she appeared transfigured.

"No!" said she under her breath.

"You see, then. You are cured! Nothing more—no terrors, no phantoms! You were forbidding yourself to think of your father because you used to be afraid of him. Isn't that true?"

She put her hand to her forehead as though fearful of what Maurecourt might be on the point of saying. He read the anxiety in her eyes and went on, with ill-concealed impatience:

"You imagine things which don't exist. Your father is no longer in a world where he can torment you. There is nothing in this room—nothing in this whole house. Do you believe me?"

He took her hand.

"I believe what you say," she repeated, simply.

He continued to speak to her, without letting go of her hand and without her understanding a word he was saying. The mere physical contact with him made her head spin. She began to tremble in every limb and felt that she was about to faint. She could see her reflection in the doctor's pupils. She could see his lips moving. Suddenly she let herself fall at his feet and uttered a piercing cry:

"Don't leave me," she wailed.

The tears seemed to spurt from her eyes; she turned scarlet and continued incoherently:

"You don't know how happy I am now. It is since you have been here. I can't tell you how it feels. If you leave me I shall go mad—I shall die. For months and months I have been thinking of you. I didn't know how to tell you. I wrote to you several times. It is all since the day I saw you on the highway."

He bent over and seized her wrists in his hands. The blood had mounted to his face and his cheeks were flaming.

"Hush! Be quiet!" he said, brokenly. "You don't know what you are saying."

She shook her head vigorously and went on:

"You won't stop my speaking. It is not my fault if I love you."

"You don't love me. The thing's impossible!"

He let go her hands abruptly and stepped away from her, keeping his eyes, however, on her face. She got to her feet.

"Why is it impossible?" she cried.

"Why, mademoiselle, the thing is out of all reason. Think of everything there is against it. First of all, my age. Do you know how old I am? Forty-five—twenty-seven years older than you. Have you given that a thought?"

She leaned on the back of an armchair.

"That makes no difference," she faltered.

"You think not?" said Maurecourt, in a rising voice. "Well, I may seem cruel, but I am going to speak to you very plainly. You can be happy—very happy. Don't you want to be? But first of all, you must understand clearly that common sense counts for at least half in any lasting and worthwhile happiness. And the mere fact that you have thought of me as—as your husband—isn't that so?—is the least sensible thing it is possible to imagine. It is just an idea, a notion that has entered your head because you live alone. If you went out, if you got to know some of the people in the town—? Didn't your father have any friends at La Tour l'Evêque? Try to meet them again. I will help you. You'll see. There are eligible young men in La Tour l'Evêque."

Adrienne raised her eyes.

"Eligible young men?" she repeated, miserably.

"Yes, indeed. I can name some."

"I don't want them."

"Why?"

"Because I can love only you."

He joined his hands and went on gently.

"I am telling you that idea came into your head some day when you were alone, some day when you were overcome with boredom. You might very well have fallen in love with another man. Suppose someone else had passed in the carriage instead of me, that day you were speaking of just now—suppose it had been a young man—"

"Why do you want me to 'suppose' all these things? Even if what you say is true, it changes nothing."

She felt a sudden resentment against this man who was making her so unhappy.

"I didn't choose you," she said. "You are quite right. But I can't go on suffering this way all for nothing. It's impossible. You must love me. Suppose I am doing wrong in loving you. I can't help it. It's just *so*."

"Let us suppose," said the doctor, after a moment's silence, "that someone told you unpleasant facts about me—I mean facts of a nature that would repel you. Suppose you heard, for instance—"

"What? Heard what—?" she asked. "What are you going to say?"

He seemed to change his mind suddenly.

"Understand this," he said. "I cannot believe that your happiness depends on me. God is good. He would not allow you to become seriously enamored of a man whom you could not marry."

"Why can't I marry you?"

He went on, without heeding her question:

"And for that reason I cannot take this seriously, or at least believe in its existence as a genuine feeling."

"Why not?" the girl persisted. "What do you want me to do to prove it? Kill myself?"

"I want to show you that you are wrong," he replied, stubbornly, "that you are deceived about your own feelings."

She clenched her hands and carried them to her breast.

"I know I am not deceiving myself," she cried. "I know that I am suffering, and I know that I am suffering because I love you. Why won't you believe me?"

He looked at her silently and said, at last:

"I cannot continue this discussion, mademoiselle."

"Why? What are you going to do? You're not going to leave me?"

He took her hand and forced her to sit down again. She obeyed, tremblingly, and watched him as he took a seat in front of her.

"I am going to tell you something that will drive you from me, once and for all, mademoiselle," he said, after a brief silence.

Her first impulse was to stop him from going on. But her desire to hear him speak was stronger.

"What is it?" she asked, in a voice hardly above a whisper.

He made an evident effort and continued:

"Just this. I am a sick man—a very sick man."

"Sick?" she repeated as though the word conveyed no meaning to her.

"Yes. That is the reason my sister could not stay in Paris where she was a teacher, and came to live here. She was too anxious. I am at the mercy of a sudden attack."

Adrienne had turned ashen.

"It isn't true," she said, feebly.

"Yes, mademoiselle," he replied, gently. "My days are numbered. In two years I shall be in my grave."

A terrible cry broke from the girl. She got up, but fell back in the arm-chair immediately. Great beads of sweat rolled down her forehead. Maurecourt was silent and did not look at her.

"It isn't true," she said at last, in a thick voice. "You say it just to get rid of me."

He shook his head sadly.

"Well, what do I care?" she cried. "What do I care if you *are* sick? That is no reason for my not marrying you. I shall die with you. What will death matter to me if you're not here?"

She jumped up and made a movement toward him, which he checked by getting up and seizing her hands.

"I should be wrong to leave you under any delusion," he said, deliberately and in a tone different from any he had used hitherto. "I do not love you."

She did not turn her eyes away nor make any movement. But in the doctor's warm grasp she felt her own hands growing colder and colder, and suddenly had the impression that her heart could not go on beating any longer and that she was falling into an abyss.

"What am I to do?" she asked.

The suffering in her breast grew intolerable. She had to heave a great sigh before she could catch her breath.

He did not answer at once. She saw tears stealing down his cheeks. He grasped her hands so tightly that one would have thought it was he who was trying to dissuade her from leaving him.

"It is a great trial," he murmured. "You must fight—not suffer yourself to be overcome."

She was not listening. She looked away over her shoulder as though he had not been there; there was no sensation in her numbed hands.

After a moment, he went away.

Chapter VII

She was alone now, still in her father's room. For half an hour she had been sitting in an armchair, before the half-open door, when she heard a voice calling her. She did not get up, but went on listening to it as it sounded, first from the parlor, then in the hall. The noise of ascending footsteps told her that someone was coming upstairs to look for her. Every minute the calls began afresh, in a different tone, passing from gaiety to surprise, and from irritation to anxiety. It was Mme. Legras. At last she reached the third floor and saw Adrienne through the open door.

"For Heaven's sake!" she exclaimed. "Why didn't you answer me?"

She stopped as soon as she noticed the girl's face.

"He came, didn't he, Adrienne?" she asked, in almost a frightened voice. "What did he say to you, my dear?"

And, as the girl did not appear even to have heard her, she came closer, laid her hand upon the arm of her chair, and leaned over her until their cheeks almost touched.

"My poor child!" she murmured. "He didn't deserve you. Cheer up!"

"Leave me alone!" said the girl.

"No," said Mme. Legras, kindly but firmly. "I will not leave you. You are going to tell me everything; that will relieve you."

Adrienne turned her eyes abruptly upon her neighbor. The words Mme. Legras had just uttered brought back to her mind what Maurecourt had said at the very beginning of their conversation. It was as though her misery renewed itself suddenly and appeared to her with a changed face. Till now she had been buried in a sort of stupor, but at the sound of this voice which seemed to be a parody of the doctor's, she roused herself and regained her senses. Shaking with sobs, she let herself fall into the stout lady's arms. Her tears were choking her; she felt the smart of them on her eyelids and cheeks. With both hands she clutched at Mme. Legras's arms and wanted to say something, but her words changed to meaningless cries. Whiffs of perfume came to her nostrils—that odor of mignonette which she knew so well and which brought back so many memories of the past few months. She heard the voice of her friend murmuring all sorts of comforting phrases as she pressed her against her ample bosom.

After a few minutes she drew back and made an effort to get up.

"Come," said Mme. Legras in a rather puzzled voice, "stay as you are awhile. What a state you are in!"

Adrienne fell back in the armchair and pressed her hands on her eyes.

"What's going to become of me?" she asked through her tears.

Mme. Legras drew a chair forward and sat down in front of her.

"My dear little child," she began, "you must listen to reason."

"I can't," moaned Adrienne.

"We shall see about that," said Mme. Legras, very suavely. "I've had pangs of the heart, and I assure you that time cures everything."

Adrienne shrugged her shoulders and hunted under her belt for her handkerchief.

"I don't want to be cured," she said in a rough voice.

"What an idea! My poor friend, everyone suffers, and sooner or later everyone gets over it. Do you imagine you're the only one? Think of all the people there are in the world—"

"No," said Adrienne, mopping her eyes. "No one—"

She writhed around in her seat, put her clenched hands upon the back of the armchair, and pressed her forehead upon them.

"Oh! Oh! Oh!—" she repeated over and over again.

Mme. Legras got up.

"Do have some courage, my child," she said in an imploring voice. "Perhaps there is still hope."

"He told me he did not love me."

"Did he say that? Are you sure you heard him say that?"

At the words, Adrienne rose and came toward her friend.

"Perhaps I misunderstood him," she said, a change coming over her ravaged face. "Do you think so?"

"It wouldn't surprise me at all," said Mme. Legras, after a moment's hesitation.

She put her arms around Adrienne and led her to the bed, on which the two sat down.

"My dear girl," said Mme. Legras after relieving her feelings with a sigh, "calm yourself and look at things sensibly. You are such a child! You don't know that often between the things a man says and what he thinks—I mean, this man may have some reason for speaking to you as he did today. It may mean nothing at all. You are young, and rich into the bargain. The devil is in it if matters can't be arranged. Come, dear girl! Get up! You are coming home with me, or, if you like, we will take a little walk in the town."

She put her arm round Adrienne's shoulders. The girl turned a face to her that was streaming with tears.

"You think that—you think that—things can be arranged?" she asked, in a choked voice.

"Yes, I do," said Mme. Legras, decisively. "But you must be brave. The first thing is not to lose your wits. Ah! as if I didn't know it! Try to think of something else. . . . Was this your sister's room?"

The two got up as she spoke.

"No," said Adrienne, mechanically. "It was papa's."

She had taken her neighbor's arm and clung to it tightly.

"Your—Oh yes! Wouldn't you rather come downstairs, dear? We can sit in your own room. I will make you a cordial."

"You're not going!" exclaimed Adrienne.

"Of course not."

They walked slowly out of the room, Mme. Legras pressing the arm of her young friend against her side and fondling her hand.

"Tell me," said she as they began to descend the staircase. "I hear you made a little journey while I was away. You must tell me about it when you're feeling better. Why didn't you think of sending me a postcard? Sometimes I think I'm no longer your friend. And, by the way, there's a little favor I want to ask of you, dear Adrienne. I hate to speak about it on a day like this, but I can't help it. There was a bill in my mail this morning from a shop in Paris. And, as I happen to be a little short for the moment and can't take a journey for a matter of twelve hundred francs—I thought of you, dear."

"Of me?" repeated Adrienne, not understanding.

"Why, yes, my dear. Of course, at Paris I could find a dozen people to advance me a little sum like this. Not my husband, no! He is having too much trouble just now with his customers and their accounts. But friends, friends like yourself, Adrienne. Besides, it is only for a few days. I am expecting a little remittance of two or three thousand francs at any moment. I am really very sorry, dear child, but if you could possibly oblige me—"

"All my money is at the lawyer's," said Adrienne. "I have only what is sent me the first of each month."

"But you have your savings, my dear. Oh, I wouldn't advise you to touch them if it was for anything else. But you can feel quite safe about this."

There was a certain impatience of her voice, which she was not altogether successful in concealing. Adrienne dried her eyes and blew her nose.

"I know—" she began. She stopped and added, "I'll see."

She took Mme. Legras into her room and opened the wardrobe with the big looking-glass in its door.

"Can you imagine," went on Mme. Legras while Adrienne was groping for her olive-wood box. "It's from my furrier. The mere thought of anyone having to pay a bill for furs on the fourteenth of July!"

Then she was silent. Adrienne had found her box and was opening it with the little key she carried attached to her watch chain.

"There you are," she said with a rather glum air.

"Ah!" exclaimed Mme. Legras.

She plunged her fingers into the box and drew out the rolls of gold coin. At this moment Adrienne remembered what her father had said about her loan to Germaine: "You'll never see it again. It's so much off your marriage dowry." She uttered a cry and made a move toward her box. But Mme. Legras was quicker than she and held it out of her reach.

"My God! how you startled me!" she cried. "What's got hold of you?"

"I can't lend you that money," said Adrienne, hoarsely. "Give it back to me!"

"I tell you it's quite safe," said Mme. Legras, getting up with the box under her arm.

"I need it at once, madame."

"Why?"

Adrienne turned scarlet.

"I can't tell you. But I must have it."

"Really!" said Mme. Legras, her face darkening. "Do you know that what you're doing is not very amiable? After having promised me the money—after putting it into my hands—"

"I'll explain to you," said Adrienne who was beginning to lose her head.

"I'm listening, Adrienne."

"If ever I marry," began Adrienne in a mournful voice—

She stopped and clasped her hands. A sigh rose in her breast.

"You're not going to get married this week, are you?" said Mme. Legras, putting down the box on a chair close beside her.

"Do you think I'll ever marry?" asked the girl after a moment.

"My dear child!" began Mme. Legras, in the tone of one who wants to restore a rational turn to a conversation. "We seem to be speaking of two different things. I ask you to lend me some money—you give it to me—that is, you lend it to me. Then you want to take it back on the pretext that you need it to get married with. Let me tell you, people don't marry as quickly as that. You will have the money back in the course of a week. Besides, this whole thing is so absurd. I wonder what we think we're doing."

She took up the box again and began to undo the rolls.

"Let us count the money," she said.

Without a word, Adrienne looked at the short, pointed fingers as they freed the gold coins deftly from their paper wrapping with the aid of a fingernail. Mme. Legras verified the contents of each roll.

"Five thousand two hundred francs," said she. "My! how rich we are!

I take twelve hundred francs, my dear. Would you like a receipt? No? Of course not. As I tell you, it is only a matter of two days, three at most. If you knew what a service you are rendering me! I shall never forget it, you may be sure of that."

As she was speaking, she slipped six of the rolls into her handbag, looking at the girl meantime out of the corner of her eyes.

"You'll see, Adrienne. Perhaps some day you may need something of me and then—*hein?*"

As the girl still failed to answer her, Mme. Legras put the box on the chair beside her handbag, and assumed a grave expression.

"Adrienne!" she said.

The girl seemed to be falling little by little into a kind of catalepsy. Her eyes were wide open, but the fixed pupils apparently saw nothing that was before them.

Mme. Legras stroked her forehead just above the eyebrows with an anxious look on her own face.

"Come!" said she in a low voice. "What is it now?"

With an exasperated gesture she seized the young girl's hand.

"Don't you hear what I say, Adrienne? Adrienne? Ah, bah!"

She took her handbag, looked again at her young friend and seemed to be doing some hard thinking.

"Supposing," she said suddenly, "that, instead of twelve hundred francs, I borrowed fifteen hundred?"

Seizing the olive-wood box, she held it toward the girl, her hand shaking slightly with excitement. But Adrienne did not seem to see this gesture any more than the others. Mme. Legras was puzzled.

"I never saw anything like this!" she muttered.

She waited a few seconds. Placing the box on the table, she opened it again, her eyes still on Adrienne's face.

"Well, then," she went on, "I add three hundred francs to the fifteen hundred you have so kindly lent me. See, I put them in my bag."

She made good her words as she spoke. Then she waited, motionless, and in deep thought.

"She frightens me!" she said, half aloud. "She seems to be looking at me, yet when I speak to her—"

She remained gazing at the girl with a mixture of fright and disgust on her face.

"What prevents her seeing me?" she said under her breath. "She isn't sick, is she? I don't believe she hears me."

She called in a louder voice: "Adrienne!" But there was no answer.

With a sudden gesture, she put her hands in the olive-wood box, seized the gold pieces which were left, and slipped them into her bag. Her eyes glistened. She set down the empty box noiselessly on the table, went nearer her young friend, and stood at her side. For a few seconds her eyes had been resting upon the gold chain which passed from around Adrienne's neck to the timepiece in her belt. She put her hand lightly upon the girl's shoulder. Adrienne did not seem to feel its contact. Then, with a rapid and simultaneous motion of both hands, she passed the golden loop over the girl's head and pulled the watch from its resting place. The whole thing took place so swiftly and adroitly that anyone watching her would have thought she was assisting at one of those conjuring tricks which make the eyes of an audience start from their heads. In one brief second the watch and chain had joined the golden coins at the bottom of the handbag.

"Oh, well," muttered Mme. Legras, as she straightened her back, "you owed me that much!"

She darted a piercing glance around her and took a few paces about the room, her lips parted, her breath coming and going a little more quickly than usual. Then she turned to the door and was gone without another word or sign.

Chapter VIII

"Mademoiselle!"

The cook was calling from the hallway. Adrienne started at the sound, but did not answer till she heard Désirée beginning to climb the staircase.

"What is it?" she asked, hoarsely.

"Is mademoiselle there?" said Désirée as she came into the room. Her keen, inquisitive eyes displeased the young girl, who remembered how they had rested upon the empty lamp the morning of Mesurat's death. Désirée was a woman whom the heat of her stove seemed to have shriveled like a twig. It was hard to imagine that any blood at all ran under the dry, tightly-stretched skin, which clung to the bones and seemed to have taken its color from them. She had a long straight nose with pinched nostrils, insolent brown eyes, and a habit of drawing her head in between her shoulders as she spoke which helped to increase her general air of suspicion.

"I thought mademoiselle had gone out," she continued. "I could not hear her walking in the parlor. I thought that probably she had gone to say good-bye to Madame Legras."

"Madame Legras?"

"Yes, mademoiselle. Did you not know that she had gone?"

Adrienne shook her head.

"Well, it's a long story," said Désirée with the utmost surprise in her face. "Mademoiselle does not know, then, that Madame Legras has slapped the face of the landlord of Villa Louise? Did she say nothing about it to mademoiselle? It's not a thing to be proud of, that is true. Well, it's all over, anyway. She has left the villa behind her for good. Did mademoiselle not hear the sound of the carriage just now?"

"No, Désirée," said Adrienne, getting up. She was breathing unevenly as she rose to her feet.

"Mademoiselle never sees a soul," went on Désirée; "that is how you hear so little, mademoiselle. Well, then, Madame Legras was shown the door. Yes! Why, it was becoming a scandal! That woman, showing herself everywhere, powdered and rouged! And insolent, too. You can be sure if they had known the kind of woman she was they would never have let her have the villa. At last the owner begins to get a little worried over what he hears and sends her a letter. Widow Got told me this, the aunt of the drapery woman, but then everyone knew about it. Well, then, Madame Legras goes to see the owner and starts her nonsense with him. It appears the lease was in the name of her friend, but she had quarreled with him, and he and the landlord were working together to show her the door. She had been to Paris to try and straighten matters out. And then she wanted money, a whole lot of money, and at once. She came to me to borrow this very morning. From me! Mademoiselle can imagine what I said to her. . . . mademoiselle, are you ill?" asked Désirée, suddenly, seeing that Adrienne had closed her eyes and was leaning on the table.

"It's nothing, Désirée," said Adrienne. "What time is it?"

"Luncheon is ready, mademoiselle."

Adrienne put her hand to her forehead, stumbled toward the armchair, and sat down again. Désirée's eyes harassed her; she felt that they were following her and studying her every movement.

"I'll be down in a minute," she said, turning away her eyes.

"Ah, good!" said Désirée. "By the way, I forgot to tell mademoiselle that someone came in to see her about an hour ago—a lady. I thought mademoiselle was out."

"Who was it, Désirée?"

Désirée jerked a shoulder toward the street.

"The doctor's sister."

She lingered on the word "doctor" with marked contempt in her voice.

"Mademoiselle Maurecourt!" exclaimed Adrienne.

"I thought she'd never go away," said Désirée, adding, in the thin acrid voice which never seemed to speak except to prepare the way for another question. "There you have folks that monsieur your father never cared for!"

But Adrienne had not caught these last words. She jumped up and took a step toward the servant.

"Désirée," she said after a moment's hesitation, "I am going to be in all day. If this lady comes, let me know at once. Do you understand? It's very important."

She seemed to have got back all her strength and spoke with an animation she did not attempt to conceal.

"Are you sure she said she would be back?"

"Mademoiselle can be quite easy in her mind. But does mademoiselle want to see this woman so much? Of course, it is none of my business, but I believe no one could be worse than that woman. I don't care how much she goes to church. You should see her grabbing the wafer. But then mademoiselle never goes to Mass."

"That's all right," Adrienne said. She would have liked Désirée to take herself off, but could not resist a desire to listen.

"I must say this," the maid went on, tossing her head, "mademoiselle is not very curious. She knows nothing, and that is her own affair. But, really, that Mademoiselle Maurecourt just now! She made me so angry I nearly told her something she wouldn't like to hear. With that air of hers—"

"What air?" asked Adrienne, mechanically.

"She's stuck up," said Désirée in a spiteful voice. "And then no one must come near that brother of hers. She's jealous. As if anyone would want him, the poor doctor! You'd think them husband and wife, except that her spying doesn't seem to amuse him much."

Adrienne turned pale.

"Désirée!" she exclaimed, "what are you saying?"

"Mademoiselle," said Désirée, shrugging her shoulders, pityingly, "you live in a dream. You imagine that others do, too. My God! mademoiselle, don't you understand that when one has secrets like yours a woman like Madame Legras is not the person to tell them to!"

"Secrets!" gasped Adrienne.

She felt her legs giving way under her and sat down again upon the bed.

"Ah yes, mademoiselle," said Désirée. "Ah, mademoiselle is fortunate to have a woman like me in the house! I can always say that things aren't true."

She stopped, fully expecting that Adrienne would demand an explanation of her words. But as the girl kept silent, she went on more boldly:

"Mademoiselle knows quite well what I mean. I say it is a blessing for her that I am cook here and that my tongue is well enough hung to give back as good as I get to the gossips in this town."

"The gossips, Désirée?" repeated Adrienne.

"Ah, yes, mademoiselle, the gossips in the market. Mademoiselle does not seem to understand. Oh, there will be plenty of chances to talk about it again, have no fear of that. In any case, I am going to give mademoiselle a piece of good advice. This is the time I can say I have a right to her gratitude. Mademoiselle, don't leave the house just for the present. That is the thing to mind now. Afterward we'll see. There are queer stories in the air about mademoiselle."

Adrienne uttered a shrill cry and jumped to her feet.

"My God! Désirée, hold your tongue. I will give you money. Do you understand?"

"Yes—oh yes, mademoiselle!" said Désirée, deliberately.

Adrienne took hold of the servant's arm. She was trembling so violently that she could hardly speak.

"Désirée," she said, "I can count on you, can't I? I will give you money, a hundred francs, two hundred. What is it they are saying about me, Désirée?"

"What are they saying? Why, everyone is saying that monsieur—that your father—"

"No, no!" interrupted Adrienne, losing her head completely. "If they were really saying so, the doctor would have told me—"

Désirée burst out laughing.

"Him!" she cried. "Don't you know he's simpler even than you? He sees all the world in a fog. He imagines everyone is as good as bread. Ah, you have a funny kind of lover, mademoiselle! I don't want to offend mademoiselle. But the drapery woman tells some funny stories. She says she got them from Madame Legras. Did you tell that woman everything, mademoiselle? As for the story about your father, even if you did not say a word"—she crossed her arms and a terrible look came upon her sordid face "—if you didn't say one word, it would start out of the ground of itself!"

"No, no!" cried Adrienne, carrying her knuckles to her mouth. With a convulsive movement she flung herself at the servant's knees and caught at her skirt with trembling fingers. "I will give you everything I have, Désirée," she moaned. "Have pity on me, Désirée! You know all this isn't true! My God! My God!"

She dragged herself along the floor to the bed and, hiding her face, clutched her head in her hands. A sort of smothered howling came from her mouth.

Certain hours seem impossible to live through. There should be some way of leaping over them, of blotting them out when necessary, and of rejoining normal life farther on. Why suffer all these tortures? They make no one any better—they bring no solution for present difficulties. Barren, barren hours—that serve only to harden the heart! So thought Adrienne as she lay upon the bed.

She had drawn the curtains at her window and was striving, not to sleep, but to rest quietly. Invariably her thoughts flew to the future, in a conscious and despairing effort to escape from reflecting upon the events of the morning. "Perhaps everything will come right," she kept saying to herself, with a stubbornness that was quite as much cowardice as courage. And the comforting suggestion seemed the more probable to her, the less reason there was to believe it seriously. She listened to every sound that reached her from the house and street. Of course Marie Maurecourt would come. She would push open the gate, she would come upstairs and she would enter the room, bringing news—surely bringing some news—or why should she have insisted on seeing Adrienne?

To this visit the girl looked now for everything, for a sudden deliverance from all her miseries, for a miracle! She could see nothing else. She would not even think of the morrow. One thing counted—the visit from Marie Maurecourt. Amid the hell of her anxiety she experienced moments of unreasoning—of delirious joy, at the thought that this woman could bring her happiness. How? She didn't know. She did not even reflect upon what she knew already of Marie Maurecourt's character. She was ready to confide her happiness blindly to her, because she knew no one else whom she could ask to help her. Everything else had ceased to exist. There was nothing left in the entire world save first the footstep of this little woman, which she would hear presently upon the garden path, and then the few minutes she would pass in her presence.

From habit she put her hand every now and then to her belt to pull out her watch, and in her trouble of mind failed to be surprised when she could not find it. She continued, all the same, to grope round her belt, and to fumble at her neck, seeking the long chain which she was so used to finding under her fingers.

At the end of a quarter of an hour she got up, almost beside herself with impatience. As she passed in front of the mirror she could not help stealing a glance at her reflection. Her swollen eyelids gave her the air of someone who had slept badly. Her face was deadly pale.

"My God!" she moaned. "She *must* come!"

She went to the door and laid her ear to the crack. She had not left her room since Désirée had come to speak to her; she had not lunched. It was probably about three o'clock. She listened, her head on one side, then, with a mechanical gesture, turned the key in the lock. For nothing in the world would she have gone downstairs. The mere thought of seeing the cook again made her blood run cold, and she put every ounce of mental strength that was left her into keeping it out of her mind. If only she could see Marie Maurecourt! . . . The idea became an obsession. She had so many things to explain to her. Everything she had not been able to explain to her brother. With Marie Maurecourt she need feel no false pride. Besides, it was her last chance. She knew it. She had a presentiment on the subject she did not dream of questioning. She would speak to this woman as she had never spoken to a living soul in her life, freely—fearlessly. She would say: "Yes, I do want to marry your brother. I am young. I am rich—well-off, anyhow. Where can he find anyone better? Would you call me ugly?"

She turned to the glass again and repeated the last words under her breath. The gloom of the darkened room did not suit her. She went to the window and flung the curtains aside. Then she looked at herself in the mirror again. The light fell full on her face. Of course she was pale, terribly so! But her eye passed to her shoulders, so soft and full that the bodice revealed every gracious curve, to her rounded arms, which she stretched out slowly and then let fall beside her hips.

"Perhaps I am not as handsome as I think," she said to herself.

She tried to recall how many people had told her she was beautiful. There was Mme. Legras. Oh yes—over and over again! But then Mme. Legras was after her money. Her father, once—yes, her father! And the young workman who had followed her at Dreux! But then, if Denis Maurecourt had liked her looks, wouldn't he have fallen in love with her from the first?

"I'm sure he's hiding what he really thinks," she muttered. She remembered something Mme. Legras had said about this hesitancy in men. And then, she continued aloud, "I love him—I love him too much for him not to love me in return."

She began an interminable argument on the subject, and suddenly, her nerves on edge from all this endless waiting, went to the window and fell on her knees before the sill.

"Why doesn't she come? Oh, why doesn't she come?" she said, striking the sill with her fist.

Abruptly, the impression had entered her mind that everything was beginning afresh, just as if nothing had happened yesterday or even this morning, and that it would be a good thing to think up some new arguments to make the doctor understand she loved him. But then, again, was it not really within herself alone that this new beginning was taking place, because within herself nothing existed but her love, while around her life was going on, faster and faster, passing from one thing to another? People were speaking, acting, all manner of events were unfolding, while she remained still as a statue. She closed her eyes and carried her hands to her ears. She heard the buzzing that she hated so, and that seemed to come from somewhere in the back of her head, begin afresh. No! She was the same as ever, with the same suffering to endure. People told her, "I don't love you." And nothing was changed at all!

At that moment she saw Marie Maurecourt crossing the street and coming toward Villa des Charmes. She leaped to her feet and hid herself behind the wall. Her heart thumped in her chest. Yet when she went downstairs it was with a sudden intuition that nothing was to be hoped for from this visit.

Just after she had sat down in the parlor, Marie Maurecourt entered the room precipitously. She had on the same clothes, which seemed to belong to someone much stouter, and which hung limply on her meager body. Her narrow-rimmed black straw hat was decorated with a bunch of grapes of the same sable hue. Although it was a very hot day she wore a blue serge jacket over her blouse. In her hand she was carrying the bag from which she had drawn out Adrienne's letters on her former visit. Perhaps she had not expected to find the girl in the parlor, for she started at seeing her, and turned a little red.

"I tried to see you this morning," she said, without any pretense at a greeting. "I could not. Doubtless you had given orders to that effect. In any case, what I have to say to you won't take long, and I intend you shall hear it."

Her voice was harsh and broken by mental suffering. A sort of palsy shook her head and made the vine leaves of black taffeta quiver on her hat. She looked fixedly at the girl, who had risen and was leaning on the back of an armchair.

"Do you know what you are doing?" she asked, and appeared to wait for an answer. In the silence her breathing was loud and awkward, almost a wheeze.

"You are killing my brother," she said at last.

Adrienne shuddered and her mouth fell open.

"Me!" she said, in amazement.

"Yes, you—*you!*" repeated Marie Maurecourt, moving nearer to her. "Don't you understand all the harm you're doing? My brother is a very delicate man."

Tears of anger and emotion began to smother her voice, but she mastered herself and went on quickly, as though afraid of bursting into sobs before she arrived at the end of what she had to say:

"Extremely delicate. His life has been nothing but a long succession of illnesses. He is frail, his heart is weak, next to nothing would be sufficient to bring on an attack. I have always taken care of him. I am ten years his senior and yet it is he who looks the older of us two. If anything were to happen to him—" a sort of muscular spasm which she could not control

2 4 7

interrupted her —"I might as well go with him. I have only him in the world. I cannot prevent him from wearing himself out, treating all manner of people who don't even pay him. But what I will not permit is that women such as you should come and torment him with their stories."

She stopped a moment and looked at Adrienne, who neither spoke nor moved.

"I say 'women like you,'" she went on, furiously, her anger getting the better of her grief. "Do you know what I have done with your letters? I have thrown them into the street. And it will be the same every time you try to write to him. And don't hope to see him again—ever! He came this morning because you enticed him with a story that you were ill. But now we know how things are. You can offer your case to some other doctor. Ask your friend Léontine Legras to give you some addresses. She ought to have plenty."

She stopped to regain breath, and went on:

"When I think of it!—He came back this morning and I thought he was going to die. He was five minutes without being able to utter a word. I have never been so afraid for him in all my life. You can believe me. He lay stretched out on a sofa in his office—"

The picture she had evoked seemed to be too much for her, and she went on even more harshly:

"I can tell you this: If anything had happened to him I would hold you responsible. There are surely laws for criminals of your sort. Finally, I have some advice to give you. You'll do best, in every respect, if you get out of this town."

The sight of Adrienne's face stopped the torrent of words and she continued more soberly:

"Come, I'm talking common sense to you. As you are not happy here, go and live elsewhere. You have means, you have no more family ties at La Tour l'Evêque."

Adrienne sat down mechanically. Marie Maurecourt took a seat beside her and continued:

"Besides, you know as well as I do that you don't enjoy a spotless reputation. Your intimacy with Léontine Legras would be quite enough. I am certain that what is necessary for you, at bottom, is to get married. Well, don't expect to find a husband at La Tour l'Evêque! People here are too much incensed against you. I would like not to believe all that is said. I know what the gossip of women like Mlle. Grand is worth. But what can one do? In a place like this lies have as much effect as truth. Go away, go away somewhere—no matter where. You have been at Dreux. Go back there! It's a much more important town than La Tour l'Evêque."

In her eagerness to appear convincing she lowered her voice almost to the timbre affected by Mme. Legras. The idea of getting rid of Adrienne by making her leave the town had come to her unexpectedly. But now it appeared so just—so advantageous in all respects that it almost made her forget her anger.

"I am certain you will be better off there. I hear there is very good society at Dreux, and plenty of it. While here—! In this hole! Ah, if only our means allowed us to go elsewhere! But you—just think! You can sell your villa, go and live at—"

She seemed struck with a new thought. Her forehead clouded. After all Dreux was fairly near La Tour l'Evêque!

"You could even go to Paris—why not?" she asked. "In any case, don't lose too much time. Otherwise one of these mornings you may receive an unpleasant visit. Do you hear me? Do you hear what I say, Madmoiselle Mesurat?"

She put her hand on the girl's arm and gave her a light shake. But upon Adrienne's features lay the same stupor as at the moment Mme. Legras left her. No emotion of any sort was to be read in her eyes. Marie Maurecourt stared at her a moment, then said, in an irritated voice:

"Good! Theatricals, more theatricals, the same as a little while ago! But you may as well know that my nerves are pretty strong. This sort of thing does not make a hit with me, this—this—this hysteria! I came here to do you a service."

Her anger again got the better of her.

"Yes, a service. And when I think of the harm you have done to me and mine! Ah, mademoiselle, it's lucky for you you have a Christian to deal with. You are in danger—danger, do you understand? Tomorrow someone may come here from the authorities. And then? What do you propose to do? Your theatrics will have no effect on them."

She got up and began to speak in the frantic tone of one whose wits have been driven astray by the announcement of some calamity.

"Go away! What are you waiting for? Pack up your things this evening! Your lawyer will see to everything else."

She leaned over Adrienne, took her hand, and looked into her eyes. "Why don't you answer?" she shouted, as though to a deaf woman. Suddenly she dropped the hand and straightened herself.

"What's happened to her?" she said under her breath.

She waited a moment, undecided what to do. At first she had thought Adrienne was mocking her. But this impression lasted only an instant. There was that in the girl's eyes which could not be simulated, a vacant stare—the stare of a person sound asleep when someone raises the lids suddenly. The blue pupils were looking at nothing—perhaps saw nothing.

Marie Maurecourt turned abruptly toward the door and left the house.

Chapter IX

Darkness was falling. It was one of those beautiful endings to a summer day of which it is difficult to say just when night begins, so limpid do the heavens remain, even after sunset. The trees had a denser shadow, the birds had ceased to sing, but the sky was still blue.

As was her custom on public holidays, Désirée had prepared a cold dinner for her mistress, and had left the house till the next day, to use her free time as she pleased. She had made no effort to see Adrienne since the conversation of that morning. Doubtless, like nearly everyone else this evening, she had gone to the public ball of La Tour l'Evêque.

The girl was alone in the parlor. She was seated on the sofa, but from time to time rose and took a few steps from one end of the room to the other. There was no hint of impatience in her movements. She walked slowly, with something absorbed in her whole attitude. But her eyes had not changed. They were always the same, fixed like the eyes of a doll. She seemed to feel the heat, and had undone the fastenings of her blouse nearest the neck. Sometimes she heaved a tired sigh, or stopped before the mirror, loosening the hair above her forehead, and frowning with a reflective air.

She had not dined. Indeed, she had not left the parlor once since Marie Maurecourt's visit. When she sat down she gazed around her with all the outward signs of close absorption, but always with the strange look which wandered from object to object without seeming to see any single one. It was growing darker and darker, but she made no move to light the lamp. She would cross her knees, clasp her hands, then suddenly, tossing her head, rise and resume pacing.

When it was too dark in the parlor to see anything, she sat down on a chair near the window and lifted her eyes toward the sky, which seemed to be growing more and more unfathomable as it darkened. The shrill peep of a bird pricked the silence and was prolonged for several seconds, like a cry of fear in face of the advancing night. All kinds of sweet scents mounted from the neighboring gardens—those heavy odors that flowers exhale in the freshness of twilight. There was not a stir in the air. Not a sound reached her from the street or from the neighboring houses, where one or two hung the tri-color. A quarter of an hour elapsed.

Suddenly a muffled report came from the direction of the town. Adrienne saw a streak of light climb the sky behind the roof of Villa Louise and break into a little cluster of stars, like some monstrous flower. A brilliant light suffused the dark vault for the space of a second, and cast its yellow reflection on the girl's face. Adrienne blinked her eyes and strained her ears to catch the admiring clamor which always followed pyrotechnic displays. More rockets mounted, some in sheaves of silver; others in spirals, growing larger and larger as they ascended, like the coils of a released spring. Still others soared quite straight and high, and disappeared in a shower of sparks among the stars. The final one took the form of a vast tri-colored bouquet and drew forth a great "Ah!" of surprise and pleasure echoing all the way to the Villa des Charmes.

Adrienne did not move. She had crossed her hands upon her knees and seemed given over to the spectacle before her eyes. These sudden fissures of light had ended by attracting her attention and fixing her gaze high up above the roof of Villa Louise. With a slight movement of the head she followed the trajectory of each rocket, and remained with her eyes riveted upon the spot where it had burst, until another rose and traced a new design in the sky. After the tri-colored bouquet had detonated she remained a long time motionless, as though waiting for more.

Suddenly, she heard the noise of a military band. It was playing a tune that was joyous and melancholy by turns, but only the lively and rapid portions reached Adrienne's ears. She listened. The piece was quite short and evidently intended as a musical hors-d'œuvre. It was followed almost immediately by a waltz whose very first bars were greeted with applause that at this distance blended into a murmur of enjoyment. The air was in fact a very popular one. All last summer it had been played, whistled, and sung until hardly a soul was unfamiliar with its languorous and hesitant rhythm.

Adrienne got up. She had often heard Mme. Legras humming the words and tune of this waltz. Perhaps she was remembering it? No! Not a thought, not a feeling of any sort was visible upon her face. She turned toward the interior of the room and took a few steps, despite the darkness. Suddenly she collided with a chair and uttered a shrill cry. She remained a moment without moving, then groped her way to the door and left the room and house.

Her feet seemed to hesitate a little as they descended the garden steps and she stopped on the path, her eyebrows drawn together, as though something surprised her—something either in the sky or the shape of the trees that she did not recognize. She looked around almost puzzled and walked straight to the gate. It was at this moment that she began to talk to herself. It was difficult to understand what she was saying, but the detached, indifferent tone of her voice contrasted strangely with a certain volubility in utterance.

She opened and shut the gate; then, still muttering, crossed the street. By now it was quite dark. But she walked rapidly and speedily gained the road to the center of the town. In the indeterminate light that still reached the earth from the sky, her beautiful face was of a uniform pallor, with great shadows that accentuated the orbits of her eyes and the curve of her jaw. An impassive expression hardened her features as though they had been chiseled in marble. Every human feeling was obliterated from the pale forehead and the bloodless lips which moved—speaking without pause.

"Five hundred francs from the notary at the end of the month, then five thousand two hundred francs of savings, that will be enough to make up my dowry. And then I can always borrow here and there, from Mme. Legras or the Maurecourts. The lawyer will advance me one or two months. I must have money. People can't get married without money. Papa will help me, I'm sure. And if he won't, I'll take my share, as Germaine did when she went away. I'll take what is left of mamma's jewelry. There's no law against that. These jewels belong to me, anyhow, because papa is dead and it's my share in the estate. Besides, what the devil does a man want with such things! Women's rings and necklaces. Papa can't wear *them!*"

She gave a muffled laugh and went on:

"And then, Germaine may as well know that I won't be spied on. I'll come in and go out as I choose. If they ever try to lock that gate to stop my going out, do you know what I'll do? I'll have another key made, for my own—yes, for my own."

She looked around her and said loudly:

"My own. And I'll go in to Germaine's room as often as I please. First of all, she owes me five hundred francs, and till she pays me I'll take her room. Do you hear me?"

The last words were addressed to an old woman who was coming out of a house across the street. She hurried away as she saw Adrienne gesticulating in her direction.

"Off with you!" cried the madwoman. "You're afraid, too, are you! Yes, you may well run! . . . She may well run," she added, speaking to herself, when the old woman had disappeared. "They'd better not upset me today. I've had enough of all these dirty sluts."

Suddenly a torrent of the grossest insults poured from her mouth. Over and over again, with terrifying energy, she repeated dirty words whose meaning she had probably never understood, but which returned to her wretched brain, where everything now was swirling in hideous confusion. She waved her arms backward and forward and walked faster than ever. Her fury had given place to a sudden gaiety, and she laughed—a deep and sinister laugh!

Suddenly she stopped. She had arrived so near the place where the ball was going on that the notes of the instruments covered the sound of her voice. At the end of the street she could see an angle of the square, festooned with little lamps, hung from tree to tree. Couples were turning round and around together. She looked at them, then took several steps toward them. These folk were dancing gravely, with clumsy movements. Their whole deportment seemed to be governed by an intense desire to make no mistake and to follow the rhythm of the band. Their feet, as they moved over the paved square, made a sort of cadenced shuffle that was louder than the music at times when the orchestra played softly. Adrienne knew the tune. It was the same old waltz, of which no one ever seemed to tire. Women's shrill voices took up the words.

Je ne vous aime pas,
Ou plutôt ce ne c'est que dans un rêve . . .

Adrienne listened. She stood in the middle of the roadway, her arms pendant at her sides, her head hanging a little forward. She seemed now to be paying the closest attention to everything she saw or heard. The lamps frightened her a little or she would have gone nearer. At last the waltz was over. The couples separated with laughter and exclamations of pleasure whose sound made Adrienne step back a few paces. In the midst of the general gaiety a male voice cried: *"Vive Fallières!"*

Adrienne retreated farther still. She imagined the people were coming toward her. Suddenly she turned around and began to run, seized with a panicky fear as unreasoning as her anger just now—as unreasoning as her laughter. She turned into a little lane which went back up toward the open country. Her heart was beating violently. She muttered something in a smothered voice and began to run faster than ever.

Presently she was on the highway. The noise of the holiday still came to her ears. She covered them with her hands and went on running. Her feet rang upon the hard stony ground. The trees to the right and left could hardly be seen against the dark sky. Between them the stars were twinkling in myriads. The night was black; in the dark only the road was visible.

At the end of a few minutes she moderated her pace and tried to recover her breath. A profound silence reigned. She had left the little town a long way behind. But Adrienne did not stop. She was walking now with uneven steps, sometimes quickly, sometimes so slowly and bowed down that it seemed as though weariness were overcoming her fears and her strength together. She was still talking to herself. But her tongue had thickened and she no longer articulated a single intelligible word.

At times her fears seemed to grow on her anew. Then she gathered all her strength and ran along the road for several seconds, as though driven by the thrust of a goad. Then her mind wandered into some maze or other of thought, and she dragged her feet.

Some peasants walking along the road came across her a little later just beyond the last houses of the next villages. She could furnish neither her name nor her address. She could recall nothing at all.